We Interrupt This Marriage

A Novel by

Evie Benson

CCB Publishing
British Columbia, Canada

We Interrupt This Marriage

Copyright ©2014 by Evie Benson
ISBN-13   978-1-77143-123-1
First Edition

Library and Archives Canada Cataloguing in Publication
Benson, Evie, 1951-, author
We interrupt this marriage / written by Evie Benson. -- First edition.
Issued in print and electronic formats.
ISBN 978-1-77143-123-1 (pbk.).--ISBN 978-1-77143-124-8 (pdf)
Additional cataloguing data available from Library and Archives Canada

Cover artwork: Groom jumping from cake top: © tiero | Canstockphoto.com

Publisher: CCB Publishing
             British Columbia, Canada
             www.ccbpublishing.com

To my family with love.

Acknowledgements

The spark that ignited *We Interrupt This Marriage* came from Stephen King's book, *On Writing,* which I highly recommend. I dare anyone to read about the babysitter, Eula-Beulah, and not break out into gales of laughter. In *On Writing,* King suggested a writing assignment: to create a five to six page short story about the disintegration of an abusive marriage. The twist was the female, the antagonist, was the abuser. The challenge gave me night sweats. I could not write about abuse, I told myself. But the alter-ego that lives inside all of us to one extent or another disagreed. I told myself you're a writer, aren't you? Then, if you're a writer, why don't you have the ovaries to write the damned thing? So I did. Write it, that is… but with an escape clause. *We Interrupt This Marriage* was written with black humor, and thus made palatable for me, the writer, with a nuance of *The War of the Roses* and a smattering of *Throw Mamma from the Train.*

As I wrote, I threw off self-imposed shackles of puritan guilt (the guilt that stopped me from writing romance novels—burning loins make me blush), and Loretta remained true to her longshoreman sensibilities. When angered—which was often—she used colorful words! I didn't feel a shred of guilt. This short story was a simple exercise. The words written were between myself and my computer.

Soon, Loretta was on a collision course across state lines, headed for sunshine as she mowed down anyone who got in her way. It became clear Loretta's story was far greater than six pages. In the end, it was a novel.

Chapter 1

Loretta connected with the side of Frank's face, satisfied with the resounding thud of cast iron against flesh and bone. The man would never learn. Day after day, he screwed up and day after day he underestimated her ability for the sneak attack. She'd timed him. To the grocery store took exactly ten minutes, grabbing a box of Pampers, three, and back home another ten. Frank had been gone forty minutes.

Loretta looked at her husband curled up on the floor in a fetal position. It suited him.

"Get up. I'm late," she said, rubbing her wrist. *The iron skillet was getting harder to lift. Then again, Frank had deserved more punishment than usual. She'd considered switching to Teflon, but realized it didn't pack the wallop she was going for. He'd been ignoring her. But that tactic wasn't going to work. She ran a strict household.*

"What did you do that for Loretta?" Frank asked, knowing that if he let go of the side of his face, teeth were going to spill out. His jaw had taken the brunt of the impact. It was locked at a cockeyed slant and the pain radiating from it was hold-the-freaking-door incredible! This, he realized, was going to take a trip to the 24-Hour Emergency Center.

If he knew Loretta, she'd be ripping out of the carport in seconds. He hoped to hell she was. He didn't think his head could take another whack. He lay looking at the ceiling, formulating what he'd tell the doctor. A fall from a ladder might work. After all, wasn't it said that most accidents occurred in the home?

On his last visit, there'd been questions. The doctor had insisted that no one was that clumsy and had tested him for Epilepsy, Parkinson's and a few other diseases Frank couldn't quite recall. Blood had been drawn and the doctor had looked down his throat (although he'd wondered at the time how his throat could be involved). Still not satisfied, the doctor had added to the day's festivities—involving a dark room and a bright light shone directly into his eyes—for what seemed like hours. He hadn't found a thing.

1

The doctor's disappointment had been palpable. It appeared an incurable disease would've made his day, maybe his whole year.

"Your tests are negative, Frank. I can't understand how you could've fallen three times in the past two months. You might think about being more careful."

That visit had culminated with an arm sling and an ice pack to the eye. The culprit was Loretta and a Louisville Slugger. At one time, she'd been the best hitter on her softball team.

Loretta reached into Frank's jean pocket and fished around for the car keys. "Now you've made me late, damn it! There's mac and cheese in the cupboard. You do know how to make mac and cheese, don't you, Frank?"

He nodded, afraid to speak, as a tooth rolled around on his tongue threatening to choke him. He remained on the worn linoleum, wincing as the kitchen door slammed shut followed by the screen door. It creaked and groaned, then collapsed off its hinges. Loretta was as hard on screen doors as she was on his physical well-being. In fact, she was hard on walls with whatever she'd hurl when the mood struck her. He tried to keep up with the damage, but it seemed she was always one step ahead of him.

She wouldn't be back for hours, thank God. She'd taken to leaving just about every night after her shift at the bottling plant. The more frequent her absences, the nastier she got. He would have expected the opposite. She *had* to be having an affair but who'd want a size 3X muumuu straddling them? There was also the matter of the truce she'd called on shaving. The black leg and underarm hair had grown in heavier than her mustache. As he lay on the floor, contemplating that fact, Frank decided it was a damn good thing she didn't wear nylons. The hair would be poking through them worse than pubes springing from a too-tight thong.

The house remained silent, which meant the kids were still in their room. They'd learned to disappear whenever she went for anything with the potential to hurt; a broom, frying pan or the Louisville Slugger. It all meant the same thing: pain!

* * *

2

The eldest, Brice, opened his door a crack and listened. All that came back to him were the sounds of his dad floundering on the kitchen floor. He rushed back to the bedroom window, pulled the curtain aside and peeked out. The station wagon was gone. In his nine-year-old mind, this was better than a trip to the candy store or getting picked first for dodge ball.

He ventured out to the kitchen, making certain he stayed inside the invisible line, the line closer to his bedroom door and safety, rather than the kitchen door.

Brice watched his dad pull himself up from the floor. The right side of his cheek was swollen to the size of a golf ball and was already turning from red to purple. It reminded him of his friend, Danny, when he'd come to school after the dentist ripped out a tooth. He grossed out the whole class when he pulled out a bloody, puss filled wad of cotton to show off the empty socket. Their teacher Miss Winegarden had gone all pale in the face, which couldn't have been easy considering she was already the color of rice pudding. She'd sent Danny off to the school nurse.

* * *

Frank managed to get to his feet as the room spun. He'd have to call a taxi, he decided. The roads had frozen over with a thin coat of ice since the day's weak sunlight had departed. There was no way he'd manage walking the seven blocks to the emergency clinic with a two and four-year-old in tow. He hit speed dial on the phone (he was organized, if nothing else), and mumbled his address to the dispatcher several times before she got it right.

"Brice, would you get dinner started?" Even through his pain, Frank was aware the words had come out garbled.

Brice watched his dad spit out a tooth. It looked like a molar and had a brown spot on it; probably a cavity. He nodded his head, afraid to speak out loud in case he started crying. Nine-year-olds didn't cry. He'd already made that mistake once and it got him sent to the school counselor's office to talk things over. Mr. Higgins had leaned over his scarred up desk and asked if there was anything wrong at home. He'd wanted to shout, *You bet your saggy ass there's something wrong!*

Wrong, Wrong, Wrong! My mom beats the shit outta my dad and he just takes it like some chicken-shit pansy.

But that's not how it went—not with a mom who got that look in her eye, telling him he'd be next. He'd looked away from Mr. Higgins' rummy eyes to stare at the wall. He was either a wuss or a drinker, or maybe both. Mr. Higgins' eyes had gone all watery.

Brice decided to check on his brothers and sister. Britney was in one of the top bunks with her diapered butt up in the air. The rest of her was covered with a SpongeBob blanket. She was wet, which was why their dad had gone to the store. They'd run out of extra absorbent diapers and the way she sucked on her bottles, they needed extra absorbent. Mark, his five-year-old brother, was sitting in the corner just like he always did when his mom was in one of her moods. He'd sit there, staring at the wall. Brice wondered what Mark saw. Maybe it was good like a guardian angel or something. Whatever it was, it was probably better than what had just happened in the kitchen.

Why didn't his dad fight back? That's what the kids on the playground did—every time. Someone would get pushed or shoved and the next thing you knew, they were rolling around in the dirt, punching each other like crazy 'till the vice principal came to break it up. Mr. Jenkins was pretty good at it, too. He'd get hold of their jackets, one in each meaty hand, and pick them up off the ground. The best fighters would keep swinging, even though Mr. Jenkins worked out every day and had a neck bigger around than the pine tree in their backyard. When that happened, he'd yell for them to knock it off. But he didn't use the F-word over and over like his mom. She was really good at that when she was pounding.

Next he went over to Brandon, his four-year-old brother. He was the crier, and always took it the worst when their mom started swinging. His face was buried in a pillow that smelled of pee. He was a crier *and* a bed wetter. Brice rubbed his brother's shoulders awkwardly as sobs shook his body. It seemed to him he shouldn't have to do this. In every Disney movie he'd ever seen, the mom rubbed the kids' shoulders.

"Come on, Brandon. I'm making mac and cheese with applesauce."

Brandon's body only shook harder. Maybe he cried better when he had an audience. Either way, it wouldn't do any good. Their mom was going to whomp on their dad as long as he let her and that would be forever.

Brice grabbed Britney from under the covers. Her blond ringlets were sticking to her head and her face was all pink and sweaty. She had on her Cinderella pajamas, her favorites, because they had a pink cape sewn on the back. When no one was looking, she could get it flying straight out if she got a head start at the beginning of the hallway and pumped her legs as hard as they would go. She might only be two but she was smart—smart enough not to try it when their mom was looking.

Curled in his arms, he asked her a question that by now was burned in to his brain. "Britney, do you have to tinkle?"

She was twirling a damp ringlet around a dimpled baby finger but paused to give him the wrong answer. "I aweddy potted."

That would be why her diaper was sagging worse than when their dad took off to the store. "When you feel like tinkling, you need to tell daddy or me. You're a big girl now. You need to go potty on the potty chair."

Her eyes grew big with imagined fear, which wasn't unusual. She had a good imagination. "Smakes in my potted."

He tried for the gazillionth time to reason with her. "I looked and there aren't any snakes in your potty chair. Remember when you got a sucker last time?"

She nodded her head in her exaggerated way and her blond curls joined in. "Lembon succer."

"Yep. There's lemon, grape, cherry, root beer, and orange suckers. If you go potty on the potty chair, you get to have one."

She nodded and tried brushing her damp bangs away from her face, missing more times than she should have. She was not very coordinated. That went for her tongue, too, because to understand her, you had to bend over and listen really carefully. But even then, most of what she said you had to guess at. The bottle she loved was part of the problem. Her words got caught up around it and they came out garbled. She didn't talk much anyway which was okay. When she didn't get her way she'd cry and their mom would start yelling at their dad how it was his fault she had to deal with four brats. He didn't think that made much sense. When he'd asked, his dad had explained where babies came from. It took both the mom and the dad so it couldn't be just his fault.

* * *

Miles away from the bedlam she'd caused Loretta tried to enjoy a quiet drive. She was still wound up over what she'd been forced to do back at the house. Soon she'd be at Jay's. The place might be a dump but there'd be music on (hopefully Marilyn Manson—her favorite), and Blue Nun chilling in the fridge. She stepped on the gas. If she was any later, Jay would get pissed and take off to a neighborhood tavern to slam down too many beers.

Her lights were on, which was a good sign. Loretta rapped on the door, afraid of the reception she'd get. She was twenty minutes late.

Jay answered the door wearing a Grateful Dead T-shirt and worn Levis. She'd shorn her dishwater-blond hair to a crew cut. It looked like shit.

"Mr. Man slip you something you couldn't resist?" Jay snickered.

Loretta was relieved. This was her good mood. Beer wafted to her through the frosty air. Apparently, Jay had started without her. Loretta walked into the apartment and sat down on the only corner of the couch free of exploded newspaper.

"Frank doesn't have the equipment to give me what I want and you know it, baby. Did I ever tell you he named it the Velvet Rocket? It should've been called the Incredible Shrinking Pinkie...now you see it...pretty sure...yep, there it is..."

Jay almost felt sorry for the guy. "Then why four kids? I mean, if you didn't enjoy it, why'd you roll over for more?"

"You don't know Frank. He's one sneaky bastard. He'd wait 'till I was asleep and play hide the winkie. I may not have liked it, but I sure as hell was fertile. Anyways, that's over now. I told him if he ever tried it again, I'd bite its head off...kinda like a praying mantis."

Jay was uncomfortable. Loretta had a nasty streak that seemed to come out whenever she talked about her husband. It was best left at home. Jay noticed red splatters on Loretta's muumuu that looked a lot like dried blood. She didn't want to know...

6

* * *

Frank took hold of Britney's chubby hand. She tended to wander and they had to make it through the emergency doors before he collapsed. He kept a cotton hankie pressed to his mouth. So far, it had sopped up the blood. He managed to get both kids through the door and settled before Britney started squirming around in her chair. Frank found a workable distraction in a children's book whose spine was coming apart.

"Brandon, read to your sister."

Brandon did as he was asked, flipping to a page that got instant results. It was filled with savanna wildlife.

"Edephents, Daddy!" Britney exclaimed.

Frank nodded, communicating with his eyes. His jaw hurt so bad tears were rolling down his cheeks.

The night shift nurse took her time coming over to where they sat to hand him a release form. Apparently, she'd seen worse. She held out her hand requesting his health care card, wondering what had brought him in this time. This time of year, most patients they saw were diagnosed with a cold or flu. Boring stuff. At least Frank kept them guessing. It was one thing after another with him. She suspected his visits weren't due to terminal clumsiness, but rather someone was using him as a human piñata.

The nurse ran Frank's insurance card through a reader and requested he follow her. Frank remained seated, looking to the two kids sitting next to him with pleading eyes.

She broke a personal rule and shared an actual smile. "Okay, go on ahead. But I'm warning you, if they get out of control, I'm sending them back to their father."

To Frank's disappointment, he was shown room 10. It hadn't been refurbished yet and the naugahyde on the examination table was dangerously slick. Shortly, the doctor stood facing him.

"Holy shit, Frank! What did you do this time? Here…open your mouth wide," he requested as he manipulated the inside of Frank's cheek with a tongue depressor. As he did, Frank confirmed what he'd always suspected. The doctor's bedside manner was why he was stuck with the night shift at this smorgasbord for the needy.

7

Frank shook his head in response. He wasn't going to be opening his jaw any further. He couldn't. The joint seemed to be locked in place. The doctor was going to have to figure something out soon, though. If he didn't get some relief for the pain, he'd be sliding off the table and doing at least a one and a half gainer before his head hit the frigging floor.

Moving his hand along the left side of Frank's jaw where the socket should have been, he frowned. "Well, shit. This is a bad one. Can you move it at all?"

Frank shook his head. Negative; no dice; wouldn't be prudent. God that hurt! He'd rather be struck with a cattle prod up an orifice than have the doctor push against his jaw again. The pain had stopped coming in waves and was now one steady, blinding freight train ready to mow him down. He was about to pantomime for a pen and paper so he could request pain meds when there was a tap on the door followed by the nurse's hasty entrance. She held Britney who was in full cry. Trailing behind them was Brandon.

"Your daughter wants her daddy," the nurse said, placing Britney on the floor who ran like a pack of ravenous dogs was after her. She collided with Frank's body, wrapped her arms around his dangling legs, and latched on tight. The impact, as small as she was, was impressive. It caused Frank to blow out the stagnating air in his under-worked lungs, along with a spray of blood; the doctor managed to duck. The resulting intake of air caused Frank to inhale the rest down his windpipe and he started to choke. The nurse took over as the doctor stayed out of range. She gave Frank a direct slap on his back and he felt his jaw pop into place. Apparently it could be heard because the nurse shot her boss a look of surprise.

"Water. Need a glass of water."

His garbled words eventually sunk in and she dashed over to the sink to fill a paper cup with lukewarm tap water. Frank drank it in big gulps, happy to have the use of his jaw back, if only partially. A pill was handed to him in a paper-dispensing cup and he tossed it back, hoping for a miracle.

In the commotion, the children had been left to their own devices. Brandon wasn't particularly happy with that and walked over to yank on the hem of the doctor's lab coat.

"My mommy hit my daddy with a big frying pan, the one she cooks eggs in. Brice said she whacked him a good one."

Well crap. What was going to happen now? Frank had visions of the Department of Social Services showing up to the house, uninvited, with tape recorders and steno pads. They weren't going to be impressed. Between the threadbare furniture and Loretta's long hauler's vocabulary, they'd be whisking the kids away before the GPS on their vehicles registered.

The nurse gave the doctor a meaningful look while the room remained as quiet as a Louisiana graveyard. But time was billable hours and eventually the doctor stood in the gap.

"I have to report this, Frank. I suggest that you file a restraining order against your wife."

He looked to the nurse in disgust. "Penny, call the police and then bring me the form."

The pill Frank had been given began working its magic as he viewed the ensuing mini-drama in the third person. In some ways he was relieved. He was tired of being Loretta's punching bag and deep down he knew the kids would be better off away from her. Revise that; they'd be better off if they were allowed to live with him and Loretta was remanded to stay out of their lives. But, he didn't trust the judicial system. A judge might allow her visitation rights and if that were to happen, they might suffer what he had for the past ten years.

The doctor resumed his examination. Pressing down on the socket he nodded. "Looks like it popped itself back into place all right. Let's see if we can have a look inside that mouth of yours."

Frank tried, but even with the painkiller his jaw wouldn't cooperate. Moving a high-intensity light inside his mouth the doctor straightened back up. "Looks like a molar's been knocked out. Far as I can tell, it appears to be a clean break, but you'll need to have a dentist take a look at it. Christ Frank, she really clobbered you a good one."

The nurse returned with a form and handed it to the doctor.

"I'll need to ask you some questions, Frank. If it's too painful to talk, you can write it down. Now…" he speed-read the first question. "Has your wife ever struck you before?"

Frank nodded his head. *This is what he got paid the big bucks for?*

"This isn't on the questionnaire, but I've got to ask. Have all these visits been a direct result of your wife's abuse?"

Frank nodded.

"Shit! She's sure not a keeper. Why would you take that from her; from anybody for that matter?"

The nurse leaned in closer, her eyes bright with curiosity as she studiously ignored the mischief the kids were up to. Drawers slammed and feet scampered.

"Penny, *will* you get those kids under control?" the doctor snapped.

Britney had located a speculum and was marveling at her shinny reflection in the cold steel. Frank cringed. How many pap smears had been pressed into service with those things? It was all too much, even through his drug haze.

The nurse grabbed it from her, giving Britney a stern look.

"This isn't a play thing, young lady!"

Britney began to cry in self-defense and Frank felt his jaw tighten up in reaction. It hurt. It hurt more than anything Loretta had been able to produce to date.

The doctor returned to the questionnaire. "This next question asks how many occurrences. We'll just take a stab at that, Frank. I've seen you at least once a month for the two years I've been onboard. I'll fill in numerous." He checked the appropriate box.

"To your knowledge, has your wife sought psychiatric help at any time?"

Frank shook his head.

"Is she on medication?" he continued.

Frank shook his head again and the doctor checked another box.

"That leads to my next question…"

Frank felt a wave of dizziness as the room began to spin. His body started to fold over as his butt muscles relaxed in preparation for a spectacular spill to the floor. The naugahyde was slicker than any teflon ever invented. The nurse caught his movements out of the corner of her eye and made a mad dash to the examining table to right him as the doctor remained a safe distance away. She kept hold of Frank while shooting glances in the kids' direction.

It was definite Britney wasn't going anywhere. She was standing in the middle of the room wailing, while Brandon tried to divert her attention with a tongue depressor. She looked at the flat wooden peace of-fering and pointed to the speculum still grasped in the nurse's hand and wailed harder. So hard that snot ran down her face and piddle began soaking her zip-up pajamas.

Frank could take no more. "Do you have a diaper?"

"What?" asked the harassed nurse.

Frank pointed to the issue at hand as the room continued to spin. The nurse's gaze fell to a small puddle on the floor. She forced Frank to lie down, pressing on his chest until his back connected with the table.

"Lay still until I get back," she ordered as she rushed through the examining room door.

Frank felt queasy; probably due to the blood and saliva running down his throat. He sat back up. The spins intensified, only this time, bright stars were popping in his field of vision like a disappointing display of fireworks.

The doctor steadfastly remained outside Frank's field of spewing; he was on his own. His thighs slid first, followed by his butt as he shot off the table with the ease of a drunk preparing to do something monumentally stupid. As his momentum picked up speed, Frank became giddy with relief. Finally, the deed would be done; not unlike looking up from tuning to a favorite radio station to discover the traffic had come to a screeching halt. There was going to be impact for certain. It was the wait between the knowing and the doing that was the best-kept secret.

It was an interesting landing and Frank gave in to the wonder of it all. His feet caught the floor first and he came to an abrupt halt— his running shoes had non-skid soles—as his body was thrown forward.

His next conscious thought was, *please not a face-plant,* but the gods weren't on his side. It was probably a ten-pointer if ever there was one. He heard the crack and was saddened to realize that it was his nose. To date, Loretta had never gone whole-heartedly for his nose.

It was Brandon and Britney who came to his rescue while the doctor remained a safe distance away. "Daddy, are you hurt?" Brandon asked in a quavering voice. Before Frank could answer he felt his tongue thicken and his mouth began the telltale saliva-letting that always precedes vomiting. It gushed out in a torrent; this afternoon's tuna sandwich and partially masticated Fritos.

The doctor moved a few steps back and was rewarded by getting clocked on the back of the head when the nurse burst through the door. He yelped and she dutifully came to a screeching halt. Parting his cropped salt-and-pepper hair with her fingers, she examined the bump. Apparently, it hadn't broken the skin. Reflected in her eyes was frustration with a nuance of disgust.

"It'll be fine. The skin isn't broken. If..." her words came to an abrupt halt when she spotted Frank lying on the floor next to his offering.

Britney had moved over to the side that remained void of stomach contents and tugged on her father's sleeve. "Go bye-bye, Daddy, bye-bye." *At least the fall had re-directed her non-ending wailing,* Frank thought. He moved the hand that wasn't pinned under his body and sought his gushing nose. The moment it found its mark, blinding pain rewarded him and his groan echoed off the sterile walls. The nurse approached, lifting Britney away for an examination. She didn't show reluctance in adding to his agony as she tweaked his sizable snout to see for herself. Frank squealed and he saw the glint of victory in her eyes.

"It's broken all right!" she announced proudly.

He swatted her hand aside, no longer willing to play the docile patient. She took this as her cue to move on to the next task. Placing the Pampers down on the table, she manhandled Frank, dragging him to the examining table's metal frame and propped him against it. Opening a cabinet, she grabbed a pair of latex gloves, snapping them on with dexterity and a touch of aplomb; she then retrieved copious amounts of paper towels from a metal dispenser mounted above the sink. The waste can was next as she dragged it to Britney's mishap. It appeared that urine was more offensive to her than chewed up lunch.

Finished, she continued to Frank's mess, got a bead on its location, averted her nostrils away from the obnoxious heap, and went to work.

This answered a question Frank had contemplated off and on while making trips to the emergency room. Working around bodily fluids appeared to remain offensive, even after years of more than a casual acquaintance.

The nurse's scrubbing became more pronounced and she looked to the doctor. "Do you need help examining his nose, Doctor?"

From Frank's vantage point (his slouch against the table's under-belly only provided a view from the doctor's Italian loafers to the edge of his lab coat), his reaction was easy to read as his calves tightened and his feet clicked together—a lot like Dorothy in *The Wizard of Oz*; there's no place like home...

"I believe Frank should be admitted to the hospital. We aren't set up to handle multiple injuries." His voice came out in a croak of self-preservation and the nurse's scrubbing increased exponentially. Frank concentrated on the blur of the hand that attacked the linoleum.

He discovered he didn't feel much pain as long as he kept his hand away from his nose. Actually, he felt pretty good now that the unau-thorized table diving was out of the way. If it weren't for the problem of what to do with the kids while he was fobbed off to the hospital, he would've looked forward to more drugs... to numb the pain ...as many as they were willing to give him.

He pantomimed writing and the nurse sprang into action. She was clearly underpaid, Frank decided.

She removed her latex gloves, tossing them into the garbage can, and grabbed a chart from a wall hook, flipping the paperwork over so he'd have somewhere to write.

There's no one home to take care of the kids, he scribbled.

Acting as intermediary, she walked his note over to the doctor whose brow knotted into two gigantic groves of concern. Whether it was concern for his patient or himself was unclear to Frank.

"Well I can't fix your nose here, that's for certain. Besides, you need to have that missing molar looked at. Do you have family nearby, someone who could look after your kids? It'll only be for tonight."

The nurse was ahead of the game and had already reached Frank with the clipboard.

He scribbled: I have an Aunt who might be able to watch them. The nurse read his reply out loud and the doctor's brow relaxed.

"We'll need her phone number," he said.

As Frank wrote it down, the doctor picked up his pace. "Penny, make the arrangements, please." He turned to Frank, almost as an after-thought. "I'm afraid you'll be required to give a short statement to the police when they arrive. They might be willing to drive you to the hos-pital. If not, you'll have to be transported by ambulance."

While Frank and the kids were abandoned in the examining room to fend for themselves, Frank went over in his mind the many reasons why asking Edith for help was a bad idea. To start with, she had a big mouth. His predicament would fly through the family tree faster than beetle kill. And once done, the family he'd disowned would give themselves permission, in a back-handed way, to meddle in every aspect of his life. Warming to the subject at hand, he reminded himself that it had been Edith who'd introduced him to Loretta. As he continued to throw out skeletons best left alone, nausea reared its fickle head all over again.

Time passed in small increments while the children leaned against the safety of Frank's chest, his breathing now shallow as the pain meds did their job. He was about to drift off to sleep when a tell-tale clop, clop, clop followed by the swishing of polyester rubbing against polyester announced Edith's thunder thighs.

Edith flung the door open and stood taking in their unorthodox family reunion in a navy blue pantsuit accented with tie-dye swirls of bright pink, orange and yellow sequins. Frank's vertigo came back with a vengeance.

She was wearing her favorite scent—deep-fried donuts. Edith was famous for her unerring loyalty to all things deep-fried to the extent she'd been recently honored with a *People About Town* write-up in the local paper. The photographer had done his best at getting her girth behind the camera but had failed mightily. He *had* caught her triple chin, though. She was standing outside the Donut Hut, squinting as raindrops fell from the sky, smiling for the camera. The article had reported that for the past twelve years, Edith had gone to the Donut Hut and ordered the same four chocolate donuts with sprinkles, along with a tall glass of milk, come rain or shine. The proprietor had framed the article for her and had an identical one made up for himself. It now hung on the greasy walls for the customers to enjoy. It was a wonder anyone ever came back.

Frank had a specific beef with the Donut Hut. That was where his life had been derailed, where Edith had met Loretta, a fellow deep-fried aficionado… to his never-ending regret.

She surveyed the room and clucked her disapproval. "Frank, what in the world happened to you?"

He could only manage a shake of his head and point to his nose, which had swollen in an odd way. He could see flesh in his peripheral vision when he looked in her direction. Unfortunately, it didn't block out the kitten-heeled shoes with ostrich feathers that were shedding the ice that had hitchhiked in with her. Edith had somehow lost her way in regards to her fashion sense. If it had glitter, rhinestones, ostrich feathers, or a Fredrick's of Hollywood tag, she bought it.

"Well, never you mind. I'll take care of things from here. Why didn't you call me earlier?"

Because you are my worst nightmare. You're the one who introduced me to my private hell and you're a gossiping old windbag, Frank thought. So as not to bite the hand that fed him, he let the unspoken words roll around in his head.

"I'll take the kids to my house. You can call me when you're released. Just wait 'till your mother finds out. She'll be worried sick!"

No she won't. She'll probably hunt Loretta down to pin a badge of accomplishment on whatever muumuu she's wearing. Next to Loretta, his mother's swinging skills were notorious. Her legend had risen to such levels within the neighborhood he'd grown up in, he'd found himself friendless. *No one* was willing to test their ability to dodge her right arm when she was in the mood to show off.

Edith grabbed Britney and her screams were smothered against a droopy bosom that spread close to where her waistline once was. Brandon's eyes grew round as he looked to his father for protection. Sadly, they had run out of options. Frank made a silent promise to himself to check out of the hospital the moment he was able to.

He forced himself to detour his thoughts in a more positive direction. Edith meant no harm. The kids would be safe, other than they'd be bouncing off the walls with a sugar high. If he knew Edith, she'd be wedging herself in the family Oldsmobile for a show-off session with her great niece and nephews at the Donut Hut first thing in the morning—*if* they hadn't released him from the hospital by then. For now, anything short of protective custody would have to do.

Their departure was replaced by a police officer who transferred the information from Frank's signed deposition to a domestic violence complaint. If he was surprised the incident was being reported by a male, he hid it well.

"Once you've had your nose seen to, you'll want to go to the court-house and seek a restraining order. Your wife won't be able to come within three hundred feet of you that way. That includes phone calls, Mr. Walch. You'll need to make sure you keep a copy of the restraining order with you at all times."

The officer turned to go but the doctor had other plans. "Could you give him a lift to Northwestern Memorial? It would save an ambulance trip."

The officer hesitated. It was near the end of his shift. All that had been on his mind the past few hours was enjoying a cold beer in front of the TV to watch a game between the Cubs and White Sox his wife had promised to tape. He took another look at Frank and felt pity. His missus had one hell of a hook.

"It isn't protocol, but what the hell. You ready to go?"

Frank got up with the help of the nurse. Standing, his pulse quick-ened and traveled to his nose with a menacing beat. Ignoring the pain, he concentrated on something he'd never dared dream of. This would be the last time he'd ever make a trip to emergency, the last time he'd have to duck Loretta's right arm, and the last time he'd have to pretend that his kids would be okay in a life filled with insanity.

Chapter 2

Frank fought claustrophobia on the trip over to the hospital. He'd been offered the police cruiser's back seat and soon discovered there were no door handles. His legs were bunched into the seat in front of him and he wondered what a criminal over five-foot ten experienced. Frank assumed the tight quarters solved a prisoner's thrashing around—there'd be no way to wind up and thrust feet through the heavy steel mesh that separated them. He could hear busy chatter coming from the police radio.

After ten minutes, Frank had almost pulled in the reins of his claustrophobia when a red Corvette whizzed past them. Without warning, the officer made a U-turn in the middle of the road and hit his siren. The officer shook his head in disgust. "Going to have to write up a ticket. This guy's been a pain in the ass one too many times."

Frank watched in alarm as the Corvette pulled to the shoulder of the road with the officer in pursuit. Hitting his brakes at the last possible second, the cruiser's grill was now only inches from the Corvette's bumper.

Frank's imagination went into warp speed. What if the guy pulled a gun? With the way things were going, it was a likely prospect. The driver had been going 90…easily. What kind of screwed up person would you have to be to be doing 90 in a 45 zone? He could be high on drugs, wanting to pick a fight and *he*, Frank Walch, AKA Loretta's punching bag, could be stuck rotting in the back seat of the patrol car until someone thought to check on the missing officer. His claustrophobia kicked in with a vengeance.

This had happened before.

His first walk into panic occurred when his mother locked him in a closet for not cutting the grass in the diamond pattern she preferred. She'd been livid. After whacking him with a razor strap (something she'd inherited from his grandfather—God rest his soul), she threw him into the hall closet amongst the musty sneakers and winter coats. Frank could still remember pounding on the door with unbound terror. What he'd gotten for his trouble was another hour of solitary.

Returning home from work, his father had rescued him, snatching him from the closet floor and carrying him into the kitchen to soak his bruised hands in a bowl of ice water.

"Why'd you lock the boy up in the closet, Donna?" he yelled.

His mother went ballistic. "You're coddling him, Lester! He knows the rules!"

This event stood out in his mind because it was the only time he could remember the old man standing up to her. It had been a terrible fight; filled with name calling and shouting. When it appeared she was losing ground, his mother grabbed the first thing within reach, the Kirby vacuum cleaner, and threw it through the living room's plate glass window. It sailed through the opening, taking the curtains with it and landed out on the lawn like a shrouded corpse. The neighbors had come over to investigate. They might've been able to ignore their constant yelling, but a shrouded corpse was another thing altogether.

That was the beginning of what Frank had come to call *the dark place*. He was ten when it started, and no other moniker fit within his limited vocabulary. The rules had been changed on all sides since the night of the vacuum cleaner, though. The following day he'd rooted around in his dad's old toolkit and found a flashlight. It was squirreled away, along with his favorite comic books, inside an old pair of galoshes at the back of that hated closet. Whenever he was sent there, and it was often, he'd tuck a coat along the crack at the bottom of the door and join his favorite heroes. Even with the flashlight and the stack of comics, claustrophobia would sometimes sneak its tentacles around him, choking off his air and balling up his fists in terror.

That was one of many punishments his mother had used over the years, but not the worst…not by a country mile. For today, *the dark place's* lessons, the ones he taught himself so he could make it through to the other side, would suffice.

He went there now and shut his eyes to begin a peaceful stroll on the beach. He envisioned a gentle surf as the froth washed against white sand, in and out, in and out…and added seashells, tumbled smooth by the undulating ebb and flow of the surf. Finally, Frank pictured himself there, feeling the warmth of the sand and the smell of the salt air. Looking off to the distance, he could feel the vertigo as the movement of the breakers rushed against his bare legs and he traveled out to sea. He was free. He'd found his hiding place.

"Sorry about that," the officer blurted as he slammed the cruiser's door. Frank's startle reflex had him throwing his arms up in the air. "Would've hated seeing that kid get off, though. We've had complaints about him. His daddy's some hot-shot attorney and that yuppie larva thinks he's entitled to ignore the law."

Frank wished he could've gotten his jaw to cooperate. He'd liked to have asked what a ticket like that would cost. Probably hundreds, maybe more.

It was another ten minutes before they pulled up to the emergency room doors.

The officer looked Frank in the eye, then away. Clearing his throat his words came out haltingly, and then picked up speed. "Listen, you need to throw your wife out of the house or find a place of your own. If you won't do it for yourself, do it for your kids. I've been a cop for over twenty years and I've never met an abuser who didn't learn it at home. You want your kids to turn out all right? Then you need to put a stop to it now. Think about that."

Frank managed a nod. The officer was right. He just hoped Loretta didn't try for a home run with her Louisville Slugger when he did.

Hospital admission was swamped and he had to wait another two hours before his name was called. In the meantime, he'd seen all manner of calamities walk through the emergency room doors. He watched as a lady was assisted to a seat, supported between two men, presumably family members. Her knee was swollen to gargantuan proportions. They got her into a chair and positioned another in front of her, in case she felt the need to rest her damaged leg. She didn't seem interested in moving as she moaned in pain. But, grading on a curve, Frank would have to say the guy sitting next to him was worse off. Beads of sweat were dripping down his face and neck. Every once in a while, the man would take out a hanky and blot the perspiration away. His cough was deep with phlegm and when he got started, it sounded like he was attempting to cough up a lung. As far as Frank could tell, each coughing fit brought him closer to a seizure. He got up and moved a safe distance away. Catching pneumonia with a broken nose wasn't a workable option.

A while later, a teenager wearing a letterman's jacket was helped to a seat by his coach. A baseball must have made a direct hit to his forehead. A small mountain had erupted on his bruised flesh, crater and all. His efforts at machismo were fading quickly as he clasped and unclasped his hands, trying to control the pain.

When his name was called, Frank rushed towards the nurse before she could change her mind. He was shown a room and told to change out of his street clothes and into a flimsy gown. He waited on the paper covered examination table with a draft to his backside for over forty-five minutes before the doctor appeared to review his admitting chart.

"It says that your wife hit you, causing an injury to your jaw and a broken molar and you sustained a nose injury with a fall while at the 24-Hour Emergency Center. Is that correct, Mr. Walch?"

Frank nodded in the affirmative.

"You know there are ways to put a stop to the abuse…" the doctor said.

Frank looked away, weary of admitting what his life had become.

"Very well then, let's see what the damage is." She advanced to the end of the table and pointed a high-intensity light up his nasal passages. Feeling along the bone, she located the break as he flinched, waiting for another flash of pain that never came.

"It will have to be set, Mr. Walch. Are you allergic to Novocain?"

"No, but could I get something stronger?" The words had come out garbled.

"Something stronger? Is that what you asked me?"

Frank nodded his head.

"I'll have a look at that mouth of yours first. Now open wide."

Frank gave it all he had and managed an opening that left the doctor frowning. Standing up straight, she coached him. "You'll need to do better than that, I'm afraid."

Frank shrugged. The jaw wasn't budging.

"Wait here a moment." She returned with his second cup of tepid water for the day and two large pills. "Take these. They're muscle relaxers, analgesics. With luck, they'll help relax your jaw so I can have a look."

Frank gingerly placed the pills on his tongue and chased them down with the water, thinking that if the doctor had any inkling of what his life had become, she wouldn't have made that crack about luck. She excused herself, promising to return within a half-hour.

Eventually, his nose was shot up with Novocain and realigned to the sickening sound of cartridge and bone as his nose was manipulated in place. His nostrils were packed with cotton and he held a prescription for Tylenol 3 and a free sample box of antihistamines. He kept the ice pack she'd given him against the swelling, frustrated his request for something stronger had been refused. For that, his insurance was going to have to cough up $780.92.

The doctor had given up on examining the back of his mouth, suggesting he see a dentist as soon as possible. He was beginning to take things personally as he was fobbed off from one person to the next.

She'd accomplished the impossible, though. His jaw had finally relaxed. Too bad it hadn't happened until after he was shown the door. The pain in his jaw had gone from intolerable to simply distracting, but his nose would soon be making up for that. He'd been instructed to take the Tylenol every 4 hours once the Novocain wore off, which Frank already knew wasn't going to touch the pain. It wouldn't have killed the doctor to give him a prescription for something stronger.

Frank stood in the hallway, deliberating. Loretta would be returning home soon to deliver a sermon on why he'd lost the WWF round in the kitchen. He had a decision to make. He thought back to what the officer had said. The kids *were* being affected. He stopped at the admissions desk to request a cab.

Several loiterers showed interest in his cab as it pulled in front of the hospital. Frank beat them to it, sprinting past the pain in his jaw, and now his nose. Apparently, Novocain had a crummy shelf life.

"You the one called a cab?" the driver asked.

"Yes. I need to get to the courthouse."

The cabbie waited until Frank settled into the back seat. "Let me guess. A bar fight and you're the welterweight that lost."

Frank looked away. He wasn't in the mood to trade insults with a stranger.

Their journey through drizzle and gusting winds was done in silence. Frank paid him with small bills and stiffed him for the tip.

"Thanks a *lot*, buddy!" the cabbie yelled as he tore away from the curb.

Frank felt sufficiently chastised. He looked to the cement stairway leading to the courthouse and contemplated the repercussions of what he was about to do. Once Loretta was served with the restraining order, there was no telling what would happen. Standing at the bottom of the stairs in the slanting rain, his overcoat flapping in the biting wind gusts, he started to do an about-face. But as he turned away from the stairs, the officer's words broke into his struggle: "*I've never seen an abuser who didn't learn it at home.*" That brought the issue to another level. His kids deserved better. He turned back and began maneuvering up the stairs, slowly, one cold slab at a time. The Tylenol hadn't made a dent in the pain since the Novocain had worn off.

It was 8:30 PM, but the lobby was packed with people who were either sitting on benches or milling about. It was impossible to sort out the guilty from the innocent. Some had on business clothes while others looked like they'd just rolled out of bed and chanced the bile of the fashion gods by showing up in what they'd slept in. A gal in an orange jumpsuit and wrist chains was being escorted through a doorway by a couple of uniformed police officers and it crossed Frank's mind that after tonight this could just as easily be Loretta. There was a better than even chance she'd retire the Louisville Slugger for something really lethal.

He searched the echoing lobby. A long line hugging the adjacent marble wall was his first solid lead. He walked over to a guy at the end of the line. "Excuse me. Is this where you file a complaint?"

The man stared back, examining Frank's ruined face. "This is it. Looks like you won't make it through the wait, though. What happened to you, if you don't mind my asking?"

"I was assaulted."

"Must've been a big guy. You really got clocked!"

Frank chose to ignore him and re-adjusted the ice pack against his nose.

"I'm here to get a writ of execution to evict a shit-for-brains renter. Caught him cooking meth in the basement," the stranger said.

Frank offered no comment and the man gave up, turning to face the long line as the courthouse doors intermittently delivered arctic blasts of wind with each new arrival.

For distraction, Frank began a head count but gave up once he reached thirty-five. It would be a long wait.

Chapter 3

The judge looked like he'd just jumped off of a two-week binge. His eyes were a jaundiced yellow with a complexion to match. He was reading the complaint Frank had finished over an hour ago. He grunted every now and then but kept reviewing a life that had come unwound. He finally put the deposition down, took off his bifocals and rubbed his eyes.

"How long has this been going on, Mr. Walch?"

"I've been married for ten years, so the answer would be ten years."

"Why would you choose to stay in such a relationship?" the judged asked.

"My wife got pregnant right away. After that, I was afraid to leave for fear she'd get custody."

"That's a commendable reason, I suppose," the judge offered. "Has your wife sought psychiatric help?"

"No she hasn't, Your Honor."

"Has she ever harmed your children?"

"No. She yells a lot, but she's never raised her hand to them."

"That, Mr. Walch, could be construed as verbal abuse, depending upon the severity."

"It's extreme all right. Whenever I confronted Loretta over it, she said it's how she was raised, and if it was good enough for her, it was good enough for the kids."

"That's a piss-poor and overused excuse, Mr. Walch. I hear it in my courtroom every day, and frankly, I'm sick to death of it. It's a matter of self-control. Lots of folks have suffered abuse and walked away to live better lives," the judge said. He seemed ready to say more, but instead he paused and took off his bifocals to rub his eyes again.

"I'm granting you the restraining order for the duration of seven days. At that time there will be a hearing to determine if the restraining order will remain in effect. Keep in mind, Mr. Walch, this by no means protects you or your children from harm. You must be diligent in your every-day routine and make certain you don't leave yourself open for retaliation. It appears your wife is mentally unbalanced. She'd do well to seek professional help and that, Mr. Walch, can be addressed at the hearing."

The judge picked up Frank's complaint and began reading the financial section. "You've indicated there is one family car and that you and your wife have a combined income of $2,750 per month. Is this information correct?"

"Yes, Your Honor."

"I'm awarding you the use of the vehicle and remanding Mrs. Walch to pay one-third of her monthly income towards child support. I'm also granting you and the children use of the home."

Frank was shocked. This was going to send Loretta into a rage. He hadn't given much thought to finances. He should have, but compared to the kids' and his safety, it hadn't crossed his mind.

"Thank you, Your Honor."

"You have stated you believe your wife is at home at this time."

"Yes, I believe she would've arrived home by now."

"Police officers will serve the restraining order this evening. You will be required to stay away from the residence until Mrs. Walch has been served and has removed her personal belongings from the home. An officer will contact you when it's permissible to return home."

"Permissible? Once she's been served with the restraining order, she'll do everything in her power to get even."

"Mr. Walch, it's not often we get complaints of an abusive wife to the extent that has been reported here. I suggest that you grow a backbone and let this be the last of it. The restraining order I'm granting requires Mrs. Walch to stay 300 feet away from you and the children at all times. She will also be directed not to make phone contact with you. If she breaks the restraining order, it will behoove you to contact the police immediately. Keep this order with you at all times," the judge said, tearing off the bottom yellow copy and handing it to Frank.

The judge stood and disappeared through a side door.

Frank leaned over the table and put his forehead in his hands, unable to move. A backbone. He'd never had the chance to grow one. His mother had chipped it away, vertebrae by vertebrae, ever since he could remember. What if it was too late? What if his life was destined to be one long nightmare? He was thirty-four years old, young by any stand-ard, but he felt like a withered old man.

The street in front of the courthouse was littered with cabs. Obvi-ously, business was booming in the land of the lost. The cotton swab-bing packed up his nostrils made it impossible to breathe except through his mouth and his eyes were swollen to mere slits. He was past exhaustion as he flagged an unoccupied cab. Once he'd given the cab-bie Edith's address, he leaned his head against the window and fell fast asleep.

"Hey, wake up!" the cabbie shouted. Nicotine breath reached him as Frank forced himself to sit up. Checking the taximeter, Frank reached into his wallet and took enough cash out to include a twenty percent tip. It might not make up for the cabbie he'd stiffed, but still, it made him feel better.

The house was lit up like Edith and Freddie owned proprietary stock in S&C Electric. Every window of the one-story bungalow cast light to the frigid exterior. At some point in time, cedar shingles had replaced asbestos siding, giving the home the look of a Nantucket beach house. Whoever had done the renovations had the foresight to accent the handsome exterior with generous moldings that were painted brilliant white around the windows, doors and even the small, mulli-oned-windowed side porch where ivy stubbornly clung. The yard was well maintained. That would be due to his uncle, Freddie. Edith might've been capable of pulling weeds from the flowerbeds, but she'd never have been able to get back up.

He watched as a figure streaked past the living room window. Judg-ing by the speed and agility, he guessed it was Brice. Frank moved to the covered porch and rang the doorbell. The figure stopped, spun around, and headed to the door to fling it open, and just as quickly, re-treated. It was Brice, busy trying to corral Britney who'd donned her Cinderella pajamas.

"She's been buzzing all over the house, Dad. I'm afraid she's going to crash into something!" Brice said, out of breath.

"Where's Aunt Edith?" Frank asked.

"She's in the family room watching TV."

"And Mark and Brandon?"

"They're asleep in the living room."

Frank wasn't surprised. It was after midnight; way past their bed-time. He bent down to scoop Britney into his arms. "And why aren't you sleeping, young lady?"

She struggled to get down, then changed her mind, and began to giggle. "Ba ba, Daddy."

Brice resumed his search of the knickknack cluttered entryway. "She dropped her bottle somewhere. Aunt Edith gave us donuts and ice cream. Britney's been hyper all night."

Frank took pity on his eldest. Too much responsibility had been handed to him. He looked his son in the eye as he struggled to keep hold of his squirming two-year-old.

"Things are going to be different, I promise. We're going to spend the night at Aunt Edith's and go home tomorrow."

"But how will you go to work like that, Dad?" Brice asked, looking at his father's swollen face.

It was a question few nine-year-olds would have to ask a parent, Frank thought sadly. "I'm not. We're taking tomorrow off."

When Frank entered the living room, Uncle Freddie did a double take. "Holy crap! What happened to you?"

Frank remained mute. It was none of Freddie's business. Besides, Edith would have already fabricated whatever she'd decided to tell the rest of the family. It's what she loved best—next to fried foods—to wring out the most salacious spin on family events. She'd placed her brother as a hit-and-run victim a few years back when the truth was he'd stepped off a curb and twisted his ankle. Before that, a grease fire, that had merely singed her kitchen cabinets, had grown into a three-alarm fire with her and Freddie's near escape a miracle.

Frank checked on Mark and Brandon. Their heads were resting on crushed velvet pillows that matched Edith's crushed velvet couch. It was his ticket out. "I fell on the ice. Listen, the boys are already asleep. Would it be okay if we spend the night and bum a ride home tomor-row?"

Edith, ever the queen of gossip, narrowed her eyes. "Mark said Loretta clobbered you with a frying pan. Your mom wants you to call her."

Frank's decision was instantaneous. He wasn't about to take the leap of calling his crazier-than-a-shithouse-mouse mother. "It's too late to call now. I'll call her tomorrow. Can we stay?"

Edith wasn't willing to be deprived. "She told me she'd wait up for your call. She's worried about you and the kids."

Like a cobra worries over its next meal, Frank thought. "I'm exhausted. I'll call her tomorrow."

Freddie took pity on Frank and volunteered himself as a buffer. "Have a seat. There's gonna be a swimsuit contest. Most of 'em are Victoria's Secret models. We been wait'n all week to see it."

Frank didn't doubt it. Freddie's face was already flushed. What a strange union. Maybe not as cracked as he and Loretta's, but close.

His nose was throbbing which meant he needed another dose of Tylenol. He wandered into the kitchen to fill a sixties-era tumbler with water. Edith was a saver. She'd probably gotten them with green stamps decades ago. When he returned to the living room, still holding Britney in his arms, he found Brice sitting directly in front of the viewing pleasure. Leggy, anorexic models strutted their stuff in thongs with little more than pasties covering their nipples. Their breasts bounced along with Brice's head as he followed the action. *Enough!*

"I need to put the kids to bed. Is it okay to use the guestroom?" Frank asked.

Edith temporarily tore herself away from the phone. "Your mom wants to talk to you."

"Tell her I'll call her later. I need to get the kids settled."

Edith gave him a reproachful look and went back to gossiping.

"Brice, I need your help." *Anything to get his attention refocused,* Frank thought. The runway extravaganza was inappropriate for a nine-year-old.

Brice disagreed. "Come on, Dad, Aunt Edith said that I could watch TV."

"And I say you can't. It's bedtime. Wake up Mark and Brandon, now."

Brice took one last peek at the contestants and went over to shake his brothers awake. They made slow progress down the hallway. Frank changed Britney's diaper and tucked them in to bed.

He'd have to sleep on the couch. There were only the two twin beds in the small guest bedroom, which was unfortunate. It meant he'd have to deal with Edith until she decided to tear herself away from the TV, and she was a night owl.

When he returned, Edith held the phone out to him. "Come on, she wants to talk to you. It'll only take a minute."

Frank looked away and thought about his absent backbone. Now was as good a time as any to begin cultivating one. "I'm hurting too much right now. I said I'd call her tomorrow."

Sighing, Edith went back to her phone conversation. "Did you hear that, Donna? Well, he said that he was in pain and that he'll talk to you tomorrow."

There was a long pause on Edith's end and Frank could hear snippets of his mother's shrill voice traveling over the phone line. Once she came up for air, Edith threw in her opinion of the situation. "He's being ridiculous, of course. Kids these days…they don't have respect."

Another tirade ensued and at the culmination, Edith placed her sixties-style princess phone back in its cradle. "She's really upset with you, Frank. You should've talked to her."

He ventured a dirty look in her direction, but his glance locked on Freddie who was nearly mesmerized by the models who slinked, en masse, down the runway for their final tits and ass exhibition. Sick.

With the segment finally over, Freddie and Edith took themselves off to bed. Frank tossed and turned on the couch. He hadn't been offered a blanket and he refused to be forced to beg for one. As the temperature plummeted since Edith turned the thermostat down to just above freezing, he suffered in silence. He couldn't wait to get home.

* * *

Twenty miles away, in a low-rent district of Chicago, Loretta was having issues of her own. She had arrived home to an empty house. She'd looked for a note, but hadn't found one. Frank must have taken the kids with him to the 24-Hour Emergency Center, which was a first. Typically, he left Brice and Mark at home. Loretta went in search of evidence. Britney's favorite bottle was missing, as were a handful of the Pampers Frank had picked up at the grocery store.

She'd waited an hour before calling his mom. "Where's Frank?"

"Where do you think he is?" Donna snapped.

"If I knew, would I be calling you?"

"Don't you get bitchy with me!"

Loretta held the phone away from her ear while Donna screamed and felt a hangover coming on. "I'm not being bitchy. I got home an hour ago and Frank and the kids were gone."

"And if he's smart, he'll stay gone!" This was screamed full-throttle, followed by a dial tone.

Loretta was pacing off her frustration and nursing her hangover with a cold beer when there was a knock on the door. Believing Frank had misplaced his house keys, she grabbed the Louisville Slugger. But instead of greeting Frank, she opened the door to two police officers.

They took in her white-knuckled grasp on the bat and moved their hands over their holsters. The gray-haired officer was the first to speak.

"Drop the weapon, Ma'am, and step back from the door."

Loretta did as she was told.

"What's this about, officers?"

As they entered, the youngest officer fished paperwork from his front pocket while his other hand remained near his gun.

"Are you Loretta Walch?"

She stood frozen to the floor.

"Are you Loretta Walch?" he repeated.

"Yes."

He leaned over to hand her the paperwork, unwilling to get any closer than necessary. "You are being served with a restraining order. You are to vacate the premises and are not to come within 300 feet of Mr. Walch, nor are you allowed to contact him in any manner, including by phone, until the court hearing."

"This is insane! I didn't do anything!"

The officers had been partners for over a decade. To date, no one being served a restraining order admitted any wrongdoing. They gave each other a meaningful look and let her drone on. She was a big woman. Neither was willing to get within arm's reach of her.

Loretta stopped screaming and settled for threats. "Well I'm not going anywhere. This is my home. If Frank wants to be away from me, he can damn well move out!"

The older officer took control. "If you don't comply, we'll be forced to take you into custody. The restraining order was signed by a judge, Ma'am. You are to vacate the premises. You have thirty minutes to gather your things."

Loretta thought about grabbing the bat and having a go at them. But when she glanced down at the Louisville Slugger, the youngest officer reached down and snatched it from the floor.

Too bad. She'd been in the mood for some exercise. How dare they invade her home and start pushing her around! She had rights, just like everyone else.

"You have twenty-eight minutes left to gather your belongings and get out," threatened the younger one, who still held the bat.

Loretta stomped off—as much as a nearly three hundred pound woman could stomp—and headed for the bedroom. The officers followed.

"Give me some damned privacy!"

"That's not possible, Ma'am," replied the oldest officer. "We've been ordered to observe you."

"Is that so? Well, let me tell you something. I'm going to get an attorney and have you guys for lunch!"

Neither had any doubt she was capable of such a feat. The woman could probably eat her way through more than what they had to offer. She was a black mark against society in twenty yards of polyester fabric.

"Where am I supposed to put my stuff? I don't know where the suitcases are," she complained.

"You could try the economy approach," said the younger one.

"What do you mean by that?" Loretta carped. She wasn't sure where he was going with his suggestion, but she was certain she wasn't going to like it.

"Plastic garbage bags, Ma'am," the officer dead-panned.

Loretta gave him a scathing look and went to search under the kitchen sink. She yanked out a box of lawn and garden bags and returned to the bedroom. Shaking the contents of dresser drawers into several of the bags, she marched to her side of the closet and started yanking her clothes from the rod, stuffing them into several more bags, hangers and all. Looking around the room, satisfied she hadn't missed anything, Loretta squeezed herself through the narrow bathroom door and started tossing her personal items into yet another bag.

The activity seemed to have calmed her. She switched to whining. "Where am I supposed to go? I don't have any money for a hotel room."

"Sorry, Ma'am, I don't have an answer for you," replied the smart-ass.

"Well, neither do I! Isn't there a half-way house; somewhere I could go until I figure things out?"

"Not to my knowledge there isn't," answered the gray-haired officer.

Loretta had exactly $35 to her name. It wasn't enough for a motel room, not even the Motel 6. Her only hope was Jay.

"I need to make a call."

"As long as it isn't to Mr. Walch," replied the gray-haired officer.

"You mean to tell me that I'm not allowed to call my own husband?"

"That's exactly what I mean. We already informed you of the restraining order, Ma'am," he answered.

Putting down the bags, Loretta scanned the paperwork. Her eyes widened in increments. This couldn't be real. No way would knocking some sense into Frank bring her life tumbling down around her like this.

"This says that he gets the car! How am I supposed to get to work, damn it?"

"Not our problem, Ma'am. Maybe you should've thought of that before you played roller derby with your husband," rebutted the smart-ass.

"I didn't do a damn thing to deserve this!"

"You can tell that to the judge seven days from now," replied the smart-ass.

Loretta went back to reading the paperwork. "One third! I'm supposed to give that piece of shit one third of my pay?"

"I suggest you make your call," the smart-ass said as he glanced at his wristwatch. "You have exactly three minutes."

Loretta saw the steel in his eyes. He'd like nothing better than to leave her stranded in the freezing cold. She picked up the phone and dialed.

"Jay, it's Loretta."

"Why are you calling me in the middle of the freaking night?"

"Because I'm standing in my living room with two police officers, holding a restraining order that Frank had served on me, that's why!"

Jay snapped to attention. "Was that blood on your Muumuu? What did you do to him?"

"I didn't *do* a damned thing to his sorry ass! It's all lies. I need a place to stay until I can figure this out."

"There's a slew of motels just down the street from you. Pick one."

"I would if I had the money. I haven't got anywhere to go."

There was a lengthy pause on Jay's end.

Swell. Her husband was tossing her out like a buggered up Kleenex... and now Jay. Loretta waited through the silence, hoping she would relent.

"You can stay tonight, but after that, you're going to need to find somewhere else."

"Could you come and get me? The judge gave Frank the damned car."

"I can't. If I get stopped I'll be facing another D.U.I. I'm not going to risk it."

Loretta tried to recall how many beers they'd downed. She was probably right about the driving. She hung up and called for a cab.

"Sorry, but your time's up," said the gray-haired cop.

"But I can't wait outside. It's freezing out there!"

"So it is. Now let's go," smiled the smart-ass.

"I don't like your tone," Loretta said. "I want your names and badge numbers. I'm gonna be talking to your supervisor!"

The smart-ass didn't flinch. "My name is Robert Coles, badge number 76554."

Loretta jotted down the information on a notepad and turned to the gray-haired officer. "And yours?"

"Sam Barlow, badge number 32248."

She tore the paper from the notepad, shoved it in her coat pocket, took hold of the bags and lumbered for the door.

"Before you leave, we need your house and car keys," said the smart-ass.

"That wasn't in the damned restraining order!" Loretta screamed.

"It's standing operating procedure, Ma'am," he smiled back.

"You can both go fuck yourselves!" she said, grabbing her keys from her coat pocket and throwing them to the floor. She slammed the door behind her to wait in the freezing sleet.

From the comfort of the heated apartment, the officers watched out the living room window for her departure.

The cab ride gave Loretta plenty of time to hash out what she was going to do to Frank. She'd start at his ankles and work up. It would be the bat this time. It was easier to get it to connect to its designated spots. Next, she'd transplant his pubic hair to his forehead and if she didn't feel better by then, she'd make a coin purse out of his furry little scrotum.

Never once did she wonder about the welfare of her children.

Chapter 4

Jay answered the door wearing long johns. They had "bite me" embroidered on the front and a trap door in the back.

"You owe me big time," Jay retorted the minute the door was shut behind them. "I have the 6:00 shift tomorrow. I need to get some rest!"

"I'm sorry, Babe. It won't happen again, but this just caught me off guard. I didn't have anywhere else to go."

Jay plunked down on a blown-out easy chair and hung her head in her hands. "Well, shit! I'll never get back to sleep now. Go fix us some coffee. Then I want to hear what happened."

Loretta grabbed hazelnut-flavored creamer from the fridge and prepared their coffees. Jay liked it extra sweet, so she added extra creamer. She felt as if she'd already worn out her welcome and if she couldn't wrangle an invitation to stay, she'd end up living on the streets. Thinking it through, Loretta came up with a plan, of sorts. Jay was a lousy housekeeper and lived off Lean Cuisine dinners—anything to avoid cutting into her party time. She could offer Jay housekeeping and cooking in exchange for a place to stay.

Carrying out the steaming coffee, she handed the cup that didn't have a chip to Jay.

"So, what happened?" Jay demanded.

Taking a deep breath, Loretta dove in. "Before I came over here earlier tonight…I guess I should say last night, Frank and I had a disagreement. The idiot called the cops and I got served with a restraining order."

There, it was said. She hoped Jay didn't go for twenty questions. It was past 1:00 in the morning. All she wanted to do was crawl into bed and get some sleep.

"That isn't the whole story. I want to hear the truth."

"That *is* the truth! Frank's been more irritating than usual. Things got a little heated and I smacked him with a frying pan, but it was in self-defense!"

"So that *was* blood I saw on your muumuu. You didn't have to go after him like that. You could've just walked out."

"You weren't there. He can be scary."

Jay snorted. "You're forgetting I've seen a picture of Frank. He's half your size! How is it you'd feel threatened by that little weasel? Hell, you could take him with one hand tied behind your back."

Loretta beamed. "You got that right. It's just that he's been doing this passive-aggressive thing lately that's been driving me crazy. He even started demanding to know where I go at night. It's like I'm not allowed a life."

Jay shrugged her shoulders dismissively. "You *don't* have a life, Loretta. You're married with four kids."

"That's not true. What've I been doing just about every night after work? I come here! Frank doesn't have the right to question every little thing I do."

"I don't know if having an affair's a little thing. I'm no prude, but you are married. Have you ever thought your kids might need you?"

"The kids are just fine. Frank spoils them and they're happier with him. We talked about this before, Jay. Anyways, what do you care? I thought you were on my side."

"I'm not on anyone's side, just pointing out the obvious. I could care less what happens between the two of you. But, I deserve to know the truth. I don't feel it's in my best interest to harbor a felon."

"Felon? Who said anything about a felony? All's I did was knock some sense into Frank. I swear to you!"

"Let me see the paperwork," Jay demanded.

"Why can't you take my word for it? I'm telling you I didn't do anything wrong."

"Could be. Hand it over," Jay insisted, holding out her hand.

Reaching into her coat pocket, Loretta surrendered the crumpled wad of paperwork.

Switching on a cheap plastic lamp, Jay began to read. It took a while to wade through a decade's worth of abuse. Several attachment pages had been added to Frank's complaint.

"He claims this has been going on for ten years. Is that true?"

"Sort of."

"It's an easy question, Loretta. Either it has or it hasn't."

"Frank's the kind of guy who needs to be reminded every once in a while. If it'd been that bad, would he have stayed?"

"I have no way of knowing that. It takes all kinds. Maybe he stayed because of the kids."

"The reason he stayed was because it wasn't that bad. We'd just get into it once and a while and I'd have to give him a reality check. That's all there was to it. I'm not some kind of monster!"

"That depends on whether you're on the receiving end or not. His statement says he had to go to the emergency room because you knocked his jaw out of its socket and busted out a tooth. That seems like more than tough love to me."

"I just hit him with a frying pan. I didn't mean to clip him hard enough to knock out a tooth. This thing's been blown out of proportion," Loretta said as she inspected Jay's newly spiked hair while she read the judge's findings. The crew cut formed little swirls where cowlicks hid. It looked worse than earlier by far.

"It says here that Frank keeps the car and you're to pay one-third of your wages for child support. Looks like you're screwed."

"I wouldn't be so sure about that. He's not getting a penny outta me! Anyways, I know where he keeps the extra set of car keys. I can sneak over there and grab the car anytime I want."

"I wouldn't do that if I were you. If you break the judge's orders, you'll wind up in jail."

Loretta felt her mouth go dry. She shut her eyes and centered herself by daydreaming about beating the stuffing out of Frank. In no time, she was herself again.

"I'm not sure what to do. I need transportation to get to work and I can't hand a third of my paycheck over for child support. I only clear $900 a month. Everyone's had their hours cut at the plant. I'll never be able to afford an apartment."

"There's ways around it. You could find someone who wants to share a place. That way, it'd cost you next to nothing. As long as you're close to a bus line, you'll get by," Jay said.

Getting by wasn't on Loretta's mind. Getting even was. But she kept that to herself.

"What if I offered to cook and clean for you? You know how you hate that. It could be in exchange for a place to stay."

"You're leaving something out. I don't want a roommate. I like my freedom, just the same as you."

By freedom, Jay meant bringing women home, thought Loretta. She would just be in the way. "Can I stay 'till I get my paycheck next week? I'm down to $25 after paying for the cab fare here."

Jay looked to the ceiling in frustration. She didn't owe Loretta a damned thing. She had gotten herself in a pickle, for sure, but it wasn't her problem. On the other hand, she was a believer in karma. When given the choice, she usually did the right thing. In this case, there was more to it than mere inconvenience. She'd grown tired of Loretta. She was a sloth and it was getting in the way of her libido. The last few times they'd been together, she'd flirted with the notion of dumping her. It just never seemed to be the right time to bring it up. Because of that, she was going to give in.

"You can stay until next week. But no fooling around. I've been meaning to tell you, you're not my type."

Loretta felt the sting of tears as her feelings of self-worth went from bad to worse. "Then what *is* your type? And how do you explain earlier tonight?"

"Frankly, my type's someone who doesn't need to wear a muumuu. Sorry, but that's the way it is. You can sleep on the couch."

"What about the past few months?" Loretta demanded.

Jay shrugged. "An error of judgment, I suppose," she said as she went to the hall closet and returned with a pillow and a moth-eaten wool blanket.

Loretta was allergic to wool. She thanked Jay anyway and watched her head off to bed, still hurt over what she had said. Throwing the cheap dime store accent pillows to the floor, Loretta was relieved to discover the extra room it gave her on the couch that would keep her from rolling off. Within seconds, she was sound asleep.

Hours later, Loretta dreamt she was falling. As her body hurled to the wooden floor, her foot caught the edge of the coffee table and a glass bowl filled with pistachios arced into the air. Jay's overflowing ashtray followed and both containers were reduced to shards, waking Loretta to her fate.

Loretta was still trying to get her bearings when the overhead light was switched on.

"What the hell…" Jay yelled, just before her bare foot was impaled on a sliver of glass. She grunted in pain, grabbed the injured foot, and did a one-legged pirouette.

Loretta missed the action. She was occupied with getting herself up off the floor while the coffee table groaned and sagged beneath her weight.

"Could you give me a hand?" Loretta called out.

"Love to. But first, let me yank the frigging piece of glass out of my frigging foot!"

Uh Oh!

Loretta watched as Jay collapsed to the floor to yank the sliver from the pad of her foot. A trickle of blood showed she was successful. She got back up and gingerly made her way to the broom closet, careful to put her weight on the heel of her injured foot.

"What the hell happened?" Jay demanded, sweeping up the glass with angry jerks.

"I fell off the couch. There isn't much room. I didn't m…"

"There'd been plenty of room if you hadn't eaten your way to the size of a highland gorilla!" Jay interrupted.

She left the pile of glass that she'd swept into a mound and walked over to grab Loretta by an arm to help hoist her to her feet. Loretta did her part, using the leverage of the rickety coffee table. She inventoried the damage from her fall. She'd have bruised knees by morning and the ankle that had struck the coffee table was smarting something awful.

"I have an air mattress in the shed," Jay said, limping to the patio doors. Soon, the sound of clanging could be heard while she routed through a lean-to next to the patio. The neighbor's dogs, disturbed by the noise, started barking, shattering an otherwise quiet night.

Jay returned holding something that resembled an over-large velour pancake and threw it to the floor at Loretta's feet. It was filthy. Dead spiders, years of accumulated dust and nameless muck had embedded itself onto the blue velvet.

From her other hand, Jay handed Loretta an air pump. "You do it. I've got to get some rest," she said, limping into her bedroom.

Loretta was satisfied she'd knocked off most of the really offensive crud from the velour, but on closer inspection she discovered a few stubborn cocoons that had to be peeled off with a paper towel. She *hated* bugs!

The directions on the air pump were hard to read. The sticker had been adhered to its shank for who knew how long. It was torn and tattered, and in places the print was undecipherable. It took several attempts before Loretta was able to start filling the mattress. She winced as she worked. The pump was noisy as hell.

When the mattress finally began to fill, Loretta leaned back against the couch to give her back a rest, hoping Jay was able to sleep past the noise. At least there was no sound coming from her room. Loretta allowed herself the luxury of letting loose some excess gas. In no time, the smell of sulfur permeated the air, staying low to the floor like a toxic cloud of napalm. She'd grabbed six McDonald's cheeseburgers and an extra fry on her way home from work. They hadn't settled well. Her stomach continued to gurgle in protest as she willed the Ex-Lax she'd double-dosed on to kick in. It was the only way she was going to get any relief.

The bed was now filled. Loretta was proud of her accomplishment; she'd never been good with mechanical things. Not trusting her first several inspections, she zeroed in on the velvet once more. A few cobwebs remained. She had another swipe at them and called it good. Finally, she was going to get some sleep.

She'd settled in and was positioning herself for maximum comfort when the side of the air mattress blew and her body was driven to the floor. Loretta laid her head against the disgusting velour while tears of self-pity welled up in her eyes.

"That's it! I can't take anymore!" Jay screamed in rage as she exploded from the bedroom.

She'd only moved a few feet into the room when she stopped cold and sniffed the air. Her mouth puckered in distaste, like someone had spoon-fed her alum. "What's... that... disgusting... smell? It smells like rotten eggs in here."

Loretta's crying picked up speed while Jay inspected the torn remnants of the blown mattress. Her inspection over, she turned her attention to Loretta who continued to sob and took pity on her.

"I give. You can share the bed with me, but tomorrow you'll need to figure out something workable," Jay warned.

Loretta pulled herself back up, only this time she had the couch for leverage, and followed Jay into the bedroom. She waited for her to choose which side of the bed she wanted, then got in as quietly as possible, fully dressed.

It wasn't long before Loretta's stomach started to rumble and gas began to build up like a pressure cooker. It had been a mistake to take the double dose of Ex-Lax, she realized, but it was too late for re-dos. She couldn't stand the discomfort any longer and let a few silent-but-deadly ones rip; hoping Jay wouldn't move the covers and asphyxiate herself. She was still worrying about the possibilities when she drifted off to sleep.

The sound of an explosion woke her. The digital clock on Jay's nightstand read 3:00 A.M. Loretta's heart raced as she listened for the source of the noise. It had sounded like a cannon had gone off, which didn't make any sense at all.

It wasn't until she laid back down, trying to get comfortable, that the awful truth was revealed.

Her Ex-Lax had kicked in. Wrong time, wrong place. What was she going to do? Humiliation washed over her as she backpedaled for a way out of her predicament. There was none.

By now, Jay was sitting up in bed, using her elbows to support herself. When she came fully awake, the look she gave Loretta was one of total, utter disbelief.

"Oh …my… God... did you just shit the bed? Tell me you didn't just shit the damned bed…" Jay whispered, then dashed to the bathroom to gag over the toilet.

"I'm sorry. I took a few laxatives last night. I didn't mean to do it," Loretta said before she started a crying jag. This time, Jay had nothing to offer.

"I'm going to sleep on the couch. Get this disgusting mess cleaned up! God, I *cannot* believe this!" Jay screamed as she marched past the bed, slamming the door in her wake.

It was another forty-five minutes before Loretta was able to get back into bed. Her muumuu and underpants hung drying over the shower rod and she was sleeping naked… for all the wrong reasons.

The following day didn't improve her mood one bit when her manager gave her the bad news with all the sympathy of a lion eating its young. Company policy forbade employee payroll advances.

Loretta had one small sliver of hope remaining. Jay had left a note taped to the bedroom door, 'Check with the Lesbian Relief Fund. They might be able to help.' The note was terse; it contained no greeting, nor had it ended with so much as a sincerely. In fact, it hadn't been signed at all. But at least Jay was still communicating with her. During her morning break, Loretta found the listing in the yellow pages. Who would've guessed?

Loretta walked the fourteen blocks to their location. It was in a dumpy part of downtown. She almost walked past it; the front of the building took up only a tiny slice of real estate that couldn't have measured more than fifteen feet across. The hand painted sign leaning in the window read Lesbian Relief Fund in block letters. It didn't look like they had deep pockets. Loretta's hopes plummeted.

Entering, her expectations evaporated altogether. The dozen or so kitchen chairs that served as seating were all occupied. Women were sitting around chatting while next to them a couple was busy with an old copying machine. They had the thing open and were alternately fiddling with and arguing over how to fix a stubborn paper jam. The gal with a shaved head and about a dozen ear piercings in each ear snapped, "Damn it, Francis, I need to get these flyers done before the rally. Let me do it."

Her partner shot her a perturbed look and went back to what she was doing.

Since no one acknowledged her entrance, Loretta decided to pass the time by playing *Name That Lesbian,* a game she had only recently cultivated. Although she and Jay had been together off and on for months, she hadn't developed gaydar. That shortcoming was problematic for Loretta, especially since Jay had officially dumped her. How could she ever hope to attract a new partner when her gaydar antenna didn't pick up the correct signals?

Loretta studied the group of women. The only commonality she could see was they all wore Birkenstocks. Maybe *this* was the code she had been looking for. Still weighing the possibilities, Loretta spied a gal tucked away in the far corner of the small space, banging away on a computer keyboard. She looked official.

"Excuse me," Loretta said when she arrived to where the woman sat.

She was fifty-something and wore her hair in a mullet; super short on the top and sides, long in the back. Apparently, she wasn't wearing a bra. Her boobs looked like lopsided dog's ears through her rainbow T-shirt.

"Yes, can I help you?"

"I hope so. A friend told me you sometimes help women in trouble."

"You *are* aware this is the Lesbian Relief Fund?" the woman asked.

"Yes, I'm aware of that." *Must've been her lack of Birkenstocks*, thought Loretta.

The woman rose and took a few steps to a dented file cabinet to wrestle with the top drawer. The rollers appeared to be off their track, but by man-handling it, she eventually got it to open and she rooted around until she located the form she was looking for. "You'll need to fill this out. It'll be reviewed and a determination will be made by the board."

"How long does a determination take?"

"Typically only a few days."

Loretta thanked her and walked over to a vacated chair. Within seconds, the metal legs protested their burden and began to fan out in small increments. Soon, Loretta was sitting slightly lower than the rest of her neighbors. She ignored the inconvenience and continued filling in the blanks.

Every once in a while the couple at the copy machine would trade insults, but then they would get back to playing tug-of-war with the temperamental machine, as if nothing had been said. It was distracting and somehow depressing for Loretta. She'd hoped for better; that relationships made more sense with same-sex couples. Apparently not—if one were to judge by the petty bullshit going on only a few feet away. She finished filling out the form and took it over to the rainbow gal.

The woman gave it a quick scan and raised her eyebrows in surprise. "It says you're asking for assistance because a restraining order was placed on you by your *husband*, rendering you homeless."

Explanations were in order.

"That's correct. I only became a lesbian a few months ago."

"That may be so…" she looked at the form for a name, "…Loretta, but we don't offer financial assistance for domestic violence when the person asking for financial assistance is the perpetrator."

"I wasn't the perpetrator. My ex lied to the judge. I asked for a divorce because I'd fallen in love with another woman and he retaliated. He wants the car, our home and child support. Because of that, I've been thrown out on the street until I get the chance to tell a judge the truth at the court hearing."

The rainbow gal's expression changed from standoffish to neutral.

"You've asked for a substantial amount of money."

"Yes, I suppose I have. I need to get a used car and find an apartment, pay for utility hook-ups and buy food. My paycheck will cover it from there. I went to my manager today to ask for an advance, but I was told it's against company policy." Loretta found herself getting wrapped up in her story and started to leak real tears that traveled down her cheeks in rivulets.

The rainbow gal grabbed a wad of Kleenex from a box on top of the metal cabinet and offered them to her. Patting Loretta on the back, she tried to calm her. "It'll be okay, dear. In no time, you'll look back on this and realize you grew as a person."

Loretta's sobs increased. Growing wouldn't do her one damned bit of good.

The women grabbed the chair Loretta had maimed and dragged it over to her desk. When Loretta settled her girth onto its vinyl seat, the legs spread further to the floor like mutant question marks. The rainbow woman watched in horror and breathed a sigh of relief when the chair's descent came to a grudging halt. The legs were now spread out at odd angles, morphed from question marks into something resembling a starfish. She made a mental note to bring a sturdier chair from home in the event Loretta came by for another visit and waited patiently for her to calm herself.

"Your request is for $2,500. Unfortunately, that's well beyond our $500 limit."

She switched tactics when Loretta went into another crying jag.

"You didn't let me finish. There are other, more useful solutions to your problem. Have you ever contemplated owning a business of your own?"

Loretta turned off the faucets and smiled, wiping her face with the soggy wad of Kleenex. "Actually, I have off and on, but there was never enough money."

"We at the Lesbian Relief Fund believe in empowerment. Instead of a stopgap solution, we prefer to help our sisters with something lasting. A business of your own is just such an endeavor. If you're granted the $500, some of it could go towards a business license and other sundries and from there we can help you apply for grants and a small business loan."

"How long would something like that take?"

"A few months. But instead of worrying over this short period of time in your life, you'd be better off looking towards your future. What kind of business did you have in mind?"

"A hot dog stand. I even have the name."

The woman grew wary. She couldn't see how Loretta would be able to stand on her feet all day. On the other hand, a food related business made sense. She put the brakes on her negative thoughts. It was unfair to jump to conclusions. She didn't even know the woman. Snap decisions were a weakness she'd struggled with her whole life.

"What would you name your hot dog stand, then?"

"L.A. Dogs. It's a good name isn't it?"

"L.A. Dogs..." *In Chicago?* "It does have a certain ring to it. Tell you what; give me a minute to find the forms and we'll get started. You can fill out a business plan and list the startup costs later. We work with the Small Business Association. They have volunteers who will help you every step of the way," she said.

When she returned with a packet, Loretta was staring down at her watch in alarm. "I'm afraid I'm already ten minutes late and work is a twenty minute walk from here. I need to go! I'll fill out the packet tonight and bring it in tomorrow at lunchtime."

The rainbow gal grabbed her purse and yelled to the women still struggling with the copier. "Francis, I need to leave for a few minutes. Can you get the phones?"

The gal with the shaved head and multiple piercings nodded. "No problem."

"Come on, I'll give you a lift," the rainbow woman said, signaling for Loretta to follow.

They went through the back door to a surprisingly spacious parking lot. Watching the woman insert her car key into the door of a 70's Volkswagen Beetle, Loretta balked.

Seeing Loretta's distress, the rainbow woman wordlessly went around to the passenger door, unlocked it, and moved the seat back as far as it would go. Even with the extra room, Loretta had difficulty squeezing herself into the tight space. Once she had settled in as best she could, her butt overlapped the bucket seat to such an extent getting the door closed was impossible. Loretta resorted to grasping the door handle so it wouldn't fly open once they were on the road. Her side of the car nearly kissed the pavement.

Even through her embarrassment, Loretta's mind was filled with grandeur. She would be a business owner! The idea for a hot dog stand had come to her on the fly, mainly because she'd had to skip lunch. She'd passed a hot dog vendor on her way to the Lesbian Relief Fund and ever since, she hadn't been able to get her mind off kielbasa hot dogs smothered in sauerkraut. Now ravenous, she added a few orders of warm, salted pretzels with melted cheese and a large Pepsi to her daydreams.

That was what she'd do, Loretta decided. The minute her shift was over, she'd walk the seven blocks to the hot dog stand. She could catch the city bus to Jay's from there. Her stomach began to growl.

The name for L.A. Dogs came from a game she and her sisters used to play when they were kids. They'd make up menus with the grossest things they could think of. Her sister had scored a direct hit with puss soufflé and later, tampon surprise. Loretta's contribution had been scab sandwiches and L.A. Dogs (short for lips and assholes). It was why their mother refused to buy them—and, truth be told, it was her only memory of her mother giving a crap *what* they ate. Her uncle was a meat cutter. His description of what went into them would've made anyone squeamish. Her hot dogs would be kosher; no entrails, eyeballs or other byproducts in them.

L.A. Dogs in lights... she couldn't wait to get started!

Her thoughts traveled to her predicament. She still didn't have a place for the night, and it wouldn't surprise her to find her things strewn across Jay's' front porch when she got there.

They pulled up to the bottling plant and Loretta said her goodbyes. "I can't thank you enough. You've given me hope"

"You're quite welcome."

"I didn't even get your name."

"Tanya, it's Tanya Brothers."

Still holding on to the door, Loretta hesitated. "I don't want to sound ungrateful, but do you have any idea where I could stay 'till I get my business started?"

"I'm glad you reminded me. I was going to ask you for your phone number. I have a few ideas, but they're just that. I'll look around and let you know."

"I can give you the number of where I stayed last night, but I'm not sure I'll be there tonight. I suppose you could leave a message."

"What about your work number?"

Loretta hesitated. Personal calls weren't allowed. But what the hell; she could tell them it was an emergency. She gave Tanya both phone numbers and squeezed herself out of the Volkswagen with a feeling of dread. This morning she had gotten on the wrong bus and was a half-hour late. And now, she was late returning from lunch.

She was hoofing it to her station when her manager started flapping his jaws. "What the hell's with you today? You trying to set a company record or something? You've been late twice in one day! You're getting a pink slip for this, Loretta, and if it happens again, you're history."

Ignoring his tirade wasn't easy, but Loretta continued to her station where she would inspect case after case of beer and pull the defective bottles off the assembly line. If she got her small business loan, and she was determined she would, she was going to pay her manager a visit to settle the score.

Chapter 5

The group counselor, Claire, looked expectantly at Frank. "Perhaps you would like to share with the group? It can be difficult to solve a problem all on your own. In group, we often offer help to one-another."

Frank looked around at the circle of females and squirmed in his folding chair. There were fourteen at the meeting. He was the only male.

Frank knew he was having performance anxiety. How could he make amends for his gender? There were thirteen pairs of eyes daring him to even try. He postponed his launch into the abyss by taking a sip of lukewarm coffee. It was bitter and carried the acrid smell of having sat on a burner too long. Looking down into its depths, he noticed a dark brown ring had built up within the cups paper lining.

The women waited silently. Frank turned his attention to the gold band on his left hand and asked himself why he was still wearing it. He could feel dents along its beaded edge as he began twirling it with his thumb. He counted twenty revolutions before the silence was broken.

"We're not here to judge you. You can share as much or as little as you like," Claire nudged.

Frank hated being lied to. From his experience, females learned to judge before they made it out of diapers. In fact, he didn't consider it out of the realm of possibility they learned it in the womb. He was being set up. If he shared too much, he'd be a female basher; too little and he'd be judged as passive-aggressive. Either way, he wouldn't be walking away from this encounter unscathed.

"I served a restraining order on my wife last night. I'm not sure where to go from here."

"And how does that make you feel?" Claire asked.

"She'll want to get even. I'm worried about the safety of my children and myself."

One of the women raised her hand. "Yes, Carrie, would you like to share?" Claire asked.

"I think that Frank should get a gun if he's worried," she volunteered.

"We've talked about this before, Carrie. You can't go around wielding a gun to solve violence," Claire admonished.

This time, Carrie did not raise her hand as she pressed her point. "It certainly worked when Hal came by to pay a visit. Nothing I'd said before made a difference; not threatening to call the police and not reminding him about the restraining order. When my 357 Magnum came out, he sprinted past the screen door and was gone! He listened all right!"

There were snickers in the group and the counselor frowned. "What if you had refused to open the door to him? There are many things we have control over that can contribute towards our personal safety. You could have called the police when he came to your home instead of threatening him with a gun."

"I could have, yes. I wouldn't be here tonight, though, because I'd be lying in a hospital bed. Hal can bang down a door in nothing flat."

Claire sighed. She'd lost control of the group.

Frank looked at Carrie and marveled. She couldn't weigh more than a hundred pounds with a heart-shaped face that framed doe eyes the color of amber. Her voice was melodious, soothing even, as she recounted pointing the business end of a 357 Magnum at her ex. Frank could picture her at a bake sale, or attending a P.T.A. meeting, but had trouble seeing her threatening a man who mowed down doors.

A middle aged woman put down the embroidery ring she'd been taking stabs at to contribute her vote. "Carrie's right. For twenty-five years, my husband beat me. Drunk or sober, it didn't matter. If his dinner wasn't to his liking, he'd slap me around. If he'd had a bad day at work, he'd go after me. If the kids upset him, his fists would come out. I think a gun would've been a great equalizer!"

Another gal with tattoos and brittle, over-processed hair entered into the discussion. She pointed to the pressed-upon counselor. "Claire, you're forgetting some of us got run over by the courts. If our old man gets visitation rights, there's no way to keep clear of him."

"But if they break their restraining order, the law will react," Claire argued.

"Fat lot of good that's gonna do when we're lying on a slab wearing a toe tag!" retorted the gal with the tattoos.

Claire stood up, clearly at an impasse. "Our time is up ladies…and gentleman. I'd like to suggest we think over what we can do, individually, that will ensure our safety *without* the use of firearms. We can discuss it during our next meeting."

The attendees vacated their chairs in varying degrees. The woman with the embroidery remained seated, pecking away at a pansy of blues and purples, showing no signs of wanting to leave her chair. Others had made for the door in a rush and a few were huddled together to grouse about the direction the meeting had taken.

"Did you hear about Susan?" one of the women asked.

Carrie, the doe-eyed gal, looked worried. "I went by her house tonight to give her a ride, but she wasn't home. What's happened?"

"Her old man knocked the shit outta her is what happened! She was on her way to her court hearing and he ambushed her in the courthouse parking lot, beating her half to death," said the woman with the tattoos. "Fat lot of good her restraining order did her."

"Where is she now?" asked Carrie, her voice barely audible.

"They just released her from the hospital. She's probably home by now. She has a sprained wrist, and her ankle got screwed up. They had to put her in an air cast. Bastard kept pounding away 'till a cop saw it and broke it up. Her ex is already out on bail."

"I should've brought her with me when I bought the Magnum. If she'd had something to defend herself with, he would've thought twice!" Carrie exclaimed.

"That's just the point," said the tattooed woman. "These bastards aren't gonna change unless they're looking down the barrel of a gun. It worked with my old man…I pointed the damned thing at his useless balls and told 'em he'd taken the last swing at me he'd *ever* take! They just gotta know you mean it."

Carrie turned to Frank and wrinkled her nose. "Sorry. I wish I could tell you it gets better. Anyway, some of us go for coffee at Denny's after the meeting. You're invited to come along," Carrie offered.

"Thanks. Anyone need a ride over?"

"We walk. It's only two blocks from here," Carrie said.

"Come on, ladies. I got a babysitter whose meter's ticking," said the tattooed woman.

While they walked as a group, Frank mulled over the fact that at thirty-four years old, he had never had anyone he could truly call a friend. It didn't take a psychiatrist's couch to figure out why. Throughout his school years, he hadn't dared invite anyone over. His mother would have done her Lizzie Borden impersonation—and, by God, she was good at it.

By the time Frank enrolled in college, he'd grown used to being a loner. And that's how it had remained until Edith had introduced him to Loretta and the start of his real problems had begun.

They'd married the summer he graduated, which was the exact moment the Louisville Slugger and frying pan came out. She must have had them tucked away in her hope chest the way some women kept a starter set of china. He might have evened the score from the beginning, taken a few reciprocal swipes back, if she hadn't gotten pregnant with Brice right away. Defying the rule of gravity, the bigger she got, the meaner and faster she got. And Loretta had super-sized at the speed of light.

"Are you glad you came to the meeting?" Carrie asked, bringing Frank back to the present.

He hesitated, not sure what to say.

"You don't have to answer that. I felt uncomfortable the first few meetings myself."

"How'd you get past it?" Frank asked with a sardonic smile.

"Oh, you mean the abuse?" she asked.

When Frank nodded, she continued.

"It's tough. My ex-husband, Hal, started in on me after our first child was born. He'd go to AA and stop drinking, then beg me to come back and I did, time after time. But when he started getting aggressive with the kids, I finally got up the nerve to leave him for good."

"How old are they?"

"Sam's ten, and Madison's eight." She looked off to the distance, breaking eye contact. "One day, Sam tried to protect me from his dad and Hal went after him. We went to a shelter that night and never returned," she said, shrugging her shoulders. "Eventually, I finished my degree so we wouldn't have to be on welfare. We lived with my parents. I can't say it was easy," Carrie said matter-of-factly.

"You must be proud of what you've accomplished. What's your degree in?" he asked.

"I'm a paralegal. The law firm I work for gave me free legal counsel to fight Hal over visitation rights. The attorney that represented me was good, but we lost. The problem is, some judges allow visitation, even when there's been abuse. My attorney submitted Hal's arrest records and proof of his alcoholism, but it made no difference. The judge justified his determination by stating that children shouldn't be separated from their parents except in extreme cases. I'd hate to see what his idea of extreme was. Maybe a chalk outline of my dead body lying on the floor might have done the trick."

"The hearing on my restraining order is in one week," Frank said. "If I don't win this first battle, how am I going to win in divorce court?"

"Was she ever arrested? It never hurts to have records for the judge to look over."

"There's nothing. She wasn't even arrested when I was granted the restraining order. She was just ordered to stay away from our home."

"What does your attorney say?"

"I can't afford one. I went to Legal Aid today, only to discover I'll need to represent myself," Frank said in a serious tone of voice. And it was serious, serious enough that if he lost, life would become an oasis of land mines just waiting to blow up in his and the kids' faces.

"What about medical records? You can present them in court. Plus, if there were witnesses, their testimony could help you win your case."

"I have medical records. The only witnesses were the kids and they need to be protected rather than revisiting their mom's insanity."

"I'd be glad to help you. Part of my job is researching court cases. I can find rulings you can present to the judge upholding a continuation your restraining order."

"It's obvious I could use your help, but before I take you up on your offer, you might want to reconsider. It involves my crazy estranged wife…someone who makes Tanya Harding look like a rank amateur."

Carrie's chuckle made Frank smile. "We'd better get started soon then. You'll need to request your medical records right away. And start jotting down everything you can remember, specifically incidents involving your children." Carrie stopped to open her purse and those lagging behind made a V around them. Taking out her checkbook, Carrie ripped out a deposit slip from the back and handed it to him. "Here's my phone number. You don't have much time and judges hate disorganization."

Frank stole a quick glance at the slip of paper before following Carrie into the restaurant. Carrie Branson. The name suited her. Most of the women had already seated themselves at a banquette. Their waitress came over and set down a thermos of coffee on the table. Retrieving a pencil from her apron pocket, she poised it over an order pad.

"What'll it be?"

Frank took in her white lace-up hospital shoes and varicose veins that exploded through her nylons and made a determination. She deserved a sizable tip.

They placed dessert orders and the waitress grabbed up their menus, disappearing into the kitchen.

The din from the dinner crowd ricocheted off the walls. Frank watched a toddler trapped in a highchair throwing his crackers and chicken nuggets to the floor and didn't try to hide his smile. This was a slice of everyday life he missed and one he'd been absent from for far too long.

The next hour they shared stories of abuse and devastation. Somehow, Frank felt comforted. He was no longer some stand-alone freak show. Sitting amongst others who'd been there, done that removed the isolation of the past ten years, turning it into something manageable. For the first time in his miserable life, Frank Walch felt like he belonged.

Chapter 6

Loretta caught the bus juggling kielbasa hot dogs in one hand and a large paper tray filled with salted pretzels in the other. The pretzels were swimming in an extra helping of melted cheese and as she climbed aboard, she left a trail of the glutinous mass.

The bus was packed and all the seats were taken. Undaunted, Loretta zeroed in on a guy with a plastic protector tucked into his shirt pocket. He reminded her of Frank. His spindly arms were about the same circumference as his neck. His pockmarked face began turning various shades of red while he studiously avoided her stare.

Loretta had no intention of backing down. She continued eyeballing him, holding on to the overhead metal rail for support and balancing her food trays with her free hand. She wanted to eat her hot dogs and pretzels while they were still warm.

"Get up," she demanded.

He ignored her outburst and looked around the moving bus for protection. Fellow travelers were watching in curiosity, but none came to his aid.

"I said get up you penciled-necked geek!"

Still no takers, he planted his feet and grabbed hold of the edge of the bench with clenched hands.

"No."

Loretta placed her pretzel and hot dog trays next to his tensed thigh, grabbed him by the collar with a meaty hand and yanked, pulling him from his seat with surprising ease. Their audience grew and a few began murmuring to their seatmates.

One of the paper trays was jostled, spilling the soggy pretzels and congealed cheese that spread like slow moving lava across the vinyl seat. Loretta flew into a rage.

"Look what you've done! If you'd been a gentleman and moved when I asked you to, I'd still have my dinner!"

Past his initial caution, the man moved his scrawny neck up and down as he inspected Loretta and offered his opinion. "Lady, it looks like you could miss a meal or two."

It was the last comment he'd make for months.

* * *

A police officer pulled up behind the ambulance with his lights flashing to take depositions from a handful of witnesses.

The most descriptive of the group explained what he had seen to the officer. "A big broad wearing an orange muumuu told that guy to give her his seat and he refused," he said, pointing to the victim lying comatose on a stretcher. "Then she yelled at him for spilling her pretzels and when he said it didn't look like she needed them, she wound up and slugged him in the face. The guy's head snapped back and he went down, unconscious."

"Which direction did she head?" asked the officer.

The man shrugged. "Soon as the bus driver pulled over to the curb, she took off at a run. I've got to say, she was faster than I would of thought, being so big and all." He pointed up the block. "She headed that way is all I can tell you."

The officer looked to the bus driver and the remaining witnesses. "Can anyone give me a name?"

They all shook their heads. He asked them to jot down their contact information, knowing all the while the trail had dried up before it ever began. They wouldn't be combing the city for a big woman wearing a bright orange muumuu.

* * *

A few blocks away, Loretta was grabbing her aching side. The taxi she'd called was just pulling up to the curb, so she stuffed the last bite of kielbasa into her mouth. They'd been delicious. She'd piled sauerkraut, sweet relish and Grey Poupon mustard on them—just the way she liked. They hadn't been as warm as she had hoped, and the buns had turned soggy, but the pencil-necked dufus had messed things up. This brought Loretta to wonder...*Why was it that she was continually under-rated? Well, she'd given him something to think about the next time he decided to shoot his mouth off! It had felt good to teach the guy a lesson. She hadn't had the chance to take a swing at anyone for too long.*

She kept a look out for the cops and squeezed into the back seat of the taxi.

"Where to, lady?"

The breath that blew back at her had Loretta curling her upper lip. He reeked of garlic. She rummaged through her purse and counted. She had exactly $17 and change. If she paid for cab fare to Jay's, she'd be broke. On the other hand, Frank was only a few blocks away. She gave the cabbie the address and leaned back.

There was a spare set of car keys at the house and Frank car-pooled to work most days. With luck, the station wagon would be waiting for her in the carport. Having wheels would solve most of her problems. She *needed* transportation. Running from the bus had screwed with her digestion.

They drove through drizzle that fast turned to ice when it hit the pavement. The cabbie slowed down. "So, are you from here?"

"What do you care?"

"Just making small talk, lady," the cabbie replied before he slipped into silence.

Left alone, Loretta calculated her cash flow. She'd be down to two dollars once she paid the cab fare. Hopefully there was enough gas to get to and from work until payday. And if Jay didn't let her stay at her place, she'd have to sleep in the damned car. Loretta made a mental note to grab a couple of blankets and a pillow once she broke into the duplex.

The cabbie pulled up and shared another blast of fetid garlic. "Do you need for me to wait?"

Loretta grabbed all but two dollars and passed it over, climbing out of the back seat without answering. The station wagon was gone.

Leaving without the car wasn't an option as far as Loretta was concerned. She'd just have to get the keys and hide out until Frank got home. Once he was in the house she'd be behind the steering wheel and peeling out of the carport before he knew what hit him.

Loretta searched through a small storage unit built into the wall of the carport until she located a rusted step ladder.

Carrying it to the kitchen window, she opened the ladder to the sound of creaking hinges and began to climb the rungs. She'd chosen this particular window because it had to be opened constantly to clear away cooking odors and was never locked. Once she reached the window, Loretta tried to judge whether she'd be able to fit through it. There wasn't much space. The only guarantee would be to get it open for a test-run. She manhandled the window along its track until, little by little, it came all the way open. She stuck her shoulders through, satisfied, until her progress was stopped. Her stomach was definitely in the way. Peering through the opening, she was disappointed again. The kitchen sink was directly below her. She hadn't thought of that. On the other hand, Loretta reasoned, if she could figure out a way to maneuver around the sink, she'd have the counter to rest on and that would make getting to the floor easier.

Undecided, she climbed back down the ladder to walk around to the back of the duplex to check the bedroom windows. They were secured with thick dowels stuck in their tracks. No amount of jiggling would budge them. Frank must've gotten paranoid. He was right to think that way. If she ever got the chance, she planned to tear him a new asshole.

The kitchen window was her only option. Things were going swimmingly until the next to the highest rung disintegrated without warning, planting her on the rung below with a jolt. On her descent, her ankle struck an exposed screw and she felt the bite of her skin being laid open. Leaning over to inspect the damage, she lost her footing altogether and thudded to the ground.

She didn't lie in the mud long. The pain radiating down her leg was now incredible. Once up, she grabbed hold of her injured ankle and hopped around in a circle, yelling an impressive string of curses to no one in particular. Once the pain changed from searing to manageable, Loretta assessed the damage for a second time. The gash was deep and blood was traveling into her Wal-Mart slip-on in a steady stream.

But hurt or not, she had no time to waste. Frank could show up any minute. She needed to get through the window and snag the keys, or she'd have to walk the twelve miles to Jay's.

Loretta moved the step ladder against the wall to stabilize it and gingerly moved up the ladder, one rung at a time, being careful to avoid the exposed screw at the missing rung and made it to the top. It appeared to be holding. Still, Loretta remained alert for the sound of stressed metal. She had almost convinced herself it was going to hold and was strategizing how she'd get around the sink when it imploded.

She dove through the window, arms first, followed by her torso. She was able to wriggle as far as her hips before she became hopelessly wedged. Loretta choked down her panic. Locating the spigot with her free hand—the one that wasn't pinned under her—she grabbed hold of the cold metal and tried to lighten the load on her pinned arm, now sending warning signals of pain while it was being crushed against the window track. The landing had knocked the wind out of her and she had to fight for breath. Squirming, she attempted to pull herself through the opening, but her body didn't budge. She felt around for a faucet handle. It was lower and might give her some leverage. But her efforts only succeeded in putting more pressure on her pinned arm. She yelled out in frustration and gave one last herculean pull. Her effort was rewarded by the faucet breaking off in her hand. Her brain didn't have time to register the implications before a steady gush of icy water blasted her full in the face.

Sputtering and gasping as the geyser sprayed her in an unrelenting torrent, she turned her face and got a freezing blast to the ear.

"What in the hell do you think you're doing, Loretta?"

It was Frank.

"Brice, take your brothers and sister to the bedroom. Now!" he demanded.

Loretta watched the kids open the front door and hurry to their bedroom, and heard Mark ask, "Is Mommy all right?" Brice didn't answer as he shut the door behind them.

"Frank, if you know what's good for you, you'll help me get down from here!" Loretta threatened.

"You don't scare me anymore. I'm calling the cops. The restraining order says you aren't to come within 300 feet of us."

"You do that, you bastard, and I'll kill you!"

"I don't know… looks like you've already laid down all your bargaining chips, Loretta."

58

"I swear to you, if you call the cops, you're a dead man! Help me get down from here, damn it!"

"You got yourself stuck, Loretta. The cops can figure out how to get you out."

"Then tell me what your favorite flowers are, you son of a bitch, because I'd hate to send the wrong ones to your funeral!"

"You're burying yourself. The judge is going to hear about this. You have no right to threaten me and no right to be crawling through the kitchen window."

"I was just picking up the things I forgot. Help me get out of this damned window, Frank. I mean it!"

In her excitement, she forgot to keep her face pointed away from the geyser coming from the broken faucet and started to choke as water filled her mouth. Turning her head to the side, Loretta went into a coughing fit.

Frank's response was to walk to the phone and dial 911. "I need an officer. My wife's just broken her restraining order and is stuck in my kitchen window." After listening to the dispatcher, he replied, "Hold on a minute, I'll get it."

Loretta watched him rummaging in the junk drawer next to the phone to grab the restraining order and then gave the dispatcher the docket number. There was another pause as Frank listened and finally, his reply, "She doesn't appear to be in distress. But either way, I'm not going to try to get her out. She's already threatened to kill me. Tell the officers I'll be waiting for them in front of the house. You might want to make sure they bring the Jaws of Life. Loretta's a big woman. It looks like she's wedged in there pretty good."

Frank hung up the phone and went in search of the water shutoff. He was disappointed at having to cut Loretta some slack, but the kitchen floor was already flooded and it looked like the living room carpet was about to be next. He found it under the kitchen sink—too close for comfort.

Now that the water was no longer blasting the side of her head, Loretta was able to yell out obscenities without distraction. Frank was unimpressed. She'd done better. The stress on her diaphragm might be the culprit. He pulled up a kitchen chair and sat down, ignoring the small lake that was soaking his shoes and socks and watched her with a wary eye. If she got herself loose, she was going to be a wildcat.

"You should have stayed away, Loretta. The judge isn't going to like this one bit."

"Fuck you! I'll come over any time I want!"

"You might want to rethink that. You just broke your restraining order. On top of that, you've flooded the kitchen. I think this might be looked upon as malicious destruction of private property. I'm no expert though… "

"When I get loose, I'm going to nail that skinny ass of yours to the fucking wall!"

"Again, you're only digging yourself a deeper hole. This'll all come out at the court hearing. I'm done being your whipping boy. You're nothing but an abusive, frustrated woman, and I use the term woman loosely. I don't know why I stayed with you as long as I did, but trust me…I'll never go back. If you lay one finger on the kids or me, you're going to regret it!"

Loretta's reaction was to take hold of the remaining faucet handle and try to propel herself through the window. She only succeeded in putting more pressure on her diaphragm and she let out an involuntary grunt as air was forced out of her lungs.

"Damn it, Frank, get me outta here!" Her voice had gone weak and as far as Frank could tell, she seemed to be panicking.

Moving in for a closer look, Frank noticed her face was turning purple and her mouth was sucking in small gulps of air, making her look like a guppy out of water. He almost felt sorry for her. Almost…

"Help will be here any minute. You'll be okay." He walked to the kids' room and opened the door a crack, not wanting them to see their mother's distress.

"Brice, keep the kids here with you. I'm going out front to flag down the police."

"Is Mom going to be all right? It looked like she got herself stuck pretty bad," Brice said.

"She'll be all right."

"Mommy hurted," Britney said, bursting into tears.

Frank scooped her up in his arms. "No honey, Mommy's okay. She isn't hurt. She just got herself stuck." He gave her a hug, breathing in the ever-present scent of milk and peanut butter and jelly.

Mark was sitting at the desk, staring blankly at the corner of the room, his eyes reflecting nothing of the hurt he must have been feeling. Brandon had crawled into the bottom bunk and buried his head under the covers. The middle boys were Frank's biggest concern. They tended to crawl inside themselves whenever the household was in an uproar, which was more often than not. He'd hoped those days were over, but he realized he should have known better. Loretta would never willingly leave them in peace.

Frank wasn't outside for long when flashing lights approached. He showed the officers his restraining order and filled them in on the situation and which window Loretta had managed to wedge herself into, then excused himself to join the kids.

One of the officers decided to get a handle on the situation while they waited for the ambulance to arrive. Walking to the side of the house and seeing Loretta, the backside of her anyway, he winced. Walking back towards his partner he called out, "He wasn't kidding about the jaws of life. Hope they remember to bring it."

He got back behind the wheel. "Didn't Lionel say something about a guy who got KO'd on the bus this afternoon? I seem to remember something about a heavy-set gal wearing an orange muumuu."

"That's the MO; a plus-sized gal in an orange muumuu. Why?"

"I think we have a winner. Go take a look."

His partner returned with his mouth puckered and his eyes squinted to slits, looking like he'd been sucking on a lemon. "That could put a guy off sex for years! I didn't know they made thongs that size. Shit!"

"Think she's the perp?"

"What? Are you kidding! I'm calling this in to Lionel. He should have the honors."

They both nodded their agreement. The officer's code of ethics only went so far.

"Lionel! You're going to love this. I think we found your perp. Orange muumuu and slip-ons. Fits your description, except you didn't mention she was wearing a lime green thong."

The officer listened to Lionel's reply, shaking his head. "*Hell* no! This is your baby. You take the overtime. She's not our type."

Lionel's voice squawked back at them as the officers chuckled. Lionel fancied himself a ladies' man. This was going to be tough on him on many levels.

"Got to go, Lionel. We'll keep in touch."

The medics pulled up behind them and the officers pointed them in the right direction. "You bring the Jaws of Life?" one of the officers asked.

"It's that bad?" asked the assistant.

"Oh yeah, and then some!" the officer replied before he climbed behind the wheel.

The assistant returned to the ambulance and took hold of a heavy metal contraption from the back. His partner had already gone ahead, probably out of morbid curiosity.

Within moments, the officers heard Loretta cursing a blue streak while the paramedics tried to pry her loose. It wasn't long before the cursing turned to screams and the officers were forced to abandon the ballgame they were listening to. Approaching at a run, they rounded the side of the house into bedlam. Loretta was sitting on the ground with her back up against the house. Her muumuu was hiked around her waist and she was swinging her arms out in a 180-degree radius, keeping the paramedics at bay.

"You need to get control of yourself, lady. The paramedics were dispatched here to help you," said one of the officers.

"Oh yeah? You're going to take me in for a restraining order that my *asshole* of a husband lied to get. All's I was doing was getting a few things I forgot last night. You're *not* taking me to jail, you bastards!"

"Mrs. Walch, I am ordering you to cooperate with the paramedics."

"You can stick your orders! I'm not getting hauled off to jail!"

"You'll have a chance to tell your side of the story. But first, you need to let the medics have a look at you."

"Do you promise? It's not like I did anything wrong. All's I was doing was..."

"You have my word. Just let them check you out, make sure nothing's broke, and then we'll talk," he interrupted.

Loretta stopped swinging, almost as if a switch had been flipped off in her brain. The medics began taking cautious steps in her direction. Once they reached her, each grabbed an arm to help her to her feet. The going was difficult and it took several attempts before she was standing. The duplex's gutters had been dripping melted ice from the rooftop and upon her slip-slide escape from the window; she'd landed in a muddy bog. Her legs and muumuu were streaked with the goo.

The medics helped her over to the gurney and convinced Loretta to lie down so they could begin their examination. The officers turned their backs and waited for a verdict.

It wasn't long before the senior paramedic reported on Loretta's injuries. "She's got an irregular heartbeat, probably stress related, but it'll need to be double-checked. Looks like she might've suffered a cracked rib and the arm that was pinned under her is banged up. Can her statement be taken at the hospital?" the medic asked.

"Oh, yeah. It can wait. There's another matter pending. We'll contact the officer involved and he can get her statement."

They watched the ambulance drive off with relief.

The rookie officer whispered under his breath, "Tell you what. That gal's a candidate for Chicago Read Mental Health Center."

The more experienced cop continued staring off to the horizon. Something told him this wouldn't be the last they heard of Loretta.

Chapter 7

The paramedics had already merged the ambulance into heavy rush-hour traffic when it dawned on Loretta she hadn't been given her say. "Where the hell do you think you're going? I was supposed to talk to that cop!"

"Lady, you need medical attention," answered the driver.

"The hell you say! If I cracked a rib, it's your damned fault. Stop this thing now!"

She was swinging her legs over the edge of the gurney, attempting to get up when the assistant medic yelled a warning. "Crap, Paul, she's unstrapped herself!"

"Shoot her up with Demerol. We need to get her to the hospital. I want to be done with this run."

"Then *you* do it. I'm not going near her."

"You've got to be kidding me, man! You're *scared* of her?"

"You bet your ass I am! If you want to poke a needle in her, go ahead."

The driver pulled over, pissed off, and slammed the ambulance into park before it had come to a complete stop. It ground to a grinding, stuttering halt.

"This is bullshit, man. I've got better things to do than corral a crazy woman." He reached around to a cabinet just behind him, coming up with a hypodermic and a vile of Demerol. Sizing Loretta up, he grabbed a second needle.

He drove the needle through the tamperproof aluminum cover and filled it with lightning speed, then filled the other.

His partner understood the reasoning. It had merit, seeing how she was the size of a small whale, but he also knew the plan was flawed. "This isn't regulation. We weren't given the go-ahead by Northwest Memorial. You can't be sure she won't have a reaction."

"We'll be at Northwest in ten minutes. The doctors can figure it out when we get her there. But first, we need to get there."

He walked around to the back and arrived at the rear doors at the exact moment Loretta flung them open. He took an impressive hit to the temple. The force was enough to spin him in a 360-degree pirouette while his partner watched from the safety of his bucket seat. He went down like a marionette on strings. His butt landed first, and then his body folded over as the side of his face that hadn't been clocked by the swinging doors landed on the pavement. Both hypodermics lay uselessly next to him.

In the bedlam, the assistant hadn't had the presence of mind to lock the doors; a fact that would later put him on probation.

Without warning, his door was wrenched open and a good-sized palm smacked him alongside his head. The side of his face went instantly numb. The bitch had clobbered him good.

"Get out!"

He didn't require a more formal invitation and scrambled out the driver's side to freedom, realizing his partner was wrong about the cracked rib. She'd laid one on him that would've made a heavyweight champion proud. He walked backwards on the shoulder of the road, never taking his eyes off her, the side of his face still stinging.

Loretta marched over to the driver's side and climbed in. "You can tell your partner for me that he's an asshole and he got what he deserved!" she yelled before slamming the door and barreling into traffic which was forced to come to a screeching halt. A chain reaction ensued, as driver after driver slammed into one-another like gleeful bumper-car drivers. It would take hours of statements and accident forms to sort out the mess.

Foremost on the paramedic's mind was calling dispatch. From the looks of things, they'd need several ambulances. Drivers at the front of the snag were already milling about. He walked up to a man dressed in a business suit holding a cell phone to his ear.

"I need to make a call," the paramedic said.

"You've got to be kidding me. I'm on hold with my insurance company. This'll be the third damned claim in a year. I'm going to be paying out the ass…"

"And that ambulance that just rocketed in front of you is the reason why. I need to call this in; my partner's been hurt."

"I'll give you the phone, but first I want your information," the driver demanded. Things were looking up. This could turn into a fat insurance claim if he played it right.

"And make it fast," he insisted. "I think I wrenched my back. That was one hell of an impact."

The medic ignored his grumbling and placed the call. "Ann, Randy here. Paul and I were transporting that woman over on Howard Street and the bitch just hijacked the ambulance."

Listening to her response he replied, "No, I'm not screwing with you. Paul got clipped with the back doors and she took off in the ambulance, causing a pile-up. There are injuries. Dispatch to the corner of Ohio and Fairbanks, pronto."

He handed the phone back to the suit and listened to a long list of complaints.

"My neck's hurting like a mother, plus I've got a headache and I'm seeing double. I don't think I'm in any condition to drive."

"There are ambulances on the way."

The paramedic hustled back to his partner who was coming to on the shoulder of the road. He gained enough control to sit up and his assistant did a double take.

His forehead looked like he'd had a monkey's ass grafted to it; actually, a monkey in heat was a better description. There was a crease running down the middle where the edge of one of the doors had connected and on either side huge red lumps had formed. His front tooth was broken in half.

The medic sat moaning and his assistant couldn't help thinking he looked like a street person auditioning for a bit part. This was going to kill him. They called him pretty boy at work; he never passed up the chance to see himself in a mirror and he was constantly screwing with his surfer's hair.

His hair wasn't doing so hot at the moment. It was coated with the residue he'd been lying in. Now grease and oil clumped it up in errant spikes.

"Let me have a look," the assistant requested. He peered into the medic's good eye—the one that wasn't swollen shut. The pupil seemed okay.

"She really clipped you. How many fingers am I holding up?"

"Four," he managed.

He'd held up three. It was probably a concussion.

"What happened?"

"You don't remember?"

Paul shook his head, dazed.

"You were standing at the back doors to give that bitch Demerol when she threw open the doors and nailed you in the forehead."

"What bitch?"

This was bad. He had a concussion for sure.

"What's your name?"

"What're you asking my name for?"

"Trust me. What's your name?"

"Paul Trundle. What's this about, man?"

"Just checking. There's an ambulance on the way. You're going to be fine."

His assistant looked across to the clogged roadway. Most of the drivers had gotten out and were comparing notes as they waited for help to arrive. Thankfully, no one seemed to be in immediate need of medical attention.

It was another fifteen minutes before the police showed. By then, most of the drivers had returned to their vehicles to keep warm. The weak sunlight had disappeared, replaced by a night chill that offered little compensation.

The ambulances followed close behind. The assistant flagged down the first in line and helped transfer his partner to a gurney.

"What happened to him? He looks like someone took a jackhammer to his forehead," the attending medic said.

"Don't ask."

"You guys are in a ton of trouble. Jake was on the phone to his insurance adjuster, throwing things around. He kept ranting about you and Paul giving up your ambulance to some chick."

Jake was their boss. The man had a hell of a temper when he was crossed.

"This was no chick."

"Come on…"

"She's the size of a fucking hippo and twice as mean."

"All I can tell you is I wouldn't show up at work until he settles down. He wants a piece of the both of you."

The attending medic looked down at Paul's mangled face. "She broke his tooth, big time. Too bad they dropped dental."

* * *

The ambulance's radio was emitting constant static, making it hard for Loretta to think clearly. She grabbed the mic and yanked. The satisfying twang of the cord being pulled from its moorings gave her a reason to smile. She rolled down the window and tossed it out on the roadway.

The medic deserved getting clocked. Smart-ass, thinking he could get the best of her! They'd acted like she was deaf, talking about shooting her up with Demerol. She had a right to defend herself.

Other than not getting caught, all that was on Loretta's mind was getting to Jay's to get her things. By now, the cops would surely be looking for the ambulance. She'd need to ditch it as soon as she could. She tried formulating her next move but realized it was hopeless. She had exactly $2. She wasn't going to get very far.

It was impossible to blend in with the surrounding traffic, so Loretta turned off from the main road and began snaking through residential streets, making slow but steady progress.

It took thirty minutes of winding through back roads before she stumbled on a trailer park near Jay's. It was the perfect place to hide the ambulance. At the back of the complex there was an open storage area for boats and motor homes. It was set back from the trailers and mercifully unlit. Loretta was about to get out to start walking the three blocks to Jay's when something occurred to her. If she was right, she'd just discovered her ticket out of Chicago.

Loretta got out to walk around to the bay doors, climbed into the back and began scrounging through the medical paraphernalia in the built-in cupboards. Blood pressure cuffs and saline drips weren't what she sought. She tossed them to the floor. Eventually, she found the mother lode: Drugs; lots of them! They'd have street value.

Now all she needed was to get Jay to share her connection. A name and phone number would bankroll her safely out of Chicago.

Jay answered the door, looking over Loretta's shoulder to the street. "What did you do now, Loretta?"

"What do you mean what did I do? I didn't do anything. You're getting paranoid."

"Cut the crap. I just got off the phone with the police. They want to know your whereabouts. And don't try to tell me they were calling for a donation. You did something!"

Jay continued to block the door, throwing frantic glances to the passing traffic.

"I went over to the apartment to pick up some things I forgot is all."

"You're full of shit!" Jay yelled.

"How'd they get your number anyway?"

"You got two strikes against you, Loretta. You're not only a wide-load, but you're dumber than dirt! All they had to do was look up your calls. My number's all over it. They're probably on their way here right now. I'm not going to let you in, Loretta. I don't want any part of this."

"I thought we were friends."

"Friends don't break apart living rooms, shit in beds and send the cops over," Jay said, standing her ground and blocking Loretta from entering.

Loretta decided to try for a sure thing. "You're right. I don't want to screw up your life any more than I already have. All's I need is the number of the guy you buy your weed from and I'll leave."

"No way! I'm not throwing him under the bus. Besides, you don't have room to negotiate."

"It's all I'm asking. Do that for me and I'm outta here. I promise."

"You don't smoke dope. Why would you want his number?"

"I need something to calm my nerves, maybe score a couple of Valiums," Loretta lied.

"You should've thought about that before you did whatever the hell you did. You're a hot mess, Loretta! You beat up on Frank for shits and giggles and then break a restraining order all within 24 hours."

Loretta's expression changed from pleading to lethal without warning. "I'm not going to leave until you give me that number, you bitch! If you want to explain to the cops why I'm here after you told them I wasn't, then be my guest."

Jay glanced back to the street thinking over her options. The cops would never believe her. And she didn't need the harassment they were bound to throw her way.

"Wait here," Jay said. She turned to a rickety table near the front door and scribbled a phone number on a notepad. "His name's Streeter. And *don't* tell him I sent you!"

The moment she handed Loretta the slip of paper Jay slammed the door. Loretta was ready for her. She hit against the door with balled up fists, forcing it back open and stalked into the living room.

"What the hell do you think you're doing? We had a deal!" Jay screamed.

"You can add liar to that fucked-up laundry list of yours. I'm not going anywhere until I get my things!"

Jay came at her in a blur. The blow glanced off Loretta's collarbone. "You're going to take your sorry ass out of here or I'm calling the police!" Jay screamed. She tried shoving Loretta towards the door to no effect. Her feet remained planted to the floor.

Loretta wound up her best swinging arm, her right, and drove her fist directly into the center of Jay's jaw. She was out before her body hit the floor. Walking to the phone, Loretta yanked the cord out of the wall and wound it around Jay's wrists, then pulled her legs up to meet her wrists and bound her limbs together. It wasn't much different than trussing a double-jointed turkey, Loretta thought, pulling the cord tight.

"Sorry, but you made me do this," Loretta said, feeling for a pulse, worried that she'd done more damage than she'd intended. Jay's carotid was still pumping. She slipped her hand into Jay's front pocket to retrieve her cell phone, tossed it outside her reach, and then went through the house to gather up her belongings. Next, she rummaged through the obvious hiding places to find Jay's emergency stash. She located it hidden in an empty waffle box in the freezer. The wad of bills was mostly tens and twenties, but it totaled to nearly five hundred dollars. It would keep gas in the tank and give her travel money for motels and fast food.

Jay's car keys were resting on an end table next to the couch. A few trips to the Hyundai and everything was shoved into the back seat. Loretta rushed to the kitchen to find a flashlight and started rummaging through the shed. The camp stove was a surprise find. Loretta threw it and the rest of the camp gear into the back seat and returned to the house. She'd need cooking utensils and whatever canned goods Jay had in her kitchen cabinets. Making a mental checklist, she was reminded to root through Jay's utensil drawer to grab a can opener. No sense in starving herself.

Loretta dialed the number she had been given from the wall phone in the kitchen. It was answered on the fourth ring.

"Is this Streeter?"

"Who wants to know?"

"I'm a friend of Jay's. She said I should call you."

"I'm listening."

"I have something you might be interested in."

"Don't know. We'd have to discuss that."

"How about now? I'll need your address."

"No address, lady. I'll meet you outside the McDonald's at Crawford and Skokie.

"I can be there in twenty minutes," Loretta said.

"Make it forty. I'm in the middle of something."

Loretta didn't bother closing the door on her way out. Jay needed all the fresh air she could get.

Familiarizing herself with Jay's car, Loretta kept the engine idling and the heater turned up full blast. The night had gone arctic: arctic enough for Loretta to reach a decision. Once she was on the road, she was heading south.

Traffic had thinned. She arrived at McDonald's twenty minutes early and got in line behind the late dinner crowd to wait her turn. The kielbasas had made her thirsty. Besides, she wanted to get something to eat before she got on the road.

In no time the interior of the car was filled with the mouth-watering aroma of three large fries, two quarter-pounders and four deep-fried apple pies. They'd been a steal at two for a dollar.

She parked away from the busy ebb and flow of the fast food junkies, bolting down the food like she was storing up for hibernation. She was on her last bag of fries when a tall, skinny guy dressed in a leather bomber jacket and a backwards baseball cap appeared on her side of the parking lot, glancing around as he strolled.

She pulled up next to him.

"You Streeter?"

"Depends."

"I'm the gal who called you earlier…a friend of Jay's."

He looked in the window of the Hyundai, suspicious.

"I've got a few things I'd like to sell. It might be better if you got in so we can talk in private," Loretta said.

"I don't like strangers telling me what to do."

"I'm just trying to help. It's freezing outside. We can do this however you'd like."

Streeter looked around the parking lot and made his decision. "Give me the keys," he demanded, holding out his hand.

Loretta frowned. She didn't like his rules. But if she was going to get out of Chicago, she didn't see where she had a choice. Turning off the engine, Loretta handed Streeter the keys and got out to walk around to the passenger's side, wondering the whole time if he planned on hijacking Jay's car. She stopped long enough to get a good look at Streeter while he settled himself behind the wheel. He looked okay. Surprisingly clean cut, actually.

"Hurry up. I have stuff to do," Streeter demanded.

Before Loretta had the chance to shut her door, he stomped on the gas and they shot out of the parking lot, landing on the roadway with a thud. He'd missed the driveway.

"So what you got?" Streeter asked, unfazed.

"Oxycontin, Phenobarbital, Novocain and Valium."

"Good shit. Let's have a look." He took the corner on two wheels and hung a sharp left that led to an unlit alleyway. Reaching overhead Streeter switched on the dome light and held out his hand. Loretta handed him the drugs and waited.

He seemed pleased with the inventory. "I'll give you $500 now and another $500 when it's been turned."

"I can't do that. I'm headed out of town. I need the money now, not later."

"You plan on getting more? I can sell this shit any day of the week."

"That depends on you. Give me the thousand now and we'll talk about more when I get back."

"Where'd you get the stuff, anyway?"

"I can't tell you that. Let's just say there's plenty more."

"You got yourself a deal." Streeter fished in his pocket and came up with a handful of cash. Counting out ten one hundred dollar bills, he handed them over. "When will you be back?"

"Not sure exactly. I'll call you. You need a ride anywhere?"

"I've got business a few blocks down," Streeter said and slipped out to be swallowed by darkness.

Loretta sat behind the wheel, stunned. She'd just made over one month's salary with one transaction. She may have hit upon something.

* * *

Frank had just about given up on hearing from Carrie when the phone rang.

His smile faded the moment he answered it.

"Is this Mr. Walch?" asked an official sounding voice.

"Yes, it is."

"This is Detective Jim Kalnoski. We're trying to locate your wife, Mr. Walch. Have you had contact with her over the past few hours?"

"I haven't seen or heard from her since the medics pried her from the kitchen window. What's wrong?"

He listened in amazement to the harried baritone on the other end of the line. Hanging up, Frank contemplated the fact Loretta had just tossed her 'Go Directly to Jail' card in the ring, so to speak, and there was no way out. He felt a certain amount of responsibility. She'd been content pounding on him while everyone else had gotten off unscathed. It appeared that without him as her whipping boy, things had gotten completely out of control.

The phone rang again and he reached for it, expecting it to be the officer calling back with more questions.

"I'm going to kill you, you bastard! When I'm through with you you're not going to need any ball room in those fucking khakis you wear because I'm going to chop 'em off! I swear…"

He hung up in a cold sweat and dialed the number Detective Kalnoski had given him. "Loretta just called, threatening to chop off my balls. She meant it."

"Did she say where she was calling from?"

"Sorry, I hung up on her."

Frank could hear the detective's exasperated sigh.

"What about caller I.D.?" the officer asked.

"Sorry, I don't have caller I.D."

"If she calls again, Mr. Walch, try to get her location."

"Loretta isn't stupid, detective. I'm the last person she'd confide in. The last time I saw her, she was stuck in a window, threatening to kill me."

"Try, Mr. Walch. We just recovered the ambulance she ditched and it appears your wife helped herself to the drugs on board. Considering what Loretta managed to pull off in less than five hours, we'll all sleep better when she's behind bars."

"What am I going to do in the meantime? I don't have a weapon."

"I can't give you advice, Mr. Walch. All I can tell you is *if* you were to have a gun on the premises and *if* you were forced to defend yourself, we'd have to ask fewer questions if her body was found inside your home than outside it. Oh, and Mr. Walch..."

"Yes?"

"Be careful."

"I will, Detective."

Frank had barely hung up when the phone rang again. He wasn't interested in falling into another one of Loretta's traps so he let the call get picked up by the answering machine. Instead of Loretta, the caller was Carrie. Grabbing the receiver, Frank tried to make his voice sound normal.

"What's wrong?" Carrie asked.

"What makes you think something's wrong?"

"I can hear it in your voice. Something's happened."

He filled her in on the day's insanity. "Loretta's really buried herself this time. She'll never find her way out."

"No she probably won't and that's going to be your insurance policy. When you think about it, it's actually a blessing."

"Not for the guy on the bus. The officer told me the man had to be rushed to the hospital. And it *sure* wasn't a blessing for the medic whose only mistake was getting her pried from the window. And her girlfriend probably won't be sending flowers either. She knocked her out and stole her car and some camping equipment."

"Did you say *girlfriend*?"

"I'm afraid so. I didn't know she'd joined the other side until to-night. I'd suspected she was seeing someone, but I would've never guessed she was having an affair with a woman."

"That must be difficult for you."

"Actually, I'd have to say it was a relief. It was peaceful when she was away."

"I mean the part about her being with another woman."

"I haven't had time to process it yet. But it's strange to think I've been sharing the same roof with someone who's been living a double life. For right now, though, I need to concentrate on what's important, and that's the kids' and my safety."

"You're right. But in many ways this could be seen as a positive. Your kids will finally have a chance to *be* kids with Loretta out of their lives."

"Exactly. I've been having a rough time adjusting to the changes. Even now, when the kids are playing and things start to get a bit loud, I'll tense up and my automatic response is to tell them to quiet down. But then I realize Loretta's not here and it's all right for them to have fun."

"It'll take a while. At least it did for me, but you'll adjust. Things will get better every day."

"They already are," Frank said as he paced in a tight circle. The phone cord only fed out a few feet. "There's something else I wanted to talk to you about. Being the only guy in the group makes me feel like I should make up for what's been done to everyone. I'm not comfortable opening up because of it."

"I can't say it wasn't a surprise to see you there. But honestly, by the end of meeting, it felt like you were one of us."

"I don't know whether to take that as a compliment or not."

"It's a compliment, trust me. You're a good person, Frank. It's nice to know there are still good guys out there."

"Come on! You could have anyone you wanted!"

"Not really. I've got baggage; I still haven't gotten over what Hal did to the kids and me and that's made me afraid to date. Besides, what are the chances I'll find a man who's willing to take on someone else's kids?"

Frank wanted to tell her to put his name on the list, but didn't. It was too soon. Besides, if he spoke his mind Carrie might see him as some kind of stalker.

"They're out there. You just have to be patient. Have you dated at all since your divorce?" Frank asked.

"Oh, sure. In between working all day, running errands, cooking dinner and helping the kids with their homework, I have about ten minutes for myself at night."

"That could change. When you're ready, you'll find time for yourself."

"I suppose so, but I honestly don't trust my judgment anymore. I figure if I find myself attracted to a guy, he's sure to be another Hal," Carrie said. "Well, enough about me. We should be making arrangements to strategize for your court hearing."

"I doubt if Loretta would be dumb enough to show up to court at this point. She's got at least seven separate warrants against her if you count her breaking the restraining order."

"Still, it wouldn't hurt to be prepared."

"True. I called the 24-Hour Emergency Center. They promised to have the records available by tomorrow. It's the least they could do. I was one of their best customers—great medical insurance, plus I was a regular."

"I'm sorry Frank."

"Don't be. It was my fault for staying. I didn't tell you what the judge said to me when he signed the restraining order, did I?"

"No, you didn't."

"He told me to grow a backbone. He was right. I took Loretta's crap for years. I told myself it was for the kids, but the truth was, I was too depressed to make any changes."

"It was like that for most of us. After a while, you lose your self-esteem. By the time I left, I was convinced that I didn't amount to anything. I had no friends because Hal had driven them all away. Even my family had stopped coming around. I was convinced I wouldn't be able to make it on my own, that I'd never be able to support the kids by myself. But I did. I have a great job, good benefits and though we may not live in a mansion, and I might struggle to pay the bills, we're happy."

"I wish I could rewind my life and feel like I did before I met Loretta."

"You will. It just takes time."

Frank felt the need to change the subject. "So, in light of today, what should I do to get ready for the hearing?"

"You need to get a copy of Loretta's warrants. Judges love concrete evidence. They're lied to all the time. Put an official looking piece of paper in front of them and they'll listen. What if we meet up tomorrow night?"

"Are you sure you want to do this? I can't pay you."

"I wouldn't take payment, anyway."

"What about your place, around 6:30? It'll be safer. But, I'll need to bring the kids with me," Frank said.

"I'll throw on a pot of spaghetti. It's my specialty."

Frank got directions, feeling equally confused and excited. He'd never attracted the ladies. He wasn't certain whether this was the beginning of a friendship, or if it held the potential for something more. By the time he shut off the bedside light, he was still turning things over in his mind. What Carrie had said about bringing baggage into a relationship was just as true for him. Who'd be willing to take on the responsibility of four kids, the youngest still in diapers? Not many, that was for sure.

Chapter 8

Loretta woke to early sunlight peeking through cheap, foam-backed curtains with a feeling of dread. She had arrived in Saint Louis in the wee hours of the morning, knowing she'd been lucky to have made it so far from Chicago—especially since Jay's car would've been reported stolen. She lay in the sagging bed, wondering if a stolen '97 Hyundai would've dug spurs into the metal of the Chicago Police…enough to go gunning for her. She doubted it. But clocking a dimwitted medic and stealing an ambulance and the drugs aboard sure as shit would!

I wasn't given a choice, Loretta thought. *If the damned medic would have stayed out of my way, I wouldn't have slammed him with the door and I wouldn't be sweating bullets in a flophouse now.* Loretta had only a rudimentary understanding of the legal system, but she was certain she'd be in big trouble if the medic landed in the hospital.

Those possibilities only strengthened her resolve to get as far away from Illinois as possible. She counted her bankroll. It totaled $1,462. It was enough to get her settled in Tulsa. That was where she was going to land. She was through with cold weather.

But Loretta's relief soon turned to disappointment when she admitted to herself that leaving Chicago meant letting go of L.A. Dogs. It was over before it ever began, and in the scheme of things, the reality was depressing. She would have been the best! L.A. Dogs could have been a chain, with franchises all over the country: a Mrs. Fields, only with hot dogs.

Loretta's meanderings took another turn. The authorities couldn't know about the Lesbian Relief Fund unless Jay blabbed. And she wouldn't have. She'd have been so pissed about her car and the camping stuff it would have never crossed her mind.

Loretta looked to the clock on the nightstand. It was 8:15 A.M.; too early to catch Tanya at the office, but not too early to call her at home.

"Hello," Tanya answered.

"Hi, it's Loretta Walch. Did the board make their decision yet?"

"As a matter of fact, I just got off the phone from your work. They said you hadn't come in today. Your loan's been approved."

"That's great news! Actually, something's come up. I got a call from my mother in Tulsa last night. She's having surgery and I'm on my way there now."

"Oh, dear. That's going to be a problem. We can't send the check out of state. The relief fund's meant for local residents."

"I won't be in Tulsa long, only until Mom's able to do things for herself. I'll be back in Chicago within a few weeks."

"I don't know… this is irregular at best."

"But you said yourself that I should start my own business. That's all I've been thinking about since we talked. All I need is a chance."

"I'll check with the board members. I'd like to help you, but rules are rules. How can I reach you?"

Something she hadn't thought about… "I'll call you. I'm staying with Mom at the hospital 'till she's released. I forgot to ask. Was I awarded the full amount?"

"Yes, they granted you $500. But remember, that's only if the board members agree to your new circumstances."

"I understand. When should I call you?"

"I should have an answer within a few days. Why don't you call me on Friday?"

"Thanks, Tanya. You won't regret this."

"I'm sure I won't, but don't get your hopes up."

Loretta hung up the phone with a sense of purpose. Tanya was in her corner. She could hear it in her voice. Now all she'd need to do was get to Tulsa and get a mailing address by Friday. She pulled a map out of her purse and traveled the distance with her index finger. She was already halfway there.

She thought over the possibilities as she drove, observing the speedometer with one eye and scanning for patrol cars with the other. She'd fill out the business plan after all. It would mean thousands in her pocket.

Continuing her route along Highway 44, Loretta's spirits rose. Once enough time had passed, she'd return to Chicago to start L.A. Dogs. She'd never have to report to some asshole manager again; there'd be no time clock to punch, no getting up at dawn for minimum wage, and she'd have the pride of owning her own business. She knew her dogs. There was nothing like a steaming kielbasa or bratwurst, smothered in sauerkraut. But it had to be the right sauerkraut; not that crap floating in vinegar. It had to be seasoned, mellow. Same with the mustard—she'd serve designer mustards. Customers would have such a variety of choices it would put her on the map! And the buns...they wouldn't be like the ones she'd had yesterday. They'd gone soggy. She'd offer sourdough that had texture and flavor, with a choice of plain, sesame seed, or onion. She'd set herself aside as *the* hot dog diva!

Thoughts of hot dogs made Loretta hungry. Starved, actually. She hadn't eaten a thing since her last gas station stop, and that had been hours ago. Her mouth began to water while she visualized designer hot dogs, topped off with a rich desert. She could go for a thick slice of double-decker chocolate cake and she would wash it down with a two-liter Pepsi.

Loretta started looking for likely freeway billboards, but none seemed promising. She held off as long as she could, finally taking the exit to downtown Lebanon. Surely they'd have a deli.

Bored with having to reduce her speed, Loretta's thoughts traveled to Frank. He'd be getting his. He'd never had the nerve to flip the shit he'd served up yesterday. He'd taken advantage of her being stuck in the damned window. When she got the chance to get him alone, she'd use *both* the frying pan and the Louisville Slugger. With any luck, she'd be able to re-arrange his head permanently.

And that pencil-necked geek had insulted her in front of a busload of people. He deserved the lesson she'd taught him, but a bleeding heart judge wouldn't see it that way, so she added him to her list of troubles. If the authorities ever connected the dots, she'd be in the middle of a shit storm. But her troubles wouldn't necessarily stop there. What if Frank got the kids to testify against her? They'd always kept quiet about what went on between her and Frank. What if that changed?

The traffic slowed and Loretta was forced to pay close attention to the road. Lebanon's main street was a long stretch of two-story brick buildings, built at the turn of the century. It was quaint with a small-town atmosphere—all of which was lost on Loretta as she salivated over her quest for hot dogs and chocolate. She drove past an ice cream parlor, a butcher shop, and dozens of small retail stores and had almost given up when she saw it.

Ike's Deli was lit up in pink neon with a bright yellow hot dog resting in the center. Hers was now the only car parked in front of the building. It was 11:05 in the morning. She was probably their first customer of the day.

Scattered inside the cramped brick walls were wrought-iron soda shop tables and chairs covered with red and white checked vinyl. From an old-fashioned jukebox Elvis crooned *Love Me Tender*. The space was chilly and Loretta regretted not grabbing a sweater from the car.

She gave her order to a bored teenager who seemed more interested in chomping on a huge wad of gum that bowed the side of her cheek than waiting on her.

"Do you have any cake?" Loretta asked.

The girl pointed to a four-tiered dessert carousel that was showing off delicacies in a slow revolution. On the second tier was a three-layered devil's food cake with dark chocolate icing. The top was decorated with whipped cream and maraschino cherries. Loretta's mouth began to swim. "I'll take three of those."

"So you want two kielbasa and two bratwurst dogs with sauerkraut and mustard, three slices of double chocolate decadent cake and a two-liter Pepsi to go," reiterated the teenager.

"What kind of mustard?"

"It's just mustard," she replied.

"I don't want *just mustard*," Loretta insisted. "I want either Grey Poupon or honey mustard."

"Let me check," the girl replied, and left Loretta standing at the counter.

She was back in seconds. "The mustard's in a serving tray. I looked for a container, but there isn't one. I could give you a sample."

"Never mind. I just think you should know what kind of mustard you serve is all."

"Do you want the hot dogs?"

"Yes I want the hot dogs. And don't get smart-mouthed with me."

"I'm not getting smart-mouthed."

"Yes you are! Just make the hot dogs before I call your boss and you and your gum wind up in the unemployment line."

The girl went red in the face but held her tongue. The woman was a witch. She headed to the back to prepare the order. As she and her gum disappeared from view, the girl made up her mind to do something she'd never been tempted to do until today. Adding extra mustard she contributed a dollop of spit to each one of the hot dogs. It served her right!

Wrapping the hot dogs in foil, she placed them in to-go bags and walked back to the register to ring it up.

"That'll be $26.80."

"Bullshit! There's no way that's right. Check again."

The girl ripped off the receipt from its feed and handed it over. "It's right."

Loretta scanned down the list with a frown. "These prices are ridiculous!"

"I don't make up the menu or the prices. I can toss them if you'd rather."

"What I'd *rather* is to walk out with my meal without having to apply for a fucking loan!"

The girl stood her ground and waited. She could've cared less whether she ended up pitching the hot dogs or they walked out the door. The $7.80 an hour she made took care of any self-interest she may have had whether Ike's Deli thrived or fell flat on its face.

Loretta banged a huge plastic purse on the counter and started rummaging through it. The teenager's attention was drawn to her knuckles. They were scratched and bruised. Curious, she took a closer look at the woman. Her dark hair was uncombed and oily and was thrown on top of her head in a ratty ponytail. She wore a drab navy blue muumuu with slip-ons—a strange choice for the cold weather. Her legs were unshaven but the girl could make out bruises that traveled up her shins through the woman's disgusting leg hair.

The woman pulled out a thick wad of cash—more strangeness. *Why would she be carting around a plastic dime-store purse when she had a bankroll like that?* the girl wondered. She opened the wad to locate smaller bills. Peeling off six fives, she threw them down on the counter.

The girl handed her back the change, never doubting there would be no contribution to the tip jar that sat next to the register. The woman grabbed up her ugly purse and to-go bags and marched out the door. The teenager placed bets that she was eating for one.

Moving to the front of the store, the girl peered out the window. The woman's car was a red Hyundai with a dent in the front bumper. She looked to the license plate as Loretta squeezed behind the wheel. They were Illinois plates. She put the number to memory.

She walked to the phone, about to set off a chain of events that would eventually put off her college attendance in the spring and stick her in limbo at Ike's Deli. But she had no earthly way of knowing that, so she dialed.

"Lebanon Police Department."

"Hey Linda, it's Kelley. Is my dad around?"

"Sure is, honey. Hold a sec."

Her father's voice greeted her. "Everything okay, pumpkin?"

"Dad, there was a woman in the deli just now. I don't know, but something seemed strange about her."

"Strange, how?"

"Well for starters, she was obnoxious. She kept yelling."

"Should I arrest her?"

"Come on, Dad. I'm not kidding around. She looked like she was on the run or something. She had greasy dark hair and wore this huge muumuu, but what really caught my attention were her knuckles. They were all busted up, like she'd been in a fight, and her legs were banged up, too. When she paid for her order, she pulled out this big wad of cash. It looked like most of it was twenties, but she was carrying this cheap dime-store purse."

Chet Caulder, Lebanon's Police Chief, smiled. With this morning's APBs was a description of a large woman, last seen wearing a bright orange Muumuu. "Did you happen to get a look at her car?"

"I can do better than that. I got the Illinois plate number." She gave it to him and continued. "It's a red Hyundai with a dent in the front bumper. Dad, she left with four hot dogs, three slices of chocolate cake, and a two-liter Pepsi. You can't miss her. The poor car dipped down on her side when she got in."

"Which way was she headed?"

"Towards the freeway."

"Okay, pumpkin. I'd better get. I'll call you later."

Riffling through the paperwork spread on his desk, he located the APB. The photo of Loretta Walch was grainy, as if it had been culled from a much smaller snapshot and enlarged. She had dark hair and looked to be in her mid-thirties. He scanned the report; Chicago resident, five-foot-two, approximately 280 lbs, thirty-four years old, Caucasian, and presumed to be dangerous. Outstanding warrants were breaking a restraining order, assault on a paramedic, grand theft of an ambulance and the drugs, assault on another male and a second grand theft auto along with the assault of the owner, a female—all within twenty-four hours. Kelly had been damned lucky she got off with just attitude.

He yelled to the dispatcher. "Linda, get Bill on the horn. He's to apprehend a woman in a red Hyundai, Illinois license plate RWB 3323, last seen traveling towards the freeway. I'm assuming she's headed south." He walked over and handed her the APB. "There's numerous warrants out on her. Tell him to proceed with caution."

"Will do," Linda replied.

The Chief hesitated. The right outcome could clinch his run for a second term. "On second thought, it wouldn't hurt for both of us to search for her." He grabbed his cap and ran out the door.

Flipping on his siren, the Chief prepared to run the downtown lights. Bill would be at O'Brian's Bar and Grill about now, busting the retiree drunks and other riff-raff as they got behind the wheel. It'd be a crap shoot whether Linda's call would catch him in the middle of an arrest or not.

He peeled out of the parking lot and proceeded through the lights cautiously with his siren blaring and gained the freeway exit in no time. Headed south, he switched his lights and siren off. His stealth approach caused the lead-foots on the freeway to let up on their gas pedal, slowing his progress when he was forced to go around them.

He reached for the two-way. "Unit KUW 556, any word from Bill?"

"That's affirmative. He's en-route to the freeway from O'Brian's."

"Ten-four. I'm headed south."

"Should I tell the surrounding counties Loretta Walch was spotted, Chief?"

"Wait for my call. KUW556, out."

The dispatcher went back to polishing her nails, having no idea the next time she saw her boss he'd be in a neck brace and sucking his nourishment through a straw.

He slowed the cruiser at the first rest stop. The perp had left Ike's with four hot dogs, three triple-decker slices of chocolate cake and a two-liter Pepsi. It stood to reason she might want to stop somewhere to eat.

He almost missed the Hyundai. It was parked at the far end of the rest stop under a big elm tree whose overhanging branches partially hid it from view. He took the exit and parked in the section set aside for semis. Now that his cruiser was tucked out of sight, the chief reached for the two-way. "KUW556, this is unit 57. Tell Bill I'm at the rest stop. The Hyundai's here."

"Should I double-check his ETA?"

"No, I can handle this on my own."

"Okay, Chief. KUW556, out."

Approaching the Hyundai cautiously, his hand near his sidearm, he stayed low. As he moved, stealth-like towards the driver's side of the car, he couldn't help but picture himself on the front page of tomorrow's newspaper with a headline splashed across the top that read *Chief Caulder Apprehends Felon Single-Handedly*. Bringing in Loretta Walch would win him another term; no doubt about it.

Loretta caught the shine off his badge in the side mirror. The officer was moving on the balls of his feet, closing the distance between them with cat-like precision.

Her only regret was having to put down the chocolate cake. She'd just finished the hot dogs. They'd been delicious, even though the mustard had been sub-standard. On the bright side, the buns hadn't gone all soggy and the sauerkraut was top of the line.

She gingerly laid the Styrofoam tray of chocolate cake down on the passenger's seat. She'd get back to it momentarily. Reaching to the back seat, she grabbed the camp stove, still in its box. The officer continued moving on the balls of his feet until something seemed to spur him on. His rush to her open window was done on tip-toe and Loretta was confident all he'd need to complete the vision she had from the side mirror was his replacing his slacks with a tutu. But his speed was impressive and it startled her enough that she put her full weight into protecting herself. The edge of the camp stove connected directly with the unprotected underside of the Chief's jaw. She heard the snap just before he flew to the ground.

Lumbering out of the car, Loretta went to inspect the damage. He was splayed on the asphalt parking lot on his back, his eyes wide in shock. Blood was oozing from a gash in the middle of his upturned jaw. She figured he wouldn't be going anywhere soon, but just in case, she grabbed the Glock from its holster. He didn't move as he watched her with his eyes glazed over in pain. Loretta decided that if she was going to take the pistol, she might as well have the ammo, so she unbuckled his holster and took that too. His only response was a garbled groan.

A crowd stood watching from a safe distance. A few were on cell phones, presumably calling the authorities. It was time to get back on the road, Loretta decided. She threw the pistol and holster to the floor-board, delicately placed the lid back on the Styrofoam container and backed out of the parking space. No one tried to stop her.

Loretta was in a tether. Now she was going to have to find another car. Barreling down the freeway, she snapped open a road map and slapped it against the steering wheel. Fayetteville, Arkansas was the next decent-sized town, but miles out of her way. So be it. They'd be on the look-out for a red Hyundai. By nightfall, she'd be driving something else.

The dispatcher got the first call moments after the Chief was attacked.

"Hey Linda, this is Bob Thornton. Better get someone out to the rest stop. Some crazy woman just clobbered Chet. Looks like his jaw was broken."

"Are you sure? I just spoke with him!"

"I'm sure. Saw the whole thing. The gal clocked him and he dropped like a stone. There's a nurse here, says he's got a broken jaw."

Linda hung up and grabbed the two-way on her desk. "KUW556, Bill are you there?"

"KUW556, yep, I'm here."

"You need to punch it to the rest stop. That perp just took the Chief down. I'm dispatching an aid car."

"I'll be there in two minutes. KUW556, out."

The radio was abandoned as the dispatcher got the EMTs on the phone. They promised to be there within ten minutes. She ignored her nails and sent prayers instead. In the heat of the moment, she never thought to alert the surrounding counties.

* * *

Loretta took the exit from the secondary road and tried to relax. She'd exhausted herself, worrying that every vehicle she saw might be an unmarked car with an officer behind the wheel bent on arresting her. There was no doubt about it, the crap in Chicago had gone on ahead of her. Why else would the Lebanon police have shown up at the rest stop? She took the first side street she came to and followed it to an alleyway. She'd be able to think better over a slice of double decadent chocolate cake. It was a shame the cop had interrupted her meal, but like always, she found herself having to use force for simply trying to live her life. She opened the container and felt elation wash over her. There wasn't a better comfort food than devil's food cake with dark chocolate icing. It was delicious, possibly the best she'd ever had.

As she ate, she mentally went over her 'to do' list. She needed another car, but the remaining $1,400 in her purse was already allotted for living expenses when she reached Tulsa. She polished off the cake and washed it down with the Pepsi. It had grown warm.

Arriving at a workable plan, Loretta took off on foot in search of a payphone.

"Domino's Pizza, this is Brandy."

"Yes, I'd like a delivery sent to the corner of Huntsville Road and Highway 45."

"I'll need an exact address, Ma'am."

"I'm having my car repaired. I don't have an address to give you."

"Hold on..." Loretta could hear her explaining the situation to someone in the background.

A man's voice came on the line. "I'm sorry, but our policy is we must have a physical address for deliveries."

"I understand. The thing is, I'm traveling and I had car problems. It's in the shop right now. My son and I are starving and I promised him

Domino's Pizza. Couldn't you make an exception just this once? I'll pay with cash."

There was a pause on the line. "I'm not supposed to do this, but what the heck. What would you like to order?"

"Two large double pepperoni pizzas and a two-liter of Pepsi, please."

"That comes to $18.15, Ma'am. The driver will be there within 30 minutes."

"Thank you so much. I'll be waiting for him on the corner."

She hung up and placed her next phone call.

"Checkered Cab, how may I help you?"

"I need a cab at the corner of Huntsville Road and Highway 45."

"We'll send someone right out."

"If they show up within five minutes, there'll be a twenty dollar tip in it for them."

"I'll relay the message," said the dispatcher.

The cab showed in four minutes.

"Is there a Wal-Mart nearby?" Loretta asked after she climbed in.

The cabbie sized up his fare and nodded. She'd be better off at Big & Beautiful but he wasn't going to be the fool to tell her.

"It's not far from here."

"I'll need for you to wait."

"That's fine, but I have to keep the meter running."

"Do I look stupid to you? I *know* the meter will be running!"

They drove the seven blocks in silence.

Loretta located the plus sizes and grabbed a sweat suit and a house dress from the clearance rack. They didn't have any wigs, so she settled for a baseball cap. At least it would hide her hair. She found the hardware isle without difficulty and bought an assortment of Philips and flat-head screwdrivers and proceeded to the checkout counter.

"That'll be forty-seven dollars and twelve cents please."

Loretta handed the clerk a fifty and grabbed up the change. So far, she'd eaten up twenty-three minutes. She should have just enough time to make it back.

"I need to be back within seven minutes," she told the cab driver.

"Hold on," the cabbie said as he stepped on the gas and merged with the traffic. They made the return trip in exactly five minutes.

A rusted pinto with a Domino's sign was idling at the curb.

"Here," she said, handing the cab driver the fare plus the twenty dollar tip he'd earned and got out with her Wal-Mart purchases.

Loretta was short of breath. She wasn't used to this much physical activity. She watched the cab disappear from sight and approached the driver's side window of the Domino's delivery car.

The radio was turned up full blast to hip-hop and the delivery boy was bumping and grinding to the music as he idled in his rust bucket. The smell of pepperoni pizza wafting from the Pinto made Loretta hungry.

She shouted for the pizza driver's attention and watched the cigarette he held fly out of his hand and onto his lap. His earlier movements didn't come close to what she witnessed next. He thrust his pelvis up, knocking the cigarette from his lap but he misjudged and it homed back down to the front of his jeans like a heat-seeking missile.

"Shit! Oh, shit!" he yelled as he smashed the hot coal with the palm of his hand until he was satisfied it couldn't do him any harm.

Turning his head in Loretta's direction, he reached over and turned down the volume on the radio.

"Are you the woman who ordered the double pepperoni pizzas?" he asked as if he hadn't been smacking his crotch only seconds ago.

"Yes, I am. How much?"

"It's eighteen dollars and fifteen cents, without the tip."

Loretta reached into her purse and found the Glock. "Could I see it first?"

"See it? Lady, they're double pepperoni pizzas. There's nothing to see!"

"The last time I ordered a Domino's pizza there were onions on it. I hate onions."

The driver gave Loretta a glare, but turned his attention to the back seat to pull out an insulated, zippered sleeve from the warming tray.

Loretta reached through the window, twisted the ignition off and yanked out the keys.

The driver whipped back around to find a Glock in his face.

"Get out of the car."

"Shit lady, don't shoot! I'll do anything you say, just don't shoot!"

"Then don't give me a reason to. All I need is your car. Do that and nothing's gonna happen to you."

The kid put his hands on top of his head. *He must've watched one too many cop shows*, Loretta thought. He motioned to the door with his bent elbow. "Is it okay if I open the door?"

"Just don't go and do anything stupid. If you do, the bullets in this Glock won't have any problem outrunning you."

"I believe you!"

Loretta watched him pull down on the door handle and get out slowly. He wasn't going to be any trouble. "Now start walking down the street. No looking back and no yelling for help because if you do, I'll shoot."

He did as he was told. Loretta watched his departure with a feeling of complete power. *She* was in control, more than she'd ever been in her life. *She* called the shots and he'd done exactly as she'd commanded.

She put the keys back in the ignition and started the car. It wasn't what she'd hoped for. It probably wouldn't push sixty on the freeway, but it would have to do. She made the corner, peeled down the alley and was next to Jay's car in seconds. She got out to work the Domino's sign free.

Inspecting the screws that held the sign in place, she tore the largest Philips screwdriver from its cardboard holder and went to work. It was rough going. The screws had rusted in place and she had to use all the strength she had, plus her body weight to get them loose. She switched to the passenger's side and repeated the process. By the time she was able to throw the sign into the bushes, she was bathed in sweat.

Time was something she had precious little of, but she needed to get the plates off the stolen Pinto. She found what she was looking for on an old Oldsmobile Cutlass a few houses down. The Cutlass was up off the ground on blocks. With luck, the owner wouldn't notice the license plates had been switched until she was safely in Tulsa.

She was getting nervous. The kid would've called the cops by now. She returned to the Pinto, installed the stolen plates and changed into a sweat suit. She had her belongings transferred within minutes. Loretta got behind the wheel, made sure her hair was tucked inside the baseball cap, and pulled out of the alleyway in a lather. Loretta forced herself to concentrate on the positive. There were only one hundred and twenty miles to go before she reached Tulsa.

*   *   *

Chief of Police, Chet Caulder, *did* make the front page of the *Lebanon Gazette*, just as he'd predicted. In the photo, he was lying in a hospital bed with his teenage daughter at his side. The headline read *Chief of Police Foiled by Woman Fugitive.*

The story was lethal; a death keel to the Chief's reputation that, depending on the townspeople's reaction, could spell the end of what he'd hoped to be a long, cushy career with the town of Lebanon. The article detailed the attack; quoting eye-witnesses who'd watched the *incident*, as the Chief now referred to it, from the safety of their cars or, in some cases, taking the short trip to the johns. Each recounting put him closer to the fruit of the month club than he cared to admit. The part where Loretta Walch single-handedly took him down with just a camp stove was eclipsed only by the witness' play-by-play of her nonchalant stroll to where he lay on the ground to relieve him of his gun and holster.

He never had gotten along with the newspaper's editor, thought the Chief.

He tried to put a positive spin on the situation, but came up empty. The election was only months away. If he wasn't re-elected, if he lost his post to that piss-pot Gordon Bradley, then Kelly might not be headed for the five-star education they'd planned on.

He looked down at the photo that took up roughly half the front page, above the fold line, and felt his blood pressure rise. The neck brace they'd put him in had forced his chin to point toward the ceiling. The camera had caught a vacant stare and the smile he'd obliged the photographer was worse—way worse. It had pixilated out as a combination grunt with a twist of grimace. Put bluntly, he looked for the entire world, and Lebanon's 11,420 residents, to be pinching a loaf in his jockey shorts. He looked…heaven help him…like a village idiot!

That would be because they'd pumped him full of pain meds a half-hour before the infamous photo op, now splashed across the damned newspaper. The Chief scrutinized the photo again. The stitches on the underside of his chin could be seen even with the piss-poor quality of

91

the photo. They resembled the leather lacing of a football. He'd have a scar there.

They had wheeled him back to his room, post-op, a few hours ago. The surgery to wire his jaw shut had left excruciating tentacles of pain traveling up his jaw and around his head that felt like a thorny vice.

His last thought before drifting off to sleep was that he should've shot the bitch when he'd had the chance.

Chapter 9

Frank pulled Britney from her car seat and grabbed the paperwork and groceries. "Okay boys, remember you promised! No rough-housing at Carrie's. We want to make a good impression."

"*You're* the one who wants to make a good impression," Brice said.

"I thought we already talked about this. Carrie is a friend who's offered to help me with the court hearing. It's important that I do everything right when I'm in front of the judge."

Brice shrugged his shoulders, refusing to make eye contact. He'd been surly ever since Loretta's disappearance. It was a lot for a nine-year-old to deal with.

Carrie answered the door holding a potholder. "You have perfect timing. I just took the spaghetti noodles off the stove. Come on in."

Frank stood in the entryway, enjoying the rich aroma of tomatoes and garlic. Once introductions had been made, Britney squirmed to be put down and headed over to where eight-year-old Madison was dressing a pile of Barbie Dolls. Frank held his breath when Britney grabbed one of the dolls without permission. To his relief, Madison only smiled and held out a floor-length gown with tiny sequins to Britney. Apparently, she'd been around two-year-olds before.

Within minutes, Brice and Carrie's son, Sam, agreed on the night's entertainment—playing Super Mario on Sam's Nintendo. Brandon and Mark trailed behind, seemingly happy just to be out of the house.

"This is a first. Usually the kids hang around the TV," Frank said.

"Well, enjoy it while it lasts. *Mickey Mouse's Clubhouse* will be on in…" she looked at her wristwatch, "exactly fifteen minutes. Madison never misses it."

"Neither do mine. All except for Brice. He's graduated to the Fashion Channel."

She looked up in surprise.

"Don't ask. The story involves my Aunt Edith, and trust me, if we went there it'd ruin a perfectly good evening."

"Then I won't ask," Carrie said with a smile on her full lips.

"It's good to see Brice hanging out with someone his own age. He never brought friends over to the house. Loretta's vocabulary tended towards the F-word for a noun, pronoun and verb."

"Been there. It was a long time after we'd moved out before Sam started asking friends over."

Frank decided to change the subject. He was still too raw from the slime he and the kids had just crawled out from under. "Can I help?"

"We could get the salad ready and if you'll hand me the garlic bread, I'll pop it in the oven."

Frank dug around in the grocery bag and handed over a foil bag. "Hope this is the right kind."

"As long as it comes out warm and swimming in butter and garlic, it'll be the right kind."

They worked side by side at the kitchen counter, chopping vegetables for a garden salad. Frank wondered if this was what a relationship was supposed to be like. If so, he'd been missing out. By the time they called the kids to the table, he'd gotten the hang of working alongside Carrie.

"Mom, *Mickey Mouse's Clubhouse* is on," Madison said as she took her seat.

"I'm one step ahead of you, sweetie. You kids can watch it from the table as long as you promise to eat your dinner," Carrie said.

Frank cut up Brandon and Britney's spaghetti noodles. All six kids were present and accounted for, yet the atmosphere was relaxed. Carrie had unearthed a booster seat for Britney and she sat proudly beside the older kids, splattering her My Little Kitty T-shirt with spaghetti sauce. All in all, it was a wonderful evening until Frank got a call on his cell phone from Detective Kalnoski.

He excused himself to walk out to his car for privacy.

"I hope you're calling to tell me Loretta's been arrested," Frank said.

"I wish I was. Actually, I just received a call concerning your wife. A Chief of Police in Lebanon, Illinois was attempting to arrest Mrs. Walch when she clocked him with a camp stove and took off with his gun and holster. The Chief had to have surgery for a broken jaw. She is also a person of interest involving an assault on a Domino's driver and the theft of his 1973 Pinto hatchback. There's been an APB issued, but she seems to have disappeared. I was hoping you'd heard from her," Detective Kalnoski said.

Frank felt like he had been catapulted into someone else's nightmare with no warning and he was left treading against quicksand that threatened to swallow him whole.

"Mr. Walch, are you there?"

"Yes, I'm here. I know what you told me must be true, but I'm having a hard time believing it. Loretta has come completely unhinged."

"I'm afraid so. Your wife is a danger to herself and others, Mr. Walch. Should I take it you haven't heard from her?"

"No, I haven't. If Loretta calls, I'll contact you right away. I need to ask you for a favor. Could you make a copy of Loretta's warrants? I have a court date tomorrow for a continuation of the restraining order. I need to include it with the others for the Judge."

"I'll have it waiting for you at the information desk. And good luck tomorrow, Mr. Walch."

Returning to Carrie's apartment, Frank kept the conversation he had with the detective to himself; even when he and Carrie got down to organizing what he would present to the court, he stayed silent. Somehow, heaping more insanity on top of what was already before them seemed like a sacrilege; as if by discussing Loretta's latest felonies, he'd be inviting her into the room with them. Tomorrow was soon enough. He'd just give himself enough time to swing by to pick up copies of the warrants and include them with all the rest.

* * *

"The court will come to order in the matter of Walch vs. Walch," called the bailiff.

The judge looked to Frank. "It appears that your wife has chosen not to make an appearance at today's hearing, Mr. Walch."

"No, Your Honor."

"Do you have legal representation, Mr. Walch?"

"No I don't, Your Honor."

"Is there anything you wish to present to the court?"

"Yes, Your Honor. I do."

"Please hand it to the bailiff, Mr. Walch."

Frank held out two folders. One contained his medical records, the other Loretta's outstanding warrants. The bailiff came forward and passed them over to the judge who began to examine them at length. When he got to Loretta's warrants, his eyebrows rose in alarm.

"The outstanding warrants you have supplied the court shows your wife has nine counts against her; two of them to include an assault on a Chief of Police and the theft of his firearm," the judge said in a questioning tone of voice.

"That is correct, Your Honor."

"Motion for a continuation of your restraining order is granted, Mr. Walch. And may God have mercy on your soul."

He slapped his gavel against its block, concluding the hearing.

Frank remained standing behind the lectern as the judge's last rights echoed in his head.

The Bailiff approached. "Mr. Walch, your hearing is over. You need to vacate the lectern."

"Did the judge mean what he said, or was he joking?"

"Judge Curtis doesn't have a sense of humor, Mr. Walch. What did your wife do, anyway?"

Frank gave him the laundry list of Loretta's warrants. "In a twenty-four hour period," he concluded.

"That's tough."

Frank moved down the aisle in a funk. He'd won the first round, but if Loretta ever caught up with him, today's decision was going to mean bupkis.

He found a bank of payphones.

"Good morning, Blackwell and Rosenthal."

"Carrie Neilson, please."

"Hold, please."

Carrie's voice broke into the elevator music.

"I was granted the continuation on the restraining order," Frank said.

"Thank God! You did your homework, Frank. You should give yourself a pat on the back."

"No. It's you who deserves a pat on the back. I wouldn't have had the first clue what to do without your help."

"What about coming over tonight to celebrate?" she offered.

Frank's face broke into a grin. He couldn't imagine a better way to celebrate his victory. "I'd love to. I don't have a babysitter, though."

"That's fine. The kids can keep each other company."

"What should I bring?" Frank asked.

"Mimosas sound good."

"And that would be…"

"Asti Spumante and orange juice."

"I'll be over around 6:30."

"Sounds great. And Frank?"

"Yes?"

"Congratulations!"

* * *

Loretta pulled into the Tulsa, Oklahoma KOA wondering if she would be able to figure out how to get the tent set up. Since adulthood she had avoided camping and she had never pitched a tent in her life. She paid the $17 fee at the office and the KOA's owner marked an X with indelible marking pen to indicate where her camp site was located. Following the directions, she stopped at campsite number twelve. The space was grassy with a large sycamore tree that shaded the site. On one side of the campsite there was a circle of river rocks that was filled in the middle with sand. Someone had placed a metal grate over the rocks, leading Loretta to assume it was a fire pit. It didn't really matter if it was or wasn't because she had no earthly idea how to start a fire. Besides, her priority was to get the tent set up while there was still light.

She used the picnic table's surface to lay out the camping gear. There wasn't much; a tent, propane lantern, camp stove, propane bottles and a sleeping bag. If she didn't find a job soon, she would be forced to purchase a cooler. The afternoon temperature had climbed to a balmy 70 degrees and iced Pepsi was sounding better by the minute.

Directions for setting up the tent were printed on the dilapidated box. Loretta had to get close to the small print and squint to be able to read them.

Be sure the tent is placed on dry, flat ground, away from an open flame. Carefully remove the restraining strap from around the tent, keeping it away from the face. The tent will automatically open and the poles will adjust uniformly. Once the tent has been set into place, attach the tent stakes using the loops on all four corners of the tent and drive them into the ground. Each tent is supplied with a rain fly. Place the fly over the tent, securing it to the hooks attached around the circumference of the tent.

Loretta pulled the tent out of the box and discovered the stakes mentioned in the directions were missing, as was the rain fly—whatever that was. She carried the tent to level ground and yanked the restraining strap. It flew out in all directions. The top of the tent slammed into her cheekbone just below her right eye. Loretta let out a yelp of pain and took out her frustration by pummeling the tent with her fists. The built-in poles reacted by giving at her every punch. She finished with a vicious kick before heading to the Pinto's rearview mirror to see what damage had been done. A one-inch gash was bleeding down her cheek and her eye had already begun to swell. Great! She would be looking for a job with a shiner.

She had left the tent lying on its side and watched as it was picked up by a gust of wind and started rolling along the ground like a crazed bowling ball. Loretta jumped out of the car and raced to retrieve it, but each time she got close, another gust of wind sent it out of her reach. She resorted to leaping on it at campsite number 9 when she'd run out of breath and energy. The landing was hard, knocking the wind out of her. She discovered the tent wasn't through with her when one of the dislodged metal spines poked through the thin nylon, stabbing her in the right breast. She gave up, put her head down on the patchy grass and started to sob. The sobs lead to full-throttle hysterics, which carried over to the KOA owner who came over to investigate.

Seeing her sprawled across the collapsed tent made it hard not to laugh, but he checked the urge with some effort and waited until Loretta gained back her composure.

"What happened?" he asked.

"The wind grabbed the damned tent. I think it's busted."

"Well, let's get it back over to your site and I'll take a look."

They each grabbed an end and walked it over. While Loretta held it in place against the wind gusts, the manager stood back to inspect the listless tent. "One of the poles is broken. I'm not sure it's going to stay up."

"It's got to. I plan to camp here until I find a job. "

"I'll see what I can do. Duct tape might work, but I can't promise anything. Where are the tent stakes and rain fly?"

"I forgot them."

He took off his baseball cap and scratched his head while scrutinizing the ruined tent. "The weather channel's calling for rain. Course, they're wrong as often as not. If it does rain, you're going to get soaked without a rain fly."

"I'll be fine. I mean how much trouble could it be if it rained a little?"

Plenty was the answer that came to mind, but he kept silent. There weren't many customers this time of year.

"I'll go grab some duct tape. It might get you through the night."

Loretta went over to the picnic table and sat down to fume. What had she ever done to deserve this? All she needed was somewhere to stay until she found a job. Was that asking too much? With a job, she'd be able to get an efficiency apartment and this nightmare would be over.

The manager inspected his handy work. It looked secure. Clouds had begun to blow in though, and he wondered at the advisability of leaving Loretta on her own. She appeared to be clueless.

"Looks like you're set for now. It'd be better if you had a rain fly and tent stakes."

"I'll get by. Are there any fast food places nearby?"

"If you get back on the freeway and head south, there's a bunch of them at the next exit."

"Thanks."

"You're welcome, but don't say I didn't warn you. We get some hellacious storms this time of year."

Loretta left the campsite, trying to decide what to eat for dinner. The double pepperoni pizzas were still in their warming jackets but when she'd checked on their condition, she'd been put off by the curling, dried edges of the pepperoni. The cheese didn't look all that appetizing either. She'd toss them out along with the warming jacket at the first dumpster she found. Her mind traveled back to yesterday's events. That cop should have left her alone. Actually, except for the Domino's guy and Jay, all she'd been guilty of was defending herself. People needed to learn to mind their own damned business!

The first drive-through she came to was a Wendy's. She pulled up to the speaker to place her order. "I'd like four bacon cheeseburgers, two orders of onion rings, and a large chocolate frosty, please."

"That'll be $13.75 at the first window," the clerk squawked back at her.

Loretta parked away from the traffic. The onion rings smelled delicious. Except for the frosty, she was finished with her meal within fifteen minutes and was wondering if she shouldn't have gotten a third order of onion rings when a State Trooper appeared. Her heart pounded in her chest as she watched him cruise by; positive the outcome was going to be a repeat of the rest stop. Only this time she didn't have anything to use as a weapon since the camp stove was sitting on the damned picnic table at the campsite, and the gun was tucked away in the duffel bag she'd stashed in the tent. The cop looked her way and appeared to be checking out the Pinto.

Loretta held her breath, willing him to keep moving. The cruiser slowed, but continued on without turning into the parking lot. Loretta let out the breath she'd been holding. She was safe for the time being. The extra order of onion rings forgotten, she pointed the Pinto back to the freeway.

Pressing down on the gas pedal, her leg shook. As soon as she got a job, Loretta decided, the damned Pinto was history.

Without a TV for entertainment, Loretta found herself at loose ends. By 8:30 she was sound asleep, with no idea the clouds overhead were about to send a whole lot of excitement her way.

It started at 1:00 AM with lightning and thunder. Loretta slept through it all, still road-weary. The storm advanced to high winds and a torrential downpour. Still, she slept. In no time, the bottom of the tent was a small lake and the sleeping bag she'd squeezed into was soaked through. It wasn't until something crashed onto the tent, collapsing it, that Loretta awoke. She'd been dreaming of treading water.

At first, her numbed brain didn't comprehend her predicament. Then panic set in. The sleeping bag was acting like a vise, its soggy fabric and stuffing constricting her movements. It took several attempts before Loretta was able to get her arms free. But worse than the vice grip of the soaking sleeping bag was the complete and utter darkness that engulfed her. She couldn't make out where the tent's zippered door was and something heavy was lying on top of her, pinning her down. It was her first introduction to complete panic.

She squirmed under the weight that immobilized her. When it refused to budge, she used both her arms and shoved. It gave a little. She tried again and heard the nylon tear. Whatever was pinning her rolled away and Loretta began to grope for the exit in sheer terror. As she did, it dawned on her the tonnage she'd just shoved off her chest could have been a bear. Did they have bears in Tulsa? God, she hoped not!

She needed to get a grip! Whatever it was hadn't snorted and it hadn't taken a swipe at her. She'd read stories about bear attacks, how they tore through nylon to get to the creamy center. The thing on her chest, whatever it was, had been dense and unyielding.

Her hand found an opening and she tore through her entombment, a scream just under the surface. What would be waiting outside for her? To hell with it! She'd take her chances. Nothing could be worse than being shrouded in wet nylon in inky blackness. With her first gulp of fresh air, she started to move in a circle, ready to take on whatever might be lurking nearby.

Loretta was halfway into her parameter check when she froze. The thing was huge! She could just make out what looked like an arm pointing up to the sky. But the arm wasn't moving. In fact, the entire *thing* wasn't moving. She listened for breathing and heard only the sound of crickets. Moving slowly, she backed up to the fire pit and grabbed one of the smaller rocks, hurling it as hard as she could. It connected with a solid thud and bounced back.

Alert for a response, she mentally coached herself. The keys were in her purse which she'd left behind in the tent. Last night before she'd turned in, she had locked the car. She considered diving under the Pinto if whatever the thing was that waited in the dark suddenly came after her, but threw the idea aside the minute it entered her mind. Diving wasn't her strong suit and she doubted she'd fit under the fucking thing anyway. The Pinto had wimpy tires, making it sit low to the ground.

Her eyes were adjusting to the dark. Squinting in concentration she saw other, smaller arms pointing from a narrow...what? Tree limb! It was nothing but a thick tree limb! She looked to the tree that sheltered the campsite and could just make out a fresh, light colored gash on the sycamore's trunk where the limb had been.

Bears, my ass!

Loretta felt a combination of embarrassment, relief and full-throttle anger. If people had left her the hell alone, she wouldn't have been sleeping outdoors with nothing but a thin piece of cheap nylon between her and the elements. She hated camping!

Her sweat suit was drenched, her hair was plastered to her head, and the wind slapping against her body was ice cold.

Loretta looked towards the office to calculate the distance. It was too far to walk. Besides, it appeared to be closed. There was only a lone courtesy light on at the front of the building. She slowly made her way back to the collapsed tent, leaned over, and began patting the wet nylon. After several minutes her hand connected with a hard, cold object. Shit! Now what? She didn't have a knife. It was locked, along with everything else, in the damned car. She'd have to find either the tear she'd made earlier or locate the zippered enclosure. She got down on her hands and knees, but lost her balance, driving her knee into one of the tree limbs that still arced across the outer parameter of the tent. Furious, adrenaline coursing through her body, Loretta picked up the heavy limb and hurled it like a javelin out into the blackness. Now that it wasn't laying across her chest in the pitch black, it hadn't been all that hard to do.

As she worked, Loretta shut her mind off to the wind that buffeted her wet clothing and the blood running down her knee. It took longer than it should have for her numbed fingers to find a way in but eventually the roughness of a zipper stopped her frantic search. It was another eternity before she had the tent unzipped but it took only seconds to grasp the strap of her sopping purse and shoot it on home.

She unearthed the car keys and trotted over to the Pinto. A heater never felt so good. Never again! Camping was for idiots, Loretta decided.

Leaving the tent and the rest of the camp gear to its fate, she drove off in search of a cheap but warm motel.

Chapter 10

Loretta arrived ten minutes early. There didn't appear to be any other applicants sitting in the lobby, but that didn't surprise her. How much competition could there be for a job shoveling dog shit from kennels? When she'd pulled up, the prevailing wind had slammed her square in the face with the unmistakable stench of dog feces.

A mousy woman wearing a smock of multi-colored dog bones approached her. "May I help you?"

"Yes, I have a 3:00 interview with Dr. Roth for the kennel technician job." Loretta handed the woman a freshly printed resume. It was consistent—there wasn't an honest thing in it.

"I'll let the doctor know you're here." The woman took the resume and disappeared.

Loretta decided to entertain herself with her surroundings. A golden lab sat at his master's feet, making eye contact with him for reassurance. Every once in a while the dog pawed the man's leg and received a pat of condolence.

"He's here to be neutered," shared the owner.

When Loretta didn't respond, he continued a one-sided dialogue. "The neighbor's accusing Jake of knocking up her prize poodle. If you ask me, he's got better sense than to hook up with that pampered, pom-pom, nail polish wearing bitch, but I can't prove it. Just doesn't seem right that he has to get them lobbed off."

Loretta looked away, leaving the man to suffer through his ordeal alone. The outside door opened to another blast of dog shit. The woman who entered was wearing a faux fur coat, holding a Siamese cat with a ridiculous fake diamond collar. The cat reacted to the lab by hissing and embedding its sharp claws into the owner's unconvincing mink.

"Sampson, stop that!" the lady demanded as she disengaged the cat's claws. She succeeded but the cat was lightning fast as he reconnected through her flimsy silk blouse.

Loretta wasn't amused. As far as she was concerned, both owners needed to get a grip.

"Dr. Roth will see you now," the woman said, motioning to Loretta.

The smell of antiseptic and fear assaulted Loretta's nostrils as she followed the assistant past several unoccupied examination tables. The doctor looked up past her bifocals, gave Loretta a cursory once-over, and pursed her lips in disapproval.

"Please have a seat," Dr. Roth requested.

"Thank you," Loretta said, trying to squeeze herself into the small upholstered chair.

Loretta checked out the desktop as the veterinarian reviewed Loretta's engineered resume, compliments of her imagination and a computer and printer she'd used at the unemployment office.

A huge stack of patient files rested on the center of the desk. Samples of dog and cat food were strewn about like four-legged party favors, and dozens of packets of medicines hawked by company drug pushers made up the rest of the cluttered desk.

"Your resume reflects you have two years experience as a kennel technician. Do I have your permission to contact your previous employer?"

"You could, but he moved to a warmer climate for health reasons. I have no idea what his new address or phone number is. I was told he retired to Phoenix."

"A shame. Tell me, what do you like most about being a kennel technician?"

Loretta's mind shuffled through the possibilities. Shoveling shit wouldn't sound convincing. Neither would the noise or the stingy wage they were offering.

"I suppose what I like most about kennel work is providing a clean environment for the dogs, making sure that they have nutritious food and seeing they get plenty of exercise. I love animals. I always have."

"What about working weekends? Do you have any specific requirements regarding the hours you're able to work?"

"No, nothing like that. I've always worked weekends. As far as the hours go, I live alone, so I'm able to work whatever hours you require."

"Tell me how you would handle a potentially dangerous animal, Ms. Simpson."

Loretta was ready for her. She'd taken the time to pull up miscellaneous information from the Internet at the unemployment office.

"I've experienced that it's important to observe an animal as soon as it has arrived at the kennel. If they show aggression, a muzzle is the best solution and, of course, keeping them away from the other dogs during exercise."

The doctor nodded her head in agreement. "Our ad mentions the job pays $8.75 an hour. Would that be agreeable with you?"

That question was a toughie. Loretta hoped this career choice would be short lived, but even then, it would be hard to make it on the slave wages they were offering. "I'd hoped in consideration of my two years of experience, you might be willing to pay a higher wage."

Dr. Roth glanced back through Loretta's resume. "I could offer you $9.75 an hour with quarterly reviews which can lead to raises commensurate with your job performance."

"That would be fine."

"Can you start tomorrow morning, 8:00 AM?"

"Thank you, Dr. Roth. You won't regret this!"

The doctor stood, indicating the interview was over. Neither had any way of knowing that of all the lies Loretta had told to date, this was the mother of them all.

Before she left, Loretta checked out the lobby. The lab had gone to sleep against his owner's legs, having no idea that fate was about to make him a falsetto. At the opposite end of the room the cat rested in his owner's arms, keeping a wary eye on its neighbor.

Loretta stopped at the first payphone she came to.

"Lesbian Relief Fund, Tanya speaking."

"Good afternoon. It's Loretta."

"Yes, how are you…or more importantly, how's your mother doing?"

"The surgery went well. The doctor told me he expects to release her tomorrow."

"How long will her convalescence be?"

"She should be up on her own within ten days or so. If it's any longer than that, I've located a CNA for home health care."

"Sounds like you have everything under control."

"As best as I can, anyway. I can't wait to get back to Chicago. I keep thinking about the possibility of owning my own business. L.A. Dogs can't help but be a success. I hope you have good news for me."

"As a matter of fact, the board has left the decision up to me. I'm leaning towards giving you the loan. If I do, you must promise not to let me down. This whole thing is highly irregular. I'd hate to discover I've made an error in judgment."

"I won't let you down, I promise. I honestly believe that once L.A. Dogs gets going, there'll be no stopping it."

"I'm glad to see that you're so enthusiastic," Tanya said. "But there's a world of difference between dreams and the actual execution of those dreams. Do I have your promise that you'll get the business plan to me within the week?"

"You have my promise. I'll send it in along with a cashier's check for the business license."

"I'll put the check in the mail tomorrow."

Loretta gave her the post office box number she'd shelled out $45 for that morning. Hanging up, Loretta grinned. Soon, she'd be saying goodbye to asshole managers and minimum wage.

The Liquor Barn's drive-through was empty. Loretta was handed her celebratory bottle of vodka in seconds. *It's about time there's something to celebrate*, Loretta thought. Returning to the motel, she realized she'd forgotten orange juice. A short trip and $3 later, she was carrying in her impromptu celebration and an empty big gulp container she'd snatched from the floorboard of the car. Inside, she mixed herself a drink and toasted to her future. She'd be a business owner, with short hours and she could sample her cooking any damn time she wanted to. Her mind fast-forwarded to chains of L.A. Dogs all over the greater Chicago area. Finally, she'd have the notoriety she deserved.

Morning found her on her hands and knees puking up the double cheese, double pepperoni pizza she'd had delivered the night before. She was covered in a cold sweat as wave after wave of dry heaves rooted her to the toilet. But sick or not, she had to leave for work. She waited for the latest spasm to pass and got to her feet.

The morning chill was serenaded by birds perched on the leafless skeletons of soapberry trees separating the parking lot from the busy road. Their warbles were wasted on Loretta. The breeze blowing in through the Pinto's open window dried the sweat that clung to her as her stomach continued to spasm which she blamed on the orange juice. It had masked the vodka and she'd gulped it down, happy with its sweet pulp until she'd gotten up to pee. The room became much like a boat in high seas; tilting and swirling and she'd barely made it to the toilet where she'd spent the majority of the night hugging cold porcelain.

Loretta arrived for her first day on the job with only seconds to spare. The outgoing kennel technician gave every indication he couldn't get away fast enough as he spit out information faster than a Gatling gun flies through bullets.

"The garden hose is there." He pointed to the connection against the outside wall of the enclosure. Opening a shed, he continued, "The food's kept here. You're expected to figure out the amount, but that shouldn't be a biggie. I hear you've already done this."

Loretta nodded her head, afraid to answer for fear the bile bubbling up from her stomach might erupt.

"Are you all right?"

She gave him a sharp look. What business was it of his if she was all right? She looked away, not wanting his concern or his scrutiny.

Moving past the awkward silence, he picked up the threads of his warp-speed instructions. "Follow me."

She trailed along with increasing difficulty. Her stomach was rolling and rumbling like an acid-washed shipwreck. If he'd go away for a minute, she could puke and get it over with.

He pointed to the kennel enclosures. "You're expected to shovel out the enclosures daily and hose them down. The feces go in this bucket."

Loretta took one look at the filthy plastic receptacle and dashed around the side of the building to produce a surprising amount of leftover pizza. Her reluctant trainer stayed in the enclosed kennel area. When she returned, nothing was said about her quick departure.

He pointed to the dog pens. "As I was saying, dump the waste out back on the compost mound. You can't miss it. The dogs are let out twice a day for exercise." He indicated a larger chain-linked area that hadn't seen grass in years. "Keep the aggressive ones away from the others. We use a muzzle on the nastiest and give them a short walk when the others are in the activity area."

"The muzzles are kept here." He indicated an unadorned wall that held muzzles of various sizes. "We don't have any problem dogs at the moment, but that Doberman pincher just showed up an hour ago." He pointed to a pen a few enclosures down. "You might want to keep your eye on him."

He glanced down at a cheap Timex. "I've got class in thirty minutes. Do you have any questions before I leave?"

Leave? What did he mean... She wasn't going to be able to do this on her own!

"I thought I'd get training. Are you coming back?"

"Afraid not. I've got a full load this quarter. If you have any questions ask Debra, the receptionist. She'll be glad to help."

He bolted away from the kennels, jumped into a 1979 Buick pimpmobile, and never looked back.

Loretta's anger made her forget her rolling stomach while she worked in the kennels of the smaller breeds. There were Yorkies, Spaniels, Shepherds, Rottweilers and everything in between. She *hated* dogs, always had. After an hour, she'd hit a workable stride and had begun to block out her surroundings, filling bowl after bowl with noxious doggie kibble.

That was her first mistake.

She'd finished feeding the smaller, more manageable dogs. It was in the Doberman pincher's pen that she encountered a problem. She was halfway through filling a dented metal bowl when a deep, confident growl raised the hairs on the back of her neck. The growl was unrelenting. Loretta moved on to her next mistake—this one of gigantic proportions. She looked the Doberman in the eye.

The beast didn't need to be asked twice. He slammed down all fours, every muscle in his sleek, fit body tense.

Instinct took over. Loretta had no interest in being this savage's chew toy. She placed the bowl down in slow motion and started to back out of the enclosure, step by careful step. She was doing surprisingly well until her butt encountered the chain link gate and she was forced to stop her retreat.

The dog stepped up his threat by exposing razor sharp canines, punctuated by full-throttle snarls. Saliva, seemingly intended for her, ran down its shiny black jowls. He struck all fours down in a heightened threat, seemed dissatisfied with the results, and launched into the air fangs first.

Loretta was paralyzed with fear. Her mind flew to something she'd read years ago. For larger breeds, and he certainly qualified as that, you were supposed to shove your balled up fist into the dog's mouth, as far down its gullet as possible. The author guaranteed results.

The dog bowl was now miles away and wouldn't have been much of a weapon anyway, considering it was made of flimsy aluminum. Loretta balled up her fist and watched as the dog continued his lunge which seemed to be centered directly at her juggler.

Once he was within striking range, Loretta shot out her fist and rammed it past some of the most serious canines she'd ever seen. She felt her knuckles being scraped on their way past his teeth but quickly forgot the inconvenience when, after blocking the animal's windpipe, he froze in shock. His body remained stiff, but immobile, as his eyes met hers in dedicated hate. He wasn't going to have his chew toy after all.

Waiting until he tried for a gasp of air, Loretta withdrew her fist, grabbed both sides of his muscled jaw, one side in each hand, and gave his head a vicious twist. The sound of cartilage and gristle was comforting as neurons were sent to his brain. He had lost the battle. As all sensation was lost he dropped to her feet in a belated peace offering.

Loretta looked down at her semi-mangled fist. "Pussy! Screwed with the wrong person, didn't you?"

The dog offered no argument as his lifeless body lay across her tennis shoes. She pulled her feet free and began the walk to the veterinary building to report the circumstances. She'd need to put the best slant possible on the incident. Thankfully, there were no witnesses to disagree.

"You *what*?" asked an ashen-faced Dr. Roth.

"I had to defend myself. He lunged for my throat!"

"Loretta, that animal was a champion, worth thousands of dollars! His owner has been coming here for years!"

"I had no choice. He would've killed me."

"Your job was to evaluate the dogs as they came in on a case-by-case basis. You knew the rules. If he'd shown *any* aggression, you should have muzzled him, not killed him. For God's sake! What'll I tell his owner? He'll sue me!"

"I *did* check his temperament. He let me pet him through the chain link fence. He was even wagging his stub. He didn't demonstrate aggressive behavior."

"Get your things. You're through!"

"You can't fire me for defending myself!"

"Bet me. Now get your things and get off this property!"

"I'm not going anywhere. I don't deserve to be shit-canned!"

The doctor turned to her assistant whose mouth was hanging open as she watched their heated exchange. "Debra, call the police. Tell them that we have an out of control employee."

"Yes, Dr. Roth."

That was all the encouragement Loretta needed. She outmaneuvered the assistant to the phone, took hold of the cord and ripped it from the wall. What followed remained a blank for Loretta.

The police gave Debra's deposition credence. She was the only witness who'd seen the event.

Allegedly, Loretta had walked over to the doctor with balled fists and began pounding on her until she collapsed to the floor. Debra's statement reported that Loretta then went to the medicine cabinet, grabbed a bottle, twisted off the cap and proceeded to pour enough tranquilizers into the good doctor's mouth to drop a horse, demanding that she swallow them, which she did.

The last part of the deposition was partially factual, partially guess work. As Debra explained to the police officers, she was afraid to follow them out through the door.

Loretta grabbed the unconscious doctor under her arms and dragged her out to the kennels (this part wasn't conjecture, as Debra had witnessed it with her own eyes). The police photographer was able to confirm her story with close-up photographs of the trail Dr. Roth's sensible shoes left in the dirt. The trail turned to streaks once the doctor's shoes connected with the cement floor of the kennel. Loretta's final act (and the one that Debra could only guess at) was to throw the doctor's comatose body into the pen of the largest canine. Now that the Doberman Pincher had been dispatched to wherever dead dogs with crushed necks went, the dog in question was a full-grown German Shepherd. The chain link gate had been closed and secured, presumably leaving the doctor to her fate.

Luckily, the Shepherd had been coming to the clinic since puppyhood. Instead of attacking the doctor, the detectives found him curled protectively against her body. Later, the Mayor would present him with a medal of honor, but that wasn't until Dr. Roth went through months of traction and intensive psychotherapy.

Dr. Roth was a minor celebrity, author of numerous books on the care and training of dogs—several of them bestsellers. The locals, protective of their celebrities whether wildly famous or not, were out for Loretta's blood. But first they'd have to find her. She had used an alias on her resume. Her references and job history led to nothing but dead ends. No one claimed to know a Loretta Simpson who fit her description.

Chapter 11

Frank arrived at Carrie's door with flowers, having no idea that seven hundred miles away, his wife had become public enemy number one in the Tulsa, Oklahoma area.

Carrie answered the door wearing a simple sleeveless jersey dress the color of periwinkles that hugged her curves. Her auburn hair was caught up on top of her head, showing off her graceful neck. Her eyes were made up just enough to highlight their warm amber depths. She took his breath away.

"You're beautiful!"

Carrie blushed. "Thank you for the compliment *and* the flowers," she said, carrying the spring bouquet to the kitchen. "Would you like a glass of wine? Our reservation isn't for another forty-five minutes."

Frank stood in the foyer, feeling awkward. This was the first time they had spent time alone.

"I'd love some wine," Frank said and he settled himself on the couch.

Carrie moved to where Frank sat and held out a bottle of White Zinfandel and a corkscrew. "Would you do the honors?"

"I'll be happy to. I'm relieved you agreed to go out with me tonight. As a matter of fact, I was surprised you said yes."

"If it had been anyone else, I would have said no."

Frank took his time getting the cork out of the bottle, carefully thinking over what he was about to say. "I'd given up on ever being happy again. I'm so glad we met." He stood, resting the opened wine bottle on the coffee table and took Carrie in his arms. He found himself drowning in moist lips that returned his pressure until they were both out of breath.

Carrie was the first to pull away. Reaching for the wine, she avoided his gaze. "I'll be right back with the wine glasses."

He followed her into the kitchen, unwilling to let the awkwardness between them stand. "I hope I didn't make you uncomfortable. I can't say I regret kissing you, because I don't. I've wanted to kiss you since the moment I met you. But the last thing I want to do is upset you."

Carrie smiled, turning his way. "Don't apologize. It was wonderful. It's just that I never thought I'd be with anyone again. It's going to take some getting used to. Does that make any sense to you?"

"Yes, it does."

"I need to tell you something and I'll only say it once because I don't want to live in the past. I loved Hal. I loved him even when he showed me who he really was; for a time, anyway. Now I don't trust myself. Every once in a while, I wonder if some chromosome that gives us discernment—the one that lets us know who to trust and who not to trust—is somehow missing in me."

"That makes us clones, then."

Carrie smiled and her cheeks flushed a little. "So, where do we go from here?" she asked.

"How about one day at a time?"

"One day at a time it is," Carrie said as she walked to Frank and they embraced.

When they pulled apart, Carrie sat down at the kitchen table. Frank found the wine glasses on the counter, and poured a glass of wine for each of them and joined her.

"I went to see Susan yesterday."

"How was she?"

"Terrible. I had to stop myself from crying. Her face was black and blue and her arm was in a sling. She's walking with a limp because of a sprained ankle and she has to wear an air cast. I just keep asking myself why no one would stop to help her. It was right there in the courthouse parking lot! She told me people passed by while her ex had her down on the cement, beating her, but no one offered to help until the police officer saw it and came to her rescue with his gun drawn. The creep listened then!"

"How's she doing psychologically?"

"She was afraid to answer the door. She's scared to death, Frank. With her ex out on bail and the hearing still a month away, she's afraid to leave her house. She's taken a personal leave of absence from work because she's terrified he'll come looking for her there. He threatened to kill her right in front of the officer. Of course, that's nothing new. He told her the day she left him he didn't have anything to lose; that he might as well kill her so he could move on with his life. He's obsessed and he's a walking time bomb."

"There's got to be something she can do. Does she have family living nearby?"

"A brother. They're estranged. She's asking the court to rescind her ex's visitation rights. If she can push that through, she'll be able to relocate."

"What's she going to do in the meantime?"

"There aren't many options. She could go to a shelter, but that's only a short-term solution. Anyway, it won't protect her at her job. There's really only one logical solution."

"And what would that be? From what you've said, she's stuck."

"I took her to a pawn shop today to buy a gun. We talked to the owner and he suggested a shotgun."

"Why a shotgun?"

"The dealer said that any man who hears the pump action of a shotgun is going to run because they know that whoever is on the business end, even if they're not a good shot, isn't likely to miss."

Despite himself, Frank smiled while a picture of Susan's ex running for his life ran through his mind. It would serve him right.

"I bought one, too. Susan and I are going to start going to the gun range. Wednesday is ladies night."

"You're kidding me, right?"

"Do you mean about the shotgun or about ladies night at the gun range?"

"The gun range."

"It's true. Apparently, it's pretty popular."

She looked to the clock on the kitchen wall and stood up. "We should probably go. We've got fifteen minutes to make it to the restaurant."

Frank followed her out, contemplating that for all Carrie's nurturing attributes, there were many layers to her he'd yet to discover.

Their discussion about Susan forced Frank to consider his own predicament. He hadn't done enough to address his family's safety. Moving would give him and the kids some wriggle room if Loretta returned to Chicago. The average person in her situation would've stayed away permanently, but Loretta wasn't an average person. She'd snapped and he knew he should expect the unexpected.

If he moved, he and the kids would have to stay with family for a while. It would take months for him to squirrel away enough for a new start. But the kids would be in a new school, where Loretta could not descend upon them to work her poison before anyone was the wiser. One thing was for certain. He was tired of swimming through the wake of Loretta's sewage.

Frank put the brakes on his thoughts as they pulled up to the restaurant. Tonight was meant for the two of them; no backwash and no skeletons allowed.

If Carrie noticed the stir her entrance caused, she didn't show it. Every male in the room had turned to stare, although the ones with female companions had the decency to be furtive about it. She didn't revel in the attention. In fact, she seemed oblivious to the sexual tension she lent to the room. It made him want her even more. They talked over a second glass of wine while they waited for their meals to be served and Frank couldn't help but wonder where the rest of the evening would take them.

* * *

Carrie's body was an amalgamation of shadows and proud curves. Her slightly rounded belly and full breasts announced childbirth without excuse. She was sex and procreation, womanly scent and silky-soft skin. She'd let down her auburn hair and it brushed her shoulders in lazy curls that caught the dimmed light of the bedside lamp.

Frank pulled back the covers and went to her as goose bumps rose on the surface of his skin. He bent his head to kiss her neck. He had never wanted a woman the way he wanted her.

"Are you sure?" he asked, worried what her reply would be.

"I'm sure. I want you, Frank. No regrets."

As they slipped under the covers, Frank felt the wonder of her soft skin and the warmth that radiated from her body. Her manicured nails traveled down his chest, leaving trails of sensation that were both confident and sensual.

116

He kissed her. Her mouth was soft and full, her lips open in invitation. Her breaths were coming in soft moans as they lay together, exploring their potential.

He moved his hands to explore her body and they began the braille of love as they moved closer to their first union.

"Frank, the phone…"

"It can wait." He placed his lips back on hers in an attempt to shut out the world.

Carrie pulled away and sighed. "It could be about the kids. We need to answer it."

He let it ring, trying to postpone the inevitable.

"Please."

He grunted in frustration and moved his arm out from the insulating warmth of the blankets and connected with the bedside lamp. The sound it made when it crashed to the floor was maddening.

Frank sat up, unwilling to admit he'd been woken from what would've been a world-class wet dream. His eyes flew open to confirm. The bed was empty except for an erection that bordered on lethal.

The phone continued to drone. He looked to the alarm clock. The hour was 1:30 AM. It would be bad news. There wasn't any such thing as a routine call in the middle of the night. His stand was now deflated as he grudgingly picked up the receiver.

"Hello." His voice carried his frustration.

"What the hell took you so long to answer the phone? Are you screwing someone in *our* bed, you bastard?"

Loretta! Please say it isn't so!

"I asked you a question, Frank. Is someone there with you?"

Frank was tempted to hang up. Her threats reached him, garbled as they threw out tin-like replicas of the shrill voice he'd hoped to never hear again.

"Answer me damn it! Do I have to drive over there to get some answers, or are you going to talk to me, you chicken-shit?"

No, not that! Anything but that…

He put the phone back to his ear in defeat. "I'm alone. You're forgetting that I'm raising four kids, one still in diapers. How am I going to have someone in bed with me, even if I wanted to?"

"Don't threaten me. You're still my husband!"

"That's a formality and you know it, Loretta. We're married in name only." *It was odd how much easier it was to communicate with her when she wasn't within striking distance.*

"I called to ask how the kids are."

They're positively thriving without you around...

"They're doing all right. Where are you?"

"What do you want to know that for?"

"I don't know...maybe because you're the mother of our children and they need to know you're okay."

Frank didn't expect the reaction he got when Loretta began to sob into the phone. He'd never heard her cry...ever...not in ten years of marriage. What had changed?

"Are you okay? Why are you calling in the middle of the night?"

"Fuck you, Frank. I'll call anytime I want!"

That was more like it.

The sobbing stopped, as if she'd turned off the lever connecting to her tear ducts.

"I'm not criticizing, I'm just concerned." *Much like he'd be concerned if a poisonous viper was curled up beside him in bed.*

"I'm just sorting things out. I've been on a diet... losing a lot of weight. The stuff keeps me awake at night."

"Stuff? What kind of stuff?"

"That's none of your business. I'm down to a size two plus."

Was she trying to come on to him? He visualized a smaller version of Loretta and his softened erection became an inny. He looked down, marveling at his body's ability for self-preservation.

"Good for you!" *Maybe if he coddled her he could get her to come clean, find out her location and alert the authorities. They'd be ecstatic.*

"I don't know. It's an improvement, but I've got a ways to go..."

Ya Think? A ways to go...it was like saying a grade school dropout had a long ways to go towards a doctorate!

"It won't take all that long, if that's what you really want." *Course, it wouldn't solve the bushy legs and underarm nests and it sure wouldn't solve the issue of her toxic personality.*

"How are you getting along?" Frank prompted.

"What business is that of yours? Have the cops been talking to you?"

He decided to share a portion of the truth so the lie didn't travel back to her and give him away. "I got a phone call about a week ago. They were asking if I'd seen you."

Her voice became deadly. "What *else* did those jerk-offs say? You'd better tell me, because if you're lying, I'll know, and I swear to…"

"Knock it off! They didn't say anything. I haven't heard from them since. Why are you so worried? You didn't do anything."

"All I did was defend myself, nothing else."

"What happened that you had to defend yourself?"

"I don't want to talk about it."

"Then we won't talk about it. Can you tell me where you are? The kids keep asking. They're worried about you."

"Yah, right...so you can go blab to the cops! I'm not telling you where I am. I don't trust you. You'd throw me under the bus!"

I couldn't. Weight loss or not, you'd get high centered.

"Come on, Loretta. We might have our differences, but you're still my wife and the mother of our children. I wouldn't narc on you."

"Sorry, my bullshit meter just went off, Frank."

"What're your plans? The kids ask about you…"

"I just got out a shovel to dig myself out of the bullshit you just heaped on me."

"Think whatever you want. It's true."

"Do they really ask about me?"

"You're their mother. Of course they ask about you. This whole thing's been hard on them."

"Would you tell them I miss them?"

"I will. But I wish you'd tell me where you are so the kids could stop worrying."

The phone went dead.

Going back over their conversation, Frank felt guilt. No matter what Loretta had done, she was still a human being. Somewhere deep down inside, she must harbor aspirations for a better life.

On the other side of the argument, she'd pounded on him for years and a part of him wanted to get even. Double-dare right he did! But not this way, not by blowing the whistle that would send her to jail.

He felt there was a strong possibility she was mentally ill. The toxicity of her personality might have a name. Manic-Depressive? No, there never seemed to be highs, so that couldn't be it. Schizophrenia? He'd never seen her delusional, never out of touch with reality. Bipolar, maybe? From what he'd read, bipolar involved a dual-personality disorder. Loretta's cruise control was set on steady nasty. Garden-variety depression? Who knew? Being able to rev to full-on bitch in ten seconds flat wasn't one of the signs of depression as far as he knew.

Still, whatever she suffered from could have a name with a magic pill attached to it, one that might make her whole. He'd never let her back into his life again, and he'd do everything in his power to keep her away from the kids, but a part of him wanted to see her get the help she needed.

It was the middle of the night, but Frank picked up the phone and called Detective Kalnoski to leave him a message. Kalnoski would now be on the lookout for a slightly thinner felon who had probably added drug use to her bag of tricks.

* * *

Loretta was showing off her newly trim body in a short skirt and see-through top. Her breasts were huge, but instead of drooping towards the floor, they were perky. How that was possible was anybody's guess. She started dancing to Madonna's *Material Girl* and her top was replaced by a gold-colored bra. The cups resembled cones as her breasts continued to defy gravity.

She danced around the bed provocatively. Frank felt nothing but revulsion. He knew that underneath the outfit lay hatred and it would spring forth the minute either one of them undid the snaps. Loretta approached him with a frown on her face.

"What's the matter, Frank? Did the Velvet Rocket disappear again? Come on, be a man."

"That's just the point, I am! You just about got the job done, though, didn't you? You almost emasculated me."

"You emasculated yourself, big boy."

Loretta broke out in a parody of *A Hard Day's Night* and her outfit changed to go-go boots and an even shorter skirt. She now wore a tube-top the color of ripe avocados with bright orange and yellow flowers embroidered on it. He was almost hypnotized by how it stayed up, considering its burden.

"I met a woman, a real woman, Loretta; someone who cares for me, whose sweet and kind and wonderful."

"No, baby, you've got it all wrong. You like it rough."

A black whip materialized and Loretta's go-go outfit was now a shiny dress made of black rubber. She wore stiletto-heeled boots that hugged her legs from her calves to the middle of her toned thighs.

"Come on baby, you know you love it. Get down on your knees. Now!"

The whip lashed out at him like Zorro on crack. Frank cringed and crawled against the side of the bed. If he had to, he could disappear under the bed. She'd never fit under there. He looked up in fear at her freshly shrunken body as the whip shot out and tentacled around his bicep. She'd fit all right.

He grabbed the whip and tried to yank it from Loretta's hands. Her long, red nails traveled along the grip in slow motion as Frank reeled it in. *Since when did she manicure her nails? Come to think of it, where had the bushel basket of underarm hair and furry legs gone?*

"What, baby, don't you want to play? I heard you've been a *real* bad boy and bad boys need to be punished. Give me the whip, Frank.... give me the whip....give me the whip..."

He woke up in a cold sweat, grasping the balled up sheet lying next to him. His heart was pounding and his stomach was doing 360's. He forced himself to calm down by taking deep, cleansing breaths. Laying there, about to head into a full-on anxiety attack, Frank made up his mind.

He was going to do the unthinkable and ask Edith if he and the kids could stay with her and Freddie until he could find a new rental. There'd be no more phone calls and no ghost of Loretta roaming the house. He'd sever the ties that were drowning his family and they would start over.

Chapter 12

Loretta studied the customers walking in and out of the Circle K. Someone was bound to call for help. So far, she'd found the Houston people to be polite. She waited patiently for a likely target. It took ten minutes.

A woman pushing a stroller emerged from the store and Loretta grabbed her chest and crumpled slowly to the ground—no sense in getting a case of road rash.

"Are you all right?" the woman asked.

Loretta felt the sting of her cheek being slapped as the woman attempted to revive her. She opened her eyes a crack and mumbled, "Call for help," and closed her eyes again. The stroller's wheels retreated back towards the store. Loretta waited.

Keds high-tops approached. "Get up, lady," a man's voice demanded

They didn't pay Circle K managers much, based on his tennis shoes, Loretta thought.

Loretta continued to lay prostrate near the front door.

"You're blocking the door. Get up!"

There must've been something about the sanctity of access into the Circle K in the manager's handbook. He seemed fairly obsessed with the situation. But, he could wait. She'd be laying there until the ambulance showed up.

An impressive crowd had assembled by the time they placed her on the gurney. Some took stabs at the cause of her collapse.

"You know, I had a cousin who dropped like that. It was a diabetic coma. Looks a lot like that to me. Her face is all beaded up with sweat, just like Naomi's was."

"How'd she do?" someone in the crowd asked.

"Deader than a door nail. Shame, too. She'd just moved in to this great little condo."

"I don't know, lady. I'd place my bets on a heart attack. Her color's all wrong. A person can't put *that* much strain on their heart and not have it catch up with them," disagreed a man.

"What about heat stroke? It could be heat stroke," said a woman who was caught up in the excitement of *name that disease*.

"Nah, it's only sixty-five degrees out. It's her heart, all right," rebutted the man. Apparently, he took his diseases seriously.

"Everybody get back," demanded the medic.

The crowd took a few grudging steps back while the medics got Loretta loaded through the bay doors.

"Bart, what's her B.P.?"

"One-thirty over ninety," the assistant replied.

"Good. Okay, call East Houston Regional. Give them an ETA of fifteen minutes."

The assistant radioed it in.

They were approximately five miles away from the Circle K when Loretta decided it was time to get the ball rolling. She reached into her purse and pulled out the Glock.

She'd had practice. Since she'd started her new career in Chicago, she'd learned the ins and outs of taking control of a moving ambulance. The trick was to scare the living shit out of the paramedics, enough to get them to turn the keys over, but not enough for the driver to overreact and head off an embankment.

While traveling further south, Loretta fine-tuned her script to an art form that was close to perfection. Of course, one of the most important aspects to hijacking ambulances was to make one or two hits in a given location and then move on to the next place before the authorities caught up with her.

Loretta was on her feet, the gun pressed against the driver's temple before either had a chance to react. "Pull over. Do that and you'll walk away. If you try anything, I'll pull the trigger."

The driver's eyes protruded from their sockets in abject fear. "I'll do whatever you say, lady."

"That's good. I'd hate to see your brains all over the windshield. It makes one hell of a mess."

The driver pulled into a strip mall's parking lot and threw the ambulance in park.

"Get out. Both of you. If you yell for help, I'll shoot."

Both the driver and his assistant nodded their agreement and their seats were vacated within seconds.

It worked every time.

Loretta got behind the wheel and pulled back into traffic. She gave herself ten minutes of driving time, and then pulled behind a warehouse. The cops would be looking for her by now.

Locating the drugs, she tossed them into a canvas bag and sat down on the gurney to change into a dark, nondescript pantsuit and granny shoes. She pulled on a salt and pepper wig and checked her reflection in a small hand mirror. She looked convincing. The final touch was a pair of thick, black-framed glasses. Satisfied with her disguise, she got out and walked to a payphone.

"I need a taxi at Big Jim's Tires. It's at the corner of Cloverleaf and Beltway," Loretta requested.

"Yes, Ma'am. Someone will be there within thirty minutes."

"Thank you"

Loretta waited patiently. She could've stood there on the street corner all day and no one would have noticed her.

The cab driver dropped Loretta off at the fringes of the Fifth Ward, the roughest area of downtown Houston. Block after block hawked adult video stores, body piercing, tattoos and female dancers with utilitarian neon signs. Their patrons didn't expect sophistication.

Loretta approached a young man leaning against the corner of an abandoned brick warehouse. He was wearing faded Levi's and a Pink Floyd T-shirt. His longish hair was pulled away from his face by a bandanna. She guessed him to be a pimp or a pusher. Either way, it was a start.

"Know where I can locate a pharmacy?"

"Do I look like the fucking yellow pages to you, lady? How would I know where a pharmacy is?"

Loretta produced a fifty dollar bill to refresh his memory.

"I'll take you there myself, as long as Ben Franklin's face is at the other end."

Loretta nodded her agreement, keeping her hand on the Glock tucked inside her purse. She'd never been enamored with back alleys, where a person could get their throat slit for less than what she'd already produced. But, it couldn't be helped.

They meandered through derelict streets, busy with the dregs of society. The guy stopped in front of a billiard room. Its wood siding was peppered with bullet holes and the plate glass window was covered with a sheet of plywood that had been tagged by graffiti.

"His name's Chance," her escort announced.

Loretta produced the hundred they'd agreed on.

"Thanks," the man said. He turned back in the direction they'd come.

Loretta stood on the pavement in front of the billiards room trying to figure out why she had such a strong feeling of foreboding. Something felt wrong. She grasped the Glock tighter and watched her tour guide's retreating back. Something felt off about him. Another wave of uneasiness sent warning signals to her brain and Loretta knew she should leave. And she would have. But heisting ambulances had gone from a way to make a living to a lifestyle and she needed meth; she had since this morning. Her introduction had happened innocently enough. A connection in Tulsa had offered her meth. "It'll help lob off a few pounds," he'd promised.

Boy had it! In only three months, she was down to a size 16. She'd never have thought it was possible, but with each passing month, she found herself needing to buy smaller clothes. She hadn't been hungry in months. It was this new found addiction that led Loretta to ignore her intuition and propelled her through the door of Greg's Billiards.

Inside, grime discolored the surface of the bar. Cracked vinyl stools hugged a gone-to-green brass footrest that ran the length of it. The soft click of billiard balls as they kissed one another was the only homey feeling the space had to offer. She walked up to the bartender who had a skull and bones tattoo on one beefy arm and a big breasted girl with huge nipples reclining against a Harley on the other.

"I'm looking for Chance."

The place grew quiet and the action at the pool tables slowed. Several in the bar turned to stare. Loretta stood at the bar, waiting, not daring to show her discomfort.

"I'm Chance," answered a man after minutes had ticked by. He had a huge beer gut, a three-day beard and from the whiff Loretta got as he approached, in desperate need of a shower. Somewhere in the past his teeth had been handed in for a set of falsies.

"I'd like to talk business with you."

"I don't do business with strangers."

"It'd be worth your while."

Chance merely grunted.

"Give me ten seconds. You won't regret it"

"You seem pretty sure of yourself, lady. Let me take his money," Chance said, nodding to a tall, emaciated man standing at a pool table, "and then we'll talk."

The men flipped a coin for the break. It didn't take long before Chance was grabbing his winnings from the edge of the pool table.

"Okay, follow me," Chance said, strolling out the back door of the billiard room.

Loretta followed him into a reeking alleyway. It was piled with debris; cardboard boxes, empty crates and miscellaneous refuse. A Kentucky Fried Chicken container filled with leftover chicken writhed with maggots that set off Loretta's gag reflex. The smell was overpowering.

"What's this about?" Chance asked.

Loretta went down the list as she pulled proof from the canvas bag she had slung over her shoulder.

"How much?"

She upped her going rate to cover the meth her body craved.

"Seems high. I'll give you $1,200."

"What's an 8-Ball of meth going for?" Loretta asked.

"Two hundred."

"Make it three hundred for two 8-Balls and you've got yourself a deal."

They'd just made the switch, his $900 and the meth for the canvas bag filled with goodies when all hell broke loose.

"Freeze!"

Loretta turned to face two plainclothes detectives approaching at a trot down the alleyway with guns drawn. Self-preservation screamed for her to run, but the muzzles of their guns were pointed at her and Chance's heads. Loretta took a step back, unsure of what to do and her decision was made for her when Chance wrapped a beefy arm around her neck.

"Bitch!" he hissed in her ear.

"I'm not a narc! Let go of me you son of a bitch!"

"No way. You're my ticket out of here."

The detectives moved in tandem, now aiming their guns at Chance. Her escort, the one with the bandanna and Pink Floyd T-shirt, had joined them.

"Let go of her!" yelled one of the men.

Chance's answer was to tighten the choke hold he had around Loretta's neck, cutting off her air. He walked backwards, dragging her with him, using Loretta as a shield.

"I said freeze!" warned the detective.

Desperate, Loretta flailed at the vice grip Chance had around her windpipe. It was no use. The muscles in his arm only grew stronger.

Loretta figured her chances of survival were zero if they made it around the corner of the building. She swung her leg out, centering all her momentum, and slammed the heel of her shoe hard against Chance's shin. She was disappointed when his only reaction was a grunt of pain and a slight slackening of the death grip he had around her windpipe. But it was enough to pull air into her lungs. Loretta lurched to the right with all the force she could muster. Chance's grip was momentarily broken. She doubled over, trying to stay outside his grasp but Chance was just as desperate and managed to reach out and grab hold of her again. As he started to pull her back against him, she heard the detectives go into action.

"Do you have a clean shot?"

"Affirmative."

"Take it!"

The impact of the bullet entering Chance's temple threw him backwards and the hold he had on Loretta brought her down in the alleyway with him. His arm, still around her neck, began to convulse in death throws. Loretta's last conscious thought was how peaceful the darkness was.

Chapter 13

Loretta opened her eyes to walls the color of goo at the bottom of a stagnant pond. She squinted and the walls morphed to a more manageable dusty green. She laid her head back down when the room started to spin. Her neck hurt like hell and shooting pains at the back of her head promised a world-class migraine. She tried to swallow but the pain wouldn't let her. A steady bleep, bleep, bleep followed by the sounds of crape-soled shoes against the vinyl floor got her attention. She opened her eyes, turning her head gingerly to locate the source of the footsteps.

Big mistake! Cartilage crunched against cartilage. The pain traveling to the back of her skull short-circuited as explosions in the form of bright flashes that temporarily blinded her. The stranger leaned over the bed and Loretta felt a burning sensation in her groin.

She forgot her pain and bolted upright. Arm restraints stopped her mid-way. "What in the hell are you doing? And why am I tied to the fucking bed?"

"I'm adjusting your catheter. You're restrained to the bed because the police have requested it," came the nurse's matter of fact reply.

"Catheter? Where am I?"

"Saint Luke's Hospital," the nurse replied.

"Why'd the police request that I be strapped down?"

"It's for our protection and they want to make sure you can't escape."

"Escape? Screw that! I'll leave if I want to!"

"You'll need to revise your plan. There's a guard just outside this door who has other ideas."

Loretta braved opening her eyes again. Her vision had returned to normal. She inspected the leather restraints. They were lined with wool. When she gave them a tug, she met with resistance. They appeared to be connected somewhere under the hospital bed.

"I'm allergic to wool."

The nurse was standing at a monitor near the head of the hospital bed, busy jotting down readings to a chart. She didn't bother to look up with her reply. "That may be, but then they'd only change them out for nylon ones. Trust me, the wool are more comfortable."

"How long have I been here?"

The nurse glanced down at the chart. "According to this, fourteen hours."

"I've been laying here for fourteen hours?"

"You were admitted last night."

"What happened?"

"A concussion, for starters. The rest is for you and the doctor to discuss."

"I have a right to know!"

"True. He'll be making his rounds in three hours. You can ask him then."

"Screw that! I want to know what's wrong with me."

"I'm sure you do, but I've already told you more than I should have. Blame it on my third cup of coffee."

"I ask for answers and you flip me attitude! I want to see the doctor now!"

The nurse moved to the end of the bed and made eye contact with Loretta. "Listen, you're in a lot of trouble. Why make this harder on yourself than you have to? Your best approach is to cooperate. You're lucky. You'll be staying in this hospital for as long as it takes for you to get well. After that, you'll be transferred to a cell. I've heard rumors jailors don't particularly care about the comfort of inmates. Make nice and for the time being you'll be a lot happier."

Loretta watched her retreat with a feeling of gloom as everything flooded back to her in Technicolor. Chance, that bastard, was dead.

The doctor was an hour late according to the clock on the wall. A stethoscope was wound around his neck and it appeared he'd borrowed the white lab coat he wore from someone way beefier. It draped over his long, skinny arms, ending somewhere near his fingertips. Judging from the fine peach fuzz that had erupted in patches on his cheeks and chin, he was testosterone deficient.

"How are we today?" he asked in a monotone voice.

"*We* feel like shit!"

He didn't acknowledge her comment as he fiddled with her I.V. drip.

"Are you an intern?" Loretta asked.

"Nope, I'm a resident, third year."

"Why didn't they give me a real doctor?"

"Look at it this way. Your care is being reviewed by the chief of staff, which means you have two doctors looking after you. I'm specializing in drug rehabilitation and you're being given the chance to kick that shit you're hooked on at taxpayers' expense. Seems like a win-win to me."

"What shit are you talking about?"

"You can cut the crap, Loretta. Blood work doesn't lie. How long have you been hooked on meth?"

She ignored his question and asked one of her own. "What happened to my neck? It hurts like hell and my head feels like it's about to explode."

"When you were thrown to the pavement, you wrenched your neck. The impact gave you a slight concussion, but that's the least of your worries."

"That's easy for you to say. It feels like someone took a hacksaw to my fucking head."

"Your biggest problem is going to be withdrawal. I've ordered antidepressants to replace the dopamine receptors that were switched off in your brain when you started the meth. You'll also be taking Tyrosine. It's been tested on meth addicts with good results."

"So, I'm being strapped to this bed to be your lab experiment? Fuck that!"

"You're strapped to the bed because you were caught selling drugs to a guy who's lying on a concrete slab in the coroner's office. My job is to try and help you, but ultimately the outcome is up to you. No matter what you decide, you'll be spending time in jail. You can spend your time getting clean, or you can continue your 'poor me' act and eventually end up back on the streets to repeat the process all over again."

"Where'd you come off so holy? I'm not being given any say-so while I'm strapped to this fucking bed!"

"Let's talk about that. You had a say when you snorted the meth. Know what's in that shit? Ammonia, Lye and Phosphorus, which is the red crap scraped from match covers. Doesn't look like much of a future to me."

"Fuck you, fuck everybody! I want outta here!"

"That isn't likely to happen. The longer you remain here, the longer you'll avoid a ten by ten cell. Think about it. I'll be checking in on you during evening rounds."

He moved off at a relaxed pace that left Loretta seething. He held all the cards and as long as she remained strapped to the bed, her future was in the hands of a snot-nosed resident who probably didn't need to shave more than once a week.

Chapter 14

Loretta appeared at her hearing in a size twelve orange jumpsuit. Jail food hadn't agreed with her. The bail set by an open-minded judge had been reasonable, but she had no one to pay homage to her character. Loretta had been forced to wait out her trial in a shared jail cell.

Her court-appointed attorney had spent exactly twenty minutes with her just the day before. Actually, it hadn't been a full twenty minutes, seeing as how his attention seemed to be zoned elsewhere. The circumstances of Chance and their run-in with the detectives hadn't seemed to hold his attention. By the end of their meeting, Loretta was sure of only one thing: he didn't give a flying fuck about the outcome of her hearing.

He now stood before the judge wearing the same worn houndstooth jacket and cheesy tie he'd had on the day before, presenting to the court exactly *nothing* to plead her case. The prosecuting attorney made up for that by calling on the plainclothes detectives, including the bastard who had entrapped her, to the witness stand. One by one their testimony had torn her a new asshole.

The bartender was the last witness the State called. He was wearing a long-sleeved shirt, presumably to cover his tattoos. When asked, he pointed in Loretta's direction to indicate she was the woman who had entered the bar and asked for Chance. His testimony came to a close after he told the judge that she and Chase had taken their business out to the alleyway, which erupted into gunfire minutes later.

Loretta wondered if the judge would mind if she asked to be led out by her wrist and ankle chains to her jail cell instead of waiting out the sham that was her trial. Undecided, she stayed seated, knowing that life, as she knew it, was over.

Her asshole attorney could've subpoenaed the doctor who had treated her for meth addiction. He would have painted her as a victim of drug addiction, which may have shaved a few years off of her sentence. But the son-of-a-bitch hadn't.

132

The prosecuting attorney announced an end to her annihilation by telling the judge he had no further witnesses.

The judge looked to Loretta with blood in his eyes.

"Please rise."

…which she did. Maybe if her body language telegraphed remorse, he might take pity on her soul.

"Do you wish to say anything before you receive your sentence, Mrs. Walch?"

"Yes, I do, Your Honor."

"Please proceed."

She had one last shot…

"Your Honor, I have just completed treatment for methamphetamine addiction. Now that I am clean, I intend to live my life differently—inside, instead of outside the law. Over these past several weeks while waiting for my trial, I saw my attorney for exactly twenty minutes, and that was yesterday, Your Honor. I did not receive fair representation." Finished, Loretta remained standing, pleading with the judge with her steady gaze.

The Judge waited out her silence before he resumed the final phase—the one that would tell her what her future held.

"Mrs. Walch, it is the opinion of this court that you did flagrantly break the law by committing a felony when you sold drugs to Mr. Chance Wycombe on the day in question. It is further the opinion of this court while considering the string of outstanding warrants against you in Illinois, Missouri, Arkansas, and Oklahoma and the magnitude of those crimes for which you must stand trial, you are a poor candidate for rehabilitation. I am sentencing you to ten years in the state penitentiary to be served consecutively." He hit his gavel at the same time Loretta crumpled to the floor.

The guards helped her get to her feet and without any warning Loretta lashed out at her attorney who prudently moved outside striking range.

"You piece of shit! You worthless, scum sucking worm! When I get out, I'm going to find you and chop your balls off and *then*, I'm going to kill you!"

At the insistence of the judge, Loretta was dragged from the courtroom; the last of her threats reverberating against the tile walls of a holding cell. No one was there to watch the guard shove her against the abrasive cement wall.

"Shut your trap, woman!" the guard growled.

"I was railroaded!" she shouted.

"Do I look like I care, lady? Shut up!" he said, giving her another shove.

Loretta was nearly catatonic during the transfer back to her jail cell. Ten years incarceration was just the beginning. Officials in four more states were wringing their hands to get a whack at her.

So be it, Loretta thought. She had no intention of sticking around to get their verdicts.

"They gave you ten years? That sucks!" responded her cell mate while she watched Loretta pace around their claustrophobic jail cell.

As far as roommates went, Belinda was blind luck, like getting in the short line at the DMV without being re-directed. Belinda insulated herself, responding only when spoken to and kept her hands off the few personal belongings Loretta was allowed in their shared cell.

"Where will you serve your term?"

"I don't know. There's a trial pending in Lebanon, Arkansas. Then there are the outstanding warrants in Illinois, Arkansas and Oklahoma. Doesn't matter. I'm not going to prison."

"What do you mean you're not going to prison?"

"What are you…*new*? I mean that I'm *not* going!"

"How're you going to manage that? If the judge says you go, then you…"

"Shut up!"

"Hey, I'm on your side. You don't have to yell at me."

"I'm not going to surround myself with negative bullshit," Loretta snapped back.

"I hope you do it, Loretta. I hope you let them have it! Just don't get yourself shot."

"It doesn't matter one way or the other. I'm not going to be locked up for ten years! *Anything* would be better than that."

Belinda slipped back into silence to concentrate on a crossword puzzle.

Later that afternoon, a jailor came to pay Loretta a visit. "Grab your things."

"Why?"

"You're being transferred."

"Transferred where? I thought I was going to Lebanon for my hearing."

"They're transporting you to Bridgeport, Texas, Women's Division. The judge has ordered that you begin your sentence now. I suppose he'll let the courts fight over who has custody of your sorry ass later," the jailor said in a slow, lazy drawl.

Loretta began gathering her belongings, her mind racing. She needed more time to figure out an escape plan. This was too sudden. She stuffed her things into the canvas bag she'd been given and handed it to the jailor's outstretched hand.

As they walked the empty corridors, the jailor slowed. "You know, you're a minor celebrity 'round here. Some of the gals think you hung the moon!"

"What the hell does that mean?"

"You're different. To my memory, you're the first prisoner we've had who knocked over ambulances. Then there's that thing 'bout clobbering the police officer and grabbing his gun."

"That hasn't been proven yet."

"Whatever," the jailor said, rolling her eyes.

Loretta was led to a holding area where she was patted down. A bright light was shone down her throat, under her tongue and along her gum line to check for contraband.

"She's clean," announced the guard. She secured Loretta with wrist and ankle chains.

They walked out to an idling van with the jailor grasping Loretta's right arm and the guard her left. They halted for the driver to run a mirror along the underbelly of the van to check for anything suspicious. Loretta took advantage of the downtime to enjoy the afternoon air. The breeze carried with it the sweet scent of magnolias and rich earth. Loretta took deep, cleansing breaths, more determined than ever to break free.

Satisfied with his inspection, the driver signed the logbook the jailor handed him and helped Loretta climb into the back seat. Once she was buckled in, the driver slammed her door, double-checked it was securely locked, and climbed behind the wheel. The mesh partition separating them seemed to give the driver a false sense of security, Loretta noticed. She planned to remedy that.

He tuned the radio to a mindless, easy-listening station. For Loretta it was cruel and unusual punishment, but it encouraged her to get busy. Feeling along the edge of the bench seat, it wasn't long before she was rewarded with a deep crack in the vinyl that she was able to work into a hole with her index finger. It took over half an hour, but eventually she found her way through the vinyl and past the foam covering to the springs below. Loretta had to widen the hole so she could use her thumb and index finger to bend the spring back and forth until it finally broke free.

Concealing it in her palm, Loretta glanced to the driver. He was rocking out to Barry Manilow's *Mandy*. Strange how anyone could get so far into elevator music, but far be it for her to complain, Loretta thought. It was her saving grace. He wasn't paying one bit of attention to what she was up to in the back seat.

She took one end of the curled metal spring and began to work it straight. It took a ridiculous amount of time before the metal coil was straightened and ready to be inserted into the lock that secured her wrists. One after another attempt ended in failure, but Loretta refused to give up. Her life, once she was transferred to Bridgeport, wouldn't be worth living. She had no choice but to succeed. Twenty minutes into her frustrating struggle, the cuffs gave. She'd almost missed the click of their release over the droning elevator music. Loretta carefully removed the handcuffs, making sure she didn't make any sudden movements that might be noticed by the driver.

Getting at the ankle cuffs was harder. She had to bend her body a little and raise her legs in the air to reach them. Within seconds, her legs were shaking from fatigue. She worked on the ankle lock for nearly forty minutes, taking rests when her legs threatened to spasm before the lock finally obliged and released her from the ankle chains. Loretta removed them in slow motion, making sure the chain didn't rattle when she lowered it to the floor.

Finally free, she forced herself to appear bored when what she really wanted to do was let out a victory cry; maybe ask the driver for a high-five. She leaned against the bench seat to wait. Eventually the driver would need to stop to refuel the van.

They tore up the miles, passing town after town until Loretta's peace of mind turned to worry. They were now on the outskirts of Irving, Texas. It was too close to Huntsville for her liking. The driver hadn't so much as glanced at the freeway signs in search of a gas station.

Frustrated, Loretta stared straight ahead and listened to the monotonous drone of the tires and moved with the sway of the van until she was nearly lulled to sleep. To stay alert, she concentrated on how she was going to deal with Frank once she broke free. The Louisville Slugger and the iron pan were retired as far as she was concerned. They'd graduated to a place where nothing but the best would do: she wanted to leave a lasting impression. There were too many possibilities to narrow the field to just one final solution, but she was getting closer. And the closer she got, the happier she became. She was positively glowing by the time the driver pulled into a Chevron Station.

The driver turned to the back seat to take a cursory glance at Loretta. Finding nothing that concerned him he jumped out to swipe a gas card through the machine. He'd already started pumping the gas when Loretta tapped on the window with her wrist that was shackled by the unlocked metal cuffs. This was the riskiest part of her plan. If he were to notice the cuffs were not secured, he'd lock her up tight and call for reinforcements.

It took several attempts before she caught his attention and he peered at her through the glass.

"I have to go," she said.

"What?" he responded, cupping his ear.

"I have to go to the bathroom!" Loretta yelled.

"It'll have to wait 'till I'm finished here," he drawled.

Loretta waited her turn anxiously. She had one shot at overpowering him. She weighed her chances. He had a gun and he had training. But she had youth, and since losing the weight, she had speed. There was one other thing that couldn't be overlooked that could tip the playing field in her favor; she was desperate.

The driver watched the pump turn its revolutions, happy for the fresh air. The ever-increasing total didn't concern him. The tab was being picked up by the State.

He left Loretta sitting in the back seat to inspect the facilities. He'd never lost a prisoner yet and he had no intention of ruining his perfect record. If the bathroom had windows that would make escape possible, he would need to look for other accommodations.

A cute blond clerk grabbed the key to the Ladies room, signaling her co-worker to take over at the register.

"It's a single stall, no windows," she explained as they walked past the front doors to the outdoor access of the restrooms. The clerk knocked on the door. Getting no reply, she slipped the key into the lock to let the official make his inspection.

"This'll do," he said.

She handed him the key attached to what amounted to be a small section of two by four and returned to her post. Strolling back to the van, the driver's thoughts were on his upcoming retirement. Looking to the back seat where Loretta waited patiently, his attention was woefully misdirected.

Later, when he was called on the carpet for his part in the upcoming calamity, he would honestly testify that Loretta had exhibited no sign of the aggression he had been trained to look for. In fact, she'd been leaning against the seat with her eyes partially closed, as if she were on the fringes of sleep.

He put his hand over his weapon that rested in its holster on his hip and opened the door to a shit-storm. Loretta flew out of the back like a major player in a martial arts movie, all assholes and elbows and connected to the driver's groin. As he went down, she connected with his windpipe. He wasn't sure which to grab first and settled for one hand on his throat and the other on his exploding crotch.

That was how the store clerk found him when she ran to his rescue. The van had already torn out of the station, causing gas to spray in an impressive geyser. The shut off to the pumps was turned on immediately, but a lethal amount of gasoline now coated everything within a fifteen foot radius, spreading a sheet of potential death. Innocent bystanders stood in awe of the scene while the clerk yelled orders.

"Ya'll stay back! Do *not* strike any matches or use any lighters. If you do, you'll blow yourselves to shit!" The last part of her warning wasn't in the employee handbook, but she was *not* a staunch believer in the public's ability to think for themselves.

She approached the driver and made another determination: The official didn't look all that official lying crumpled on the ground with one hand clutching his nuts, and the other, his throat.

Were her feet held to the fire, she would have had to admit her priorities weren't exclusively centered on the driver's emergency or with the gas spill. With this calamity, she'd be lucky to leave work before midnight and the jock she was dating needed to be on the football field by 7:00 AM the next morning for practice. The evening they had planned was now a total loss.

Resigned to her fate, she helped the driver get to his feet and together they made it safely past the gas spill to the front of the store. Once out of immediate danger, the driver fell back to the ground, clutching his crotch again.

"Can you make it inside?" she asked.

"Have the cops been called?" he gasped.

"Yes, they have. Do you feel any burning, any smarting of the eyes?"

He shook his head in disgust. "Oh yeah, I feel burning all right. But it isn't in my eyes. Which way did that bitch go?"

"She took off for the freeway."

"Shit! Call the cops back and make sure they're on their way!"

"Are you sure you're okay?" the clerk persisted. She had her priorities. The manual clearly stated anyone involved in a HASMAT injury was to be given medical attention.

"Nothing's hurt but my pride. I can't believe it... I *cannot* believe I let this happen!"

She had nothing to add or subtract from his statement. If he hadn't just ruined her lifetime achievement award with the jock, she may have mustered up a little sympathy.

* * *

Loretta took the northbound exit and gunned the van to eighty. It shook and shimmied as it lumbered down the freeway. The pavement was dry and the traffic was relatively light as she wove in and out of the three lanes. Her goal was the next exit.

Most of the drivers she approached prudently moved out of Loretta's way as she bore down on them, but the more dimwitted were dealt with by being narrowly missed when she swerved around them at the last possible second.

Taking the exit, Loretta removed her foot from the gas pedal to make the sharp curve of the off-ramp. She was happily surprised when the van maneuvered with all four tires planted firmly on the ground. Loretta scanned both directions of the intersection for a place to hide. Less than a block away was a vacant pancake house. Without slowing, she took a sharp right and continued into the empty parking lot and bounced her way to the lifeless structure. She stomped on the brakes as soon as the van was tucked from view of the roadway behind the building.

Loretta's heart was beating out of control. Even after leaning her head back against the headrest and willing herself to relax, her heart refused to return to normal, forcing Loretta to admit that if she didn't put an end to all the drama in her life, she'd be six feet under.

She sat that way for quite some time, reliving her flight to safety. She should have grabbed the driver's gun, but hadn't. Without it, her chances of stealing a car were drastically narrowed. But her mistake didn't matter now. There'd be no re-do.

An answer to her dilemma arrived in the form of country-western music that reached her through the van's open window. She got out and listened to *Bubba Shot the Jukebox,* and walked to the end of the building to watch customers come and go from the bar across the street. They seemed to be enjoying themselves. A few who'd had too much of a good thing staggered to their vehicles. Her mind made up, Loretta began her search on foot.

She struck out with the first several dozen vehicles. It was through the driver's window of a shiny new Dodge Ram pickup that her hope was renewed. There, dangling from the ignition was her deliverance. She tried the door and was pleased with the ding-ding-ding that greeted her. She climbed into the cab and started the engine. The tank was full, which reminded her of another problem. She didn't have any cash. When she'd been arrested, the bastards had taken everything she had.

Loretta guessed the truck would get around eighteen miles per gallon *if* she was lucky. She pulled out of the parking lot, determined to concentrate on the positive. What was in the tank would take her 400 miles towards Chicago, her final destination.

Chapter 15

Frank arrived home to bedlam. Edith was at it again. The evidence lay on the kitchen counter—an empty Donut Hut box that would've easily held a couple dozen donuts. All that remained was a skid mark of maple sugar frosting and a few chocolate sprinkles.

"Before you say anything I only let the kids have two," Edith said in self-defense.

"I thought we talked about this. They can't handle that much sugar. Mark's teacher has started hinting I should have him tested for A.D.D. He can't concentrate when he's pumped full of sugar! Plus, Britney hasn't been sleeping well. She keeps waking up in the middle of the night with nightmares."

"You're overreacting. How are a few donuts going to make a difference? What's really happening is they're upset about their mother disappearing like she did."

Frank wasn't ready to give up. "If you want to give them treats, why not get them fruit? They love grapes or those fruit roll-up things."

"You know I go to the Donut Hut every day. It's easier to pick up their afternoon treat there. You need to let me spoil them a little."

Throughout their conversation, Britney was racing back and forth between the kitchen and living room, meeting up with one wall and pushing off to race to the other. She had on her Cinderella pajamas and the cape was streaming behind her proudly, stopping only when she did.

Brice was sitting on the floor, watching Edith's favorite runway show. Mark and Brandon were in the corner, fighting over who got the last donut. The issue was solved when Mark grabbed it from Brandon's grasp and it broke in half.

"Why's Brice sitting in front of the TV? I thought we agreed he wasn't allowed to watch the Fashion Channel. I don't want him looking at half-naked bodies. It isn't natural."

"Sure it is! He's an inquisitive little boy. It doesn't hurt for him to appreciate the female form. Besides, I change the channel when there's something racy on."

Frank threw up his arms in surrender. The only solution was for them to move. He had received his damage refund for his old rental and along with what he had tucked away over the past two months, he had enough to start looking. At lunch, he'd gone through the classifieds and found several places he could afford. One of them was a townhouse duplex. Two levels would keep the kids' noise contained. Since Loretta had gone missing in action, they'd adapted to their new freedom without a hiccup and quiet had been replaced by pillow fights, rug wrestling and laughter.

Frank made his decision. He'd get the kids under control and make a few calls. Walking over to the TV, he turned it off. "Brice, you know you're not allowed to watch TV until you've done your homework and you aren't allowed to watch the Fashion Chanel."

"I didn't turn it on, Dad. Aunt Edith did."

"Does that mean you have to plunk yourself down in front of it?"

Brice looked away, unable to come up with a workable excuse.

"Okay boys, time to do your homework," Frank commanded.

Brice and Brandon settled in around the coffee table and started rifling through their backpacks. Mark was sitting on the couch swinging his legs back and forth, unable to wind down from his sugar high.

"Mark, that means you, too. You boys need to get your homework done as quickly as you can. We might be looking at a house later tonight."

"Does it have a big backyard?" asked Brandon.

"I don't know. That's why we need to go look at it," Frank replied.

"Well, I want a big backyard with a tree house!" Brandon insisted.

"If you had a tree house, you'd probably fall out of it and break your arm," Brice said, still smarting from being banished from the Fashion Channel.

"I want a tree house, too…with a tire swing," added Mark.

"We'll see. Now get your homework done," Frank repeated, swooping Britney in his arms before she made another round between walls.

"And you, young lady, get to pick out a movie." He put her down and she raced to the bookshelf. He knew what her choice would be before he set her on her feet. *Mary Poppins* was her all-time favorite. She would've watched it a dozen times a day if given the chance.

"Mawee Possims, Daddy," Britney said holding out the DVD to Frank.

Frank got it started and sat down with a sigh. It would be nice to be surrounded by their things again. Peace and quiet was a fragile commodity in Edith's household. He was reminded of that when she rounded the corner of the kitchen. Actually, rounded wasn't quite accurate. She teetered. She had traded a pair of sensible low-heeled mules for backless four-inch stilettos. Frank supposed they were meant to go with the rhinestone-embedded leggings she wore. The matching top was garnished with ostrich feathers along the neckline in day-glow pink that shed as she approached him.

"What's this I hear about your looking for a place? I thought you were happy here."

"We are," Frank lied. "But we can't stay here indefinitely."

"I just think you should stay here a little longer and put aside enough for emergencies before you commit to a rental."

"I'm only looking, Aunt Edith. It'll probably take months to find something I can afford that's livable."

"That's my point exactly! Wait another month or two."

"We'll see," Frank said. He got up from the couch and headed for the bedroom. It was the only sanctuary he had, and he wanted to make calls without Edith breathing down his neck.

Edith's voice bellowed after him like a heat seeking missile. "By the way, your mother wants you to give her a call."

The hair on the back of Frank's neck stood up in reaction. Of all the many possibilities to ruin his evening, calling his mother would be it, Frank thought.

"Did you hear me, Frank?"

"Yes, I did! I'll call her later tonight."

Her voice grew louder as she teetered down the hallway after him. "Why do you insist on being so mean to your mother? All she wants is to talk to you every once in a while."

The every once in a while was actually several times a week, which Frank attributed to her fascination with calamity—whether she generated it herself or it was brought on by happy circumstance. Frank was reminded he needed to get an unpublished number when they moved. It was a luxury he couldn't afford to pass up.

He dialed the number for the townhouse and was relieved when his call was answered right away.

"This is Frank Walch. I'm calling about the townhouse duplex you have advertised for rent. Is it still available?"

"Do you have any pets?" inquired the landlord.

"No, I don't."

"Then, yes, it's available."

"Is there any possibility I could see it tonight?"

"What time?"

Frank looked at the bedside clock. "Would 7:30 be okay?"

"That'll be fine. Come to the adjoining duplex. I'm requesting first, last and deposit."

"How much is the deposit?"

"One month's rent."

It was as if the landlord had psychically connected with his wallet. It would take everything he had. "That's no problem," Frank said. His actual thoughts were if the townhouse was right for him and the kids, they'd have to tough it out by eating macaroni and cheese for a month and he'd need to wait to have the telephone and cable hooked up. It couldn't be helped, though. If he stayed at Edith's, it wouldn't be long before he was throwing breadcrumbs at himself like some crazy person in the park.

Hanging up, Frank reread the ad: 3 bedrooms, 1½ bath, and a fenced yard on a cul-de-sac. And it was affordable. The location was in a decent part of town and the school district was one of the best in the Chicago area. If the place was even borderline livable, he was going to grab it up.

He pictured Edith circling the hallway and decided to stay behind the bedroom door to review his divorce paperwork. The official filing date stamped on his copy made it real. It represented the final step to kick Loretta out of their lives for good. He had followed the advice of one of the attorneys Carrie worked for and had already placed the third of four notices of his impending divorce in the newspaper. Apparently, Loretta's fleeing across the country wouldn't stop him from being granted a divorce. One week from today he would be sitting before a judge.

When Frank returned to the kitchen, the boys were still working on their homework and Edith was taking a vat of lasagna out of the oven. It was dripping with melted cheese and tomato sauce. Garlic bread followed. Watching Edith sit everything on the counter, Frank's thoughts turned morbid. Were there mortuaries that specialized in big and tall, or did they deal with issues like Edith one customer at a time?

"I'd planned on taking the kids to McDonald's," Frank said.

"Now why would you want to do that when there's a delicious meal right in front of you? I swear, Frank! You can be so obstinate when you want to be! Your mom and I were just discussing that the other day. It's as if…"

Frank tuned her out. He was getting fairly good at it. If he didn't, it would be the breadcrumbs for sure.

"Okay, are you boys about ready? We're going to look at a duplex right after dinner." In unison, they slammed their books shut and abandoned their paperwork to stuff everything into their backpacks. Frank went to check on Britney.

She was curled up on the couch holding the cover of *Mary Poppins,* crashed from her sugar high. He decided to let her sleep.

Freddie returned home from work and gave Edith a perfunctory peck on the cheek. "Smells great! Want me to get a salad started?"

This was Freddie's mantra, it seemed. Every night, he'd promote greens and every night Edith would get defensive.

"There's enough here to feed an army. We don't need a salad," she replied with an edge in her voice.

"Who wants garlic bread and lasagna?" Edith asked, looking to the kids.

Busy hands grabbed for plates, undermining Frank's plans for McDonald's, just as Edith knew it would.

"Put the plates down and go wash your hands," Frank said.

"Are you going to watch the swimsuit contest with us, Frank?" Freddie asked once the grown-ups had seated themselves.

"I didn't know about it until now."

"You bet. Edith and I've been looking forward to it. That gal from Italy's sure a looker."

"That's what you always say. I think the girl from Sweden has the Italian model beat, hands down!"

"Too flat-chested for my taste," argued Freddie.

"I'm going to have to pass on that, Freddie. The kids and I are headed out to look at a duplex," Frank said, relieved the boys were busy washing up in the bathroom and out of hearing range.

"Well, if you ask me, you're jumping the gun. There'll be plenty of places to choose from once you have the money to go looking," Edith said.

Frank ignored her.

Within a half-hour, they were on the road. He started to relax the minute he shut the front door and Frank didn't have to second-guess why. Brice had been paying way too much attention to Freddie and Edith's conversations. His determination to move was only strengthened.

"Will we have to go to another school if we move, Dad?" Brice asked.

"It depends. If we like this place, the answer is yes, but the good news is Madison and Sam goes to the school you'd be transferring to."

That seemed to calm any fears Brice had because there were no further questions from him.

"Has Britney eaten her sandwich?"

"Most of it. The rest, she's wearing," answered Brice.

"Grab the Wet Ones and clean her off, would you? We're almost there."

Frank realized his descending on a landlord with four kids in tow was pushing it. The least he could do was make sure they were presentable.

"When we get there, I want you boys to be quiet and to behave yourselves."

"Can we check out the backyard to see if there's a tree house?" asked Mark, the most tenacious of his kids.

"That's okay, just don't roughhouse. We need to make a good impression with the landlord."

"Why wouldn't he want us to live there if we roughhoused?" asked Brandon.

"Because some adults don't like noise," Frank answered.

"Like mom, Brandon. 'Member when she'd start yelling when we made noise? Some grown-ups just get mad," explained Mark, suddenly an expert on the subject of noise.

They pulled up to the curb. The duplex was a sixties brick with a simple bay window facing the street. Frank was relieved to see a tall fence at the back of the property. The kids would have a safe place to play. Frank turned to the back seat for one last pep talk.

"Now remember, no yelling, shouting, fighting or roughhousing. I need you to stay in the car until I come get you."

Britney started to wail past the straw she had stuck in her mouth before he'd even gotten the door closed. It was 7:30 on the dot. He decided to ignore her outburst in exchange for punctuality. Surely he wouldn't be held responsible for one distraction out of four.

The man who answered the door was wearing a white T-shirt with stains under the armpits and dress slacks with red suspenders. The fashion police would have arrested him.

"You here to see the duplex?" he asked.

"Yes. I'm Frank Walch. My kids are out in the car. Would you mind if I went to get them?"

"How many?"

Frank's blank look forced the landlord to repeat himself.

"How many kids?"

"Oh. Four. I have four kids."

"How old?"

"The oldest is nine, then five, four and two."

"Where's their mother?" the landlord asked, narrowing his eyes.

Frank hadn't considered the possibility he'd have to answer to an inquest. He stood on the stoop and mulled over what he was willing to share. "She disappeared. I have full custody of them."

A half-truth at best, or maybe just wishful thinking, but it was as much of an explanation as he was willing to give.

"At least there won't be any fighting. Hate that. I had to kick out a couple once over something like that. They'd go at it; fists through walls, cops being called all hours of the night."

If he knew Loretta, he'd have slammed the door in my face, Frank thought. *Her brand of evening the score made the landlord's description seem like foreplay!*

148

The kids were borderline scary as they slipped through the empty rooms. They never said a word. Either his warnings had sunk in or they were as anxious as he was to leave Edith and Freddie's house.

The rooms were spacious with plenty of closets and cupboards for storage. The dining room was large and was situated directly off the kitchen and the area shared the same vinyl flooring which solved the problem of Britney's constant spills. The only negative was the carpet. Not only was it an ancient, high-low, rust color shag, it reeked of cat urine.

"Were you planning on replacing the carpet anytime soon?" Frank asked.

"You mean the cat piss? Didn't find out they'd snuck the little sucker in here until they moved out. Go figure. I lived one wall between them and never had a clue."

"I don't have pets. I'd like to rent the place if you'd agree to replace the carpet."

"If I did that, I'd have to charge you more. Carpet doesn't come cheap," the landlord grumbled.

"This place is perfect for the kids and me, but I don't know if I could commit to a higher rent. I have an uncle in the carpet business. Maybe he could offer you a deal."

"Think he'd be willing to do that?"

"I'm pretty sure he would. We're staying with him for the time being. I could ask him tonight and call you back."

"It might work. This place's sat empty for nearly a month because of the cat smell."

"Dad, could we see the backyard?" Brandon asked.

The landlord opened patio doors off the dining room and turned on the backyard lights. The boys took off to investigate with Britney in tow. Every now and then, Brice and Brandon would pull her off her feet and swing her forward as she giggled. The camaraderie reminded Frank of a clip from *The Sound of Music,* all warm and fuzzy and touching. They were laying it on pretty thick.

The yard was the best part of their tour. The fence was six feet tall and made of cedar. Ferns and shrubs hugged the fence line. Several old-growth trees were grouped together that would shade the yard in summer.

"Your kids are well-mannered," the landlord offered.

"Thanks. It's been rough on them since their mom left. I'd like to rent the place if you're willing to replace the carpet," Frank said. "It's in a good school district and it's an easy commute to my work."

"I'll get the rental agreement."

Frank drove off, smiling. The duplex was the perfect size and it was a bargain. But grading on a curve, the best part about it was Loretta would never find them.

Chapter 16

Loretta took the downtown exit for Ozark, Arkansas cursing her luck. Her money and her gun were in the custody of the Texas Penal System. Because of that she was stuck without a dime and the gas light on the truck was warning her she was sucking fumes. With mounting frustration, she pulled up in front of a Winn Dixie and watched in awe as her answer walked out of the store. It was almost brutal in its simplicity.

The area was made up of consecutive strip malls. Within minutes Loretta located a Dollar Store. The place was packed, which was what she was hoping for. Entering, she glanced down the first few aisles. They were crammed together and overfilling with useless crap. She located the toy section against the back wall, selected the most realistic pistol they had, and continued to browse, walking up one aisle and down the next. The clerks were busy with a steady stream of customers. It was now or never. She bent over, pretending to be inspecting an item on a lower shelf and stuffed the toy gun in her bra.

No one gave her a second glance when she exited.

Before she returned to the truck, she did some dumpster diving and found a plain paper bag. It was all the props she'd need. All that was left was to find a target with a full cash register. But she'd need to choose someone she could intimidate, because bluff was all she had.

She cruised past several strip malls before she slowed to watch a lone clerk ring up a purchase from the only customers in the place. Loretta slipped the plastic pistol in the paper bag and loitered outside the large plate glass window.

The couple in line was busy playing grab ass. The man took his hand away long enough to collect his change and they left the liquor store with their purchase.

Loretta walked through the electric doors and up to the register. The clerk was arranging mini sample-sized bottles looking bored. She wouldn't be bored for long.

"Open the cash register," Loretta demanded, pointing the bag at the woman.

The clerk took one look at the unmistakable outline of a hand gun pointed at her chest and collapsed to the floor in a dead faint. Loretta looked down at the clerk's prostrate body and cursed. She was hoping for an easy target, not some Scarlet O'Hara. She moved behind the counter, stepping over the clerk's body and hit key after key until the register sprung to life at No Sale. Grabbing the bills from the till, Loretta guessed there to be well over $1,300. It would bankroll her trip back to Chicago with more than enough spending money until her next ambulance heist.

She was stuffing the last of the bills into the paper bag when a young man walked in. From his vantage point, he couldn't see Miss Scarlet wasting space on the floor.

"Could you tell me where the Jack Daniels is?" he asked.

"I haven't got a clue. It's my first day. Sorry."

It was time to go.

Chapter 17

Frank walked in on the group who had formed a protective circle around Susan. She was holding the arm that wasn't shackled to a sling around her middle, sobbing.

He walked over to Carrie. "What happened?"

She left the group of women and moved where she and Frank could talk in private. "Susan's ex-husband came to her house last night. He broke through a window this time. She managed to chamber a slug in the shotgun and had it pointed at him when he broke down her bedroom door."

"Did the cops come?"

"Eventually, but first she had to threaten to shoot him. He ran out the back door, yelling that he'd kill her the next time!"

"He's bluffing."

Carrie gave him a look of exasperation. "He wasn't bluffing when he beat the crap out of her in the courthouse parking lot."

"But now she has the shotgun."

"It saved her this time, thank God, but she's convinced he'll come back with more than his fists."

"He still hasn't had his hearing for the last assault charge. Can't the court revoke his bail and throw him in jail?"

"They could if they can find him. Now that he's broken bail, bounty hunters are after him, too. But he's not going to be walking around with a sign announcing himself. He'll just show up one night to kill her!"

"What's the answer, then? They can't post cops outside her door around the clock."

"Exactly. I'm going to invite her and the boys to live with me."

"But if he tracks her to you, then you and the kids are at risk."

"I've got a few ideas."

"What about a shelter?" Frank asked, grasping at straws.

"We've already had this discussion. A shelter's only a temporary solution. Besides, I want to help. This could just as easily be me and the kids."

She spoke with such conviction; Frank decided to drop the subject. He'd have to try and talk some sense into her later.

Claire called the meeting to order. There were no takers. She tried another approach. "Okay, let's have a seat. Maybe we can come up with ideas for Susan during group."

One by one the women broke rank to claim a folding chair. Claire waited until the last straggler sat down.

"Susan, do you feel like sharing?" asked Claire.

Susan blew her nose into a wad of Kleenex and took a deep breath. "I don't feel like sharing as much as I'd like to get that son of a bitch in a room; his fists and my shotgun. We'd see who comes out on top then!"

"But you proved last night violence isn't the answer. If it had been, you wouldn't have just threatened him."

"To tell you the truth, I tried to pull the trigger, but my bad arm wouldn't cooperate and I froze. I'm regretting that now. He's going to come back and this time he *will* kill me."

"And he's broken his bail. The authorities will be looking for him."

"They're not going to find him. He's got low-life friends all over Chicago. He can camp out with any one of them."

"What about work? They could arrest him there."

"That's not going to happen. He hasn't worked a steady job for years. He goes to one of those day-job places and grabs odd jobs. He doesn't keep a regular schedule."

"What about a shelter? You and the kids would be safe there."

"I've already tried that, more than once. I don't want to go back to a place like that, not if there's another answer. My boys were miserable, I was miserable..."

"But at least you'd be safe until you could figure out something better."

"What about family?" suggested one of the women.

"The only family I have is a brother. He and I haven't spoken in years."

"Maybe you could mend bridges, tell him what happened and ask for a place to stay," Claire said.

"That's what started our argument in the first place. A few years ago, my ex-husband put me in the hospital. The authorities placed the boys in protective custody. When I called him for help, he said, 'Good luck' and hung up!"

Carrie turned to Frank with a look of vindication.

For the remainder of their one-hour session, Susan's situation was discussed, but no one came up with a workable solution.

The group session broke up and Carrie waited until the last person said their goodbyes. "Susan, do you want to grab a cup of coffee at Starbucks?" Carrie asked.

She looked confused. "I thought everyone was headed to Denny's."

"I'd rather talk to you in private. Do you mind if Frank comes along?"

"I guess not. What's this about?"

"I'll tell you when we get there," Carrie said, leading the way out the door. "We'll take my car."

They brought their coffees to a corner table where they could talk privately.

"You and the boys aren't going to be safe if you stay at your apartment. We both know that. You could go to a shelter like Claire suggested, but that's only a stopgap solution. I'd like for you and the boys to come live with me, for as long as you need."

"I can't do that, Carrie. If my ex ever found out where I was, you and your kids would be in danger."

"I've given that some serious thought. No matter where you're living, you won't be safe unless you quit your job. It makes it too easy for your ex to follow you home."

"How would I survive? It could take a while to find a new job and I'm living hand-to-mouth as it is. I don't have any savings and I've never seen a dime's worth of child support since my ex and I split."

"It's doable, Susan. I'll cover the rent and utilities. All you'd need to worry about is food."

"And how would I get a decent reference if I quit without notice?"

"Your manager wouldn't fault you for protecting yourself and your kids. It isn't like she doesn't know what he's capable of and if you tell her he threatened to kill you, she'll probably be relieved you're giving your notice. She has to take the safety of the other employees and herself into consideration," Carrie said, clearly frustrated. "I'm worried that you're letting your ex back you into a corner. You're frightened. But as far as I can see, if you keep going in the direction you're headed, you're letting him win."

"You weren't there last night when the window got smashed out and you weren't there when he was tearing the damned bedroom door off its hinges, threatening to kill me. And you weren't the one whose sons hid in the closet in terror!"

Carrie waited for Susan to calm down. She'd been there, all right. It had been a while, but the fear and the memories would never leave her as long as she drew breath. Most people would never understand what it was like to peek inside the darkened interior of a car before daring to open the door, nor could they understand how the sound of footsteps on an unlit street could make you break into a run, your heart pounding in your throat. And, thank God, most had never experienced the unconditional terror reflected back from their children's eyes when they'd given up hope.

"If I could, I'd go back to last night and be with you and the boys, and this time, the damned trigger would be pulled!" Carrie exclaimed.

Susan's response was laughter through tears. "I wished we could. I've never liked funerals, but his would've been fun. We could've had a good old-fashioned Irish wake and partied 'till we dropped."

"There's always the next time. Hal saw the light when I pointed the Magnum at him. He hasn't been back since, and from what I've heard, he's moved from Chicago. He'll probably die of natural causes. But your ex is still in the running."

Susan laughed harder. Frank was hard pressed to see the humor, but he kept his silence, just as he had throughout the evening. He felt as if he'd been thrown to the back seat, a useless appendage. Had they asked his opinion, he'd have told them they had pretty much lost their minds.

Susan got control of herself and blew her nose. The soggy Kleenex wasn't doing the trick so Frank handed her his napkin.

"You're right, Carrie. I'll have a talk with my manager tomorrow and hand in my resignation. When can the boys and I move in?"

"Tonight. You'll move in tonight."

"I need to pack our things."

"No you don't. At least not tonight. It isn't safe. We can go by in the morning before work and grab what you need. Your ex isn't an early riser is he?"

"Not unless he's changed his lifestyle, he isn't. What about my furniture?"

"It might have to wait, unless you can afford a U-Haul and a storage unit."

"We both know the answer to that," Susan said.

"You have the rest of the month to figure it out. With luck they'll find him and throw him in jail."

"The boys are at the babysitter's right now. I haven't felt safe leaving them at home with a sitter for ages."

"Then we'd better get going," suggested Carrie.

Once settled in the car, Frank broke his silence. "If the two of you are going to pick up Susan's things in the morning, I'm coming along. I'll be your lookout."

The women smiled their thanks, which was a happy surprise for Frank. He'd expected an argument. On the drive, Frank felt relief over having rented the duplex. Even so, his thoughts kept traveling back to Susan's children hiding in terror from their father. No one, especially a child, deserved to live a life filled with abject fear.

Chapter 18

Loretta slid the half eaten mound of home fries and catsup away and grabbed a newspaper to kill time. She wasn't meeting Streeter for another half hour. Seeing nothing interesting on the front page, she skipped to the job classifieds and read a handful of ads before she realized she was only fooling herself. She wasn't going to be working a regular job. She had moved past regular months ago.

Loretta was re-folding the newspaper when her name jumped out at her in bold type. She laid the paper flat on the table. There in the legal notice section was her first inkling Frank was divorcing her.

Notice of Action for Dissolution of Marriage

To: Loretta Walch, last known location, Chicago, Illinois.
You are notified that an action has been filed against you and that you are required to serve a copy of your written defense, if any, to it on Frank Walch. If you fail to do so, a default may be entered against you for the relief demanded in the petition.

The Frank she knew couldn't possibly be that stupid. He would have known who he was screwing with and would have stopped short of posting their divorce in the notice section of the classifieds.

She grabbed the plate of cold fries and catsup and threw it against the wall, not waiting to watch the pattern of grease and catsup streak down its bead board accent. The kitchen staff ran to the front just in time to watch her stalk past them and out the door.

Jamming the keys in the ignition, Loretta tried to get herself under control. But no matter how she approached it, she was trapped. If she showed up in court to fight Frank, they'd cart her off to jail for sure. Loretta's knuckles tightened around the steering wheel, turning as white as a two-day-old cadaver. He was a dead man...

How had he recovered his balls? Loretta wondered. Maybe his mother had loaned them back to him, like some sort of twisted timeshare arrangement. As far as she was concerned, that was a shame. The years she'd spent training him seemed to have been flushed down the toilet. She wanted names.

* * *

Sitting in the McDonald's parking lot, watching the customers filing in and out was maddening. Since getting hooked on meth, her ability to sit for long stretches at a time had disappeared. She got out to stretch her legs and decided to give Streeter another twenty minutes. If he didn't show by then, she'd cruise around downtown to find his replacement.

She almost missed him. When he finally emerged from behind the dumpsters she was already headed for the road. Streeter was wearing the same leather jacket he'd worn the first time she'd met him, plus a black eye. Looking closer, she saw abrasions across his left cheekbone and chin.

She called his name and he turned in her direction, seemed to reconsider, and continued walking towards the street. She gunned the truck to within inches of his lanky frame, in no mood for games.

"Watch where you're going, lady!"

It finally dawned on Loretta that Streeter didn't recognize her. She'd lobbed off nearly one hundred and fifty pounds...of course he didn't recognize her.

"Streeter! It's Loretta, Jay's friend."

He walked to her open window and squinted. "What happened to your face?"

Loretta flinched at his insult. Even coming from a pusher, it hurt. "I could say the same about you, asshole!"

Streeter shrugged with disinterest. "The other guy's worse. I did okay."

"If you say so," Loretta retorted.

"You dropped some tonnage. Last time I saw you, you were the size of a cement truck."

"I lost a bit."

"A bit? You lost a whole other person!"

Loretta was tired of their word games. She had better things to do; like planning how to send Frank to his great reward.

"I need some meth."

"You should have said that in the first place."

They did the transaction and Loretta took off for the first seedy motel she could find. It had been fifteen hours since her last hit of meth. She paid for the room with cash and was given a flimsy aluminum key that was a perfect match for the flimsy lock on the door.

Placing a mirror on the bedside table, Loretta used a straight razor to chop the meth into a fine powder, arranged it in thin, even lines and snorted it up greedy nostrils. She shut her eyes, smiling. It was a wondrous thing, that first rush of euphoria.

Loretta woke to Latino music blasting through the two-inch gap at the bottom of the door where weather stripping should have been. Even being woken up at 7:30 in the morning didn't ruin her good mood. She had what she needed in a baggie next to the bed.

The drive to the courthouse nearly made her forget her good mood. Traffic was heavy and the steady, slanting rain dampened her spirits. She braced herself for what she'd find. Frank was out of control. But not for long.

Moving to a bank of computers, Loretta typed in Walch vs. Walch and opened the divorce complaint. She jotted down the docket number and then waited in line for what seemed like hours. Handing Loretta the file, the clerk announced the rules: "You can copy what you need, but the file cannot leave this room," she instructed, pointing to a row of copy machines. Loretta read through Frank's complaint page by page, printing copies as she went. He was asking for full custody, the furniture and the station wagon, the bastard! At least he hadn't requested child support.

It didn't matter anyway, Loretta thought. *Even if the judge gave him what he was asking for, he wasn't going to live long enough to enjoy it.* The divorce hearing was in two days. She gathered up her copies and all but threw the file at the clerk on her way out.

She used the truck to dump her rage, swerving her way in and out of traffic on the way back to the motel. Her new best friend waited for her in a baggie. She did her best thinking when she was high.

Chapter 19

A knock on the door caught Frank wrestling a dresser up the stairs. "I'll be there in a minute!" he yelled.

He stopped when he got the dresser as far as the landing and squeezed past it to race down the stairs. He had one day to get as much done as possible. The boys were at their new school, Britney was at her new babysitter's and he'd taken the day off to organize the place. It was a tall order, but he had a goal in mind: he wanted to bring stability back into their lives as soon as humanly possible.

Edith stood on the doorstep. Today's fare included a sequined top with matching leggings in the same shade of bright orange. Her shoes were kitten-heeled pumps accessorized with sequins made of dyed-to-match orange satin. But most outrageous was the pair of jumbo-sized sunglasses with chunky white frames that had been liberally bedazzled with rhinestones. She looked like a parody of Elton John.

Edith held out an unopened box of donuts. "I thought I'd drop off a treat for the kids. I would've called, but then I remembered you don't have a home phone and you know how I detest calling your cell. They charge such ridiculous rates."

He took the box of donuts with a feeling of dread, hoping this wasn't the beginning of an unwelcome habit. "Thanks, Aunt Edith."

"Don't pretend you mean it. I miss the kids already. How are they doing?"

"So far, they've made friends with a few of the neighbor kids. And Brandon and Mark keep nagging me about building a tree house."

"A tree house was all they talked about after you came back from seeing this place, which is one of the reasons why I came by. Freddie and I talked it over and we'd like to help you out a little."

"Aunt Edith…"

"No, don't interrupt. We talked about it and we'd like to supply the materials for the tree house. And we want to buy a swing set for Britney. You know, one of those wooden ones with a jungle gym. No reason for her to be left out."

"Aunt...."

"You didn't let me finish. Freddie and I know you don't have the money to get a phone or cable TV, so I went over today and paid for them." She reached into her coat pocket and produced the receipts and slapped them down on an end table.

"The kids love the Disney Channel and we want them to be able to watch it. And before you start to object, it's not like Freddie and I can't afford it. We never had kids...our whole lives we've been putting money aside. For what, I don't know. Maybe it was for now. It's what we want to do, Frank, and you have to admit you can't be without a home phone. What if Loretta showed up and you couldn't get to your cell, or the stupid thing had a dead battery? Why, you and the boys wouldn't be able to call the police for help." Edith finished a little out of breath but as determined as he'd ever seen her.

"I'd need to pay you back."

"Don't be silly. It's already done. There's a saying, '*You'll never see someone pulling a U-Haul to their funeral.*' Now isn't that the truth! Freddie and I aren't young anymore. We'd like to start spreading it around a little while we're still able to enjoy it."

"I appreciate it, Aunt Edith, I really do. But I'd feel better if I paid you back."

"You're a stubborn one! You always have been, ever since you were a little boy. But, if it's the only way, then fine, you can pay us back. But the tree house and the swing set are gifts from Freddie and me."

Edith hesitated and walked over to the living room blinds with her back turned to Frank. "I've never told you how proud I am of you. You've given the kids stability, and let's face it, four kids is a huge responsibility. Yet, I've never heard you complain. I'm proud you're my nephew. I just wanted to tell you that." Edith turned around to face him. "If I'd known who Loretta was, I'd never have introduced you to her. Why did you keep it a secret?"

"Embarrassment, I suppose. Maybe even pride. Deep down, I thought one day Loretta would wake up and see how much she had to be thankful for, and somehow she'd change. But that never happened."

"Some people are happiest when they're spreading hate. I'm afraid Loretta is one of those people," Edith said. She looked around at the boxes that were piled up in the middle of the living room. "What if I helped you get unpacked? I could get the kitchen organized."

Frank wasn't sure how he felt about the unexpected offer. Part of him would've been happy to see Edith's broad butt bouncing off to her car. She'd been a pain in his side his whole life; always ready with the gossip and controlling everyone within her circle of influence. But today, he had seen another side of her. She clearly cared for the kids and they needed someone in their corner.

"I'd appreciate some help. I was hoping to be unpacked by the end of the day so I could surprise the kids."

"Well then, if you'll show me where you want your things to go, I'll get started."

The remainder of the day was spent listening to an oldies radio station Edith was partial to while they unpacked boxes. By the time Edith left, the townhouse actually looked good; as good as it could look with worn out furniture, anyway. While Frank slid the couch and end tables in place, he made a decision. Once the new carpet was installed, he was going to ask Carrie to join him to knock around garage sales and maybe a few thrift stores. The sagging couch and beat up dining table had to go. It was time to begin the business of living now that Loretta was MIA. He'd start by improving their new surroundings.

By the time he picked up the boys from school and Britney from the babysitter's, the cable was working and the phone had a dial tone. Either Edith had connections or she'd played the pity card and told them his story.

The kids were thrilled with the news about the tree house and swing set. Once he'd convinced them he couldn't rush out that night for materials, they'd settled for a half hour in front of the TV before they started their homework. Frank realized he would need Freddie's help to get the tree house built and the swing set put together. If someone were to put a computer in front of him, he could work magic, but when it came to carpentry skills, he was lost.

Brice got up from the couch when *SpongeBob Square Pants* came on. "Dad, can I watch TV in your room?"

"As long as it isn't the Fashion Channel."

"I knew you were going to say that."

"It's a rule, Brice."

"I wanted to watch Animal Planet, anyway," Brice said. He hesitated before he headed up the stairs. "Thanks, Dad."

"For what?"

"For fixing up the house. It looks really nice."

"You're welcome, Brice."

Frank watched him climb the stairs. Since Loretta had been gone, Brice had begun to relax. Britney's antics and his younger brother's noise was no longer something that needed to be kept in check. Not that it ever should have been in the first place. It was going to take time for them to heal. Hardest of all, Frank realized, would be gaining back Brice's respect.

Attending group had brought that to the forefront. He'd also come to realize he'd invited Loretta into his life to try and right the wrongs he'd lived with as a child. As if by turning Loretta around, he'd be fixing his past, reliving the nightmare—only with a better ending. But he couldn't get the job done. Loretta hadn't wanted to be fixed, and no matter how hard he had tried, no matter what he had done, he would never have been given the chance to put the perfect life he envisioned in a box, wrap it with a bow, and give himself that gift based on will alone. It didn't work that way.

* * *

Frank received the call on his cell phone just as he was crawling into bed. Getting a call at 11:00 at night never involved good news, but with Loretta being on the loose, it gave a whole new meaning to what he might be inviting into his life by answering the incessant ringing.

"Hello?"

"Frank, it's Detective Kalnoski. I wish I was calling with better news, but the truth is your wife's had a busy few weeks."

"What do you mean by busy?"

"She was busted in Houston, Texas. Seems she was mixed up with a drug dealer by the name of Chance. Plainclothes detectives showed up and there was a shootout. The dealer was killed and Mrs. Walch was admitted to the hospital. When she was released from the hospital, she stood trial..."

"Why wasn't I told about this before?" Frank interrupted.

"I just found out myself. They should have notified me, but when multiple felonies across state lines are involved, it sometimes gums up the works."

"At least she's behind bars. How much time did she get?"

"That's why I'm calling. The judge gave Mrs. Walch ten years for her involvement with the drug bust in Houston and ordered her to be transferred to the Bridgeport, Texas Women's Division while the rest of her court appearances could be worked out. She injured the jailor who was transporting her, and stole the transport van. They found it, but it appears Mrs. Walch is on the run again."

"So you called to tell me Loretta could be anywhere, possibly even headed back to Chicago?"

"I'm afraid so. You'll want to be careful, especially at work. If she decides to show up, she'll likely follow you from work since your move."

"Will this ever go away? Loretta's a loose cannon. How am I going to protect my kids from someone like that?"

Frank hung up to stare at the ceiling, fresh out of ideas and totally out of hope.

Chapter 20

The bailiff stood to instruct the audience about court protocol and then played a video on court procedure. Turning off the TV once the video was finished, he stood. "Hear-ye, hear-ye! All rise. The court will now come to order; the Honorable Judge Thomas, presiding."

Frank stood with the rest of the hopefuls while a black-robed judge emerged from behind a door near the bench and seated himself.

"The matter of Walch versus Walch is called to order," announced the bailiff.

"Are both parties appearing in this matter?" the judge asked.

"Mrs. Walch is not here, Your Honor," the bailiff responded.

"Please step forward, Mr. Walch," the judge requested.

Standing at the lectern, Frank sent desperate prayers to a God he hoped existed.

"Do you have representation, Mr. Walch?"

"No, Your Honor. I am representing myself pro se."

"Proceed, Mr. Walch."

"Your Honor, I am seeking a divorce and asking for full custody of my children. I am also requesting the restraining order against Loretta Walch be continued. I have provided the court with records proving ten years of abuse by the defendant along with a string of outstanding warrants which include the theft of a controlled substance, the theft of a transport vehicle and the wounding of the jailor who was transporting her. The authorities haven't been able to locate her, Your Honor. Also included in the warrants I supplied to you is the assault and hospitalization of a Chief of Police and the theft of his firearm. Additionally, I have submitted financial records proving I can provide for my family."

Frank took an uneasy gasp of air and the judge nodded and began scanning the divorce petition and documents that rested in a thick pile on his desk.

Minutes later, the judge looked up from the paperwork to resume his questioning. "Has the defendant attempted to contact the children, Mr. Walsh?"

"No, Your Honor, she hasn't."

"Was there ever abuse perpetrated by the defendant on the children?"

"There was constant verbal abuse, Your Honor, but no physical abuse."

"It appears, Mr. Walch, that your income is barely sufficient to meet your monthly obligations. Was it your intention *not* to seek child support from the defendant?"

"That is correct, Your Honor. Due to the volatile nature of the defendant, I believe it is in the best interest of the children and myself to sever all ties."

The judge kept Frank waiting while he reviewed the evidence in front of him.

"The articles of submission you have provided the court proves your allegations," the judge said, almost in the form of a question.

"Yes, Your Honor."

"Motion for divorce and continuation of Mrs. Walch's restraining order is granted," were the judge's final words as he slammed down his gavel.

Frank managed to rise and head toward the courtroom door. Carrie caught up with him from where she sat in the gallery. They got as far as the lobby when Frank collapsed on a bench. It was done. Ten years of marital hell were over.

"Once the authorities find Loretta and throw away the key, she's out of our lives," Frank spoke out loud. The words were true—he'd just heard them from the judge—but it was going to take time to believe it.

"You were terrific. Judge Thomas is tough. I've heard he's one of the toughest," Carrie said.

"And you waited to tell me this because…"

"It wouldn't have done you any good to show up to court more worried than you already were."

Once they were settled in the car Frank turned to Carrie.

"We need to celebrate. We should do something special tonight," Frank said.

"What about taking the kids to a movie?"

"I was thinking of something a little more romantic."

"I'd agree, a romantic night together sounds like heaven, but finding a babysitter on a school night might be next to impossible."

Frank wasn't willing to give up. "We've got hours before the kids are out of school. What about going to my place? I don't feel like walking into an empty house when I should be celebrating one of the best days of my life."

"Now that sounds like a workable plan," Carrie said, giving Frank a meaningful look.

"I may be the luckiest man on the planet. I have a beautiful woman sitting next to me who I've been wanting to get alone, and I just won the rights to my life back," Frank said, squeezing her hand as they drove off into the early afternoon traffic. Their first stop was to a video store.

"I was thinking about renting a romantic comedy," Frank said.

"In that case, I'd have to say you know women."

"No. I know you," Frank replied as he sought her mouth.

They made out like a couple of horny teenagers until a customer pulled up next to them and they were forced to draw apart. Frank looked to the fogged up windows with pride. Finally, he knew what most of his high school had bragged about around the lockers. It had only taken him a couple of decades to get there.

Carrie looked at his condition and started laughing. "It might be better if we wait a while."

"Think they'd arrest me?" he asked.

"It's a possibility."

By the time the fire was crackling, filling the living room with the rich aroma of wood smoke, and they were each holding a Bailey's and coffee, they had four hours before school let out. As far as Frank was concerned, a week would've been far better.

Chapter 21

L oretta zeroed in on the **FOR RENT** sign posted in the front yard. Cutting through the alleyway, she checked out the backyard. The boy's bikes were missing and dead grass outlined where Britney's sandbox had sat.

Angry, she took off for the boys' school. Within minutes, she was idling across from the school playground with the heater turned up. The recess bell clanged and soon the cyclone enclosure was busy with kids tossing balls, playing on the jungle gym or, to a lesser degree, beating the snot out of each other. Hard as she searched, she couldn't locate the boys.

Loretta was convinced Frank didn't have the imagination or the guts to move outside the Chicago area. Luckily, she didn't need to call the psychic hotline to find him. She'd get the truth out of his big-mouthed mother.

Donna answered the door in a robe Loretta recognized. She and Frank had given it to her for Christmas years ago. It was ugly then and even uglier now. Her scalp was decorated with pink curlers.

Donna stood in the doorway, puzzled until she finally figured out who was standing on her doorstep. Her eyes popped and her mouth formed an exaggerated, empty cavern. She hadn't gotten around to putting in her dentures yet. Her next move was to slam the door.

Loretta was prepared. The door merely deflected off the tennis shoe she'd wedged in the jamb. When it bounced back, Donna put her weight against it and the two of them engaged in a silent tug of war until Loretta grew tired of the game and went low, putting all her momentum into the center of the door, and slammed her ex mother-in-law to the floor.

"You're going to tell me where my kids are!" Loretta screamed, stalking past Donna.

Scrambling to get back on her feet, Donna's face was flushed and her breathing came in frantic gasps.

"Tell me where Frank and the kids are!" Loretta repeated.

Donna managed to seat herself in an easy chair but her breathing remained labored and her cheeks had turned a blotchy shade of purple. Her balled up fists told Loretta she had no intention of sharing. Time was slipping by. Loretta decided on something more creative.

Nestled in an entertainment center, highlighted by a halogen light, was something Donna loved more than life itself: a museum-quality piece of Ming Dynasty china. Her great-grandfather had won it in a heated game of poker and it was priceless. Donna called it her insurance policy.

Loretta had it snatched from its resting place and held above her head in seconds. To her amusement, Donna yowled like a cat whose tail had been stepped on—hard.

"Loretta, if you don't put that down, I'm going to kill you!" Donna said in a breathless squeak.

"Then tell me where the kids are. I'm their mother. I have a right to know!"

Donna knew better than to point out that Loretta had given up her rights about the same time she'd gone mental. She looked to the hands that held the china and stifled a scream. She'd do it all right!

"I'm giving you to the count of five. Either you tell me, or I swear you'll be gathering up shards." Loretta paused for effect.

"One..."

"I don't know where they are!"

"Two..."

"I'm not lying. Frank even got an unlisted number. No one knows where he's moved!"

"Three..."

"He and the kids were living with Edith before he found his new place. She probably knows."

"Four..."

"Call Edith!"

"Five!" Loretta pitched the vase towards her mother-in-law who demonstrated amazing agility with a dive to the floor, catching it inches from impact.

"Edith better have the information, or I promise you, I'll be back!" Loretta stormed out of the open door while Donna lay sprawled on the floor, cradling the priceless relic.

Donna was weak with exhaustion, which she felt was a shame… she'd liked to have peeked out the window to get a description of what the bitch was driving. The last she heard of Loretta were tires peeling out of the driveway. The smell of burning rubber reached her through the open door and Donna threw up from the strain of it all.

It took a while before she was able to get up off the floor. When she did, it was done in dainty increments for worry she'd be sick again. Once up on her feet, Donna concentrated her fury on filling a pan with hot, sudsy water and returned to the oriental carpet she'd soiled to clean it before it could leave an unsightly stain. She took her time. It was almost new and she'd be damned if she'd give Loretta the satisfaction of having to replace it.

She leaned back to inspect her work. It looked immaculate, just as she'd hoped. But her relief soon turned to frustration when she considered getting involved with whatever fresh hell Loretta was planning to serve up. On the flip side, it could all blow up in her face if the family ever discovered Loretta had paid her a visit and she had said nothing to warn them. She had two choices: to call the police or to call Edith.

The police would waste precious time and she had plans. She picked up the phone and hit speed dial to Edith. Donna didn't miss a beat when the phone was answered.

"Loretta was just here and she's headed your way!"

She listened to Edith's tirade and returned fire. "Of course I didn't tell her anything! She was crazed, worse than I've ever seen her. She's looking for Frank and the kids. When I told her I didn't know where they were, she said she was coming to your place. I wouldn't be there if I were you."

Donna had to pull the receiver away from her ear while Edith bellowed and waited for her to come up for air.

"You can do whatever you want, Edith. Call the cops, don't call the cops. But I'm telling you Loretta's gone berserk! I wouldn't want to be the one to cross her. She must've dropped over a hundred pounds. There's only one way she could have done that in such a short time and that's drugs. Drugs can make even a sane person crazy and we both know Loretta hasn't had a sane day in her miserable life!"

Before Edith could respond, Donna slammed the phone back in the cradle. It was in Edith's hands now. She walked to the garage with the priceless china. It was going where it should have been all along—to a nice, safe bank vault. Once it was safely tucked away, she was going to return to the house to pack her bags because she was headed for Scotts-dale, Arizona. Surely that would be a safe distance away from Loretta's carnage.

*   *   *

Twelve miles away, Edith ran to her Oldsmobile, nearly tripping over an extra-long boa of ostrich feathers that got tangled in her high heels while she was on the phone with a 911 dispatcher. "I'm telling you my nephew's wife, Loretta Walch, is on her way here, threatening me and the rest of the family. She has outstanding warrants against her clear across the country!"

At the suggestion that she wait until an officer arrived, Edith nearly hopped the curb and smacked into the neighbors cement birdbath. "I *know* I couldn't have just heard you ask me to stay here. If she shows up before the cops do, I'm a dead woman! Call me on my cell phone when they've arrested her. I'll identify her and give a statement then." Edith hit the end button without slowing down.

She made it to Frank's place in minutes. Her biggest concern was the kids. She needed to be there when they arrived home from school. On a normal day, she wouldn't have headed to Frank's for another half-hour. But this wasn't a normal day. This was a day where all bets were off…the bitch was back!

Edith was sorely disappointed she was going to miss her standing date with the Donut Hut, now going on thirteen years. But it couldn't be helped. She swung into Frank's driveway and dialed his office. The receptionist informed her he was out on calls.

"This is an emergency. Please tell him his wife's back in town. Tell him I'm picking up the kids and that he's to meet us at the Albertsons across from his office."

Edith sat in the car with the heater turned up full blast. It had to be, as it hadn't worked properly for years. She turned on the radio to an oldies station. Ella Fitzgerald was bantering with Louis Armstrong *Let's Call the Whole Thing Off* and Edith cringed. Too bad she hadn't thought of that before she'd introduced Frank to Loretta. It would be a millstone she'd wear around her neck for the rest of her life. The next song was The Platter's *Harbor Lights*. It brought her back to when she and Freddie were dating and Edith became nostalgic, remembering the romantic drives they used to take.

Edith sat bolt upright in the seat. Freddie! She hadn't called Freddie. How could she have forgotten? To hear Donna tell it, Loretta was out for blood, anyone's blood!

"Affordable Flooring."

"Freddie, its Edith."

"What, you don't think I'd recognize your voice after thirty-eight years?"

"I'm serious! Loretta just left Donna's house. She's looking for Frank and the kids. Loretta threatened her and then tore off for our house."

"You're not calling from there, are you?"

"Of course not! I wish you'd pay attention. I'm calling to tell you not to go home. Donna said she's gone off her ever-loving rocker."

"And you're just figur'n this out? Loretta's been off her rocker since day one."

Edith cringed. He didn't need to rub it in. "All I'm telling you is not to go home. At least not until the police find her."

Freddie's voice went up a few octaves in frustration. "You're tell'n me I can't go to my own home? What am I supposed to do? Wait for the cops to catch up with that crazy bitch?"

"That's exactly what I'm telling you! Come on, you know how nuts she is. We need to keep out of her way until she's in jail."

"I won't do it, Edith. We can't let her run our lives. I'm not afraid of her."

"Normally, I'd agree with you. But what about the kids? We can't do anything that might endanger them. If Loretta finds out where they are, there's no telling what she might do."

Freddie remained silent as he mulled over her words. "What's your plan, then? Seems like you got all the answers," he retorted.

"You don't need to get sideways about it. And I don't have all the answers! I'm at Frank's place now, waiting for the boys to get home from school. Then I'm picking Britney up from the sitter's. I left a message for Frank to meet us at the Albertsons across from his work. After that, I don't have a clue. I'd like for you to meet us there. Maybe we can come up with something that makes sense."

"You called the cops, right?"

"Of course I did. Do you think I'm some sort of an idiot?"

"Not some sort...just gard'n variety."

Edith snapped her phone shut. He blamed her. He'd always blamed her for Loretta. She was still fuming when the boys came running up to the car.

"Where's our donuts, Aunt Edith?" asked Brice.

There was the rub. It's what they asked every afternoon, without fail.

"I have a surprise. We're going to pick up Britney and then, we're going to the Donut Hut so you can pick out exactly what you want."

Brice looked doubtful. "But dad always picks Britney up after work."

"Yes, he does, doesn't he? I asked him to meet us at Albertsons to-night. I've decided to treat us all to fried chicken. Do you boys like chicken?"

"Not as good as pizza. Can we go to Chicago's Pizza instead?" Mark asked.

"Tell you what, tonight we'll have chicken and the next time we'll get pizza."

Pulling away from the curb, Edith didn't notice the white Dodge Ram parked at the curb a few houses down.

*　*　*

Following Edith had been almost laughable. She'd had the damned phone to her ear nearly the whole time, never once checking her rear-view mirror. Loretta decided there must be a recessive gene that ran in the family. Neither Edith nor Donna could anticipate her next move any better than Frank could when she'd meet him at the door for a wake-up call.

Frank's new place was nicer than she'd expected and she looked forward to doing a little snooping. Brandon had run into the townhouse with his book-bag and returned empty handed to jump into Edith's back seat. With luck, the door had been left unlocked.

Loretta turned the handle and it opened to a life she felt she'd left years ago. The sectional couch still had the sag in the middle where the strapping had come undone and the dining table was marred from a black Sharpie Brice had experimented with when he was two.

The rooms were clean and empty. She stood in the middle of their new life knowing she wasn't needed. Sadness descended upon her. But it didn't come from the sadness of missing the kids, which on its own heaped guilt on her. It was more the sadness of not belonging to any-one. She was aware of the mood swings she'd been experiencing lately. One minute she'd be angry and furious, the next, sad. Worse was the paranoia. Whenever she was in a public place, she felt as if everyone was staring at her, judging her. Most days, she'd feel all the above... like flashes, breaking up her day into hectic blotches of time that had no end.

She shook herself into action. Frank would've put his extra keys in the junk drawer. He was disturbingly neat and predictable. The junk drawer would be directly below the telephone which in his new place was mounted above the kitchen counter. She wasn't the least bit sur-prised when she found them laying neatly in a drawer organizer.

She knew she should leave and go back to the motel to plan Frank's future, but a curiosity grabbed hold of her. Opening the sliding glass door off the dining room, she walked onto the cement patio. Lying on the lawn was a huge box with a picture of a fancy cedar swing set on it. Further back near a group of trees were piles of lumber and an old door. It looked like the makings for a playhouse, which completely confused Loretta. Frank didn't have money for a fancy swing set and besides that, he couldn't drive a nail to save his soul.

Locking the patio door, Loretta continued upstairs. Frank's bed-room was the first room she came to. His bed was made with the same comforter they'd slept under for years. A notepad on the top of their scarred dresser caught her attention. Turning on the overhead light, she read Frank's handwriting: Carrie, dinner Friday 7:00 – Elaine's Restaurant.

Loretta was instantly furious. She might not want Frank, hadn't wanted him for more years than she could remember, but seeing the name of another woman scribbled on a crummy slip of paper stung her ego. She decided to rummage through his drawers and see what else he'd been up to. She started with a bedside table. There were no condoms, or body oils, or marital aids—not even a dirty magazine. It appeared Frank wasn't involved in an affair, but clearly he'd taken the first steps towards one.

An intriguing idea came to Loretta. She could go on their date with them! Well, maybe not *with* them, but she could certainly spy on them. Why not? With the weight loss, a convincing wig, and the right make-up, Frank would never recognize her. She'd get to see this Carrie up close and personal.

Walking faster now, Loretta opened the second door down the long hallway. It was Brice and Brandon's room. The bunk beds had been separated and were made up with matching Star Wars bedspreads. That would be Brice's influence. He loved anything Star Wars.

She moved across the hall to the last bedroom. Britney's Sponge-Bob blanket lay crumpled at the bottom of her bed. Her teddy bear, the one she insisted on at bedtime, was lying on the pillow; one of its arms flopped onto the pink gingham sheets. Mark's bed was against the opposite wall. A Cars bedspread was thrown haphazardly across it. It smelled of urine, which meant that he hadn't stopped wetting the bed.

The alarm clock on the nightstand read 4:10. It was time to go.

* * *

Edith pulled up in front of the Donut Hut, which pleased her to no end. She had been able to keep her sterling attendance *and* show off the kids.

"Brice, is Britney's face clean?" Edith asked, already having a pretty good hunch what his answer would be. But she was a woman who believed in the powers of positive thinking.

"It's crusted over with her lollipop," he answered.

"You boys go on in, but watch for cars! I'll be there in a minute." Edith grabbed a container of Wet Ones and went to work on Britney's gooey mouth.

"I swear, young lady, you can certainly make a mess!"

Britney tried to dodge the clean-up by twisting her face in the opposite direction as the cloth approached. Edith was used to this game and had Britney cleaned up in seconds. "Now, let's go inside and get your donut."

The boys were already being helped by the owner.

"I want that one," Mark said, pointing to a maple bar.

The owner looked to Brice. "Have you decided, young man?"

"I want the one with the whipped cream and chocolate."

In no time, a Neapolitan was selected from the tray with a paper tissue. "And you?" he asked Brandon.

"I want a cinnamon roll."

Edith approved of his choice. Next to their chocolate cake donuts with sprinkles, the cinnamon rolls were her favorites.

"Clyde, would you put those in separate bags with napkins?"

"Will do. The usual for you, Edith?"

'Yes, and throw in a strawberry donut with sprinkles."

"I was wondering about you when you didn't show up at your usual time."

"Well, I'm here now. Where is everybody?"

"My guess would be home getting dinner started."

His comment reminded Edith of the chicken dinner waiting for them at Albertsons. She threw the boys a sharp look. "You need to save these for dessert. And no cheating! I don't want you spoiling your dinner."

"Could we bring them into the grocery store with us?" Mark asked.

"I don't see why not," Edith said.

Albertsons was busy. She sat the children at the last available table and went to the deli counter to order a family bucket of chicken, raspberry Jell-O with whipped cream, and biscuits with plenty of butter and honey. They were almost finished with their meal when Frank and Freddie showed up within minutes of each other.

Edith whispered in her husband's ear. "Keep an eye on the kids." She motioned to Frank to follow her.

"What happened?" Frank asked.

"I got a call from your mom this afternoon. Loretta broke into her house, insisting she tell her where you and the kids were. Before Loretta left, she told Donna she was coming over to our house and if she didn't get answers, she'd be back."

"Where's Mom now?"

"You know how high-strung she is. She isn't answering her phone. She's probably afraid to."

"I'll bet she took off. She'll be thinking about saving herself with Loretta on the rampage."

"Please don't talk about her that way. I know she isn't perfect. None of us are. But I don't think she'd be capable of running off at a time like this."

Frank had bigger things to worry about and decided to drop the subject. "How am I going to keep the kids safe with Loretta in town? Did anyone call the police?"

"I called them right after I heard from your mother. They promised to send a cruiser over to the house and I left my cell number in case they find Loretta, but I haven't heard back from them yet."

"Did you make sure you weren't followed when you drove over to pick up the boys?"

"I left right after Donna called. Loretta wouldn't have had time to reach my place to follow me."

"Then you don't know Loretta. Did Mom say anything more?"

"She told me Loretta's dropped a lot of weight, over a hundred pounds. Your mom didn't recognize her at first. She said Loretta was acting crazy."

"How crazy is the question. Did she get a look at the car she was driving?"

"She didn't say, but I'll keep trying to reach her."

Frank scribbled the detective's number down on a slip of paper and handed it to Edith. "If she shows, whatever you do don't open the door! Call this number. It's Detective Kalnoski's cell number. He's promised to respond right away. They want her brought in as bad as we do."

"Until they find Loretta, I can't keep watching over the boys at your house, Frank. It's too dangerous. And I can't have them at my place for the same reason," Edith said.

They remained standing in the condiment aisle, trying to come up with a workable solution. Edith was certain of one thing: she loved the kids, enough that Loretta would have to walk over her dead body to get to them. But so what? Dead wouldn't keep them safe.

An inkling of a solution came to Edith and she grabbed at it. "Maybe Britney's babysitter could watch the boys after school for the time being. She's within walking distance of the boys' school. Or, they could catch the bus to her place. Freddie and I will pay. I know you don't have the money right now. The important thing is for them to be as far away from that bitch as possible!"

Frank was surprised at Edith's use of words. But Loretta's showing up had changed the rules for everyone. Her idea about the boys joining Britney after school had merit. He hated having to accept Edith's help, but pride wasn't going to keep his kids safe. A daycare that Loretta didn't know anything about would.

"I appreciate your offer, Aunt Edith."

She gave him a hug before they returned to Freddie and the kids.

On the way home, Frank kept checking his rearview mirror. Once they reached the house, his worry kicked into overdrive. He could feel Loretta's presence. The negative energy seemed to have a life-force of its own.

"Brice, stay in the car with your brothers and sister, and hit the door locks. I want to check out the house, okay?"

Frank waited to hear the click of the door locks before he let himself in through the front door. As soon as he crossed the threshold, he smelled her. It wasn't perfume, or soap, or deodorant, but it was definitely Loretta: the smell of musk and desperation.

Frank paced the circumference of the first story, looking for anything she may have left behind; something that had dropped out of a pocket or been laid down accidentally, but he came up empty handed. He followed the stairs to the bedrooms and continued his search. Everything appeared the same as when they'd left this morning, but here, where the spaces were tighter, her scent grew stronger.

If he hadn't been so exhausted from the moonlighting he'd done to put the townhouse in order, he would have noticed that the small notepad he'd left on the dresser was missing.

He'd kept the kids in the car long enough. Frank made the call to the babysitter from his cell phone while herding the kids into the house and was relieved when she agreed to watch the boys after school. Frank locked the deadbolt after them. It wasn't until Brice and Mark requested he unlock the car so they could retrieve their backpacks that he started to connect the dots. Brandon's backpack was sitting on the dining room table.

"Brandon, did you bring your backpack into the house before you left with Aunt Edith?"

"Yes," he answered.

"Did you lock the door after yourself?"

Brandon shrugged while he continued to search through his backpack.

"He never locks the door Dad...ever!" Brice answered with heart-thudding conviction.

That was how Loretta had gotten into the duplex without breaking out a window or jimmying a lock.

"Okay, change of plans! Everybody grab school clothes for tomorrow. We're going over to Carrie's."

Clothes, diapers and pajamas were stuffed into plastic bags and loaded into the station wagon. Backing out of the driveway, Frank realized he'd forgotten Britney's bottle. Fear, that had built to borderline terror, lead to his decision to stop at a grocery store to buy a replacement.

The drive was quiet. The kids had picked up on his frantic mood. He looked in the rearview mirror for the hundredth time. It didn't appear they had company. He pulled into a grocery store lot, put the station wagon in park and sat idling while he kept an eye on who came and went. He was afraid to leave the kids in the car, but he was just as worried about bringing them with him should Loretta suddenly materialize.

"Dad, how come we're just sitting here?" Mark asked.

"We're not just sitting here. I need to get a bottle for Britney."

"You've been acting weird all night, Dad!" Brice said.

"Okay Brice, make sure to keep the doors locked. Don't unlock them for anyone, you hear? I'll be right back."

"Why are we going to Carrie's so late and why do you keep telling me to lock the doors?" Brice's voice carried his frustration.

"That's a lot of questions in one breath. We'll talk when we get to Carrie's. Everything's going to be okay. I just need to grab some milk and a bottle for your sister. And remember, don't unlock the doors for anyone!"

Brice's scowl remained but he managed a nod.

"I mean it, Brice. No opening the door!"

"I heard you Dad! I won't open the door," Brice snapped.

Frank took off at a jog. He ran down the baby aisle and grabbed the first bottle he found. Britney wasn't particular about her bottles as long as she had a nipple popped in her mouth. He continued to the dairy isle, grabbed a quart of 2% milk and raced to a checkout stand.

He was seventh in line and the wait was nerve-wracking, but it gave him time to think. When they got to Carrie's, he was going to have a talk with Brice about his mother's re-appearance. It was a lot to put on a nine-year-old boy, but keeping the truth from him wasn't the answer either.

Carrie answered the door wearing a pair of faded jeans with her auburn hair pulled back in a ponytail. She looked more like a teenager than the mother of two. She looked to Frank with Britney laying fast asleep in his arms, and motioned for him to follow her down the hallway. "It'll be quieter in here," Carrie whispered, tucking Britney into her queen-sized bed. They crept back out as silently as possible.

The boys remained standing in the middle of the living room, as if they hadn't been to her house dozens of times before. Carrie's heart went out to them. Whatever had happened was almost palpable. She decided to try and lighten the mood. "So, would you boys like popcorn?" They said yes, but from what she could tell, it was more out of politeness than genuine interest. "Okay, then. Madison and Sam are in Sam's room doing their homework. Why don't you boys go in and say hello."

Throwing a packet of popcorn in the microwave, Carrie made nervous small talk, certain whatever Frank had to tell her was going to be bad news. "Susan and the boys are at the mall. They'll be back soon."

"Would it be possible for us to stay here tonight?" Frank asked.

Her eyebrows shot up but she managed to keep her voice neutral. "Of course you can. You and the kids are always welcome. Now, why don't you tell me what happened that brought you here on a school night looking like you're ready to implode?"

He gave her an abbreviated run down.

"But how can you be sure Loretta was in your house? I mean, you didn't find any evidence, right?"

"True. I don't know how to explain it, other than to say I could feel it."

"Well, there's that."

He looked at Carrie, unsure of whether or not she was patronizing him. He saw nothing but concern on her face.

"Have you got a game plan?" she asked.

"I called Britney's sitter when we got home and she agreed to watch the boys after school. As far as keeping the kids safe at home, I haven't figured that out yet."

"It might not be an issue. You said the Chicago Police are looking for her, right?"

"There's more that I need to tell you," Frank said, and then he gave her a rundown on Loretta's crime spree he'd kept hidden from her.

"The three of us need to sit down and think this through. Between you, Susan and me, we should be able to come up with a workable plan. Maybe the real question is whether or not we can live a normal life and at the same time protect our kids. Is that even possible?" Carrie asked.

"I don't have the answer to that."

"Well neither do I, but we've got to try."

She looked down at the plastic bowl that held the popcorn. "It's cold. Think the kids will notice?"

"As disjointed as this day's been, I doubt it. I promised Brice we'd talk. Do you have any ideas where we could do that?"

"I'd suggest Susan and the kids' room, but she's not here to ask. I'm sorry. This place has zero privacy."

"We'll go to the station wagon. No one will interrupt us there."

"True. But are you sure it's a good idea to tell Brice about his mother?"

"He already knows something's wrong. If there was a way around it, I wouldn't tell him, but he's the oldest, and considering Loretta's mental state, it's safer for him to know the truth. What if she were to show up at the boys' school one day? Anything's possible. And to think I made a promise to Brice that he'd finally have the chance to be a kid."

"You're a good father. You need to stop blaming yourself, Frank. Look how far you've already come. You have a new home in a better neighborhood, the boys are doing great at their new school and you've told me they're much happier." She wrapped her arms around Frank's neck. "Everything's going to be okay. They'll find Loretta and they'll lock her up. In the meantime, I'll help with whatever you need, which includes your staying here for as long as you need."

Frank's response was a heavy sigh as he leaned into Carrie and stroked her back.

"Mom, where's the popcorn?" Sam yelled from the hallway.

Carrie drew back. "Sorry," she said.

"You've got nothing to apologize for. You're wonderful."

Carrie reached around him to open a cupboard door, grabbed a small bowl and shook some of the cooled popcorn into it.

"This bowl is for Brice," Carrie said, handing it to Frank. "He doesn't deserve to hear about his mother *and* miss out on buttered pop-corn all at the same time."

"Carrie, thank you."

"No thanks are necessary. You'd do the same for me."

She walked down the hallway with her ponytail swaying with her movements. To Frank, she was the sexiest woman alive.

Starting the car to get the heater going, Frank got down to the pain-ful business of taking his son's innocence away, one tiny slice at a time.

Brice listened with his head down, as if he were ashamed. It broke Frank's heart.

"So if Mom comes to our school, what am I supposed to do?"

"You should ask for help from one of your teachers and don't go with her. I'm contacting the school first thing in the morning so they'll be aware of the situation. I'm sorry, Brice, but your mother isn't to con-tact you or your brothers."

"I won't go with her, Dad," Brice said in little more than a whisper.

They'd started back down the walkway to the front door when headlights bounced at them from the street. The lights were too bright to be able to make out either the car or the driver. Frank went into fight or flight mode.

"Brice, go inside and lock the door! Don't open it until I tell you to."

Brice reacted with a burst of speed. The door slammed and Frank was relieved to hear the deadbolt get thrown. He searched for something to defend himself with, but there were no lawn tools and no Louisville Sluggers to be had. The best he could come up with was a cement urn.

He grabbed its abrasive lip and had it hoisted over his head at the same time the car's headlights went out.

It was Susan.

She walked around him in a daze, so pale she looked like she'd donated too much blood. Frank set the urn back down on the walkway next to the plants and potting soil he'd overturned. Apologies weren't necessary. She didn't even notice him.

He followed her to the door where they were forced to wait for it to be opened. Brice had taken his warning seriously and Frank had to give him the all-clear before he unlocked it.

Susan remained staring straight ahead, got as far as the ottoman and flopped down on it as her boys and Brice made a beeline to Sam's bedroom.

"What happened? I hope it isn't something terrible. I don't think my nerves could take it," Carrie said to Susan.

"It isn't terrible," Susan replied.

"Then, what is it?" Carrie persisted.

Susan sat up from her prone position and looked around the room, still dazed.

"I'd just finished buying Josh new shoes. Remember when I told you his coach kept nagging about how the black bottoms of his tennis shoes were leaving marks on the gym floor?"

"Yes, I remember," Carrie said.

"Well, we'd just bought his new gym shoes and I was in such a great mood. It felt good, *really* good to get out of the house." At that,

Susan looked to Carrie. "Please don't take that wrong. I love it here. It's just that I haven't been out of the house for days."

"No worries," Carrie said.

"I decided to treat us to dinner at the food court. We were just sitting down with our trays when Brenda walked by."

"Who's...?" Frank asked.

"Brenda is Susan's ex sister-in-law," Carrie volleyed back.

"I tried to make as small a target as possible and turned away from her but she saw the boys and came running over. I haven't talked to her for over two years and she was going on and on, as if we were best friends."

"How did you handle it?" Carrie asked.

"I was civil to her, but it was horrible. I kept expecting her to tell me my ex was somewhere in the mall and wouldn't it be nice if she found him so we could all share a table together. But Brenda didn't say anything like that. She visited with the boys and then she told me something that made me wish I'd been hooked up to a Valium drip."

"Susan, I like intrigue as much as anyone, but tonight's not the night. Would you get to the point?" Carrie said.

"That's where I'm headed! She told me her grandmother had passed away and there'd been a reading of her will last Monday. She was filthy rich. Her grandfather invented some sort of machinery...I can't remember what exactly. Anyway, the family's worth millions."

"But what does that have to do with you?" Carrie asked.

"Now you're nagging! I'm getting there. Just let me tell the whole story because if I don't, I'll probably have a stroke."

"Then by all means, tell the whole story."

"Anyway, like I said, she was rich. At the reading of the will, her grandmother had requested that her attorney read a letter she'd written to the family. In it, she told my ex what she thought of him."

"There *is* a God!" exclaimed Carrie with enthusiasm.

"It gets better. In the letter she said my ex had shown himself to be an abuser, a terrible husband, and a worse father and because of the embarrassment he'd inflicted upon the family name, and for his flagrant disregard of his financial responsibility to his children, he wasn't going to receive a penny of her inheritance."

"But that's great Susan. I can't imagine a person who deserved to be disinherited more than he did."

"If you think that's great, wait till you hear the rest. She'd outlived the rest of the family except Brenda, my ex, and their father. My ex father-in-law and she had a huge fight years ago and hadn't spoken since. He was left out of her will as well." Susan drew a deep, cleansing breath and continued. "The estate was split right down the middle—half to Brenda and the other half to the kids and me."

"No way…" Carrie whispered.

"It's true. The attorney has been trying to get in touch with me. He hit a dead end with my old phone number and address, of course, and again at my job. Brenda said when my ex learned she wasn't leaving him a dime, he went ballistic and threw a chair through the attorney's penthouse window. My ex is being sued."

"This will kill him."

"Actually me. It'll kill me if he finds out where I'm living."

"I hadn't thought of that. I'm sorry, Susan. How will you protect yourself? If he was violent before, he'll be doubly so now," Carrie said.

"Bodyguards. Lots of bodyguards are the only answer. He won't be able to get near the kids or me that way."

"They're expensive. You'd need round the clock protection," Frank warned.

"Let's just say that with what was left to us, I could hire enough bodyguards for the entire Chicago Metropolitan area and it probably wouldn't make a dent in the principal."

"Thank God! You'll never have to worry about your ex again," Carrie said with such enthusiasm, it might as well have been her who'd been handed the windfall.

"I'm going to the bedroom to call the number Brenda gave me. It's the attorney's home number. If he doesn't answer, I'm to call him on his cell phone, day or night. It appears money and power linger long after the body's grown cold. I still can't believe it," Susan said as she took off down the hall to her bedroom.

Carrie watched her progress with a smile that lit up the room. "She'll be safe now. When God closes a door, he opens a window. In this case, that window's the size of the Sears Tower!"

Chapter 22

Loretta's errand list was a mile long; get with Streeter for meth, find a wig, buy make-up, and she'd need to find a dress for her evening out. Crashing Frank and Carrie's dinner still ranked at the top of her priority list, but she was running low on money.

Another ambulance heist was the answer, but every time she would start to make plans, that same sinking feeling she'd had outside the billiards room came back to haunt her. She was down to less than $400. If she didn't figure out something soon, she'd be living on the streets.

Her hook-up with Streeter was in fifteen minutes. Traffic was light. It was just after the morning rush hour and before the lunchtime crunch. When she pulled into the McDonald's parking lot, she found Streeter loitering near the dumpsters, which she'd come to think of as his office. He was wearing his uniform: a bomber jacket and worn Levis. He was *not* a creative dresser.

Loretta parked and walked to the fetid dumpster where Streeter held out a baggie. She grudgingly gave him the crumpled bills for the 8-Ball that brought her closer to homelessness.

"I'll have something for you by tomorrow," Loretta said.

"Just give me a call. We'll meet here."

Loretta climbed back into the truck for a day of pampering. She started at a kiosk in the middle of the mall that sold cheap nylon wigs. The darker colors and blond tones were eliminated right away. They made her skin look sallow. The reds tones would draw too much attention. She settled for a wig in a soft golden brown that reached her shoulders. It was a huge improvement over her natural hair which had turned dry and brittle and was beginning to thin at an alarming rate.

Next was make-up. Loretta went to the Estée Lauder counter at Macy's and waited her turn. Having never worn make-up, she was going to take whatever advice she was given but purchase the make-up at a drugstore. She couldn't afford their prices. The clinician was a petite blond with impeccable skin and a full, pouty mouth that looked like it had been stung by dozens of pissed-off bees.

Seeing what she had to work with, the clinician searched her drawer until she found a box of latex gloves and slipped a pair on over her long, manicured nails. During her training, it had been impressed upon her that she could not turn anyone down. But she'd never been told she couldn't protect herself with gloves. Loretta's skin was a mess. Given a guess, she'd have said the culprit was drugs. She'd begun seeing more and more customers like her, even with high school girls. She reached for the only product in her arsenal that would cover most of Loretta's skin eruptions.

"For your skin type, I'd recommend an overall cover." She showed Loretta the designer tube before applying some on her latex fingertips and began applying it to Loretta's ruined skin.

"How much does it cost?" Loretta asked when she saw the miraculous transformation reflected back in the mirror.

"$39.95," the clinician replied without flinching.

"For *that* little tube?" exclaimed Loretta.

"It's on sale. It's usually $44.95. If you want overall coverage without looking like a wax mannequin, this is the best product on the market."

The woman frowned at Loretta's mustache. "You might want to do something about that unwanted facial hair. You could purchase a depilatory cream. We have several to choose from, or you could go to a beauty parlor. Most of them offer waxes."

"Does it hurt?" Loretta asked.

"It hurts like the dickens! But you'll find your make-up will go on a lot smoother."

"Throw a depilatory cream in with the face make-up," Loretta requested.

"What eye shadow color do you prefer?" the clinician asked.

"You decide. I'll be wearing a light brown wig."

The clinician was relieved. The woman's hair resembled what you'd find on the floor of a bikini wax establishment. In her everyday consultations, she'd improved the love lives and self-esteem of countless women, but common decency wouldn't allow her to go so far as to suggest a wig.

"Golden brown will be perfect for your coloring. Is this makeover for a special night out?"

"It's a surprise for my husband," Loretta answered with a straight face.

"What color is your dress?"

"I haven't picked it out yet."

"Well, let's see." The clinician stood back from Loretta, warming to her task. "You'd look good in winter colors. I'd say royal blue, red or even some deep yellows, but whatever you do, stay away from mustards! I haven't met a woman yet who could pull that off! Your brown eyes and skin tone would work well with greens. What if we go with a touch of green eye shadow?"

"It's worth a try," Loretta replied, losing interest. This was a makeover, not a beauty pageant! *Whatever was up with this gal, it wasn't normal*, Loretta thought. *No one* could be that hung up on looks. Or maybe they could, because the woman kept flapping her jaws as if her efforts were going to turn her into the next big find, maybe playing the love interest opposite Matthew McConaughey. Like *that* would ever happen.

"I think we should apply neutral shades with a tiny bit of emerald green extended away from the eye. It'll give you an exotic look and open up your brow area."

"Anything would be an improvement." She gave up! The woman was hopeless.

The clinician got to work like she was painting the Mona Lisa. In some ways, she was. Loretta had never looked so good. In fact, walking down the cavernous interior of the mall, she experienced something outside the norm. Several men had turned to stare when she passed by.

Breaking the promise to herself of not purchasing at the Estée Lauder counter couldn't be helped, but it left her $67 poorer.

If she was going to have enough money to pay for dinner at Elaine's, Loretta fretted, she'd need to look for a marked-down dress. She'd also need dress shoes. All she had was a pair of cheap flip-flops, some slip-ons and the tennis shoes she'd bought for her job shoveling shit at the veterinarian's. And nylons, she'd need nylons, too. This afternoon's outing was going to break her!

Loretta found her jewel hidden at the back of a clearance rack at 70% off. It was a dress of light celery-green silk that complimented her skin and eye color. To get the full effect of her new look, Loretta took the nylon wig out of its bag, gave it a shake and put it on, smoothing the strands that flipped up slightly around her jaw line in the jagged, random cut that had become so popular.

Loretta stood back to look in the full length mirror, happy with what she saw. The dress was a size twelve and it fit perfectly! She was looking back at a stranger.

She found the shoes on a sale rack at Payless; simple camel-colored pumps. The nylons were marked down to $1 a pair, so she purchased two. Glancing in the mirror as she modeled the pumps, she made a mental note to shave her legs.

Her last stop was at Walgreens where she bought a package of disposable razors, a travel-sized shaving cream, lipstick in the same shade the clinician had applied, eye shadow and blush. The day's shopping, including the meth, had done substantial damage to her cash flow. Loretta was now down to $15.75. But it was worth every penny. Frank would never know what hit him!

*   *   *

Sitting behind the tinted windshield of the truck, Loretta watched Frank stroll arm-in-arm into the restaurant with an auburn-haired beauty. She was petite, no taller than five foot two, with a slim figure. Loretta hated her on sight.

She gave them ten minutes to be seated and followed.

The hostess smiled at Loretta as she entered. "Good evening. Do you have reservations?"

"Yes, for 7:15."

"Your name?"

"Loretta Smith."

The hostess ran a pampered nail down the reservations book and nodded. "I'll be seating you in a moment. If you'd like, you can take a seat." She gestured to a silk upholstered bench the color of dusty raspberries.

"No, I would not like. I'd like to be seated now," Loretta said and remained standing.

"It'll be just a moment. I need to confirm that your table is ready."

The hostess made a dash to a handsome middle-aged waiter with impeccably clipped salt and pepper hair and an olive complexion. He carried himself like a queen's butler, but told such filthy jokes, he was a favorite with the kitchen staff.

"Marcus, table three's just arrived. She's insisting on being seated now."

"No can do. I've got two tables that need to be delivered and another waiting for me to take their order."

"And I've got a tweaker blocking the lobby."

"Is she of the celebrity gold coke spoon on a chain genre, or just a run of the mill crack whore?"

"Come on Marcus, help me out!"

"You're going to owe me."

"Done!"

She headed back to her station, her head held high in triumph. The woman hadn't moved. "If you'll follow me, please."

Things were going well until they reached table three and the hostess slid a chair out for Loretta.

"I don't want to sit here."

"Excuse me?"

"I said I don't want to sit here. I like that side of the room better." Loretta pointed to the busiest section of the restaurant.

"Ma'am, this is the only table available."

"I want to be seated over there," Loretta insisted, raising her voice in agitation and pointing across the busy room.

The waiter's timing was impeccable. "Hello, I'm Marcus, your waiter for tonight. Is there something wrong?"

"Well, yes. I want to be seated on the other side of the room," Loretta said, pointing to where Frank and Carrie sat.

He looked to the hostess. "I'll take care of this, Dawn."

She all but ran back to her Lucite podium.

"If you'll follow me, Ma'am," he said, leading the way.

Loretta interrupted their follow-the-leader by pulling out a chair of her choosing. "I'll sit here."

As far as the waiter was concerned, the table was a curious choice. It was too far away for the pianist to be enjoyed properly and it was directly in the path of employee traffic to and from the kitchen. However, Steven, the only waiter Marcus detested was working this station. The woman gave him the impression she would be a stingy tipper and she'd make up for it with constant demands.

Marcus smiled. "As you wish, Ma'am," he said, standing aside while Loretta seated herself.

"And stop calling me Ma'am!"

Even in a whisper, her meaning was heartfelt. The waiter excused himself, eager to give the bad news to his co-worker.

Loretta's heart was pounding. She couldn't remember ever being quite so nervous, even when heisting ambulances. She took a quick glance at Frank holding hands with Carrie and instantly felt like rushing their table to knock the disgusting smiles off their faces.

Getting control of her rage, Loretta leaned forward to eavesdrop on their conversation.

"Deep down I know the kids are safe, but for some reason I can't stop feeling guilty about us taking time for ourselves. Sometimes I daydream about all of us: you, Susan and me taking the kids and running away to somewhere remote where no one could ever find us; not Susan's ex, not Hal and not Loretta," Carrie said.

Loretta's eyebrows rose in surprise... *Was Frank into a ménage à trois...some sick three-way? He couldn't be! His libido wouldn't be up for the challenge. He liked sex occasionally, in the middle of the night, with the lights out and a sleeping body lying next to him. At least that was the way it had been for years with him. Maybe he'd rejuvenated the Velvet Rocket for something kinkier.*

"What would we do at this remote hideaway?" Frank asked.

"I haven't gotten that far. How about you?"

"I'd design computer software. Technology is changing so fast, there are gaping holes left where there should be programs. A good example is inventory. A person could solve a merchant's inventory control problems and make a good living doing it."

"Why haven't you already done it, then?"

"No time. I had to make a living and then the kids came. After that, I was busy keeping them and myself out of Loretta's reach."

Loretta felt her hackles rise. He was making her out to be some kind of monster! She'd never laid a hand on the kids. She wouldn't have gone after him either, if he hadn't asked for it day in, day out.

"Did I tell you Susan's got a real estate agent looking for a place outside of town with acreage? She wants enough land to keep a horse for the boys."

"She's been given an incredible opportunity."

"She wants the kids and I to live with her once she's found a place."

"What did you tell her?"

"It's tempting, but I can't. I need to make my own way. We'll visit as often as we can, though. Imagine how much fun it'll be for the kids."

"I envy her, to be able to get away from the traffic and crowds," Frank said.

Loretta was getting a little queasy listening to Frank's sappy voice. Maybe his mother had only time-shared back one of his balls. The other must've contained the testosterone.

"Where would you live if you had your choice?" Carrie asked.

"I don't have a clue. I was born and raised in Chicago. I haven't spent time anywhere else."

"When I was a kid my parents took us to Oregon every summer. My grandparents had a farm there. They raised goats and kept chickens. It was wonderful."

"Would you like that...to move to the country?"

Loretta had trouble keeping a straight face. Frank was not some knight in shining armor. He would not be galloping up on a white horse to whisk Carrie to some farmhouse. He didn't have the bankroll.

"Someday, I would," Carrie said, pausing when their waiter arrived to refill their wine glasses.

Loretta scowled. Eavesdropping was tedious. Their conversation was a yawn and she'd already let her lobster bisque grow cold. Her appetite, as usual, was non-existent. She forced herself to take a bite of the sourdough roll that had arrived with her meal and found it tasteless.

She was having trouble following their conversation. What had Carrie meant when she said the kids were in safe hands and who, exactly, was Susan? Loretta added to the evening's frustration by having a quick look at the money remaining in her purse. Her meal would cost every bit of what she had, even without a tip. As far as she was concerned, this evening's sleuthing was a waste of time.

Loretta walked away from the disappointing evening with one lasting impression: she wanted Frank on her turf. When she was finished with him, she doubted the prom queen would want what was left.

Chapter 23

Frank felt relief as he watched Freddie's Oldsmobile pull up. The boys had been threatening mutiny. Investigating the tools he had already laid out, they'd convinced themselves they could start the tree house on their own.

All morning he'd had to get on them about not going out front to wait for Freddie.

Even the bodyguard stationed at the front door, compliments of Susan, didn't ease Frank's worry about Loretta swooping down on them. Two days ago, he'd discovered the extra set of keys he'd put in the junk drawer were missing. He'd had the locks changed, but it didn't solve the issue over why Loretta had stolen them, *if* she had stolen them.

Freddie got out and walked to the back seat to grab his tools. As he did, he flashed a mile of plumber's crack.

"Thought I'd never get outta the house! Your aunt made me watch that swimsuit finalist thingy so she could call in my vote. She'll call it in all right, but my vote'll go to *her* gal," Freddie said. His comb-over caught a gust of wind and stood at attention, now resembling a bird's broken wing.

Freddie stopped short when he saw the bodyguard, roughly the size of a standing freezer, leaning against the side of the house. "Who the hell's that?"

"That's the bodyguard I told you about."

"I'd hate to be the one who pissed him off. He looks cross," Freddie commented, lowering his voice.

"Not cross, just doing his job."

"Does he always stand with his arms folded like Mr. Clean, frown'n?" Freddie asked.

Frank shrugged. "I guess so, unless Loretta shows up."

"Well hell's bells! From the looks of him, he could do the job just by staring her down!"

"It's his job to look serious."

"How long will he be here?"

"I'm not sure. Susan and Carrie ganged up on me. I'm not comfortable having a stranger here," Frank said, then decided to change the subject. "Are you ready to get started? The boys nearly drove me crazy."

"That's what I'm here for. We're gonna build a tree house that'll stop traffic from the street, it'll be so amaz'n," Freddie said, smiling at the boys who'd broken the rules again and were standing in the driveway.

Freddie kept his gaze on them and continued. "Now don't you go get'n on your high horse. If we're gonna build this thing, you best follow directions. Whoever doesn't is gonna get clean-up duty."

The boys nodded in unison and followed Freddie inside to the dining room table where he fanned out the papers he held in his hand.

"Now, see here?" Freddie said, pointing to the tree house plans. "These're just basic plans. I had Aunt Edith find 'em on the Internet and print 'em up. You boys have a look at 'em and tell me which one you like the best. It can only be one, though."

The men left them to their decision and went through the sliding glass doors to the backyard.

"Have you heard from the detective?" Freddie asked.

"As a matter of fact, I called him this morning. They haven't found Loretta, but he assured me they won't give up until they do."

"Ha! Half the police force is the Donut Hut's best customers. If you ask me, they spend too much time eat'n and not enough time look'n!" Freddie said with conviction.

"This one's personal. It looks bad when an ambulance goes south, plus Loretta took out a Chief of Police," Frank disagreed.

Freddie shook his head. "She's a crazy one!"

The boys came running out with a floor plan. "We want this one with a trap door in the ceiling. Could we have built-in bunk beds and a rope ladder?" Brice asked.

Freddie scratched his head being careful not to muss his comb-over. "If we put a trap door in the ceil'n, we'll have to build your tree house with a flat roof and it'll need to have a rail'n around it. Otherwise, you'll go flying off the thing!"

"We won't go flying, Uncle Freddie. We'll be careful," Brandon argued.

"Well, if we're putt'n in a trap door, we're putt'n up railin's. And we're add'n a play area underneath for Britney," Freddie said.

The day was clear and crisp and it didn't take long before jackets were thrown off in exchange for sweatshirts as they worked up a sweat.

At lunchtime Edith showed up with homemade soup and a platter of sandwiches.

"My, you boys are busy! I can already see how nice it's going to be!" she exclaimed.

"You should go on up and check it out, Aunt Edith," Brice said, pointing to an aluminum ladder leaning against their work area.

Edith looked down at the shoes she was wearing. They were her most casual, made of navy and white denim, but impractical for climbing ladders because of three-inch Lucite heels. "I'll leave that to you boys. I haven't climbed a ladder in years," she demurred.

"How's it going?" she asked Freddie.

"We'll be done by next weekend if the boys keep go'n like they've been."

"Don't forget Britney! She's going to love her playhouse."

"She'll have her playhouse and I'm think'n you can find her a kitchen set."

"That would be perfect. What about a fridge, sink and stove? She'd play out here for hours. I'll pick up some play food and a little grocery cart and pots and pans and dishes—unbreakable, of course. What color?"

"That's your department," Freddie said, quickly losing interest.

"It'll be pink. Britney loves pink. While I'm at it, I'll find a table and chair set. I can stencil flowers on them."

Frank cringed. Edith had stenciled every wall in her house with flowers, including some of the furniture. Her place looked like a botany test site. But he held his tongue. It was a nice thing they were doing for the kids.

"Are you planning on putting up drywall?" she asked Freddie.

"It wouldn't be a li'l girl's playhouse without walls, now would it?" Freddie answered.

"Then, it needs a light. You never know…"

"Now you're go'n too far Edith! She doesn't need no damned light!"

"A light, Freddie! And make sure the ceiling's taped nice because I'm going to paint it with clouds." Edith paused to make eye contact with the boys. "Come on into the house, everybody. Lunch is ready."

Freddie gave Frank a look of frustration. There wasn't much doubt who'd be winning the battle.

"I suppose we could run a heavy-duty extension cord from the ceiling. We'd have to do the same for the boys, though," Freddie grumbled.

They walked into the kitchen, neither admitting the real boss was laying out their meal.

"Did you make sure you weren't followed?" Frank whispered to Edith.

"Yes, I did. Thanks to Loretta, I'm constantly looking in my rearview mirror. She's finally done it. I've become paranoid. I'll be glad when they find her."

"That makes two of us. Have you heard from Mom yet?" Frank asked.

Edith's cheeks turned red with embarrassment. "No I haven't, but when I do, I'm going to give her a piece of my mind! To think that she'd just take off at a time like this. Well, I never thought she was capable of such a thing."

Frank left it there. It served no purpose to include his mother in an otherwise perfect day.

Edith had made enough food for the entire neighborhood and they did her proud, heaping their bowls with homemade soup and grabbing sandwiches.

"Aunt Edith, did you bring donuts for dessert?" Brandon asked the minute he scooped the last spoonful of soup from his bowl.

"What do you think?"

"I think you did," he said in a hopeful voice, "…didn't you?"

Edith grabbed the box she'd hidden on top of the refrigerator. "You get to pick out one," she said, daring Frank to say anything by shooting him a belligerent look.

The boys ran out to the backyard to eat their dessert, sitting amid the sawdust and lumber scraps while Frank wondered: at what point in time would his kids need fillings? Edith was tenacious, if nothing else.

He watched her help herself to four chocolate cake donuts with sprinkles.

"Freddie, you'll be home by 8:00, right?"

"I'll be there. Why?"

"Because the swimsuit contest results are going to be in."

"It'll be the Italian model," Freddie said.

"No, it'll be the one from Switzerland. She's the prettiest."

"No, she ain't!" he disagreed.

"You never did have the sense God gave a goose!"

Before things got too out of hand, Frank stood in the gap to redirect the conversation. "So what are you going to stencil on the table and chairs, Aunt Edith?"

"I was thinking about wildflowers done in pastels with pretty blue ribbons. I'll have Britney help me choose the colors," Edith said, standing in the middle of the kitchen, dreamy-eyed.

The second he and Freddie returned to the tree house, the boy's requests started. "Dad, could we build a table so we have a place to eat?" Mark asked.

Frank looked to Freddie and got a nod.

"Yes, we can. Do you want it built in or something you can move around?" Frank asked.

"Built in."

"We need a piece of wood for our sign, too," added Brandon.

"What's this sign going to say?" Frank asked his four-year-old.

"It's going to say *No Girls Allowed*."

"You'll change your mind about that in ten years," laughed Freddie.

"Is it going to have a carpet?" asked Brice.

"We got remnants in the warehouse I can get for free," Freddie offered.

"Do you have blue?" Brice persisted.

"There's lots of blue."

"Then it's settled. You'll have a built-in table, wood for a sign and carpeting," Frank said.

"Could we put in a skylight, so we can see the stars at night?" requested Sam.

"It's doable. All it'd take's a piece of Plexiglas, some flange and caulking, but that's it, boys. No more requests," Freddie said.

By the end of the day, they had a good portion of the tree house built and the walls for Britney's playhouse were studded out.

"That'll do'er 'till tomorrow. I'll be here early. Probably around 9:00."

They followed Freddie out to his car while Frank nervously kept a lookout. He knew he should relax. What could be safer than to have an experienced bodyguard standing inches from your front door? But it was Loretta who posed the threat, and considering her track record, paranoia was a reasonable approach, Frank decided.

"Can I spend the night, Frank?" Sam asked when they returned to the house.

"If it's all right with your mom, it's fine with me."

Sam didn't waste time getting his mom on the phone. "Frank, Mom wants to talk to you. She said yes!" He put the receiver down on the counter and ran out to the backyard.

"Hello there! How's Britney doing?" Frank asked.

"Couldn't be happier. So far, she and Madison have cut the hair off two Barbie Dolls and Madison's showing Britney how to use finger paints as we speak."

"How's your house holding up?"

"Fine. I covered the table with a plastic tablecloth. We're baking chocolate chip cookies in a little while."

"You're a saint."

"Nope, just a mom. Since Sam's spending the night at your place, what if I keep Britney here?"

"You sure you're up for that?"

"I'm sure. She's having fun. It would be a shame to send her home now."

"Has she asked for her Cinderella PJ's yet?"

"Only a couple dozen times," Carrie said, laughing. "So, what do you think about the hired help?"

"It was nice of Susan to offer, but having a stranger standing right outside the door seems like overkill."

"I agree. It's going to take some getting used to. On a brighter side, Susan just got back after seeing a ranch house on fifteen acres. It's got a stable and a corral. The previous owners raised quarter horses."

"Is she going to buy it?"

"Well, the boys were chattering like magpies about it. It's got an in-ground swimming pool and a hot tub. I could tell she liked it, but she told me she's afraid she'd get lost in a house that big."

"She'd get used to it."

"She might, but it's got seven bedrooms and five bathrooms, a huge living room, plus a family room. She brought up the possibility of my living with her again."

"And you said…"

"That I'd think about it. It's hard saying no, but I can't imagine being happy living in someone else's house."

"Selfishly, I'm relieved. I'd rather have you living close by."

"Is that so?"

"It's so. Listen, if you don't have anything planned, I thought I'd barbeque some hot dogs and a couple of steaks for the grown-ups tomorrow night. Think you could make it?"

"I'll be there. Sam gave me a glowing report. Is it true the tree house is going to have a skylight and a wrap-around deck?"

"Don't look at me! Freddie's out of control."

"Something tells me he's not the only one. Anyway, I'll bring corn on the cob and watermelon for the barbeque. Do you need anything else?"

"Only you."

"Funny guy! I'll see you tomorrow night, then."

Frank hung up hating that he wouldn't see her until the next day. He was completely, totally in love. The more time they spent together, the stronger his feelings grew. He wondered how he was going to tell her and when he did, what Carrie's reaction would be.

Chapter 24

Loretta paced around the cramped motel room in tight circles. She'd run out of meth. Her skin was crawling and her thoughts were all over the place. She shouldn't have put off heisting an ambulance. She hadn't thought clearly since yesterday when she'd snorted the last of the 8-Ball.

Desperate, Loretta grabbed her purse. There was a Red Lobster down the street. It was as good a place as any. She found a safe parking spot within running distance of the restaurant. Something kept telling her that her luck had run out. If that gut feeling turned out to be right, she wanted to be as far away from prying eyes as possible.

She walked the three blocks to the restaurant and waited in the lobby for a table. The lunch-hour crowed was surprisingly heavy.

"Loretta Rhodes," the hostess called out.

As soon as Loretta stood, the room started to spin. She grabbed hold of the bench she'd been sitting on to regain her equilibrium.

"Are you all right, Ma'am?" asked the hostess.

"Fine. I'm fine, just a little dizzy."

"If you'd rather have a seat for a bit…"

"Is there something wrong with your hearing? I said I'm fine!"

Several customers turned to stare.

"I'm sorry. I was just trying to help."

"If you want to help so bad, then point me to my table so I can get something to eat."

"Very well, Ma'am. Please follow me."

"And don't call me Ma'am! We're about the same age. How would you like to be called Ma'am?"

The hostess stole a quick glance. The woman looked forty-five at best. Her skin had an unhealthy gray cast to it, bloodless almost, and her face was broken out with open sores.

She seated Loretta in a hurry and went to warn her manager.

A waiter showed up to take Loretta's order before she'd had a chance to look at the menu. She kept him waiting, finally ordering a large bowl of soup, cheesy garlic rolls and their largest order of shrimp appetizers. She needed nourishment if she was going to be successful. Besides, she wouldn't be paying for her meal. She could afford the very best.

The waiter delivered her food in minutes.

"Would you care for anything else?"

"A glass of milk," Loretta replied, biting into a shrimp slathered in cocktail sauce. It was delicious. While Loretta savored the shrimp, she tried to remember how long it had been since she'd eaten. To the best of her recollection, it had to have been two days ago.

The milk was set down and her waiter disappeared at a trot. It was obvious he was keeping his distance, which Loretta attributed to the meddling hostess. She must have given him a heads-up. Loretta looked around at the packed restaurant. More than one pair of eyes were watching her. In fact, it seemed like just about everyone in the restaurant had turned their attention in her direction. She wiggled in her booth, uncomfortable with the scrutiny. *What did they know, anyway? They should mind their own damned business!* Loretta was unaware she'd spoken her thoughts aloud.

"Is everything okay?" asked a man who suddenly appeared at her table.

"Who the hell are you?" Loretta asked.

"I'm the manager and I'm asking you if everything's okay," he repeated.

"I'm fine! What's with you people anyway? Can't someone just enjoy their meal in peace?" she yelled.

"Typically, the answer to that would be yes, but you're disturbing the customers. I'm going to have to ask you to leave."

"You're *what*?"

"I'm asking you to leave. Now."

"Well, I'm not going to leave! I have just as much right to be here as anyone else."

"You did until you insulted our hostess and started yelling at the customers."

"I wasn't yelling at the damned customers!"

"Like you aren't yelling now, I suppose."

"Listen you asshole, I'm going to sit here and enjoy my meal and if you don't get the hell away from my table, I'll fillet you with my dinner knife!"

"If you don't leave now, Ma'am, I'll be forced to call the police."

There was no warning.

Loretta shot up out of her chair and grabbed him by the necktie, slamming his face into her soup bowl. Two men seated at nearby tables rushed forward to help but not before his body started to twitch and his arms flailed out as he tried in vain to free himself. It took both of the men to break her death hold. While they were otherwise occupied wrestling Loretta to the floor, the manager slumped over the table, gasping for air, his face covered with small blisters from the hot potato and cheese soup.

Loretta was pinned to the carpet. If there was one thing she hated, it was being held against her will. She was relieved when one of the men disengaged himself to come to the manager's aid. Now she had a fighting chance.

Centering all her rage into freeing herself, Loretta gave a herculean shove and managed to push the man from on top of her. Twisting her body and pulling legs to her chest for momentum, she delivered a brutal kick to his face, bloodying his nose. When she got to her feet, he followed. Loretta settled the matter with another swift kick, this time to his kneecap and he crashed to the floor.

A siren approaching the front of the restaurant was Loretta's signal to exit through the emergency door. She ran until her lungs felt like they would explode. Climbing into the cab of the truck, Loretta started the engine and peeled away from the curb.

Back streets served as her escape route until a Pizza Hut materialized, which Loretta took as a sign. She went in and placed an order, taking a seat near the front. This was important to her game plan. It wouldn't do to collapse if no one was looking.

When she grabbed her chest and fell to the floor, Loretta experienced the best customer service Pizza Hut had to offer. The manager was a vision of synchronized discipline as she yelled for a clerk behind the register to call 911 and started performing CPR. In the spirit of fair play, Loretta realized she should have popped a breath mint before her collapse.

The EMTs cuffed her for blood pressure and connected her to a portable EKG machine. They were stumped when they weren't able to find anything wrong with her.

"Tom, call it in," demanded the senior medic.

The emergency room supervisor ordered the patient to be brought in. It would be the last he'd hear from the medics for days.

Loretta lay on the gurney, letting the excitement of the moment pass. When she estimated they had reached the midway point to Chicago Medical Center, she reached in her purse for a roll of duct tape. The rest of her plan involved luck.

She waited until the driver stopped for a red light. Throwing off the blanket that covered her, she jumped up and yanked the fire extinguisher from its wall mount and slammed it over the driver's head. When he collapsed against the wheel, Loretta reached over to throw the ambulance in park, keeping a wary eye on the assistant. Just as she expected, he went for the door handle. She grabbed him by the shirt collar and pulled him back into his chair.

"If you don't want some of what your partner just got, you'll stay put."

"Lady, you're nuts!"

She took hold of the roll of duct tape and with her teeth fed out enough to secure his wrists. "If we're going to get along, you'll have to improve your people skills," she mumbled past the tape still in her mouth.

She looked over to the driver. He hadn't moved. "Put your hands in front of you."

The paramedic looked at the strip of duct tape and dove for the door. This time, Loretta grabbed the waistband of his pants.

"Keep it up, and you're going to wind up with one hell of a headache. Now hold out your fucking hands!"

"KZH657 to unit five, come in...."

Loretta looked down at the squawking radio. "Turn that damned thing off!"

"I can't. It automatically goes on whenever the engine's running. The only way to turn it off is to shut off the ignition."

"What happens when you don't reply?"

"I don't know. I suppose they'd send someone. This ambulance is set up with a GPS system. They track our location with it," he said, hoping the crazy lady would believe him. "Listen, why don't you go now while you still can? They're probably already headed this way."

"Do like I told you and hold your fucking hands out!" Loretta yelled, reaching for his hands.

The paramedic looked to Loretta to judge his chances. The eyes looking back at him resembled hockey pucks: black and void of all emotion. He jerked free, grabbed the door handle and made his break. As he ran, he told himself the distance between them was increasing with every pump of his legs.

But he made one mistake and it was of gargantuan proportions. He twisted his body around to see if she'd followed. She had...and she was close on his heels. The medic lost his footing and crashed to the shoulder of the road, face first. Loose gravel abraded the side of his head like number 10 grit sandpaper. He had just enough time to lift his head from the shoulder of the road and look towards the highway for help.

When Loretta finally caught up with him, the attack would've rated a three on a scale of one to ten before she punctuated the insult by sitting on him. Grabbing his arms, Loretta pulled his wrists together and wound tape around them in crazy eights at least a half-dozen times.

Even with her on top of him and the blood trickling down his face and duct tape wound around his wrists like a cheap pair of handcuffs, the paramedic held out hope.

The roadway was busy, and the few seconds he'd had to scope it out had been promising. Several of the drivers had come to a halt while others had slowed to a crawl. The law of averages alone meant someone was bound to stop to help him. He sorely hoped it would be someone who was not afraid of a crazy woman brandishing a roll of duct tape and a fire extinguisher.

"You know you're going to pay for this, don't you?" Loretta yelled, and then waited for a reply that never came. "I'm going to get you to your feet and you're going to cooperate. Any more crap, and I'll rip your fucking head off!"

He believed her.

Loretta pulled him to his feet and grabbed the back of his shirt, dragging him towards the double doors at the back of the ambulance. He estimated they had another fifty feet to go when a car pulled over to the shoulder and stopped. This was his chance, the only chance he might get with this crazed, fire extinguisher-packing bitch. He threw himself out of her grasp. Diving to the ground, he set off a chain reaction when his body clipped Loretta's legs, forcing her down on top of him, hard enough to knock the wind out of him.

"What the hell's going on here?" the driver yelled through his open window.

Loretta got up, walked the six feet to the Mercedes and slammed the fire extinguisher into the windshield. She was zeroing in on the passenger side mirror when the Good Samaritan peeled back into traffic, his tires squealing on the roadway, while drivers tried to move out of his way.

The paramedic watched his would-be rescuer's retreat with dread.

"Now get up, damn you! I swear if the cops show up, you're a dead man!"

Loretta was convincing, but the way the paramedic saw it, she'd probably try to kill him whether he cooperated or not. He had no illusions. His refusal was going to make her as crazed as a rhino on angel dust.

"I said get up!"

He remained on the ground, unwilling to play. Maybe his tombstone could read *Stubborn 'Till the End*...or something to that effect. The impact of the fire extinguisher against the side of his head delivered blinding pain. He flipped over and shot his legs out, connecting with her knees. Loretta toppled over yelling a string of curses.

His hands were useless. The tape binding his wrists was acting like a vice. He swung his legs back as far as possible and then thrust them at her throat. The momentum should have qualified as a boiler-maker, but he miscalculated and his kick merely glanced off her cheek, which only succeeded to bring her to her feet in a wild rage; the kind of rage he was unaware humans were capable of. She was feral; something that crawled out of sewers in the dead of night.

Grabbing hold of the paramedic's shirt collar, Loretta yanked him to his feet and started dragging him to the ambulance. His survival instinct took over again—albeit a bit weaker and he dug his heels in, trying to slow their momentum. Unfortunately, Loretta had moved away from the graveled shoulder. His feet now bounced along the rumble-strip, forcing his body to dance and vibrate like he'd been strapped to a jackhammer. Without warning, a strange emotion washed over him: laughter. He felt like letting out a good, old fashioned belly laugh at the absurdity of it. He was being dragged, in full daylight, by a female lunatic along a rumble-strip that had been designed for safety.

His shirt collar was now a tourniquet. They had nearly arrived to the ambulance doors when from behind closed eyes he saw crimson and indigo swirls that rushed at him with intimidating speed. His world went black.

Loretta had trouble shoving the paramedic's comatose body into the bay. He wasn't a large man, but his dead weight made the going tough. Traffic was grid-locked. She kept her eye out for interference. Several drivers held cell phones to their ears. Some, or all, would be 911 calls. She needed to get away as quickly as possible. One last yank and the paramedic was lying flat on his back on the ambulance's bay floor. She had his ankles bound with tape within moments—the duct tape wound around his wrists had weathered the struggle just fine.

His partner was easier. Loretta trussed him where he lay passed out in the driver's seat. Satisfied with her work, she maneuvered his legs over the bucket seat's console and then shoved him to the passenger's side.

The shoulder of the road remained clear. Loretta took it, driving as fast as she dared. Approaching sirens gave her added incentive and she forgot caution. Her foot pressed the gas pedal to the floor and the ambulance careened around the cloverleaf exit on two wheels, threatening to flip. Hitting the brakes was impossible. Loretta let up on the gas and held on tight to the steering wheel while the ambulance fishtailed. The rear end hit the guardrail and the momentum slid the ambulance sideways, stopping only inches from the busy intersection.

Loretta laid her head down on the wheel and tried to catch her breath. The sirens were getting closer by the second. She took a tight grip on the steering wheel and slammed on the gas at the first break in the heavy traffic.

The sirens now carried with them the sharp bleat of horns. They'd already merged onto the busy roadway close behind her.

Loretta had run out of time. The hilly roadway she travelled hid the ambulance from view, but not for long. An alleyway was her only option. Which one was the gamble she would have to take or risk being caught. The sirens continued to reverberate, but it was impossible to tell if they were coming from behind, or ahead, or both. Loretta knew if she made the wrong choice, she'd be trapped. She zipped past one alley, then another, playing with time, which on a deal or no deal conundrum could prove to be lethal.

Coming up to the next alley, Loretta saw what appeared to be the metal sheen of a garage door. At the last possible second she cranked the wheel hard. She'd misjudged the length of the ambulance and the back end collided with the corner of a warehouse. From the rearview mirror Loretta watched bricks spray the alleyway.

Turning her attention from the rear-view mirror to the alleyway, she breathed a sigh of relief. Just ahead was the battered door of a garage. Newspapers affixed to the narrow windows near the top had long since gone yellow. But Loretta's attention was centered on the flimsy lock which was rusted with neglect. With luck, it wouldn't take much to break it free from the hasp that held it.

Sirens were screaming from all directions. Loretta ran back to the ambulance for the fire extinguisher and slammed it against the rusted lock several times before it fell to the alleyway with a metallic clang at the same time the fire extinguisher came to a valiant end with a shower of white foam that erupted from a hole ripped in its side. Loretta tossed it into weeds growing between the garage and the next building. Getting the metal door open was all that was on her mind and she put everything she had into raising it on its tracks. It wouldn't budge.

She frantically pushed and heaved, banged and swore. There was nowhere else to go, therefore Loretta reasoned, it had to work. If it didn't, she was going to be spending the rest of her life behind bars wearing an orange jumpsuit. She looked like crap in orange!

Finally, Loretta heard a squeak of submission. She continued to rock the metal door up and down, coaxing the rusted track to cooperate. Her efforts bought her a few more inches. She tightened her grip on its lip and gave a yank upwards and gained another foot. She kept at it until there was enough clearance for her to disappear into the darkness of the garage.

Getting the ambulance through the opening was a lot like putting a condom on an elephant. She had to settle for scraping her way in. On its downward trajectory, the garage door rolled on the track with surprising speed. Sitting in total darkness, her surroundings were now darker than a proctologist's worst nightmare. She turned on the ambulance's headlights, but the cavernous, greasy space still gave her the creeps.

The medic in the passenger seat was coming to, which was both a relief and a nuisance. She didn't have much time to find the drugs and disappear to freedom. She had to step over the assistant to get the back dome light on and confirmed he was alive by the movements of his chest as his lungs drew in the fetid air of the garage. At least if she was caught, she wouldn't be facing manslaughter charges, she thought.

Moving to the built-in cabinets, Loretta tossed out the refuse till she got to the good stuff. The end result was a disappointment. There were fewer drugs than there'd been on other heists and she was reminded once again of her feeling that this time was going to be different. It was different all right and it would be her last.

Throwing the drugs into a pillowcase, Loretta got out of the ambulance and moved to the side door of the garage. Unlocking it, she stuck her head out and looked both ways down the alley. The coast was clear as far as she could tell; no cop cars were blocking the way, no blue uniforms were on foot searching the area. But the sirens hadn't given up. They weren't going to call a truce until they were slapping handcuffs on her.

The area was littered with broken bottles and debris and smelled of mold and urine. Sunlight must have never made it to the meager twenty feet of space between the tall buildings. Damp cold seeped through her clothing, raising goose bumps on her flesh. A police cruiser raced past, lights on, and siren blaring. Loretta instinctively hugged the wall of the building nearest her.

A sign nailed to a door directly across from her was promising: it announced Joe's Smoke Shop in weathered lettering. She reasoned the alley was used for smoke breaks judging by the spent cigarettes at both sides of the doorway. She tried the door and it swung open onto an unlit storage room. She had to stop to let her eyes adjust to the darkness. Snippets of conversation reached her through the closed door leading from the storage room to the front of the shop. Loretta burst through the door, startling the clerk who was resting his arms on a glass display case only feet away from where she emerged.

"Excuse me! What the hell do you think you're doing?" he demanded.

"Does this door lock?"

He ignored her question and frowned. "Maybe you weren't listening. I asked you what you're doing."

"A man followed me down the alleyway just now. I used the back door to get away from him. Does this door lock?" she asked.

Without bothering to answer her, the clerk moved to the door and twisted the lock.

"Why were you walking down an alleyway in this part of town? Do you have some kind of death wish?" he asked.

"It's a free country! All I did was take a shortcut. I need to use your phone."

He simply stared, first at Loretta, and then his glance moved to the pillowcase she held clutched in her hand.

"I need to call a cab. The man who was following me is probably still out there and I'm not leaving until I see a cab pull up."

"Shit, Jimmy, all she's asking for is to call a cab. Give her the damned phone," rasped the customer standing across from the clerk, obviously angered.

The clerk gave Loretta a sour look. "My gut's telling me different. Maybe those sirens I've been hearing are for you."

"You need a description of the guy? Would that make you happy?"

"Actually, I'm thinking I should be the one on the phone calling the cops."

"Go ahead. At least I'll be safe."

The clerk thought it over and grudgingly handed Loretta a phone book and pointed to a phone mounted against the wall. "Make it fast."

Loretta got yellow cab on the line and had to ask for the address from the clerk to give to the dispatcher. She hung up the phone and walked to the front of the shop to watch for her ride while she drummed her free hand against a glass cabinet displaying pipes and roll-your-own paraphernalia. Each time a siren was heard, she stiffened.

The clerk had no way of knowing his observations would prove extremely beneficial to the detectives who eventually followed her trail; first to the cast off fire extinguisher, then to the injured paramedics, and finally, to Joe's Smoke Shop. He was able to supply them with the first description of Loretta since her hundred and fifty pound weight loss, including brittle hair, bad teeth and worse complexion.

The cab pulled up. Her parting smirk, however slight, latter made it to the police rendering.

Chapter 25

Frank sat the platter of hot dogs down on the table and yelled for the kids. Mark's head popped out of the tree house.

"Can we eat in the tree house, Dad?"

"I don't see why not. Hurry up, though. I don't want dinner to get cold. Tell your brothers and Sam to get down here pronto!"

Sam and Brice took turns lowering themselves down the rope while Frank held his breath. "They're going to break their necks. Maybe we shouldn't have agreed on the rope."

"And take away their fun? So far the escape hatch and the rope are their favorites. You and Freddie did a terrific job. I especially like the *No Girls Allowed* sign," Carrie quipped.

"But they made an exception for you."

"I'm not a girl, I'm a mother. Mothers bring popcorn and cook meals and fix boo-boos. Therefore, we tend to get exemptions."

"You're all girl as far as I'm concerned," Frank said, putting his arm around Carrie's shoulders. Carrie leaned in to him, drinking in his warmth.

"I'll take that as a compliment."

"Good. It was meant to be one. I only wish we were alone, so I could prove it. What do you think our chances are of getting the kids interested in a movie once Edith and Freddie go home?"

"If we let them play outdoors and wear themselves out, I'd say we have a good shot at getting them to settle in upstairs and we can cuddle up on the couch," Carrie said.

"Hmmm…they've already been climbing up and down that rope swing for an hour. We'll be curled on the couch and I'll be nibbling on your ear in no time," Frank said, drawing Carrie close and stealing a kiss. "Are the girls still in the playhouse?" he asked.

"The last I saw, Madison was busy showing Britney where the kitchen set should be. She's already gotten my promise to sew curtains for the windows."

"But the walls aren't even finished."

"That may be, but we girls think ahead."

The boys gathered around the picnic table to grab hot dogs, wedges of watermelon and fistfuls of potato chips, then ran back to the tree house and placed their overflowing plates, one on top of the other, into a metal bucket.

"What're you boys doing?" Frank asked.

"It's our hoist, Dad!" Brice answered in the voice he used when his brothers were being dense.

"A hoist. Of course it's a hoist…silly me," Frank muttered. "We may never see them again. Did you ever see *Swiss Family Robinson*?"

"Of course. Hasn't every kid?"

"I suppose so. I hope so, anyway. I remember when I saw it for the first time. They swam out to the shipwreck and brought back the wood to build the tree house and used palm fronds for the roof. They had a bucket hoist to haul their water. That's what this reminds me of."

"Yes, it does, doesn't it? This has been good for them, doubly good because you and Freddie let them help build it."

"I'm glad we did, but you and I need to make a pact. Next weekend needs to be spent finishing the tree house, but the following weekend is ours. I want to take you out to dinner and a movie."

Frank was leaning over for another kiss when the girls emerged from their ground floor, soon to be frilly playhouse. He sighed and hung his head in frustration.

"Come on, it isn't all that bad," Carrie laughed.

"That depends on your definition of bad. I need a night alone with you. Just you and me, some soft music and a crackling fire."

"I'm flattered," Carrie said and gave him a chaste hug. "Where are Freddie and Edith? Their steaks are getting cold."

"Fighting in the kitchen," Frank replied.

"Fighting over what?"

"I'll let that be a surprise. I'm sure they'll be happy to share. But just so we don't end up playing referee, I'm fixing each of them plates. With luck, they'll decide to eat in the kitchen."

They helped the girls prepare their hot dogs and at their insistence helped carry their plates back to the playhouse. It was finally Carrie and Frank's turn. The steaks were New York strips, barbequed over mesquite chips and nearly tender enough to cut with a fork. They prepared four plates with steak, baked potatoes with all the trimmings, and fresh fruit.

"I'll be right back," Frank said, grabbing Edith and Freddie's meals.

Edith was positively glowing in a tailor-made caftan of deep purple that had dyed-to-match seashells crocheted around the neckline.

"I'm telling you, that Swedish gal has it, hands down," Edith said.

"Not in the butt department, she don't. You could balance a plate on the buns of the Italian model," argued Freddie.

"Oh, get over it! Ever since J-Lo, all anyone ever talks about is butts. Your gal has a saggy chest. Why, you have more than she does."

Freddie looked down and flexed lazy pecks through his tank top. "Nah, the Italian has more'n me. Plus, she's a looker!"

"Oh, so now you're saying the Swedish gal isn't a looker? She has those ice blue eyes, a lot like Cameron Diaz's. She's way prettier than your pick."

Freddie looked to Frank. "She's still pissed the Italian won," he said, winking.

"Here are your steaks. Enjoy them while they're warm," Frank said as he placed their plates on the dining room table.

"Why don't you and Carrie join us?" Aunt Edith said.

"No offense, but I'm enjoying a little alone time with Carrie. With six kids involved, it's not all that often that we get uninterrupted time," Frank replied. He slipped through the open patio doors, leaving them to battle over whose pick deserved the win.

It was the first warm day of spring and Frank and Carrie were content to enjoy the fresh air and each other's company. "Susan put earnest money down on the ranch house I'd told you about, and her offer was accepted," Carrie said.

"That was fast!"

"It probably had a lot to do with her boys. They couldn't stop talking about it. The move will be good for them. Right now, they're crowded having to share Madison's room."

"You're going to miss her, aren't you?"

"Yes, I will. It's been nice having her around. She's become like a sister to me. But it has been cramped and it's a wonder we did so well in such tight quarters."

"The reason is simple. You're a nurturer, Carrie."

"That reminds me. Has anyone heard from your mother?"

"Not a word."

"It's hard to believe she'd leave in the middle of such craziness."

"If you knew her, it wouldn't be. She was a terrible mother and a worse grandmother. The kids have never gotten a birthday card or a Christmas gift from her. Her world revolves around one person: herself."

"She's missing out on the best part of life, then. Has she always been self-centered?"

"As far as I can remember, she has."

Carrie saw Frank's body begin to tense up. He hadn't talked much about his childhood, but clearly it had been a difficult one. She decided not to pursue the subject. There was enough going on without ripping open old wounds. Someday, soon, she hoped he would decide to trust her.

Chapter 26

Loretta snorted the last of the meth and let the euphoria take over. The rush wasn't as long-lasting as it once was. It might be she'd need to increase her intake. If so, Streeter would be there as long as she had the money.

That was the good news. The bad news was she didn't *have* any money. She'd sworn off ambulances. The last job had been a complete nightmare. She'd watched the local news and read the papers for several days after the heist. She wouldn't have been surprised to see her face on *America's Most Wanted*, but there hadn't been anything, not one word. It could be that city officials had quashed the story so they could lick their wounds in private. It could be, but she doubted it. The only thing she was sure of was the shit-for-brains paramedics were bound to be recuperating on Labor and Industry's dime.

Her thoughts were traveling at lightning speed, which was a comfort. It seemed she gained IQ points the moment the meth disappeared up her nose. She continued to sift through the possibilities, pawing at the ground of one half-baked idea after another for her cash flow dilemma. Suddenly, a light bulb came on. Tanya! She'd go see Tanya. How had she forgotten? By now, the paperwork she'd submitted for L.A. Dogs would have been processed, maybe even approved. She could be a business owner with plenty of cash flow to support her habit.

Loretta grabbed her purse and pulled out the cash she had remaining from the last ambulance heist. It totaled to $461. It wasn't enough to rent even a miserly studio apartment, and besides, the meth would eat it up within the week. She couldn't turn to her family for a loan. She hadn't spoken to any of them for nearly twenty years. And she never would. If she ever saw her father again, she'd have to hook him up to that pulley he'd used to dress out the deer he hunted, and do a little dressing of her own—starting with his pecker.

Her mom was just as bad, only in her case the problem stemmed from her being certifiably nuts. Loretta decided to stuff her memories. She wasn't going there. Not today, and maybe not ever…

Traffic was brutal. She idled with the rest of the bumper-to-bumper traffic and contemplated how she'd explain her lack of follow-up to Tanya. She could say her mother had an unexpected relapse and she'd been forced to return to Tulsa to help nurse her back to health. Tanya couldn't fault her for that.

Cutting into the alleyway, it was easy to snag a parking spot. The Lesbian Relief Fund might be an embarrassing dump, but the parking was stellar. Glancing in the rearview mirror, Loretta frowned at a fresh breakout that resembled the craters of the moon. She fished around in her purse and located the tube of Estée Lauder cover-up and went to work.

Tanya didn't recognize her when she entered through the back door.

"Hey there! It's me, Loretta."

Tanya's mouth dropped open while she processed Loretta's newly svelte figure with difficulty. Gaining her composure, she went on the attack.

"Where have you been? I've been trying to reach you about your business license, but your work maintains you disappeared like vapor; no notice and no contact. I even called the friend you'd been staying with. No one returned my messages."

Thank God! There was still hope, Loretta thought.

"My mother had a relapse and I had to rush back to Tulsa to help her. I'm sorry for not contacting you. The situation was overwhelming. I didn't have time to call."

"Loretta, you've put me in a terrible position. I vouched for you and got you the money you asked for. I've been dodging bullets ever since!"

"But I'm back now. I really am sorry. Mom had a slight stroke. The doctor said it was because she stopped taking her high blood pressure medicine. She needed round-the-clock care and Medicare only covered a part-time nurse. I had no choice but to go back."

"What about skipping out on your job? I've got to tell you, Loretta, it doesn't look good."

"When I talked to my boss about Mom's health issues and asked for time off, he went ballistic. I tried to work it out with him, but in the end, I was forced to quit. I couldn't leave my mom to take care of herself when she couldn't cook for herself or make it to the bathroom on her own. Come on! What would you have done?"

Tanya's expression softened but she clung to the core of her anger with another question. "Explain to me why you never called."

Loretta did a pirouette and threw up her arms. "Look at me! I dropped one hundred and fifty pounds. Why? Because I was running my ass off! I didn't have a minute to myself. Mom had to be carried to the bathroom, couldn't feed herself, couldn't even talk so that someone could understand her. The only spare time I had was when she went to bed, and by then I was too exhausted to call."

Something broke loose and Tanya's face reflected compassion. She was a gay Joan of Arc. "Okay, here's where we stand. Your loan has been approved, pending your submission of the start-up costs. Plus, we need a verifiable physical address. I can almost guarantee you they'll be checking it. You've lost all credibility at this point."

Loretta was stumped. Even if she were to kick the meth, she wouldn't have enough for the apartment she needed for a physical address. Besides, she'd tested the possibility of sobriety and failed.

"The address could be a problem. I coasted into town on fumes and I had to sleep in my truck last night. I don't have money for an apartment."

"Truck? Did you say truck? The last time we spoke, you were without transportation. You said your husband was awarded the car."

Shit! She'd screwed up. She needed to be more careful, keep her story straight. Tanya might have thawed, but she had her bullshit meter turned on full blast.

"Actually, it's Mom's. She's in a convalescent home now. The doctor's forbidden her to drive."

Tanya was scrutinizing her, taking mental notes as her glance travelled up and down Loretta's meth-slim body.

Loretta forced herself to relax. It wasn't easy, considering the meth she'd just snorted was coursing through her bloodstream, messing with her nervous system.

"I don't know, Loretta. I want to believe you, but there are too many inconsistencies."

"What inconsistencies?"

"Your weight loss for one. A person doesn't lose that much weight naturally! Have you been taking drugs?"

"No! I don't use drugs. I never have. They scare the shit out of me. I told you how I lost the weight. You ought to try carrying dead weight around and working non-stop day and night. The weight just dropped off."

"Okay, then. Let's say you're telling the truth. What guarantees do I have that if I help you again I won't end up looking like a fool for a second time?"

"You have my word."

"And judging from your actions your *word* isn't worth much, Loretta!"

"That's awfully harsh. I...I..." Loretta turned on the waterworks.

"Knock it off! Tears aren't going to get you anywhere."

But Tanya's actions said differently when she grabbed a handful of tissues and handed them to Loretta.

"Tell me what to do. I need this chance and all that's standing in the way is that I have an address. I've been dreaming about L.A. Dog's ever since we talked about it. You were right. I'll never make anything of myself as long as I'm working a minimum wage job. I want...no, I *need* an opportunity to change my life. I know I'll be successful."

Tanya reached into her desk and pulled out a business card. "This is a halfway house for women in transition. I was going to give you this after your first visit, but it turned out you didn't need it. Give them a call. They might be able to help."

Loretta hugged her benefactor. "I can't thank you enough! I promise you won't be sorry."

"I seem to remember your saying something similar the last time I helped you and it nearly cost me my credibility. This place means everything to me. Don't screw me over again, Loretta, or I swear I'll kick your ass myself!"

Tanya's words had been said in jest, but Loretta's reaction was instantaneous. Her body stiffened and she went into defensive mode. She didn't like threats, not from Tanya, not from anyone.

Chapter 27

By the time Loretta hunted down a payphone that offered privacy, rivulets of sweat were running down her sides and she was ready to tear the head off of anyone who got in her way. She dropped quarters into the slot and dialed.

"New Beginnings, this is Roberta speaking."

"Hello, Roberta. A friend of mine suggested I contact you," Loretta said.

"What is your situation?"

"I had to leave an abusive situation and the past couple of days I've had to live in my truck."

"We have a room available. You can come in and fill out an intake form. As long as you pass the background check, we'll be able to give you a room tonight."

"A background check?"

"Don't worry, we run one on everyone. It's only to screen for felonies. Do you need directions?"

"No, I have your address. And thanks, Roberta."

Loretta hung up, feeling trapped. Her driver's license was in the custody of the Texas judicial system, and even if she had it, her outstanding warrants would be caught in a nanosecond. Jail was not the type of accommodations she had in mind.

Her next call was for damage control.

"Streeter, it's Loretta."

"I thought you'd never call."

"I need a connection for a new I. D."

"Well shit, Loretta, I'm in pharmaceuticals, not fake I. D.'s."

"But you know someone, right?"

"For a finder's fee…"

"That's fair. I'll catch you the next time I see you."

"No way."

"Come on Streeter! Have I ever let you down?"

"There's always a first time."

"You'll get your fucking money! You owe me, Streeter, and I need an I. D."

"I don't owe you jack."

"You do and you know it. Come on, all I need is a name."

There was a long stretch of silence on Streeter's end, but eventually he gave her an address and phone number. "Name's Jerome, but if you tell him I sent you, the pharmacy's closed. You got that?"

"Yeah, I got that. Thanks, Streeter."

"Whatever," Streeter said. The phone went dead.

Within an hour, Loretta was pulling up to a dilapidated Victorian. The place looked empty. There were no cars in the driveway and no lights reflected from the leaded glass windows. Her knock was answered within seconds.

The man standing at the threshold resembled a mutant Q-Tip. He was well over six feet tall and painfully thin with a thick head of curly white hair. His complexion was pasty gray which competed with a bulbous nose peppered with huge pores. But it was the coarse black nose hair poking out of his nostrils that Loretta found the most revolting.

"Come in. We don't need an audience."

Loretta took a last look around the neighborhood. There wasn't a light on anywhere; not next door and not across the street. Zip. Who the audience was that he was referring to was anyone's guess.

Entering the drafty parlor, Loretta was assaulted with the overpowering stench of dirty socks and body odor. Heavy brocade curtains sucked up every bit of light from the few lamps that were on. Brittle, dark paneling and a massive fireplace gave the place a spooky feeling. Loretta had no problem imagining the creaky Victorian sharing space with long-dead apparitions that rattled doors and slid down the ornate banister in the dead of night.

"I'm Loretta, the gal who just called."

"Don't waste my time by stating the obvious. Driver's licenses are $375. If you want a birth certificate, it'll cost you another $350. I call it my two-for-one special," he said, chuckling.

Loretta couldn't see the humor. If he was trying to grab business with a bargain bin approach, he'd need to work on his delivery. The driver's license would cost just about everything she had.

"A license is all I need."

"What state?"

Loretta calculated her choices. "Illinois."

"Wish people would be more creative. Age?"

"Thirty-four."

"They'd never buy it. You should shoot for somewhere in the forties."

"But I *am* thirty-four. I'm the one paying for the license. I'd like to use my real age."

"Whatever you say lady, but I'm warning you, nobody's gonna buy it."

Loretta was already sick of Q-Tip's rudeness, but she ignored his comment. "The first name has to be something close to mine…maybe Lori and the last name's got to be Walch."

"You don't want much, do you?"

"I'm having something delivered where I'm staying. The I.D. has to be close enough to my real name so it won't get sent back."

Loretta plunked down on an antique settee, uninvited. The velvet had worn off in places and musty-smelling horsehair stuffing was peeking through the worn areas. The place was suffocating.

"I need the I.D. tonight," she said.

"You came to the wrong place, then. What weight?"

"One-forty. What do you mean I came to the wrong place?"

"It takes time, that's all. You want to have a believable license? I can have it ready for you in the morning."

"This'll be used for a background check."

"I'll have you looking like you just stepped out of a nunnery. But, I'll need until 10:00 tomorrow morning."

Loretta pried herself from the hollow she'd made in the settee and walked towards the door, anxious to get away.

He let her get as far as the door before stopping her. "You're forgetting something."

"What do you mean?"

"I'm paid up front."

"I'll give you the money in the morning when the job's done."

"Not happening."

"What about half now and the rest when I pick up the license?"

"I don't do business with people who don't trust me."

"Trust you? You make fake I D's for fucks sake!"

"Take it, or leave it."

Loretta dug into her purse and counted out the money. She had exactly $86 left. Not enough for a motel and Streeter's going rate. Handing the bills over, she turned to go.

"You're not very bright, are you?"

"Do you always insult your customers after they pay you?"

"Just the stupid ones. I need to get your picture for the driver's license," he said, pointing to an empty corner of the room. "Stand over there. I'll be back in a minute."

He returned with a digital camera and snapped several photos. "That should do it. I'll see you tomorrow," he said.

God, she hoped so! Loretta thought as she left the Q-Tip to his ghosts.

*   *   *

The marked down blanket and pillow were placed in a Target bag.

"That'll be $12.72 please," the clerk requested.

Loretta paid and went out to the parking lot. It was ten minutes until closing. She contemplated sleeping there; the truck was a gas guzzler and she was down to half a tank. She was forced to re-think her plan when a security guard cruised past. They probably did spot checks throughout the night.

Driving around the vicinity, Loretta scoped out possibilities. Gas stations were too well lit and grocery stores weren't the best choice, either. It was when Loretta saw the Walmart sign that she made her decision. They were open twenty-four hours and the parking lot was fairly busy, even this late in the evening.

Loretta picked a spot far enough away from the building for quiet, but not so far that the truck would draw the attention of one of the rent-a-cops circling around. Settling in was difficult. The back seat was narrow and hard as concrete. Loretta shifted the pillow for maximum comfort and pulled the blanket over her head to block out the parking lot's floodlights. She was nearly asleep when a car door slammed shut followed by a couple's loud conversation. They'd taken their happy hour to Walmart.

By morning, Loretta had logged four hours sleep. She still had three and a half hours to kill and a spine that felt as if every vertebra had been fused together. She unfolded herself and gingerly got out of the truck to the frosty morning chill and the only entertainment available at such an undignified hour—the warm interior of Walmart.

*   *   *

When Q-Tip answered her knock, Loretta realized she'd been holding her breath. She'd given it better than even odds he'd be a no-show and $375 richer. His color looked worse in the daylight

The interior hadn't improved. A small crack between the heavy curtains highlighted dust motes that floated in the stale air and the smell, if anything, was worse. Loretta switched to breathing through her mouth.

"Here it is," Q-Tip said, handing Loretta her new driver's license.

Loretta glanced at the photo and winced. She looked terrible! Her scalp showed and the picture highlighted the breakouts on her face. She should've applied more cover-up, Loretta realized.

"This picture isn't very flattering," Loretta complained.

"Were you going for realistic, or fantasy?"

"You're an asshole!"

"Maybe. But I'm an honest asshole."

She looked back down at his work. Other than the disappointing photo, the license looked authentic.

*   *   *

Loretta felt relief when Roberta returned with a printout, smiling. "You're golden!"

"Boring might be a better description," Loretta said, smiling back.

"Why don't you get your things and I'll show you to your room."

Now was the sticky part. If it failed, then *she* failed. Tanya had been very specific about her needing a verifiable address.

225

"I've been working with a woman at that Lesbian Relief Fund on a business loan. Part of the requirement is that I supply an address and phone number. If I get a call or mail from them, it's important that I'm notified. If they haven't fixed their mistake, the mail might be sent to Loretta Walch."

"We strive to protect our guest's anonymity at New Beginnings. Giving out our phone number and address is against the rules."

"I wasn't aware of that. I already gave Tanya this contact information on the way over here. If they're not able to reach me, I'll lose my loan."

"We all have to make sacrifices now and then. I'm sorry, but I can't make an exception," Roberta said. Her mouth was set into a rigid, no-nonsense line of displeasure. Loretta backpedaled, trying to come up with something…anything that would get her to change her mind.

"Have you ever had a dream so big you never really expected to have it come true? Well, owning my own business is mine. I've worked all my life at an assembly plant for minimum wage. This is the first chance I've been given to better myself. It means everything to me!"

Roberta stared past Loretta, deep in thought. "Is this the only contact that has our information?"

"Yes, it is. I can assure you Tanya would never give out the information to anyone."

"Then we'll just keep this to ourselves."

"Thank you! You won't regret it!" Loretta said, which was the kiss of death for Roberta, but she wouldn't be finding that out for a while.

Loretta grabbed her things from the truck in record time. She was afraid to leave Roberta enough time to stew over her decision and change her mind.

The room Loretta was shown smelled of Pine Sol and was sparsely furnished. There were no pictures on the wall and the bed was covered with a simple white chenille bedspread. A plain nightstand was squeezed tight against the bed. The only other items in the room were a chrome lamp and an alarm clock that crowded the surface of the nightstand. Loretta sat her plastic bags on the bed. As far as she could tell there was nowhere else to put them and still be able to walk around the room.

"You'll find reading material in the recreation room as well as a phone for local calls. Breakfast is served at 7:30, lunch is at 12:00, and dinner is at 6:30. The residents are expected to share in the daily chores. You're required to put your name on the chore list no later than tomorrow." Roberta handed Loretta a pamphlet. "Please read the rules and regulations and sign the back sleeve to acknowledge that you will agree to them. Your stay is dependent on need. When you're able to afford a place of your own you're expected to inform us immediately so the next person on the waiting list can receive help. Actually, you were lucky. We're usually filled to the brim." Roberta turned to go, but seemed to change her mind midway and turned back to face Loretta. "How did you hear about us again?"

"A friend. Her husband used her for a punching bag and New Beginnings helped her get back on her feet. When she found out what I was going through, she gave me your information."

"That's odd. Usually our referrals come from social workers or the medical profession. As you are already aware, the women we help are asked not to give out our information."

"Kind of like an exclusive spa, right?" Loretta said, smiling.

Roberta gave her a sharp look. "No, kind of like a New Beginning. Are you sure you didn't call last night?"

"You already asked me that. I didn't call."

"Then you have a clone because the lady I spoke with on the phone sounded just like you."

"I appreciate your help, Roberta. I don't know what I would've done without it."

"You're welcome. Get some rest now. You look exhausted."

Loretta fell asleep mulling over the many ways she could screw up and give herself away. She'd need to be careful, very careful.

Chapter 28

Frank shoved the last bag into the back of the station wagon. "Brice is your sister ready?" he yelled towards the front door.

"She was until she spilled orange juice down her dress," Brice yelled back.

Frank returned to the house at a run, hoping to speed things up. Carrie and Susan were expecting them in twenty minutes. Even with the light Saturday traffic, the drive would take them forty minutes.

Britney was sitting in the hallway, bawling.

"She won't let me change her," Brice said.

"What's wrong, honey?"

Britney picked up the hem of her pink dress, while tears coursed down her cheeks, and covered her head with its ruffled skirt. Frank noticed her diaper needed to be changed.

"Daddy needs to put another dress on you, Britney," Frank said.

Britney pulled her dress back down and shook her head, crying harder.

"Don't you want to see the horse and go swimming?"

"Pink dess!"

"It's dirty, Britney. Tell you what. You can wear your blue one with the ruffles."

Her response was ear-splitting hysterics.

"She's tired, Dad," Brice said with authority.

"Grab her blue dress and a diaper, please, and then tell your brothers to get in the car. We're late!"

"Do you think there'll be any hot dogs left?" Brice asked over Britney's screams.

"There'll be plenty. Make sure the boys packed their swimsuits."

"I already did," Brice said.

Guilt grabbed hold of Frank when Brice handed him the diaper and clean dress. He'd promised him a childhood, but so far Brice had been stuck helping with his brothers and sister more than he should have.

Frank concentrated on getting Britney's soaked dress over her head. She squirmed at every attempt.

Temporarily giving up, he tried another tactic. "Britney, if you don't behave, you're going in time out!"

She stopped her wiggling, looking at Frank to judge his mood. Seeing the steel in his eyes, Britney went limp. Within minutes, they were buckled up for the long drive.

"I told you Britney was tired. She's already asleep," Brice pointed out just before they reached the freeway.

In their frantic dash, Frank hadn't noticed the quiet.

"Good. She'll be in a better mood when we get there."

"You should talk to Aunt Edith. I think she's giving her too many sweets."

"I will. In the meantime, let's concentrate on having fun. You boys get to go horseback riding and swimming."

"What kind of horse?" asked Brandon.

"It's called a Paint, like the ones the cowboys and Indians used to ride. His name is Cochise," answered Brice.

"Is he nice?" asked Mark.

"How should I know? If you're scared, you shouldn't ride him," Brice taunted.

"I wanna ride the horse!" Mark yelled, offended.

"That's enough boys. Everyone's going to get a chance to ride the horse. Carrie says Cochise is a gelding. He's gentle."

"What's a gelding?" Brice asked.

Frank cringed. He should have left that part out. "Never mind. Let's just enjoy the ride. Why don't you boys play eye-spy?"

The trip livened up as they ripped through the alphabet grabbed from signs, storefronts, and license plates. Frank took advantage of the lull and tried to come up with something for Carrie's birthday present that was only a few days away.

Maybe a diamond necklace, one that fit his budget, but nice enough to show her how he felt. The more he thought about it, the more convinced he was that a necklace would be the perfect gift. Decided, Frank enjoyed the rest of the long drive in relative peace.

"We're here! Boys, grab the bags from the back," Frank said, glancing at his watch. They were twenty-five minutes late.

Susan's home looked more like a one-story mansion than the ranch house she'd described. Both wings of the house were connected with a tall wrought iron fence and a heavy, ornate gate. Frank carried Britney who was still asleep and received a nod from a now familiar bodyguard standing to one side of the massive front door.

They were surrounded by lush plants that lent an atrium feel to the open courtyard. Some of the foliage had been allowed to take root in the soil that skirted large slabs of flagstone while others were contained in colorful ceramic pots of varying sizes. A mosaic waterfall mounted against the wall released a cool mist, which woke Britney and she began to squirm to be put down.

"There you are!" exclaimed Carrie as she opened the door to greet them. She was wearing jeans and a long sleeved peach-colored sweater cut low enough to display a bit of cleavage. Frank had to force himself not to stare.

"I'm sorry we're late. Britney had a mishap."

"I'm just glad you're here," Carrie said, offering him a warm smile.

She leaned at the waist to be nearer the boys. "If you hurry through the back," she said, pointing to a bank of French doors on the opposite end of the cavernous living room, "you can catch up with the other kids. They're headed to the stable."

The boys took off, racing through the empty room and their footfalls echoed off the orphaned walls.

"That only leaves us adults and one little girl," Carrie continued, smiling at Britney. "What a beautiful dress! Did you pick this out all by yourself?"

Britney held out her arms and Carrie grabbed her up, putting her face into Britney's curls and breathed deep. Frank felt a lump form in his throat. This was something only a mother would do, to breathe in the scent of a child they loved. It was both primal and poignant.

"You smell wonderful. And I love these ruffles!" She looked to Frank with a question. "Did you bring her sippy cup?"

"Of course, and her swimsuit, diapers, clean-ups, and her favorite teddy."

"Let's get you some apple juice," Carrie said to Brittney while she adjusted her on her hip and led the way into the kitchen.

Frank took one more glance at the living room. Susan's beat-up couch and coffee table were dwarfed by the huge space. Her furnishings might as well have been doll furniture on loan from Madison.

"No worries. Susan's asked me to go furniture shopping with her. She wants this place to look inviting," Carrie said, reading Frank's mind.

"How's that possible? Susan could host a football game in there."

"We're thinking about large, overstuffed couches with plenty of tables and plants. It'll need paintings for the walls and a couple of oversized rugs to warm up the tile floors."

The kitchen was a slightly scaled-down version of the living room, only with miles of glass-fronted cupboards. Frank walked over to an alcove that was finished with burnished adobe on the exterior and weathered, soot stained brickwork on the interior.

"What's this?"

"It's a brick pizza oven."

"Of course, who could imagine having a kitchen without one?"

Carrie laughed and pointed to something large and metal that was recessed into the wall.

"And that would be?"

"A cappuccino maker. Would you like one?" Carrie asked.

"I'd like something cold, if you have it."

Carrie walked to a sub-zero refrigerator and opened the door. "Let's see. There's beer, lemonade, Pepsi or apple juice."

"Lemonade's fine. A beer would've been my first choice, but I have to drive home."

"That's negotiable, actually. The kids and I are staying over. Susan plans to invite you and the kids."

"Are there enough beds?"

"The bedrooms are furnished. It was the first thing Susan did."

"Change that to a beer, then," Frank said, taking Carrie in his arms for an embrace. "I have missed you these past few days."

"I've missed you, too," Carrie said.

Britney's sippy cup was filled with apple juice and Frank was handed a cold bottle of Coors before they meandered through a dining room that would've made Trump proud and out through adjoining French doors. Frank reached the flagstone patio and stopped short.

"Impressive, isn't it?" Carrie asked.

"I don't think that's a big enough word," Frank said. "That's an Olympic-sized swimming pool, isn't it?"

"It sure is, plus the Jacuzzi," Carrie replied.

Frank continued taking in their surroundings. Further, beyond a wooden fence that traversed the property, stood out-buildings and the stable. Part of the wooded area had been cleared for an outdoor riding rink while the rest was left to nature.

"Hi Frank! Come on over and get comfortable," Susan called.

She was sitting at a glass-topped table with seemingly not a care in the world. And why not, Frank asked himself. Her troubles had evaporated with the reading of a matron's will—a matron who'd smelled a rat.

Frank took Britney from Carrie's arms and they settled in.

"This place is incredible," he said.

"Thank you. But, no matter how much time goes by, I'll probably never get used to it. Apartment living has always been my comfort zone."

"Don't underrate yourself. You and the boys needed protection and a safe place to live. Your ex's grandmother just saw the need and filled it. Bottom line, there's no price tag that can be placed on happiness and security," Frank said with conviction, looking to Carrie.

Susan flashed a Cheshire smile. "It's nice to see the two of you so in love."

The comment was unexpected and Frank was left floundering over how to respond when Mark offered a distraction by tearing through the gate leading to the patio.

"Dad! Come here. You need to see the horse!"

"We'll both go," Carrie said, getting up. "I'd like to give you a tour of the stables."

"Leave Britney with me," Susan said. "We'll hang out and dip our feet in the pool."

Their walk was done in silence. There was so much Frank wanted to say, but the words refused to come. Entering the stable, they were greeted by Brandon who was currying Cochise. The horse was dealing with the attention by standing stock-still, staring at the opposite wall with his tail swishing every now and then. Frank wasn't certain whether or not it was a warning.

"Brandon, why don't you give Cochise some time to rest?"

"But Dad, all I'm doing is brushing his coat. Sam says he likes it."

"He'll be okay. He's used to kids," Carrie whispered in Frank's ear.

"Well, keep a look-out. If his ears go down, that means he's had enough."

Carrie gave Frank a guided tour of the stable. It was set up with eight stalls, including one that was much larger that was meant for foaling mares. A wood-sided tack room held Cochise' saddle, bit, reins and other riding gear.

"Susan's been thinking about boarding horses if the situation with her ex ever gets under control," Carrie whispered once they were away from earshot. "She's discovered she likes working with horses. It keeps her busy while the boys are in school."

"Mom, can I ride Cochise?" Sam asked.

"You can after dinner. You kids need to be back at the house in 30 minutes for hot dogs."

"But a half-hour's enough time for a couple of us to ride him," Sam disagreed.

"And who's going to get the saddle and the bit on him? You can ride him after dinner. Have fun kids, and we'll see you in 30 minutes." Carrie's voice was pleasant, but her determination was unmistakable.

On the way back, Frank noticed another guard patrolling the back of the property.

"Has Susan's ex been after her again?"

"Not so far. Why do you ask?"

"Because I just noticed a second bodyguard."

"That would be because given the size of the house and property, the agency felt she needed two guards."

"So there's something to be said for small spaces," Frank said hopefully.

"We're low maintenance compared to this."

"Does that bother you?" Frank asked.

"Does what bother me?"

"Take your pick: that you have to work while Susan is able to relax, that you rent while she lives in a mansion, or that you have to struggle to put food on the table."

"That's easy. I don't begrudge Susan a thing. I honestly like my life, especially since we met. I'm happy! No amount of money could buy that."

Frank took hold of her hand to stop their progress. He needed to be able to look in her eyes when he told her how he felt.

"What Susan said earlier is true. I love you, Carrie," Frank said, drawing her into his arms. He gave her a long, lingering kiss, not caring if the whole world saw them.

Carrie returned his kiss without hesitation. "I thought you'd never say the words. I love you too, Frank."

"I've loved you from day one. There isn't a moment I'm not thinking about you. When we're apart, all I want is to be near you. I love it when we're all together, the kids and the dinners and the conversation. Even having to sit through another Disney movie is something I look forward to. And now that I've met you, I can't imagine life without you. Would you marry me, Carrie?"

As soon as Frank said the words, he wished he could take them back. It was too soon. He was rushing her.

Carrie's eyes filled with tears. "Yes, I'll be your wife!"

With her words, Frank felt he had been handed a gift. They would build their life together and leave the past behind where it belonged. "Carrie, I want to make you happy. I'm going to turn things around and start working on a few of those computer programs I talked to you about. If I'm successful, you'll be able to stay at home with the kids. Would that make you happy?"

"I'm already happy. It doesn't matter to me whether I work or not. Just promise me one thing."

"What's that?"

"I want us to have a baby to blend our family. Boy or girl, I don't care."

"Are you sure seven kids won't make you crazy?"

"*Twenty* kids wouldn't make me crazy."

"Somehow, I believe that. We'll have as many as you want."

"Oh, one will do!" Carrie said, laughing through her tears.

They strolled back to the house, hand in hand to tell Susan the news.

"I bought a bottle of champagne to toast the new house with, but this is way better!" she exclaimed.

The low-key celebration went on as the kids rode the horse and later took turns doing cannonballs into the heated pool. By the time they all turned in, Frank was exhausted and happier than he'd ever been. The only way the day could've been better would be if Carrie was lying in his arms.

* * *

Frank woke to shouts just past his bedroom window. He still hadn't come fully awake when a bullet struck the window and showered the bed with shards of glass. Its final trajectory embedded into the wall in a cloud of drywall dust. Frank threw off the covers and jumped out of bed on rubbery legs while his heart tried to find a way through his chest.

"Halt!" Frank heard a man's voice command. Frank made it past the glass that peppered the carpet when a second bullet narrowly missed him and slammed into the mirrored closet door. It was still cascading slivers of mirror when he made it through the door.

Carrie had already run to the hallway as Frank sprinted towards the room where the boys and Britney were sleeping. "Get Sam and Madison into the hallway!" Frank yelled to Carrie.

While he ran, Frank comforted himself with the thought that the only gunfire he'd heard had been accounted for: two bullets, both slamming into his room. The kids would be unharmed. They had to be. Still, when he turned the doorknob on their door, he felt physically ill with worry. Frank took in the scene in seconds. Brice was holding Britney in his arms. She wasn't fully awake and her head lay against his shoulder. With his arms full, he was shaking the bed with his foot, trying to wake up Brandon and Mark.

"Brice, take Britney into the hall and stay with Carrie. I'll get the boys."

Frank threw back their covers and grabbed each of the boys in his arms.

"What's wrong, Dad?" Mark asked, still half asleep.

"We'll talk about it later," Frank said, still confused over who had transformed his window and the closet door into lethal graffiti. Just as important was who had screamed the command to 'halt'. The man's voice had sounded official, but he had no way to be sure.

Now that he knew Carrie and the kids were unhurt, Frank allowed himself to relax long enough to start piecing together what had just happened. When the second bullet took out the closet mirror, he had heard the sound of breaking twigs and a grown of pain. If someone had been hurt, and that someone wasn't Susan's ex as he suspected, the groan could have come from one of the bodyguards.

Frank was still thinking over the implications when he caught up with Carrie who was keeping herd on the kids. Her expression was one of complete terror. Before he could go to her, Susan tore out of her son's bedroom and into the hallway, both of her sons in tow.

"Come on! We need to get downstairs to the wine cellar!" Susan yelled.

Frank delivered Britney into Carrie's arms and scooped up Madison. They followed Susan's head-long dash down the stairs with the older kids following behind. At the bottom of the stairs, Susan turned to the right and continued at a run until they came to a narrow door where she stopped and hurled the door open.

"Hurry up!" she shouted, and hurried the children through. Frank and Madison were the last to enter. Susan slammed the heavy door behind them and threw the deadbolt. Hands shaking, she slid a thick metal plate through brackets attached to either side of the frame.

Susan gave the adults a look of relief. "This was designed as a fall-out shelter by the previous owners. The walls are lined with lead and no one, and I mean no one, will be able to get past this door," Susan said.

"Tell me what happened," Susan continued, looking to Frank, then Carrie.

Frank hesitated. The kids were frightened as it was. Talk of gunfire, exploding glass and the sounds of someone being wounded wasn't the answer. He motioned the women to the far corner of the cellar.

He kept his voice low. "I don't know for sure. I was woken to the sounds of shouts and gunfire, then the bedroom window exploded. Another bullet took out the closet door. I heard someone shout and crash into the bushes. I didn't stick around after that."

"It's David. It *has* to be him," Susan whispered in a shaky voice.

"Mom, its cold in here," complained Michael, Susan's youngest.

"Honey, we need to stay here until the bodyguards tell us it's safe."

"It's Dad, isn't it?" Michael said, and started to cry.

Susan turned to Carrie with a look of pure anguish etched across her face. She went to her son and got down on her knees. Putting her arms around Michael she drew him close.

"Remember when Mommy hired the bodyguards? I did that so we would be safe. Daddy can't hurt us anymore," Susan said.

"Then why are we down here if we're safe?" Michael asked.

"Because that's what the bodyguards and I decided we'd do if anything happened. We agreed that if your daddy or anyone else ever came over without permission, we'd come here where it's safe until the bodyguards came to get us."

"But he could have killed them and then no one can help us," Michael said, pressing his face into Susan's shoulder and sobbed harder.

She stroked his back and waited for him to calm down. His sobs turned into shuddering breaths. Moving back, she placed her hands on his shoulders and looked him in the eye, making sure she had his attention.

"Sometimes people lose their way and get confused over what's good and what's bad. That's what happened to your daddy. He forgot how to be good and he needs help. Those men are here to help us *and* your daddy. He can't hurt them because they know how to protect themselves."

"Like the army guys on TV?"

"Yes, just like the army guys."

"Or they could be angels," Madison said hopefully.

"To me, they are. So, I suppose that makes them a little bit of both: army guys who will protect us and angels who will protect us, too. That makes us doubly safe!" Susan exclaimed.

"Angels are the best though, because God sends them and they can't get hurt, ever! You could even shoot them. It would go right through them, huh Mom?" Madison insisted.

"Yes, that's true, honey. Nothing can hurt them," Carrie agreed.

Frank was relieved and saddened. Now that the initial shock had passed, the kids appeared to be coping. That on its own was a sad testament to the life their children had come to expect.

"Let's sit close together. If we do that, we'll stay warmer," Frank said.

One by one, they got down on the floor to huddle together. Their wait was uncomfortably long and Frank's mind kept travelling to the worst case scenario.

A half-hour passed before they heard tapping against the door. Frank shook his head and Susan and Carrie nodded their understanding. If it was one of the bodyguards, they'd know to announce themselves.

"It's Matt Jacob," said a man's voice. To Frank's relief, it was the same baritone he'd heard yell "halt" past his bedroom window.

Susan was on her feet in seconds. She twisted the bolt open and slid the metal plate away from its holders.

"What's happened?"

"You'll want to settle the kids down first so we can talk in private," he said.

"Is it safe?" Susan asked.

"Very, Ma'am."

Susan looked from Carrie to Frank in shock. *Very* could have many connotations, not all of them good.

* * *

"We'll be back in a few minutes. The rules are no one leaves this room until the movie is over," Carrie instructed.

A hand shot up. "I have to go to the bathroom," Mark said.

"There's a bathroom right there," Carrie said, pointing to a closed door in the corner of Susan's oversized bedroom.

Frank could see a look of indecision on Carrie's face and he understood. Susan needed her for moral support, but being separated from the kids after what they had just been through was unbearable.

"I'll stay with them," Frank offered.

Carrie shook her head. "Thank you, but Susan needs both of us. Okay kids, now remember, you're to stay here until we get back...no exceptions."

Frank and Carrie entered the living room together to the sound of Susan's sobs.

"He's dead. The stupid bastard had a gun! How will I ever tell the boys?" she said between jagged intakes of breath.

Carrie went to comfort her. "There's no argument this will be hard on them, Susan. On the other hand, if you hadn't had protection, he would've killed you. I'm sorry to have to say this, but he was pure evil. He brought this on himself. With time your boys will understand that. In the meantime, I'll be here for you and so will Frank. You won't have to go through this alone."

Frank looked to the guard who had freed them only minutes ago.

"He discharged his weapon. We weren't given a choice. The police have been called. They'll be here soon," he said.

Frank wondered how he'd feel if the tables were turned and this was Loretta who had been shot and killed. The truth was he honestly didn't know.

Chapter 29

Meth. It was the last thing on her list of to-do's for the day, but for Loretta it had become an obsession. She couldn't function without it. Now that she'd sworn off ambulance heists, she'd need to sell the truck or suffer withdrawals.

She felt hungry, which was a nuisance. Dumping loose change from the bottom of her purse onto the passenger's seat, she counted $2.40. It was enough for two junior burgers at McDonald's. She watched the truck suck the gas gauge closer to empty while she idled in the snarl at the drive-up window. The chop-shop had better be close or she was going to have to borrow gas money from Streeter.

Streeter was an hour late by the time she took the last bite of rubbery cheeseburger. That evening her chore at New Beginnings was vacuuming, which was good. It didn't come with an exact timeline and Roberta wouldn't have an excuse to get on her ass until 9:00 PM, when the rules posted on just about every available wall requested quiet time. She had already been late for her daily chores twice, which Roberta seemed to relish pointing out at every opportunity.

A rapping on the window made Loretta jump. Streeter's face was pressed to the window.

"You scared the shit outta me!"

"Let's go. I've got a schedule to keep," Streeter said with a straight face.

"*You've* got a schedule? That's rich! I've been waiting over an hour."

"Are you going to bitch, or are you going to drive?" Streeter said.

"Don't go all Dr. Laura on me. You're not bitchy enough!"

The rest of the drive was spent listening to a hard rock station Streeter selected. They arrived at a broken down garage on the outskirts of town. Bare blackberry bushes appeared to be the only thing holding up the south wall.

"Let me do the talking," Streeter said.

"Why?"

"Because you'll get hoovered…right up the 'ol poop-shoot."

"I didn't think you cared."

Streeter led the way to a door whose varnish had long since bubbled to the texture of alligator scales. His knock was answered by a short, pudgy guy in overalls.

"You Streeter?"

Instead of answering, Streeter pointed to where the Dodge Ram sat amongst the day's mud puddles.

"That's it."

The man held out his hand. "Give me the keys."

Streeter nodded and Loretta reluctantly handed them over.

The guy had to hoist himself into the cab to start the engine, which struck Loretta as funny. She had to bite her tongue to keep from laughing. Continuing to watch him inspect the truck, she decided he deserved the nickname of Shorty.

"Why'd I just give him the keys?" she demanded of Streeter.

"Are you dense? He's got to check the gauges, make sure it's running okay."

"When do I get to see the trade-in?" she demanded.

"When he's done checking out the truck," Streeter said in exasperation.

They stood in the waning light and watched as Shorty hopped out and got down on all fours to have a look at the undercarriage.

He nodded to Streeter. "It'll do."

As far as Loretta could tell, the deal was done in code. A few grunts…silence, more grunts and then, finally, a word or two. Boring shit!

"So, you wanna check out trade-ins?"

"Yeah," was Streeter's contribution.

They followed Shorty out back. Parked amongst the brush and tall grass were half a dozen pieces of crap.

"They're legit; registration, plates…mostly from customers who couldn't pay their repair bill."

"Lovely," Loretta blurted, to which she received a dirty look from Shorty and a poke in the ribs from Streeter.

"Shut the fuck up," Streeter whispered in her ear.

Loretta bristled. She'd only said the truth. There wasn't a car there that looked like it would make it to the end of the block.

"You wanna do business or not?" Shorty snipped.

Streeter pointed to a Vega on blocks. "What about that one?"

"No engine. I could have it ready by the end of the week."

To keep the peace, Loretta just shook her head no.

"What do you have that could go out today?" Streeter asked.

Shorty walked over to a Chevy Nova, circa 1980. "This one and that Falcon over there," he said, pointing to a white station wagon that was rusted beyond recognition. Loretta couldn't have guessed its age, but then, she didn't care. Driving a piece of crap like that, she might as well spray paint her name and contact information on the windshield in day glow orange. *No way* would it blend.

Having learned her lesson, Loretta nodded to the Nova with a sinking feeling. She'd be lucky if it had a working heater. She leaned into Streeter and whispered, "Mileage and tires. Ask him."

"How're the tires and what's the mileage?" Streeter complied.

"Tires are okay, and the tabs are current. Plus, I'll throw in a one-month warranty."

Warranty? Did chop-shops actually give a warranty? Loretta wondered.

"Mileage," she reminded Streeter.

"Could you check the odometer?"

"Why? It's a beater! It'll get you around, barely, 'till you switch it out. At least it's legal," Shorty said.

Loretta had to admit, Shorty had a point.

"What kind of cash for the switch?" Streeter asked.

"You never said noth'n 'bout cash. The truck's hot. There isn't much to work with."

"Don't fuck with me. There's plenty of room for negotiation. You're getting a new truck with 10,000 miles on it in exchange for a piece of shit. What kind of cash are you willing to throw in?"

Silence reined as Shorty rubbed his balding scalp. It looked like it had taken direct hits from dozens of oil changes. *He certainly hadn't been blessed in the looks department*, Loretta thought, as she continued her scrutiny while the men played their control games.

"I don't know…how 'bout $500?"

"How 'bout two grand?"

"Don't bust my nuts! I'll get *maybe* two grand total outta the whole deal."

"Then let's split it down the middle, one thousand."

Shorty walked out through the side gate to have another look at the truck. He didn't say anything, just stood there.

Shorty hoisted himself back into the cab and started the engine, checking the dials. He did a combination jump-slide out of the cab and they didn't see the top of his head again until he'd made it around to the other side.

"How 'bout $750?"

"It's worth a grand," Streeter said, sticking to his numbers.

"I don't like getting strong-armed."

"And I don't like getting fucked by short, fat, bald guys."

And to think I got been reamed over saying lovely! Loretta thought.

"I'll be right back," Shorty said. They watched him disappear into the garage at as brisk a pace as possible on his abbreviated legs.

"That went well, right?" Loretta asked.

"Better than I expected. The guy must have a thing for muscle trucks."

"Do you think the Nova will make it for a while?"

"Who knows? Thing is, you've got no future with a hot truck, ambulance heists or not."

Shorty returned with a wad of cash and a set of keys held together by a piece of twisted wire. Walking to Streeter, he held out the roll. "Count it."

Streeter flipped through the bills and nodded to Loretta. "It's all there."

"What about the warranty?" Loretta asked, figuring it was okay to talk since the deal was done.

"Lady, you'll just have to trust me."

"Trust you? Why should I trust..."

"Never mind her. She's got commitment issues," Streeter interrupted-ed.

"Well, it's insulting. I've been doing business for decades and I've never screwed nobody!"

I've never screwed nobody! Ha! What'd he call buying hot cars and selling them on the black market? If that wasn't bullshit...

"I think..." she began.

"Shut up! We'll get your meds as soon as we're back on the road," Streeter interrupted. Looking to Shorty, he winked. "Bipolar."

"I knew it! I knew there was something wrong with that bitch!"

Loretta gave no warning as she tore after Shorty. Thinking fast, Streeter shot out his leg. She barely had time to throw her hands out to cushion her fall. Her right wrist took the brunt of the impact. She rolled over grabbing it and went off.

"You pig fucker! You dirty son of a whore! What'd you do that for?"

As he bent over to hoist her from the grease-splattered dirt, Streeter hissed in her ear. "You want the money? If you do, you'd better shut up!"

"I don't like you lady!" Shorty barked.

"There's nothing *to* like. She's a pain in the ass, especially when she's not on her meds," Streeter said, and took Loretta by the arm, her bad arm, and shoved her towards the backfield and her new crap-mobile.

Her wrist was smarting something awful and Loretta was beginning to wonder if it was broken. How was she going to get the vacuuming done? She needed a roof over her head and Roberta, that bitch, was already looking for a reason to throw her out on the street.

"I think it's broken," Loretta complained to Streeter.

"It isn't broken. It's just scraped up a little."

"Then what do you call this?" Loretta shouted as she stuck her swollen wrist inches from Streeter's face.

"Anyone ever tell you you're a hypochondriac?" Streeter said.

He was already behind the wheel of the Nova and the blast from its missing tailpipe drowned out her retort.

"How am I going to drive this? I'll get stopped for sure!" she yelled over the horrendous noise. Blue smoke continued to rise in a dark cloud, making her cough.

"I'll be right back," Streeter announced, hustling towards the side door of the garage.

Loretta had another look at her wrist. She twisted it to the left, then the right. It hurt, but at least she could move it. It was probably just a sprain, but the swelling was getting worse by the minute.

"He'll have a muffler on it by tomorrow," Streeter informed Loretta as he strolled back to the car.

"How are we supposed to get home?"

"I called a taxi."

"Why would you do that without asking me?"

"Easy. I got business."

"Then, we're splitting the cost."

"Fine by me."

"By the way, asshole. I want my money," Loretta said, holding out her hand.

She shoved the wad he handed her into her pants pocket with her good hand and then had another look at her wrist. It was turning blue at the joint. "We'll need to stop at the drugstore. I need a wrist thing."

"You're still on that?"

"Yes, I'm still on that! It hurts like hell."

"Not as bad as looking at you. You need to drop the meth."

"Is that the advice you give to all your customers?"

"No. Just the ones going bald with a face that resembles pizza."

"I didn't ask for your opinion, Streeter."

"I'm giving it anyway. I almost like you. *Almost.* It's time you thought about unlatching from the addiction tit."

"Maybe later."

Their taxi pulled up and conversation ceased. When they reached Streeter's drop-off at McDonald's, Loretta held out her good hand for his half of the cab fare, which he counted out to the penny.

"Wait here a sec," she said to the cabbie.

"It's your dime, lady," he answered, turning the radio up and leaning back for maximum comfort.

"I need a bag," she whispered as soon as she caught up with Streeter.

"I thought we talked about that."

"You talked, I listened."

"I'm not gonna whip out a bag in front of the frigging cabbie!" Streeter whispered.

"Then let's go around the corner."

"The meter's running," the cabbie yelled as they disappeared from view.

They started negotiations behind the dumpster. Loretta had to control herself from gagging from the stench.

"Give me one 8-Ball. I'll cut back a little."

"You need to stop. You're killing yourself."

"Why the concern? I mean, you do this all day long!"

"Yeah, I do. I meant it when I said I almost liked you. I'd rather not watch your hair fall out or your face turn into something from a horror show."

After a heated debate Loretta was holding a bag and Streeter was gone, leaving her to wonder if there wasn't some sick, demented friendship brewing.

* * *

Loretta was wearing the brace she'd purchased on the way to New Beginnings, propelling the vacuum cleaner with her left hand. Her right was now swollen to double its size.

"Can you get your kid under control?" she yelled as a toddler made a third pass down the hallway, blocking her progress. He was around two Loretta guessed and hyper as hell.

"He's just playing," the mother bleated defensively past her partially open door.

This called for diplomacy, Loretta realized, something she had never warmed to. "I didn't mean to be rude. It's just that I twisted my wrist today and I'd like to get the vacuuming done before I fall on my face."

The toddler's mom stuck her head out from the doorway to confirm, and then advanced to where Loretta was doing the push-pull with clumsy inefficiency. Looking down at the bruised, immobile wrist, she clucked, "You need to get some ice on that."

"Tell me about it! I'm going to as soon as I'm finished."

"I'll finish it for you. How much do you have left to do?"

"The rest of this hallway and the rec-room."

"Piece of cake!"

"Thanks," was all Loretta got out before the toddler whizzed past them, now free of his diaper. "Who'll watch him?" Loretta yelled over the noise of the vacuum cleaner.

"You of course! His diapers are in the top dresser drawer," she called back as she showcased her vacuuming acumen. It was impressive. Loretta followed the pint-sized streaker into the cramped bedroom and was soon asking herself if she'd made a good bargain when the little terror rushed at her, cushioning his landing against her damaged wrist. She let out a yelp of pain and collapsed to the floor. To the toddler, Loretta's fall represented a fun opportunity and he grabbed a wooden pull toy and crashed it over her head.

Loretta was left to wonder if he could be the spawn of the devil in cherub's garb. Maybe they made little zip-up suits to disguise the ugly horns and hooves.

"Knock it off! Get the hell away from me, you little heathen!"

Unfortunately those were the words Roberta heard while she stood, statuesque, in the doorway with her arms folded officially around her midriff. Loretta remained clueless to her audience when she received a smack to the side of her face with a nursery rhyme book. She grabbed the naked doppelganger and positioned him over her lap, ready to administer a little tough love when the sound of Roberta clearing her throat stopped her momentum and she looked up.

"Just what do you think you're doing?" Roberta demanded.

Loretta considered answering her question honestly, that she was getting ready to have a little house-warming party with his backside, but stopped herself.

"A diaper change. I was about to change this little guy's diapers."

"Don't lie to me! You were getting ready to spank him. I saw it with my own eyes."

"That's not what you saw at all. I'd never spank someone else's kid," Loretta argued.

"You are a liar! Where is his mother? Poor little angel…"

"His mother's vacuuming."

"So this is how you repay her for doing your job? Spanking her son?"

"I wasn't spanking him. I was laying him down to put a diaper on him."

"You make me sick. Get your things together and get out, or I swear I'll call the police myself."

Loretta's initial response was to tell Roberta what she thought of her. She'd start with her stupid wig. It looked like a parody of an old *Dynasty* re-run—platinum and winged. Next, she'd move on to her orthopedic shoes that laced up the middle. With luck, there'd be time to discuss how everybody gossiped behind her back. She was hated by nearly everyone at the shelter, including the volunteers. But she couldn't say any of those things. If she did, she'd draw the police card that would take her directly to jail.

Loretta rose and handed the doppelganger to Roberta and the maven of New Beginnings was amply rewarded when he let loose down her flowered silk dress. The spray soaked her right side and as she moved him out of range, the left got preferential treatment.

Judging by the look on Roberta's face, Loretta figured it was time for her to gather her things. Marching to her room, she didn't try to hide the smile on her face. By tomorrow, Roberta's rules would include *No pissing on the help.*

The dresser contents were the first to get dumped into a plastic garbage bag. The toiletries were swiped from the top of the dresser into another. Loretta was finished in minutes.

The rec-room was empty except for the unattended vacuum cleaner. She grabbed the communal phone and dialed Streeter's number.

Loretta got right to the point. "Can I spend the night?"

"I said I almost liked you. I didn't mean I wanted to poke you."

Loretta sighed. "I know that! Don't you think I know that? I just need a place to crash for the night."

"I don't know. My girl's possessive. She might get jealous."

"Jealous? We're talking about me Streeter, the gal who's going bald and, as you so kindly put it, has a face that resembles something from a horror show."

"True."

"So, can I stay?"

"One night. But that's all."

"Give me your address."

"I don't do addresses over the phone. Go to McDonald's. I'll meet you within an hour."

"Thanks."

"Whatever!"

Again, the dial tone. Had he ever considered saying goodbye?

She called a cab and waited outside in the slanting rain the weatherman had forgotten to mention. Fuck!

Streeter was on time, which was so unusual it put a smile on Loretta's face.

"What happened?" he asked.

"Life. Life happened and I was just standing in the fucking way. How far's your place?"

"About a mile or so."

Almost immediately Loretta's damaged wrist began throbbing like a tom-tom, spelling out flashes of pain. It felt like hours before Streeter halted, motioning Loretta to follow him along a pathway.

"But this is an old folk's home," Loretta said.

"So?"

"You're not old…"

"I get free rent in exchange for caretaking the grounds. Follow me. My place is out back."

He led the way to what appeared to be an old carriage house. It had a slate roof and mullioned, leaded glass windows.

"This looks like something Disney threw up," Loretta said.

"So," Streeter said defensively.

"So, I can't picture you here."

"Well, neither can I."

The interior was interesting. At some point straw had been added to the plaster walls which had been whitewashed. Loretta supposed most would consider it quaint.

The windows and doorways were arched and on the fireplace wall were built-in bookshelves. Most surprising to Loretta was how clean the place was; no dirty socks or leather motorcycle jackets thrown anywhere. As she looked closer, she took dust off the list as well.

The place was decorated in Caribbean colors, mostly lime greens and turquoise. A collection of green-ware was displayed on top of the bookshelves to either side of the fireplace.

"Do you really collect glassware?" Loretta asked in surprise.

"Sometimes. They were left to me when my mom died. I just add to it whenever I stumble on a piece I like."

"What else don't I know about you?"

"For starters, I don't like answering questions about my personal life."

"Point taken. Sorry I asked."

He disappeared through an archway that Loretta assumed led to the kitchen. The sound of clanging was followed by running water.

"Do you want a roast beef sandwich?" Streeter yelled around the corner.

The meth had taken care of Loretta's appetite, but she didn't want to be rude. "I'll take half a sandwich, if that's all right."

"What would you like on your sandwich? Mayo, horseradish, lettuce…"

"All the above, thanks."

"Do you want root beer or orange juice to drink?"

"I'd love something with alcohol if you have it."

"I don't drink, so you're out of luck."

"I'll take a root beer."

Within minutes, Loretta was balancing a plate on her knee and complaining about Roberta to Streeter.

"She's like this mongo-bitch. She micro manages everybody."

"Some folks are like that," Streeter said, giving Loretta a meaningful look.

"Are you comparing me to her?"

"Probably. Until this afternoon, I've never seen you break a smile. You're all the time running around, grabbing onto the negative."

"Do pushers usually get a smile?" Loretta asked, genuinely curious.

"Yeah, once in a while."

"How odd."

"Why does it seem odd to you?" Streeter asked.

"Addicts don't seem like happy people is all."

"Some are, some aren't. You're one of the aren'ts. Why is that?"

Loretta was speechless. No one had ever asked her that question. It may have occurred to Frank when she was teaching him his lessons, but he'd never asked.

"I had a bad childhood is all."

"Bad as in I didn't get enough attention, or bad as in I got the shit beat out of me?"

"Bad as in I got to be a stand-in for my mother, including what she refused to do with my dad."

"How'd you handle it?"

"Apparently not great! You didn't cross my dad. If you did, you got the wrong end of a belt, unless he'd been drinking. Then, it was worse."

"What about the rest of the kids? You had brothers and sisters, right?"

"Six. There were six of us, one brother, four sisters."

"Did he treat them the same way?"

"The beatings, yes. I never asked my sisters about the other. I never caught him in the act with any of the rest. But they knew what he did to me most nights. We shared a room for shit's sake. The crying and the begging for him to stop...I remember his breath the most. It smelled like stale cigarettes and alcohol. Then one month, I missed my period. They drove me to a place in Des Plains and I stayed there 'till the baby came. It was a boy. I'd heard stories about what happened to babies like him. They were born deformed, maybe even crazy. He looked okay to me, but they wrapped him in a blanket and whisked him out of the room like it never happened. The other girls told me it's what they did, so we weren't tempted to keep them. What they didn't know is I didn't want to see him. I hated every minute it was growing inside of me, pushing out my belly like some disgusting growth. That's all it was to me, a disgusting growth.

"I never went back home and I haven't spoken to my brother or sisters since. Hell, I wouldn't even know how to find them. But it's a sure bet they left as soon as they could."

Streeter shook his head in sympathy while Loretta wiped away the first honest tears she'd shed in decades.

"That's not right. Your old man should have been brought up on charges."

"He'd have lied anyway, and my brother and sisters would have been too afraid to testify against him."

"Where was your mother during all of this?"

"Good question, excellent question as a matter of fact. She was just doing her bit for survival, I suppose. Most days, she'd sit on the couch, fixating at the wall. I was the eldest, which meant I did the cooking and the cleaning and took care of the kids.

"He beat her too. She'd just curl up in a ball and take it. My first memories of her were different, though. I can remember her trying to get her licks in a few times, but eventually, she gave up…just laid there and took her beatings, like a cowering dog."

"What about when you got pregnant? Did she ever talk to you about it?" Streeter asked.

"Nothing was ever said. It was like it never happened. I don't think my brother or sisters ever knew. I sure didn't tell them. I was too ashamed, like it was my fault, like I went begging for it!"

"But you didn't."

"No, I didn't." Loretta wiped her eyes as the tears ran down her cheeks.

"Is that why you got fat?"

"What?"

"Is that why you got fat?" he repeated.

"What's one thing got to do with the other?"

"Lots, actually. If you're fat, then nobody's going to want you."

Loretta looked Streeter's way with a blank stare on her face, realizing she had never thought about it that way.

Streeter continued, "It could be why you went for the other side."

"Other side?"

"You know…Jay. It might be why you hooked up with Jay."

"Who told you about Jay?" she asked in alarm.

"She called the night you tied her up with the phone cord. She was looking for her car. Man, was she pissed!" Streeter started to chuckle, which turned into full-blown laughter.

"Why didn't you say anything to me?" Loretta asked.

"Say what? Excuse me, but I can't do business with a woman who ties people up with phone cords and steals their cars and camping shit."

"I don't know. Maybe."

"Jay was okay, but I've got to say, I thought it was kind of humorous in a demented sort of way."

Loretta mulled that over. Streeter wasn't passing judgment. But even so she felt like some kind of experiment; one that pitted his ability to shrinker-size himself against her screwed up life. It dried her tears and sent her into defensive mode.

"Fuck you, Streeter! You're just a piece-of-shit pusher. Who voted you the fucking thought police?"

"No one. And you don't have to get your panties in a wad over it."

"The hell I don't! You're dissecting my life like you're some kinda guru, like you have all the answers! Where's your fucking degree?"

"It's waiting for me to finish this last semester."

Loretta jumped up from the couch and looked at Streeter as if he'd morphed into an alien, something with two heads and black, almond-shaped eyes.

"The hell you do!" was all she could come up with on the fly.

"It's true. Sixteen more credits and I'll have an embossed certificate by the state of Illinois to counsel whoever walks through my door."

"What? Are you gonna dispense that shit you sell out of some fancy bowl in your waiting room?" she yelled.

"No drugs. I'll have a degree in psychology, not a doctorate. Doctorates are the ones who get to write scripts."

"You're telling me that while you've been on the street pushing shit, you've been collecting credits towards a degree?"

"That's exactly what I'm telling you."

"If you want to help people so damn bad, why would you push your shit?"

"Fair question. The truth is it's been getting to me. I see folks like you and I feel guilt. It's why I told you to stop. You're not the only one I've tried to reach."

"But that's nuts! You get them hooked and then you preach to them!" Loretta yelled in his direction.

"I didn't say it was an exact science. When I started selling, it was just a way to get through school; a little here, a little there; mostly pot or ecstasy, for people like your friend Jay. Eventually, I opened shop for the real shit; coke, Oxycontin, meth. I wasn't proud of it. I wouldn't have done it if I wasn't losing customers. People go where their drug of choice is. I did what I could and started to talk to my regulars. Some of them went for help."

"That's supposed to justify your being a pusher?" Loretta demand-ed.

"No, it doesn't justify it. I'm just getting by, like everybody else."

"Getting by, and selling drugs to anybody with the cash to buy them," Loretta shot back.

"Not exactly. I don't hang out around playgrounds and I don't sell to minors."

"Well, that makes you a regular prince, doesn't it?"

"I'm as fucked up as everyone else. The difference is I'm honest about it."

Loretta slammed her glass down on the rattan trunk Streeter used as a coffee table but didn't get the effect she was going for. The uneven surface toppled the glass over and the root beer splashed out, dribbling through the open weave of the table.

"What's that supposed to mean?" she demanded.

"It means that you seem to like using loved ones for dart boards. Jay spent a lot of time venting the night she called," Streeter said in way of explanation.

"I was just evening the score. Frank needed to be taught a lesson once in a while." Her voice sounded whinny, even to her ears.

"Like your father did to you?"

"You're sick! You don't know the first thing…"

Streeter jumped up from his overstuffed chair and interrupted what was winding up to be a world class bitch-a-thon.

"Listen, I've got to go. You can sleep on the couch. You'll find a pillow and blankets in the chest," he said, pointing to the dripping rat-tan. "And don't answer the door while I'm gone," he called on his way out.

"Whatever," was all Loretta was allowed before the door was slammed shut.

Streeter had slipped back into his pusher mode, the armchair psy-chiatry dropped at the threshold for survival on the streets.

Loretta finished her sandwich, which would have been surprisingly good if it hadn't soaked up some of the spilled root beer. It didn't mat-ter anyway, she decided. Her appetite had flown south.

She needed a drink. She was angry over Streeter's crawling into her head. Thoughts of her past kept trying to creep back into her head like

254

uninvited parasites. Fuck it! That was a no-fly zone, a place with a no-return address…

"Put a lid on it, girl!" is what her dad would say when he was raising his meat-cleaver hands to her and always when he climbed on top of her after the lights went out. "Put a lid on it!"

She'd tried, but couldn't.

Why had Frank taken what she dished out? Deep down she knew the answer. She'd always known. He'd learned it from his mother. And to be fair to Frank, she hadn't started swinging 'till the dishes had been stowed away in the cupboard of their first apartment. Did that mean they'd made some sort of secret arrangement that the abused ferreted out before choosing a mate? Maybe a smell, or a certain look that said, "Hey, lookie here! We'll get together and it'll be just like the good old days when you got the ever-loving shit beat outta ya!"

It must have been something like that, because she'd curbed herself before the wedding. After that, Frank was on his own. And what about the fat she'd packed on, and after that, years after that, Jay? Had it all been to drown out her kiddy-diddling father? Enough! It was enough. She couldn't go there, *wouldn't* go there. Because if she did, she'd lose control and control was all that had ever done her any good.

Taking her plate and the sticky glass out to the kitchen, Loretta rummaged around for a bottle with one hundred proof in it. Streeter had to be bullshitting about his not drinking. As hard as she searched, she didn't find a bottle in the cupboards, or above the stove, nor under the sink.

Unsuccessful and frustrated, she turned her attention to locating the source of the cloves she'd smelled when she and Streeter had entered the cottage. It wasn't until she returned to the small living room that their fragrance grew stronger and she located a bowl which sat on the rattan coffee table, filled with little clove buds, now swimming in spilled root beer. Go figure.

Streeter wasn't anything like she'd guessed and the surprises continued as she snooped around the living room. The bookshelves were filled with leather-bound classics: *Tom Sawyer*, *Moby Dick*, and *Little Lord Fauntleroy*. Present-day was represented with *The Art of War* and *The Late Great Planet Earth* among dozens of psychology books. How truly odd.

Loretta settled herself on the couch wondering what she should do over the weekend. Saturdays with Frank had never been eventful. When they were getting along, they'd watch TV. When they weren't, she'd warm up her swinging arm. But tomorrow might be different. Frank had another woman in his life. And there was nothing she'd like better than to mess with their plans.

She was fast asleep under a soggy blanket by the time Streeter passed the couch on the way to his bedroom—the one room Loretta hadn't snooped in out of grudging respect. Honor amongst thieves...

Chapter 30

Loretta leaned forward in the backseat to get a better look as Carrie pulled into Frank's driveway. In a flash, she felt overwhelming jealously that was even stronger than the night she'd followed them to the restaurant. Her determination to get back at Frank for his replacing her went to the very top of her priority list. But that was going to be next to impossible with an armed bodyguard hovering next to Frank's front door.

"How long are we going to sit here, lady?" asked the cabbie.

"As long as it takes!" Loretta snapped.

Carrie walked to the back seat of a newer model SUV and waited patiently as two kids disengaged themselves from seatbelts. She was wearing worn 501 jeans that were probably a size four. Her ponytail was letting loose little wisps of auburn hair that curled around her graceful neck and framed her heart-shaped face. Even with no make-up, she was beautiful, and another strike was checked off in Loretta's little black book of vengeance.

She continued to watch as Frank greeted Carrie and her kids at the door, flinching when they embraced. The guard stood at attention, seemingly oblivious to the PG rated groping.

Britney appeared in the doorway and extended her arms to Carrie who swept her up. Loretta saw red.

The boys streaked past the adults and climbed into the back seat of the station wagon. Frank took Britney from Carrie's arms and settled her in her car seat in the station wagon. Within minutes both Frank and Carrie's cars pulled out of the driveway.

"Follow them," Loretta commanded.

The cabbie tore out from their look-out point, happy for some action.

"And don't be so obvious about it! You can catch up with them on the main road," she warned.

Her plan was to seek and destroy, not to be discovered before the fun even began. The cabbie slowed. Once they'd reached the main road, the cabbie eased up on the gas to let another car get between the cab and the station wagon and continued following in the lazy Saturday afternoon traffic. The drive would have been boring for Loretta had it not been for her rage.

They turned on Cannon Drive and into Lincoln Park Zoo's crowded parking lot. It was a sunny day with cumulous clouds meandering slowly against a backdrop of bright blue sky. *The zoo will be crawling with parents and kids*, Loretta thought with a frown. She would have preferred somewhere more private for this confrontation.

"I'll get out here," Loretta announced.

"That'll be seventy-one fifty," the cabbie said.

Loretta shoved the bills at him, never taking her eyes off Frank and Carrie's progress. It took a while for them to find parking spots, but eventually Frank surfaced to stuff bills into a battered drop box.

Loretta stood only a few hundred feet away from Frank, studying a zoo pamphlet she'd snatched from a nearby rack.

Wearing the shoulder-length brown wig she'd bought for the restaurant and trendy sunglasses, the kind that covered roughly a third of her face, Frank never gave her a second glance. This morning she'd slipped on leggings, a lightweight jacket (both size ten) and the barely worn tennis shoes left over from the vet fiasco. Frank and the kids remembered her as a size three-plus. Loretta planned to use that to her advantage.

The older kids tried to run ahead of the adults the moment they passed through the zoo's turnstile, but were corralled by Carrie. Frank held the back of their little group with Britney still in his arms. It was all Loretta could do to keep from confronting them right there. But drama could wait. She needed time to formulate a plan of attack first.

"Dada, potted," Britney insisted as she yanked at her diaper.

So, she'd finally grasped the concept! Loretta thought.

"Come here, sweetie," Carrie said, holding out her arms.

"Potted," Britney said with conviction, resting against Carrie.

"The kids want to check out the new wolf pups. I'll take Britney to the restroom and meet you there," Carrie said.

Loretta hung back, biting her tongue and watched her replacement head for the public bathrooms with her daughter cradled in her arms. Soon, Carrie would learn her lessons.

Keeping her distance, Loretta looked on as the boys' attention was drawn to a litter of wolf pups. The most aggressive pup tired of playing with its littermates and turned its attention to its mother's flank, nipping at her fur with his sharp milk teeth.

After a few minutes, the mother wolf grew tired of his antics and corrected him with a half-hearted snap that connected with his snout and then laid her head back down to rest. The bully sat back, sneezed and shook his head, eventually transferring his energy to the tallish grass growing in half-hearted clumps and began ripping it out from its roots.

Observing her sons, Loretta wondered why she felt nothing. It had been months since she'd had any contact with them, but the anger she felt was not about being cheated over time with her children. It was centered almost exclusively on jealousy.

When Carrie returned they moved on to the small mammal house to watch a dwarf mongoose burrow down to the cooler soil beneath and from there, an exhibit of fruit bats.

Loretta continued to lag behind as they headed for the African Journey exhibit. They didn't get far.

Mark took hold of Frank's hand, stopped, and looked earnestly up at his father.

"Dad, could we have a puppy?"

"No, we can't. The landlord won't allow it," he answered.

"Why not?" Mark persisted.

"Because puppies go to the bathroom on the floor and they chew up couches and…"

"If *we* got one, he wouldn't do that!" Mark interrupted.

"That's where you're wrong. They *all* do that."

"But…"

Carrie stepped in to play referee. "It's already 2:30! How about going to the Big Cat Café for some flat-bread? They should still be open for lunch," she said, looking directly at Mark.

"We've never been to the zoo before. Is it good?" Brice asked.

"You're in for a treat, then! After lunch, maybe we could rent a couple of paddleboats," Carrie said, looking to Frank with a puzzled expression on her face.

Of course she'd be puzzled. She probably took her brats here every damned weekend! Loretta thought.

"I want to see the hippos and giraffes first," Sam said.

Getting a smile from Carrie, the boys raced on ahead. Once they were out of hearing range, Frank spoke softly. "I could've taken them on my own. It isn't like they reject parents at the gate for not coming in pairs. Loretta never wanted to move from the couch on her days off."

Loretta's hands balled up into tight fists. *Was this what he did with this woman, complain about their life together? Well, she had a few thousand complaints about him, too!*

"Don't beat yourself up. You're already changing things around. Just look at the fun they're having!"

Frank took hold of Carrie's hand and gave it a squeeze. "Thank you."

It was another hour before they reached the paddleboats and Loretta had reached her saturation point. She was no closer to a game plan than when she'd crashed their outing, but she was willing to ad-lib.

Carrie snagged a comfortable bench while Britney slumbered against her shoulder. Once Frank made sure they were settled in, he joined the kids.

The boats seated four. Frank nodded to Brice. "You're the oldest. Why don't you get behind the wheel and take your brothers? Madison and Sam can ride with me."

"Hey, let's have a race!" Sam yelled out to Brice once they had climbed into the boats.

"You'll lose!" Brent called back.

Loretta paid the $12 for a paddleboat while keeping an eye on Brice and the boys. Her plan was to ram Frank out of the water. Nothing less would do. She wouldn't be able to do that if Brice's boat got in the way.

Frank was sitting in the boat's molded seat, waiting for Brice to catch up while he relaxed by soaking up the spring sunshine. His head was turned towards Carrie's kids. He was laughing and gesturing, clearly enjoying the day's outing. His attention was definitely not on what was barreling down on him at breakneck speed, and for that, Loretta was eternally grateful.

Months of anger and frustration traveled from Loretta's fevered brain that was transformed into manic action. Her legs interpreted her pent-up rage which now resembled the piston action of an out of control locomotive. She thought about Frank replacing her with Carrie the prom queen and her legs pumped even harder. Soon, they were a blur as she bore down on Frank, narrowing the gap between them by the second.

Loretta looked to the boys' paddleboat and was relieved to see the three of them pointing towards Frank's boat apparently debating which side to approach that would let them to win the race. They were barely moving when she sailed past them and didn't pay one bit of attention to the wake she created as their boat rocked from side to side.

The harder she peddled, the hotter the sun felt. Soon trickles of sweat were escaping from Loretta's cheap wig that now felt like a hothouse sauna under the heavy nylon backing. Sweat streamed from her face and armpits and her clothes now clung to her like she'd yanked them directly from a washing machine and thrown them on. Exhaustion overtook her, and the harder she pumped, the heavier her breathing became. Moments before she collided with the back of Frank's paddleboat, he stiffened in what appeared to Loretta to be recognition.

This was not in Loretta's playbook. She would not be denied the heads-up she'd planned to give Frank just before impact. It was the one satisfaction she had obsessed over since following Frank to the paddleboat rentals. The look on his face when he realized he was about to be dispatched on a one-way trip to the bottom of the algae filled lagoon would be, in Loretta's mind, priceless.

Before Frank was able to turn all the way around, Loretta pulled as much air into her lungs as possible and shattered the idyllic quiet with a primal scream. "Fuck you, asshole!"

The look on Frank's face, now that he was finally facing her, was more than Loretta could've hoped for. Reflecting back at her, now only feet away, was sheer terror. Had Loretta not been on the verge of heatstroke, she would've laughed out loud. As it was, the grin that spread across her face was so wide it nearly split her face in two.

"Watch out!" was all the warning Frank could manage to Madison and Sam before their collision. Their paddleboat lifted out of the water, teetering. Frank locked his arm tight across Madison and Sam, shielding them as best as he could from being thrown out of the boat while the paddleboat made up its mind whether to complete a somersault or right itself.

"Mom!" Mark yelled from the other boat.

The boat slammed back down on the water and Frank began peddling frantically. When he had gained a safe distance away from Loretta, he looked back at his sons. They all wore expressions of disbelief and his heart broke for them.

Continuing to pump his legs, Frank's imagination took over. Maybe Loretta had damaged her boat...enough for it to take on water and sink—with her in it. But looking back, he was sorely disappointed. Loretta was grunting and straining while her legs pumped furiously. They were only twenty feet from impact.

His next thought was Carrie. She was bound to have seen the whole thing from where she sat. She'd be worried sick. Continuing to piston his legs, trying to widen the gap that separated them, he looked to the bench where he'd left Carrie and Britney. It was empty.

"Frank! When I catch up with you, you're a dead man!" Loretta screamed.

While Frank was hoping the strain would be too much for her and she'd keel over her plastic steering wheel with a stroke, Loretta was gaining on him. Her smile of victory resembled a clown's grimace.

She was now only feet away from success when her foot was grabbed. Sitting up in her seat, Loretta tried to kick herself free. As she did, she looked down and was surprised to find Carrie. Her face held nothing but grim determination. Loretta fell back into the seat in surprise.

Carrie took the advantage and gave a determined tug and was rewarded when Loretta's butt began to slide off the boats molded seat. Loretta kicked out with her other foot and Carrie grabbed it, yanking with all her might. Loretta flew out of the paddleboat and plunged into the stagnant lagoon.

The shock of the freezing water tightened Loretta's diaphragm. For every gasp of air, she managed only enough oxygen to keep from passing out. She was still huffing and puffing, desperately trying to fill her lungs when Carrie grabbed her and twirled her around. They were now face to face.

"You're crazy, Loretta! You could've hurt my kids!" Carrie screamed as she put her hands on top of Loretta's head and pushed down. As she did, she lifted her torso out of the water for leverage.

Loretta thrashed about, trying to shove Carrie's hands away. But she didn't have the strength. Soon, she was past caring as the dark water enveloped her. Just before Loretta passed out, Carrie released her hold and Loretta's head bobbed above the water line.

Pulling air into her lungs, coughing and sputtering, Loretta had the presence of mind to realize her mistake. Carrie was crazier than she was, enraged and out for blood! Loretta frantically rubbed the water from her eyes so she could see well enough to defend herself.

It was Frank's face that came into focus.

A smooth breast stroke caught Loretta's attention and she watched as Carrie's even breast strokes brought her to her kids. Carrie grabbed hold of the swaying boat and hoisted herself aboard, baptizing her kids with frigid water that cascaded off her clothes in sheets.

"Someone call security!" Frank yelled to the onlookers who had congregated at the edge of the lagoon.

His grasp on Loretta's upper arm was surprisingly strong and she figured her best chance for escape was to bluff her way out. "You're no match for me, you bastard! I'm gonna make you pay for getting custody of the kids!" she spat, and attempted to wrench herself free.

The look Frank shot her was maniacal.

"Security's on their way. Your own stupidity's going to land you in jail."

The reality of her situation meant nothing to Loretta. She'd be going to jail if they caught her, but between then and now, she had an uncontrollable urge for revenge.

"Let go of me, you prick!" she screamed.

"Not until the police get here. I've had enough of your crap! If you had any decency, you'd have left the kids and me alone."

Out of the corner of her eye, Loretta saw dark blue uniforms approaching the bank of the lagoon. Their badges announced them as zoo security. She moved her mouth over the hand that restrained her and bit down until she drew blood.

"Damn it!" Frank cursed and yanked his hand back to inspect the wound.

Loretta took the opportunity to swim outside Frank's reach. She looked towards the uniforms, realizing whichever direction she swam was going to be a crap-shoot. She chose the opposite bank. It was further to swim, and it might give security time to catch up with her, but as far as she could tell it was her only chance for escape. While she swam, she made herself a promise. She'd either get away to freedom, or she'd die trying. Living behind bars was not an option!

Loretta made it to the opposite bank and climbed out, exhausted. The uniforms had remained where they were, across the other side of the lagoon, which was curious. But this wasn't the time to loiter, nor was it a time to give in to her exhaustion.

As Loretta took to the footpath at a trot, she heard sirens approaching the parking lot. She followed the exit signs at a flat-out run, never slowing. The path opened onto the front of the zoo and she vaulted over the turnstile while a woman at the ticket booth watched with her mouth gaping open.

Two patrol cars raced into the parking lot just as Loretta dove into heavy shrubbery bordering the parameter of the zoo's fence line. To stay hidden meant crawling through the dense shrubbery on her hands and knees. Twigs poked her through her wet clothing and her heart felt like it was going to explode out of her chest, but she couldn't slow down. The woman at the ticket booth would have already alerted security. Soon, the cops would be headed in her direction.

She continued through branches that scraped and poked her exposed skin. The damp soil filled her nostrils with the sickening stench of rotting vegetation. In spots the ground was left bare. Exposed to the previous day's rain, it was treacherously slick. More than once, her hands slipped out from under her and she went down in a face-plant.

Maneuvering between the dense shrubbery, Loretta began to see glimpses of daylight. After another thirty yards, the daylight increased and she was rewarded with the view of a grassy knoll. She grunted in relief. She could roll down to a copse of trees at the bottom and on to safety.

Out of breath, she flopped to the ground.

"Rocky, come on boy!" a man called.

There was a sliver of silence as she crouched lower. With no time to rest, Loretta picked up the pace, slipping and sliding over a particularly tricky patch of ground.

The silence was broken once again with an ear-piercing whistle. "Rocky! Come!" the man commanded.

Loretta stayed low, moving towards the opening. It was then that she met the soft brown eyes of an Irish Setter. She sighed in relief. At least it wasn't another damned Doberman. She'd had enough of Dobermans to last her a lifetime. Irish Setters were family dogs; friendly, playful and loyal, Loretta told herself. She had nothing to worry about.

She quickly had reason to change her mind. The dog started a low grumble from deep within his chest. His hackles rose and he moved stiff-legged towards her, narrowing the gap between them. Loretta took in the red collar and the leash that dangled from it. Rocky was now *her* problem.

"Hey there Rocky, you're a good boy," Loretta cooed.

The Setter sat down and cocked his head, as if trying to decide what to do with the stranger he'd stumbled upon. His movements showed his confusion while his gaze turned first to where Loretta hid, then back towards the parking lot where his owner called his name.

"Go boy...go...go on," Loretta encouraged.

Peering beyond Loretta towards the asphalt parking lot, the dog got up, wagged his tail, and bounded away.

Loretta slunk back down onto the muck, trying to figure out what to do. The cops were probably already searching the parking lot, and when they caught her they'd slap her in handcuffs. But if she made a break for it, the damned dog was sure to follow. She remained crouched behind the last of the shrubbery, undecided. Her indecision switched to action when she heard the sound of pounding feet against the parking lot's pavement.

"Have you seen a woman around five-two, one hundred and fifty pounds with wet clothing?" a man asked.

"I haven't seen anyone. What'd she do?" Loretta heard the dog's owner ask.

Instead of a reply, Loretta heard the sound of footfalls reverberating towards her hiding spot.

It was now or never. Loretta crawled the rest of the way out. The knoll was steep. With any luck, they wouldn't see her tumble to the bottom. She held her breath and pushed off, letting her body roll down the steep decline. She soon picked up speed. The trees were now a blur, as was the sky and the grass. The dog hadn't given up. His furious barks were non-ending.

When she reached flat ground, Loretta stood and ran for the dense copse of trees, but she felt like she was on a tilt-o-whirl. The ground and the sky were spinning out of control. She looked like a quarterback running for a touchdown, compensating by spreading her legs further for balance. She reached the shelter of the trees and flung herself to the ground. The smell of pine needles greeted her. She'd made it! Loretta held her breath and listened. All that came back to her was the persistent yapping of the dog.

She scrambled her way through the trees to disappear into the neighborhood beyond. But melding was not possible. Women pushing strollers, kids on bicycles, and drivers slowed to stare at her. The dirt and smaller debris clinging to her sopping clothes resembled a three dimensional finger-painting made of brown dung. The best she'd been able do was take a few swipes at the worst of it and call it good.

Loretta picked up her pace, past upper-end homes, and on to a small strip of quaint shops in search of a payphone. It was at a trendy coffee shop that she finally found one. The ten-minute wait for her cab was spent over a steaming mocha while Loretta ignored the customers' stares.

Today had been a bust. Cab fare had eviscerated her cash flow, but worse…far worse, was being the recipient of Frank's new backbone.

* * *

Two police officers approached where Carrie and Frank were comforting the kids.

"We're still looking for your ex-wife, Mr. Walch. She couldn't have gone far," one of the police officers said.

"Did you check her warrants?" Frank asked.

"We pulled it up. She's been a busy gal," the officer replied.

"She's crazy. If you catch her, it'd be best not to underestimate her," Frank warned.

The officer nodded. "You might as well head home. There's no way to know how long this'll take."

"Will you call?" Frank asked.

"You'll hear from us, one way or the other," the officer promised.

Walking to their cars, Frank slowed, letting the kids go ahead of them.

"What happened back there, Carrie? What made you come after her like that?"

"Well, I don't know for certain. When I saw Loretta ram your boat, I lost it. She could've killed you and the kids! I passed Britney over to that grey-haired lady and dove in. I didn't have time to think about it, I just jumped in. If you hadn't stopped me, I'm afraid I would've drowned her."

"No, you wouldn't have. You'd have stopped yourself."

"I'm not sure I would've, Frank. Something just snapped. All I could think about were all those years of abuse, when I'd cower and take Hal's crap. I was at the end and I couldn't stand by for anything more. I don't even remember making a conscience decision to push her head underwater. I just had to stop her."

"You stopped her all right! Where'd you learn to swim like that?" Frank asked.

Carrie turned to him and smiled. "I was captain of the swim team in high school."

"Yet another thing I didn't know about you. What else haven't you told me?"

"Stick around. I have the feeling we have plenty more to share."

Frank took hold of her hand, giving it a reassuring squeeze as they caught up with the kids. Frank mulled over the day's insanity. He had some changes to make, starting with telling Susan he would no longer need her offer of a bodyguard. He had accepted because until today, he wasn't sure if he could hit a woman, even in self-defense. But after Loretta's stunt today, he had his answer. If she ever came after him again, he was going to deck her.

Loretta might *never* give up, but for him, things had changed in both small and large ways. He no longer feared her.

Chapter 31

The cab pulled up to Streeter's and Loretta paid the fare. Her mud-caked clothing had already begun to dry. When she moved, she felt like she was wearing filthy armor. Her skin was itching something awful and her hair was dreadlocked into a mass of mud, twigs and unnamed grime. All she could think about on her way into the cottage was climbing into a steaming shower to get clean and warm.

Streeter was sitting in his armchair reading a textbook when Loretta walked through the door. He lowered the book to stare with his mouth hanging open.

"What the hell happened to you?" he asked.

"It's none of your business," Loretta said and continued her determined stride to the bathroom. Looking in the mirror was a shock. Her hair was filthy and plastered against her scalp, her face was streaked with mud, and her clothes stuck to her like a filthy shroud.

Streeter followed her in. "The cab's already come and gone. You said 2:30."

"Well, something came up," Loretta said, still looking at her reflection. There were scratches on her arms and face where branches had scraped her exposed skin.

"Does this have something to do with a new vocation…maybe mud wrestling?"

"Shut it, Streeter!"

"I'm not dropping it, Loretta. You just walked through the door, hours late, looking like something that crawled out of a swamp. What happened?"

"Get out of the bathroom! I need to take a shower," Loretta said, peeling off her T-shirt.

"Not happening. First, tell me what's going on."

"Screw you!" Loretta said, peeling away the rest of her filthy clothes, oblivious to Streeter's gaze. She was going to get clean, wash the twigs and the mud from her. He could wait for an explanation!

Soon, there was an oozing pile of clothes on the vinyl floor. Loretta leaned over to adjust the water temperature to hot and disappeared behind the shower curtain.

"I've got to tell you, Loretta. That was kind of sexy, in a demented, filthy sort of way," Streeter said with a smile in his voice.

"You can kiss my ass," Loretta said over the spray of the shower. The hot water cascading over her body was heaven.

"Better watch it. I might oblige. Grading on a curve, your ass isn't all that bad."

She selected a shampoo and liberally squirted the bottle over her hair, then used her hands to work up a lather. Locating errant twigs, Loretta yanked them one by one from her matted hair.

"Maybe we should get your girlfriend on the line, ask her to come over for a vote."

"That was cold. Why'd you have to break the mood like that? I was just trying to pay you a compliment."

Done soaping and rinsing herself, Loretta let the hot water play against her body and relaxed. It wasn't long before the water turned tepid, forcing her to twist the handle further towards hot in small increments. When the spray became sub-arctic, Loretta called a truce.

"Streeter, are you there?"

"Where else would I be?"

"Hand me a towel, would you?"

"I was hoping for some full-frontal nudity," Streeter complained.

"Give me a damned towel and get out!"

"Are you going to let me in on why you walked through the door looking like a swamp creature?"

"If you'll hand me a towel, I will. Just let me dry off."

The shower curtain was slid open. Streeter stood with a smile on his face, extending a bath towel.

"I'd thought with all the weight loss, your skin might be hanging from your body like a loose drape. You're actually doable."

Loretta snatched the towel and threw the curtain closed. By the time she'd dried off, Streeter had left. She vigorously went after her hair until it was merely damp, ran a brush through it, then wrapped a towel around her body and walked into the living room.

Streeter had returned to reading his textbook, but placed it face down on the end table when she marched past him to plunk down on the couch.

"So, give."

Loretta sighed. "I followed Frank, Carrie and the kids to the zoo today."

"Why would you want to do that?"

"Because I have a right to know what he's up to and I wanted to see the kids."

"From the looks of it, things didn't go so well," Streeter said, meeting her eyes.

Loretta filled him in on the day's events, starting with the stake-out and finishing with Carrie's pulling her into the freezing lagoon and her scramble to freedom.

"You can't blame her. You could've hurt her kids," Streeter said.

"How's a little paddleboat gonna hurt her kids?"

"Oh, I don't know...drowning comes to mind."

"No one got hurt! I am so pissed Frank got away!"

"Is this it, then?" Streeter asked.

"Is *what* it?"

"Is this the end of your tormenting Frank?"

"No, it's not! Frank hasn't begun to pay."

Instead of arguing, Streeter headed for the phone. "I'm calling for a cab. We need to get your car before the garage closes. Why don't you get dressed—unless you plan on flashing Shorty a little skin."

Loretta grabbed her mangled trash bag that sat near the couch and dug through clothes until she'd found a warm outfit. She could still feel the cold of the lagoon.

* * *

Streeter turned the key in the ignition and the Nova purred back. "Sounds good!"

"At least I won't get picked up for driving it," Loretta agreed.

"So, where are we headed?"

When Loretta didn't reply, Streeter drove through the open chain link gate and made a left. Neither bothered to look back as Shorty swung the gate back into place and slapped on a fat padlock.

"Where are you headed?" Loretta asked.

"Not sure. What about Vegas? I hear the weather's great this time of year."

"Bite me, Streeter."

"I'm not joking. Why *not* Vegas?"

"I can think of a few good reasons why not. You've got college, I don't have any money and you have a girlfriend somewhere in the Chicago area. Plus, I have a vendetta to settle."

"By that, you mean Frank. Didn't you learn your lesson today? You're a train wreck waiting to happen, Loretta, and if you don't cut the shit, you're going to wind up dead or behind bars."

"There's more to it than that. Frank took my kids…cried like a little bitch to a bleeding-heart judge and got full custody of the kids."

"And your point would be?"

"He doesn't deserve them!"

"And you do? You've said yourself they're happiest with him. Besides, you're not in any condition to take care of kids. First, you'd have to get clean."

"So what if I did?"

"Vegas isn't just for gambling. There's a rehab there that's pretty well known. It's run as a non-profit on a sliding scale. Considering your scale's zippo, the price is right. You have the fake I.D. As far as they are concerned, they'd be treating Lori Walch from Chicago who's squeaky clean, no record of any kind, with no paycheck to attach."

"I already tried it. When I was arrested in Houston, they chained me to the fucking bed and put me on antidepressants and Tyrosine."

"That was different," Streeter said with conviction.

"Oh yeah? How so?"

"Simple. It wasn't your choice. This time it *will* be."

"What about the girlfriend?" Loretta asked.

"She's just a figment of my imagination. I made her up in case you wanted to jump my bones."

"Then who's gonna pay for the gas? It's what…almost 1,800 miles to Vegas."

"I will. In fact, now would be a good time to start," Streeter said, pulling into a Chevron station.

Loretta looked at the gas gauge. The needle was buried on empty.

"What about school?" she hollered out to Streeter as he sauntered into the station to pay.

"I'm out for spring break," he called back.

Loretta sat in the bucket seat trying to wrestle her demons to the ground, where she could get a good look at them. Streeter was right. She was playing Russian roulette with her drug use and her luck was running out. Most of the time she felt like sucker-punching whoever she came in contact with. The meth…well, the meth made things worse.

What if rehab in Vegas was the answer? What if there actually was someone at this rehab who could explain to her why she'd lived her whole life as an outsider, taking pot-shots at caring, sometimes approaching something close to feeling, but always stepping back, afraid to commit. If that person existed, where would it lead her?

She had no fucking idea.

Taking off for Vegas would mean postponing L.A. Dogs. On the other hand, she wouldn't mind growing her hair back and finding skin under the eruptions that had become her face.

Could she get clean? The meth wasn't just about the chemicals. Part of the whole drug thing was the chance to flip the finger at everyone she came into contact with. That, and the euphoria. It made her happy, and happy was a commodity that had been lacking in her life. Happy was everything...

Streeter returned and started pumping gas. Loretta got out and asked him the only question that mattered.

"Why are you offering?"

"Atonement. I've done some shitty things."

It sounded fair and just raw enough to be believable.

"Are you going to steal my car?"

"Just borrow it 'till you call me to be picked up."

"You'd have to promise me something. If it didn't work out, you'd come get me."

"You're asking if I'll still be your friend and the answer to that is yes."

"I'm not saying I'll do this, but I'll think about it. If I do decide to go to Vegas, there's something I'd need to do before I leave and I'd need your help."

Streeter shot Loretta a suspicious look. "Will this something have the potential to put us behind bars?"

"No, but that's all I'm willing to say. First, I have to decide whether or not to go to Vegas."

"Don't take too long."

Chapter 32

Loretta was adding a garnish of sliced black olives and chopped green onions to a platter of nachos when Streeter wandered into the kitchen.

"Have you gone domestic, or is this just a temporary setback?" he asked, grabbing a nacho covered in hot cheese and dipped it in a bowl of freshly made guacamole.

"Call it a temporary setback. The truth is I'm not feeling the rehab thing and I needed something to take my mind off it. I mean, why now? I'm doing fine. Why turn things upside down and hand over the keys to my freedom to some rehab? From what I've heard, once I sign an admissions form, they can hold me as long as they want. I don't like the idea of having my life planned by people I've never met."

"Maybe you should go because your meth use is a symptom of the problem, not the root cause. If you dig a little, you might be able to figure out why you're so toxic to yourself and the people closest to you. Think about it: it's all kinds of messed up when the first time you saw your kids in months, you tried to drown their dad right in front of them. Something has caused you to disconnect, Loretta, and it might involve more than what your dad did to you, which was bad enough. Until you face it, you'll never have a normal life."

"Aren't you the swinging dick? You spew your little gems of wisdom, telling me my life's a hot mess while you still push your crap on the street."

"You're right. We're not that different. The exception is I don't get a kick out of smashing people's faces in. If you could rein that in, you'd be happier. It's time for you to make a decision, Loretta. The call I got earlier was from the rehab center. A room's opened up, so they have space for you."

Streeter ignored Loretta's silence by filling a plate with nachos and guacamole. He brought it into the living room, leaving Loretta to fight her demons in private. She would never agree to rehab unless she felt it was her decision. He channel surfed to the bio channel. It was a segment about Pamela Anderson's boob reduction, which interested him about as much as the Theory of Relativity did.

Loretta settled herself on the couch with a plate of nachos, refusing to make eye contact with Streeter. "Here's the deal. Before I go, *if* I go, I want to see the kids and I'll need your help to do that."

"How could you show up without Frank calling the police?"

"I've been thinking about that. Britney's turning three on Saturday. Frank will have a birthday party for her later in the day if he sticks to his usual routine, but if we showed up early in the morning, he'll be preoccupied with the party preparations, and he'll be easily distracted. I could see the kids before I left."

"You're not making any sense, Loretta. Do you honestly think you'll just knock on the door and Frank will let you in?"

"Of course not. But we could create a distraction, then I could slip inside and say goodbye to the kids."

"Why the sudden interest in your kids? You never talk about them. You don't even keep photographs of them. And now you want to show up for a visit when there's warrants out for your arrest. If you're caught, you'll be behind bars for years."

"I've been thinking about all the undone parts of my life. I want to connect with the kids before I leave for Vegas. The truth is, I won't be coming back once I get out of rehab. I need to start over and leave all my old baggage behind."

"Where do you plan to do this dropping out?"

"Well, I'd had L.A. Dogs stuck in my head, but then I realized it was more for the independence than it was about making hot dogs and it started me thinking. There's a lot a person can do that doesn't revolve around food."

"Like what?" Streeter asked, finishing the last bite of nachos and turning off the TV so they could talk in quiet.

"If I tell you, do you promise not to laugh?"

"I'll try."

Loretta shot him a look of death.

"I'm just saying…"

"I've decided to move to Alaska and become a Madam."

Without saying a word Streeter got up and slammed himself behind his bedroom door. Loretta followed.

"You didn't even hear what I have to say," Loretta shouted past his closed door. "I read an article about Alaska a while back. In some places, the men outnumber the women two to one. They're lonely and most of them have money. I figure if I have to live with warrants hanging over my head, I might as well do it on my terms."

Streeter opened the door and gave Loretta a look of complete disbelief. "You don't even like sex. And you bitch about the cold. You're not making any sense."

"But that's the beauty of it, Streeter. With L.A. Dogs, I'd eat up all the profits. As a Madam, I could hire a stable of girls and manage them. I wouldn't be tempted to sample the wares, because you're right. I don't really like sex. I didn't like it with Frank, and it wasn't all that great with Jay. I wouldn't even need a bouncer. I'd be the bouncer. It would be a win-win situation and I could call the shots. If I have to dodge the law the rest of my life, I might as well do it while bankrolling a new life."

Streeter looked confused as he walked over to sit on the edge of the bed. "What's scary is you're almost making sense. But why Alaska?"

"Where else could I disappear? I need big open spaces where people aren't expected to conform. I would fit in in Alaska and there's likely to be fewer questions asked. If I supply women where they're needed, doesn't it stand to reason I'd receive a little favoritism, where folks are just as likely to look the other way as to go digging into my past?"

"Where would you find the girls?"

Loretta rolled her eyes. "Funny how you become a detail guy only when you're digging into other people's business. I don't know exactly how I'll do it, I just know I will. It couldn't be all that hard. And I'll run a classy establishment: no street-walking, and no dates with strangers in seedy motels."

Streeter was clearly warming to the idea. "Would you want company? My last quarter's almost complete and selling pharmaceuticals has lost its appeal. I'm ready for something new."

Loretta smiled a rare smile. "I'd like that. We'd have each other's back. But what about helping me see my kids one last time?"

"I won't promise anything, but I'm willing to toss around a few ideas."

For the rest of the afternoon, they threw out what ifs until they were confident they had a plan that worked.

* * *

They circled the block several times before they found a parking spot. Loretta was the first to get out of the rented Celebrity. She held an oversized gym bag in one hand and with the other, she got busy digging in the bottom of her purse for quarters.

"Just how long do you think this is going to take? You just put over $3 in that parking meter," Streeter said.

"Do I look like a psychic? I don't have a clue how long it'll take. But if this is going to work, you'd better pull that plank out of your ass. You look guilty."

"That might be because we're about to do something so stupid, we deserve to be arrested just for thinking it up. Which reminds me: you should seriously investigate why you like living on the edge of annihilation once you've checked into rehab."

Instead of answering, Loretta walked to Streeter and yanked his T-shirt up.

"What are you doing?" Streeter asked.

"Just checking to see if you're wearing a teddy under that thing. Streeter, you need to man up! This'll be easy. In and out. Just relax, already."

"I can't relax. This area's crawling with cops. What in the hell were you thinking? I'm beginning to wonder if the meth hasn't drilled holes in your brain."

"Just shut up and follow me," Loretta said, leading the way through the door of a dry cleaner's.

It was early Saturday morning. The place was as dead as Loretta suspected it would be. There was a lone clerk standing at the counter with no one else in sight. Streeter dumped the contents of his duffel bag on the counter and Loretta got down to business.

"Do you have a bathroom?" Loretta asked

"Sorry, it's not for public use. There's one at the coffee shop at the end of the street."

"That would be fine if I could make it that far. I'm sorry, but I really need to use your bathroom."

The clerk looked torn and Streeter decided to play the pity card. "They did an ultrasound. Made her drink about a half-gallon of water," he said just above a whisper.

"It's located in the back on the right," the clerk said.

While Streeter kept the clerk busy, Loretta scanned the mechanized clothes rack and found what she was looking for almost immediately. In seconds she had the clothes stuffed in her gym bag. She continued to the bathroom, relieved the first leg of their plan had gone so smoothly. By the time she returned, Streeter was finished checking in his clothes and he was holding a claim slip.

"Thank you," Loretta said to the clueless clerk on their way out.

Streeter waited until he'd climbed into the passenger's seat and they had merged into traffic before he spoke. "I take it back. That was easy."

"Of course it was easy. The dry cleaner is only two blocks from the police station. They were bound to have uniforms," Loretta said. "You didn't give the clerk your correct address, did you?"

"Do I look like an idiot to you? I'm surprised you think so little of me. And now, some shelter's gonna receive half my wardrobe, which, by the way, included a few of my favorite sweaters."

Loretta reached to the back seat, grabbed the gym bag, and dropped it on Streeter's lap. "Hope the size works."

Streeter pulled the uniform out of its martinizing bag to inspect the tag. "It'll do. How much time do we have?"

"Not much. Need a place to change?"

"Not really," Streeter said, slipping the starched police shirt on over his T-shirt. "I still think showing up at Frank's without a badge is a monumentally stupid idea."

"Like I've already told you, Frank has a thing for authority. It would never dawn on him to ask for a badge. Just stick to the plan and we'll be all right."

By the time they reached Frank's neighborhood, Streeter was wearing the uniform and a leather holster. Loretta had scored a realistic looking Glock at a prop shop, which was tucked into the holster, completing Streeter's impersonation of one of Chicago's finest.

"Okay, I'm parking here. Once Frank takes off, let me in through the back door," Loretta said.

"What if this backfires?"

"If Frank gets suspicious, and he won't, we'll leave. It'd take the cops at least 30 minutes to show. By then, we'll be across town. They'll never find us."

"This idea of yours sucks. There's too much that can go wrong. What if Frank asks why I didn't pull up in a cruiser?"

"You know, you really need to grow a pair. That's why I rented the Celebrity. It looks like every unmarked cop car on the road. You're forgetting, this was *our* idea. All you need to do is tell Frank his Aunt Edith had a heart attack and then offer to stay with the kids until someone else can get there. He'll call the bitch, of course, but even so, I'll have plenty of time to see the kids before Carrie shows. Afterwards you get to throw me to the wolves."

"I'm not throwing you to the wolves, Loretta. You'll just be kicking the meth, so you won't self-destruct. The truth is, I'm trying to save you from going postal and getting picked off some tower that everybody gets to hear about on the six o'clock news. You don't realize it now, but you'll be thanking me some day."

"Whatever. Now get going!" Loretta snapped.

Loretta watched Streeter knock on Frank's front door. The two of them spoke on the front porch, away from the kids. Frank disappeared but left the door open, which Loretta took as a good sign. Long minutes passed before Frank re-emerged wearing a jacket and carrying his car keys. Loretta remained behind the wheel until the station wagon disappeared down the street. Getting past the back gate was easy. It had been left unlocked. Streeter saw her before the kids did and opened the sliding glass doors.

Without warning, Loretta felt her resolve evaporate. She and Streeter may have rehearsed how to get the police uniform, and how they would get past Frank. It had all gone so smoothly. But the one thing Loretta hadn't rehearsed was how to face her children. She couldn't make up for the harm she had already done to them, and she couldn't pretend she wasn't hooked on meth. The last time her kids had seen her, she was otherwise occupied trying to drown their father. It suddenly became crystal clear. Streeter was right. She didn't deserve her children. Maybe she never had.

Streeter watched Loretta's expression change from triumph to resignation. Meeting Streeter's gaze, she shook her head and slowly walked away, past the kid's toys, and the tree house, and the swing set, through the unlocked gate and on to the car. She'd wait for Carrie to come to the kids' rescue, as Loretta knew she'd do for as long as they needed her, and then she and Streeter would drive the 1,800 miles to a rehab she detested the thought of. It represented the only chance she had left.

About the Author

Evie Benson lives on Alki Beach in Seattle, Washington where she enjoys beach-combing with her German Shepherd, Smalls, and supports her love of writing as a barista. *We Interrupt This Marriage...* is Evie's debut novel. Look for the sequel, *Frost Heaves,* coming soon.